Between Conformity and Resistance

THEORY IN THE WORLD

Edited by Gayatri Chakravorty Spivak and Hosam Aboul-Ela

Published by Palgrave Macmillan:

Between Conformity and Resistance

Essays on Politics, Culture, and the State

Marilena Chauí

Translated and edited by Maite Conde
Introduction by Maite Conde

BETWEEN CONFORMITY AND RESISTANCE
Copyright © Marilena Chauí, 2011.

All rights reserved.

First published in 2011 by
PALGRAVE MACMILLAN®
in the United States—a division of St. Martin's Press LLC,
175 Fifth Avenue, New York, NY 10010.

Where this book is distributed in the UK, Europe and the rest of the world,
this is by Palgrave Macmillan, a division of Macmillan Publishers Limited,
registered in England, company number 785998, of Houndmills,
Basingstoke, Hampshire RG21 6XS.

Palgrave Macmillan is the global academic imprint of the above companies
and has companies and representatives throughout the world.

Palgrave® and Macmillan® are registered trademarks in the United States,
the United Kingdom, Europe and other countries.

ISBN: 978–0–230–10900–1

Library of Congress Cataloging-in-Publication Data

Chauí, Marilena de Souza, 1941–
    Between conformity and resistance : essays on politics, culture,
    and the state / Marilena Chauí ; translated by Maite Conde.
        p. cm.—(Theory in the World)
    Includes bibliographical references.
    ISBN 978–0–230–10900–1
    1. Politics and culture—Brazil. 2. Popular culture—Brazil—
History—20th century. 3. Brazil—Cultural policy—History—20th
century. I. Title.

JL2431.C48 2011
306.20981—dc22   2010035419

A catalogue record of the book is available from the British Library.

Design by Newgen Imaging Systems (P) Ltd., Chennai, India.

First edition: September 2011

10 9 8 7 6 5 4 3 2 1

Printed in the United States of America.

Contents

Theory in the World: A General Introduction

"Theory" is an English transcription of the Greek *theorein*. Corresponding words exist in the major European languages. Our series, "Theory in the World," works within these limits. "Theory" has been creolized into innumerable languages. Yet the phenomenon of "seeing or making visible correctly"—the meaning in Greek that will still suffice—does not necessarily relate to that word— "theory"—in those languages. That describes the task of the editors of a translated series of theory in the world.

Heidegger thinks that truth is destined to be thought by the man of "Western Europe."[1] Our series does not offer a legitimizing counteressentialism. Take a look at the map and see how tiny Europe is, not even really a continent, but, as Derrida would say, a *cap*, a headland.[2] Such a tiny place, yet who can deny Derrida's description, which is a historical and empirical observation? Look at the tables of contents of the most popular critical anthologies, and you will see corroboration of the essentialist conviction that goes with the historical claim. The counteressentialism is reflected in the choice of critics from "the rest of the world." Just being nonwhite is the counteressence.

The influential *Norton Anthology of Theory and Criticism*, for example, lets in only Maimonides before the modern university system kicks in.[3] But, even if they had let in Khaled Ziadeh, Marta Lamas, Marilena Chauí, and Arindam Chakrabarti, the material would be determined by the epistemological procedures of that system. Norton lets in W. E. B. Du Bois, the first African American to get a doctorate from Harvard, the man who felt that "of the greatest importance was the opportunity which my *Wanderjahre* [wandering years] in Europe gave of looking at the world as a man and not simply from a narrow racial and provincial outlook."[4] Then we get Zora Neale Hurston (Columbia), Langston Hughes (Harlem Renaissance via Columbia), Frantz Fanon (University of Lyons), Chinua Achebe (University College, Ibadan), Stuart Hall (Oxford), Ngũgĩ wa Thiong'o (Leeds), Taban Lo Liyong (Iowa), Henry Owuwor-Anyuumba (Iowa), Spivak (Cornell), Houston Baker (UCLA), Gloria Anzaldúa (UCSC), Homi Bhabha (Oxford), Barbara Christian (Columbia), Barbara Smith (Mount Holyoke), Henry Louis Gates, Jr. (Cambridge), bell hooks (UCSC). The point I am making is not that these wonderful writers have not challenged Eurocentrism. It is that they are sabotaging from within and this is a historical fact that must be turned around so that there is a chance for truth to reveal itself. Fanon stands out, not because he is not a university man, but because he is the only one who clearly operated outside the Euro-U.S., though he was what Du Bois would call a Black European, literally fighting Europe, also from within, located in a geographical exterior.

(In the next most influential anthology, the rest-of-the world entries are almost identical, but for Audre Lorde [Columbia], Geraldine Heng [Cornell], Ania Loomba [Sussex], Chidi Oklonkwo [Georgia Tech], Jamaica Kincaid [Franconia and the New School]).[5] Again, Fanon is the only working "outsider." I am sure the general pattern is repeated everywhere. I have myself been so tokenized through my long career as representing "Third World criticism" that I am particularly alive to the problem.[6]

Yet our list is not really different. Marta Lamas teaches at the National Autonomous University in Mexico, founded in 1551; Khaled Ziadeh went to the Sorbonne, and Marilena Chauí is a Professor at the University of São Paulo. Lamas repeatedly assures us that affirmative action for gender justice works in the "developed countries," Chauí offers us Spinoza, and Ziadeh recommends modernity via an earlier imperial formation, the Ottomans. So what is the difference?

Our position is against a rest-of-the-world counteressentialism, which honors the history versus tradition binary opposition. We recognize that a hegemonic Euro-U.S. series can only access work abroad that is continuous with Euro-U.S. radicalism. To open ourselves to what lies beyond is another kind of effort. Within the limits of our cause, we focus, then, on another phenomenon.

The history of the past few centuries has produced patterns of bilateral resistance. The formation is typically my nation-state, my region, my cultural formation over against "the West." These days there are global efforts at conferences, events, and organizations that typically take the form of the Euro-U.S. at the center, and a whole collection of "other cultures," who connect through the imperial languages, protected by a combination of sanctioned ignorance and superficial solidarities,

ignoring the internal problems when they are at these global functions.[7]
The model is the fact and discipline of preservation. By the Nara document of 1994, Japan insisted that preservation should be not only of
built space but also of intangible cultural heritage. What started was
the model that I have described above. It is now a tremendous capital-
intensive fact of our world.

In and through our series, we want to combat this tendency. We want
not only to present texts from different national origins to the U.S.
readership, but also to point out how each is singular in the philosophical sense, namely universalizable, though never universal. We are not
working for area studies niche-marketing, though the work is always
of specialist quality. In the interest of creating a diversified collectivity
outside of the English readership, the editors plan to hold annual conferences, interactive on the Web.

The story begins for me in a conversation with the Subaltern Studies
collective in 1986—asking them if I could arrange the publication of a
selection—because they were not available in the United States. A long
term preoccupation, then. To this was added Hosam Aboul-Ela's 2007
consolidation of a thought that was growing inside me: from the rest of
the world literary editors wanted fiction, poetry, drama—raw material.
Theory came generally from "us." When Palgrave Macmillan called on
me, I called on Hosam to be my coeditor for this series.

In the intervening three decades a small difference had imposed
itself. Earlier I had felt that my brief within the profession was to
share and show the work overseas was really "theoretical" by Western
sizing. (I use the word "size" here in the sense of *pointure* in Derrida.)[8]
Hence "strategic use of essentialism." Now I also feel the reader must
learn that "theory" need not look the same everywhere, that for the
independent mind, too much training in producing the European
model in stylistic detail might hamper. (From my teacher training
work in rural India I understand that it is the illiterate man who
understands things best because his considerable intelligence has not
been hobbled by bad education or gender oppression. The lesson here
is not that everyone should be illiterate, but that strong minds should
not be ruined by bad education or imperatives to imitate.)

This caution applies to *Neighborhood and Boulevard* by Khaled
Ziadeh—not bad education, obviously, but the imperative to imitate
"French Theory." Ziadeh theorizes by space and repetition; Hosam
Aboul-Ela's Introduction walks us through it. There are plenty of peo-
ple writing in Arabic who produce work competitive with the best in
European-style "theory." Reading Ziadeh, as Aboul-Ela points out, we

have to learn to recognize "theory" in another guise. My own work profits from his account of the de-Ottomanization of the city by the French
into an "Islamic" space; because I think de-Ottomanization, still active
in our time, has a history as old as the Fall of Constantinople, and,
reterritorialized, backward into Byzantium.

Our series has only just begun. I have described our goal with appropriate modesty: to translate theoretical material operating outside the
Euro-U.S., not readily available to metropolitan readership but continuous with the episteme, even as "hybridity" keeps the local elsewhere.
Yet there are also singular enclaves in many places where teaching and
thinking apparently take place in less continuous epistemic formation.
To acquire texts from these enclaves would require the kind of preparation, partly traditionalist, partly anthropologistic, that I do not possess. Perhaps, if our initial forays succeed, we will be able to fling our
net wider: particularly important in the context of sub-Saharan Africa,
where strong theoretical writing in the imperial languages (also languages of Africa, of course) flourishes and holds influence. For theoretical writing in the indigenous languages, not necessarily imitating
the European model, contained within internal conflict, avoiding the
anthropologist in the name of tradition will be on our agenda.

For now, I have arrived, after an initial meeting at the Modern
Language Association, to an understanding of an activist "Task of the
Editor," that I have outlined above: to combat the bilateralism: my place
and your Euro-U.S., that legitimizes Eurocentrism by reversal.

We start our list with Marta Lamas, *Feminism: Transmissions and
Retransmissions*. Lamas is a feminist who theorizes as she practices. Her
work is full of singular Mexican specificities. My own work can build
on hers. As Jean Franco writes in her Introduction: "Lamas remains
required reading." I will spell out how Lamas and I relate. The human
being and advanced primates are defined by the difference between what
they need and what they can make. In this difference rise art, capital, the
intuition of the transcendental, and human continuity as history. Each
one of these is medicine and poison. This difference is theorized—and
it is silly to think the primitive is incapable of theory—in terms of the
only difference empirically available to us—sexual difference. It is this
that Lamas calls "the invariable traits of biological difference." Gender
(or "what we now call gender," Lamas again) is the grounding instrument of abstraction. I could go further, but for the series introduction,
this is enough.

Next comes Khaled Ziadeh, of whom I have already written, and
Marilena Chauí, *Between Conformity and Resistance: Essays on Politics,*

Culture, and the State. Chauí's specificity is Brazil, as Étienne Balibar's is France, and Partha Chatterjee's India. Readership of English and French have had no difficulty in finding what is universalizable in the texts of these latter two. We hope that they will proceed in the same way with Chauí. In "Brazil: The Foundational Myth" she speaks to India, Africa, Israel, and many other countries. Her discussions of citizenship and democracy have worldwide application. Her comments on the administered university is right on target for that phenomenon everywhere. Her discussion of popular religion has validity for discussions of secularism today. Her analysis of ethical philosophy, diagnosing "ethical ideology" as a do-gooding that presupposes victimhood and therefore evil, is applicable to the presuppositions of human rights and the international civil society. When she writes about Spinoza, it is an implicit critique of the digital idealism of Michael Hardt and Antonio Negri's recent work, which takes Spinozan categories such as "multitude," "singularity," and so on, and simply empiricizes them, ignoring that Spinoza was writing from within a position that could theorize only the righteous state. Again, there is much more material that I could cover, but I will stop here and let you enjoy the text for yourselves.

(I am sorry that she opposes a caricatured "postmodernism," especially since she herself is sometimes perceived as a "postmodern" writer.)[9]

Down the line, we are planning to bring forward proposals for translations of Luis Tapia, *History and Politics in the Work of René Zavaleta*, as well as a text by the "Bolivian Gramsci," René Zavaleta Mercado himself; *Deho, Geho, Bandhutto*, a text by Arindam Chakrabarti, and Nasr Hamid Abu Zayd, *Discourse and Interpretation*; we are negotiating for women's texts from China, Korea, and Japan.

Our translators share with us the problems of translation for each unique text, at least hinting to the reader that, although the activity of translating is altogether pleasurable, to accept translations passively as a substitute for the "original" closes doors. We will not give up the foolish hope that a careful translation, sharing problems, will lead to language-learning.

Read our series as a first step, then. Come to the annual conferences where all of the authors and translators will gather, to ask: what is it to theorize, in our world?

GAYATRI CHAKRAVORTY SPIVAK
Columbia University

Sources

The texts used have been taken from published journals and books listed below. The essays are published in English for the first time and are translated by Maite Conde unless otherwise indicated.

"The Engaged Intellectual. An Extinct Figure?" (O intellectual engajado. Uma figura em extincao?). Taken from *O silêncio dos intelectuais*, Ed. Adauto Novaes (Sao Paulo: Companhia das letras, 2006): 19–44.

"The Integralist Imaginary" (O imaginário integralista). Originally published in *Ideologia e mobilização popular* (São Paulo: Ed. Paz e Terra, 1978): 19–49.

"Notes on Popular Culture" (Notas sobre cultura popular). Originally published in the periodical *Arte em revista* Ano 2, 3 (1980) (São Paulo: CEAC Universidade de São Paulo): 15–21. English Translation by Dylon Robbins.

"Popular Culture and Authoritarianism" (Cultura popular e autoritarianismo). Originally published in *Conformiso e resistência* (São Paulo: Ed. Moderna, 1982): 121–179. English Translation by Dylon Robbins.

"Ethics and Violence. A Difficult Democracy" (Ética e violencia). Originally published in the magazine *Teoria e debate* 39 (10/12): 31–43. This updated version was provided by Chauí for this collection.

"On the Present and Politics" (Sobre o presente e a política) provided by Chauí for this collection.

"Power and Liberty: Politics in Spinoza" (Poder e liberdade: A política em Espinosa). Originally published in *Cadernos da ética política* 4 (2002): 9–44.

"Brazil: The Foundational Myth" (Brasil. Mito fundador). Originally published in *Brasil. Mito Fundador* (São Paulo: Perseu Abramo, 2000): 57–87.

"Religious Fundamentalism: The Return of Political Theology" (Fundamentalismo religioso: a questão do poder teológico). A version of this paper was published in the book titled Filosofia Política

Contemporânea: Controvérsias sobre Civilização, Império e Cidadania, Ed Atilio A. Boron (Buenos Aires and São Paulo: Consejo Latinoaericano de Ciencias Sociales and FFLCH, 2006): 125–144. This version has been significantly adapted for this collection and for an American readership.
"The Winds of Progress. The Administered University" (A universidade hoje). Originally published in *Escritos sobre a universidade* (Sao Paulo: Ed. Unesp, 2000): 175–195.

Acknowledgments

I would like to express my thanks first of all to the series editors Hosam Aboul-Ela and Gayatri Chakravorty Spivak for their enthusiastic support of this project. Thanks also to Dylon Robbins who first highlighted Marilena Chauí's work as an ideal addition to the series and who took the time out of his busy schedule to complete some of the translations. Carlos Alonso and Graciela Montaldo were extremely helpful in the initial stages of this project. Lucia Villares also helped in reading through some of the translations. Many thanks as always to Tariq Jazeel for his assistance and invaluable opinions on the content of this book. Finally, my deepest gratitude to Marilena herself.

This book was completed with the support of a three-year research fellowship at the Brazil Institute, King's College London, provided by the Banco Santander.

MAITE CONDE

A Note on Translation

The essays contained in *Between Conformity and Resistance* were originally published between 1978 and 2010, and they were written by Marilena Chauí as seminar papers, book chapters, and journal articles. This edition that you have before you is, therefore, not the translation of a book. It is a collection of essays, each of which focuses on a specific topic relating to a particular moment or an issue in Brazil's cultural, social, and political history, as well as society and politics in general. Nevertheless, as readers will note, there are common themes and ideas that run through the essays, producing a body of work that illuminates Chauí's own ways of thinking about Brazil and its place in the world at large. In spite of their differences in focus, the essays respond to each other, and shed light on one another. I would like to thank Chauí for her input and support in selecting the essays collected here. Whilst this book is in this sense an authorized translation, any infelicities remain the responsibility of the translators.

To the Anglophone reader and to the community of scholars and critics familiar with Chauí's work, I would like to point out a number of words and phrases that indicate the limits of the translated essays that follow. Taken together they constitute a reflection on the untranslatable, a situation encountered by every translator at some point or another, as well as an aporia worthy of its own philosophical reflection. I highlight them here not because they interfered with the task of translation, but because they were a crucial part of the engagement with Chauí's work.

Where to start? Perhaps the best place to start is at the beginning, that is, the very origins or foundations of Brazil. In "Brazil: The Foundational Myth" Chauí draws attention to the invention of Brazil, a process that took place in the sixteenth century, and was imbricated in reinterpretations of Christian scripture, the legibility of a religious cosmos, and the formulation of new ways of thinking about history and geography, or time and space, that developed in Europe. Taking their cue from biblical texts, these ideas conjured up the image of Brazil as a utopian land of plenty, a paradise in which there was no conflict and that was inhabited by innocent, cordial people. As Chauí notes, these ideas have been endlessly replayed in a number of variants in the country's national imaginary, as historians, philosophers, politicians, and writers transcribed and translated the mythical ideas that cemented the modern foundations of Brazil. Brazil's modern identity itself thus came into being through a process of translation, as European ideas of Brazil as paradise played a part in forging the cultural, ideological, and political foundations of the country. This reminds us of the colonial production or "invention" of Brazil itself, whose foundations were never always already in place but relationally produced and legitimated.

Chauí's work engages with and exposes the ways in which this translation has been reiterated in various guises, reading them against the grain to expose their political effects. The relationality that Chauí exposes as key to the production of Brazil is also at the heart of the essays here. Many of the essays here highlight and develop from a concern with a local or Brazilian history; they also reveal an intricate dialogue and engagement with universal intellectual ideas and theories that have been involved both in the very invention of Brazil as well as its critique. The promises and limits of translation are intimately woven into Chauí's engagement with the various intellectual discourses and philosophical ideas. Thus though some readers may be unfamiliar with the essays themselves, they may recognize the debates and topics they feed into. Some of these debates have been translated in different ways elsewhere. An example is Roberto Schwarz's work, specifically his seminal essay "As Idéias fora de lugar," which is referred to in a number of essays in this collection. Well known to the Anglo-American audience through its translation by John Gledson as *Misplaced Ideas*, Schwarz's essay has been translated here as *Out of Place Ideas*, in order to capture the sense of the spatial disjunction and incongruity—central to Schwarz's text—between Brazil's social and economic reality and its foreign forms of ideological sustenance. In this sense *out of place ideas* echoes its common usage in archeology, as a phrase that refers to objects found in seemingly impossible contexts that, therefore, challenge conventional and hegemonic history. This translation seems more salient to Chauí's *specific* use of Schwarz's essay, which has often been held up as a totalizing and wholesale diagnosis of a postcolonial condition. Chauí uses his work instead to explore the theoretical workings of an authoritarian imaginary that precisely played on and exploited the notion of the inadequacy and inappropriateness of foreign ideas, of ideas formulated elsewhere, for the Brazilian context; an imaginary that foregrounded notions of dependency implicit in cultural copying as well as the need for autochtonous economic and political models, central to the 1930s and the 1950s. Similarly, in the essays that follow Chauí's quotations from Schwarz's essay differ slightly from Gledson's translation in order to bring out the common and specific elements between both Brazilian theorists.

The word *letrado* also emerges in Chauí's essays that focus on the role and place of the intellectual in Brazil. This term may be familiar to Anglophone readers because of its centrality to literary debates, most notably Angel Rama's *The Lettered City*. This collection has maintained the word in Portuguese. The translation of *letrado*, "man of letters," is wholly inappropriate in Chauí's work, which characterizes the *letrado* by his proximity to the law and the juridical foundations of the state. The *letrado* in this context is a lawyer, lawmaker, or a public statesman, the member of a professional class or *estamento* to use Raymundo Faoro's term, whose educated or enlightened opinion is capable of intervening in matters of state legislation, administration, and control, as well as educational policy. It is this legal figure that Chauí's work discusses, focusing on the *letrado* as an intellectual figure linked to the legal and juridical, and the political, foundations of state formation, rather than the literary figure who controls written forms of representation. Other words and phrases have also been kept in Portuguese in their English translation, their explanation often central to the essay itself. This is particularly true of Chauí's essays dealing with popular culture, in which highly localized figures, places, and practices, such as *boteco*, *pedaço*, or *colega*, as well as the everyday urban slang of city residents and migrant workers, contest the literal status of any translated word, revealing the impossibility of and resistance to translation that is central to political intervention. In keeping these words in Portuguese I have hoped that they may find a home within the English context.

In many of Chauí's essays, the inclusion of the reported speech of migrant workers and urban inhabitants consciously draws attention to the fissure between the language of their author, Chauí, and those subjects whose speech she reports. The translations here have attempted to preserve this fissure, finding urban equivalents for the Portuguese slang where possible but also recognizing the impossibility of this. The translations have also aimed to maintain Chauí's informal and idiomatic style, in which the author's personal opinions are made transparent. They have tried to respect Chauí's distinctive pace and rhythm.

The excursive style, which tends toward meditative and explanatory digressions in between sentences, has been kept, as has her tendency to clarify previous examples and sentences, a mark typically employed in scholarly Portuguese. Now and again, where a concept is cast over the length of several sentences, I have felt it necessary to repeat the initial reference or to divide long sentences and paragraphs without impairing the ideas conveyed.

"O dever-se" has been translated throughout this collection as "the ought." This translation renders the philosophical sense of a normative order that can be uncoupled from the natural order of things, that is, the ways things should or ought to be, as opposed to the way things are. This meaning is salient in Chauí's Spinozan or Spinozan-influenced essays, where it refers not to a literal sense of duty or obligation, but to a normative order that impinges on human actions and human freedom, forcing individuals to act contrary to the prescripts of the order of nature. Drawing from Spinoza, Chauí critiques the imposition of a normative order, the view that human beings "ought to be" governed by normative ideas, rather than the more descriptive laws that govern the rest of nature.

Finally, let me turn to the title of this book itself. Readers familiar with Chauí's work will recognize its reference to her 1986 study, *Conformity and Resistance. Aspects of Popular Culture in Brazil,* from which the chapter "Popular Culture and Authoritarianism" has been taken. Initially planned for a foreign audience, this study examines popular culture in Brazil, attempting to define and understand its internal dynamics, in ways that challenge the exclusive paradigms of enlightened views that had posited it as a form of conformity or resistance to hegemonic culture. Exploring various forms of popular culture, from religion through urban networks to housing projects, Chauí's work challenges this exclusive paradigm to trace the emergence of popular cultural practices as internal to dominant practice, and to look at how it creatively appropriates, uses, and manipulates it. This creativity is at play in Chauí's own work and its engagement to broader intellectual theories and philosophical ideas that are brought to bear on Brazilian culture, politics, and society.

Introduction

Maite Conde

In a national culture of notable variety and depth, philosopher Marilena Chauí is one of Brazil's most well-known and outspoken thinkers. A *paulista*, she was born and educated in São Paulo. She studied philosophy at the University of São Paulo where she has been teaching since 1967, the year she defended her master's thesis. In a career spanning four decades, Chauí has published numerous books, articles, and essays, and she regularly contributes to the country's press. Amongst her many books and essays, she has written on philosophers as well, such as Maurice Merleau-Ponty and most notably Baruch Spinoza; her study *A nervura do real* (*The Nerve of Reality*) was published in 2004, the culmination of thirty years of research on and engagement with the seventeenth-century Dutch Jewish philosopher.

It would be no exaggeration to say that Chauí's works have led to her consecration as one of Brazil's foremost philosophers, well known not just in academic circles but way beyond as well. Her 1984 book *O que é ideologia?* (*What Is Ideology?*) became a bestseller, an extraordinary phenomenon for a work of philosophy. This kind of success testifies to Chauí's own desire to dismantle the notion of philosophy as something specialized and remote, to see it instead as another conception of the world and in doing so to restore to philosophy a coherent and critical specificity. Indeed, many of Chauí's books, such as *Conformismo e resistência* (*Conformity and Resistance*, 1986), *Cultura e democracia* (*Culture and democracy*, 1989), and *Escritos sobre a universidade* (*Writings on the University*, 2001), critically engage with and philosophically reflect on specific political scenes and concerns that have shaped and impacted the social and cultural landscape of Brazil since the years of the dictatorship.

The military coup of 1964, paradoxically dubbed "a revolution," saw the collapse of the utopian spirit that had previously marked the country's political landscape. Direct physical repression, the systematic use of censorship and torture, and political assassination marked the ensuing years. These repressive measures were designed to create favorable conditions for Brazil's "economic miracle," based on massive multinational investment and the country's complete integration into the world economy. The so-called return to democracy in the mid-1980s was marked not so much by the overthrow of the previous regime as by its gradual replacement by a series of transitional governments that restored electoral government yet maintained many of the economic policies of the past.

The same period also saw the emergence of a new political protagonist with the growth of a number of grassroots social movements that started to demand reforms. These included women's groups, the gay movement, the landless workers' movement, and most significantly the *Partido dos trabalhadores,* or PT (the Worker's Party), Brazil's ruling party since 2002. Struggling to create rights and to define citizenship, this new historical subject radically challenged the playing field of Brazilian politics, leading to the reassessment of concepts and categories—the state, civil society, democracy—all of which are central to Chauí's philosophical inquiries.

Chauí's career and work cannot be thought of in isolation from these transformations. Under the gradual onset of the dictatorship in the late 1970s, she was one of the founding members of the PT and has been an active member ever since. In 1989 she was appointed São Paulo's secretary of culture in the PT administration of Mayor Luiza Erundina, a post she held until 1992. As secretary of culture Chauí implemented a number of new programs in São Paulo. This included the project called *Cidadania Cultural* (Cultural Citizenship) that saw the introduction of several *casas de cultura* (cultural centers) throughout the city's peripheral or marginal areas. The project was part of a broader initiative to establish culture as a right for all citizens, and to provide all citizens with the right to participate in decisions regarding the practice of culture.

This emphasis on broadening cultural participation informs not just Chauí's political activities but her philosophical work too. Chauí's intellectual trajectory combines a vocation for politics with a desire to know. Blending philosophical commitment to truth and reflective judgment with political participation, Chauí embodies what Pierre Bourdieu calls the paradoxical nature of the intellectual, challenging the classical, and false, opposition between autonomous reflection and intervention. It is this difficult synthesis between autonomous reflection and intervention that makes Chauí, as she herself says, an engaged intellectual.

An important part of the origins of Chauí's engagement lies in reassessing the role of intellectual, and indeed philosophical, ideas in the political process of culture and state formation. This reassessment is undoubtedly informed by the context in which Chauí's work emerged, namely, the period of redemocratization. Yet far from reflecting on this specific period, Chauí casts a wider gaze back in and across time to look at how intellectual ideas and systems of thought have played a part in forging and perpetuating what she refers to as the authoritarian structure of Brazilian society. Writing forcefully in 1986, a year after the election of Tancredo Neves, which saw the end of more than two decades of dictatorship, Chauí dispels the celebratory idea that the country has *returned* to democracy. Brazil is an authoritarian country, she writes. It is a country that has yet to realize the liberal principles of republicanism; it is a country in which traditional hierarchies persist and in which social relations are dictated by arbitrary practices of tutelage, clientelism, and favor; it is a country that "came to know citizenship through the new type: the *senhor-cidadão*, who reserves citizenship as a class privilege, making of it a regulated and periodic concession to other social classes that can be taken away when the dominant class decides (as during dictatorships)." For Chauí, the curtailment of civil and political rights during the dictatorship should not be considered a temporary aberration but rather part of a political model rooted in Brazil's authoritarian structure. What is important, therefore, is to show how intellectual ideas have helped to forge and perpetuate this social structure, and also how they may participate in constructing an alternative political landscape: a politics of absolute democracy, following Spinoza.

In her essay "Brazil. The Foundational Myth," Chauí explores and exposes the ideas that lay behind the "invention" of Brazil, a maneuver that recalls the narrative creations of imagined communities explored in much recent cultural criticism.[1] If this work sought to go beyond the narratives of an originary identity, Chauí, on the other hand, consciously returns to the very source and originary moment of Brazil's identity and its mythological foundations. "Myth in the anthropological sense: an imaginary solution for tensions, conflicts and contradictions that cannot be resolved in reality. Myth in the psychoanalytical sense: repetition, compulsion due to the impossibility of symbolism and above all as a barrier to the passage to reality. Foundational myth because like every *foundatio*, it imposes an internal link with the past that does not cease, that does not allow the work of temporal differences and that maintains itself perennially present."[2]

Chauí's focus is not a discourse of nationalism, but rather a particular narrative of origins that has functioned in the name of "the nation," that is, "Brazil," the "people" or "Brazilians" making them the subjects of theological-political power. This narrative has its roots in theological-political ideas that were forged in Europe in the age of conquest and colonization. These ideas rested on three interrelated concepts: first, the vision of paradise—the idea of Brazil as a Garden of Eden, with an exuberant nature and inhabited by a cordial, happy, and peaceful people, an idyllic land free from all conflicts; second, the theological and providentialist history that asserts that Brazilians are part of God's providential plan, the new chosen people for a new covenant, revelation, and redemption of faith at the end of time. Allied to this is a prophetic-messianic notion of history, based in a cosmic battle and struggle against the forces of evil. And third, a juridical and theocratic notion of the divine or absolute ruler who is responsible for the enactment of the prophetic providentialist notion of history. These ideas invented both Brazil's identity and its political power, the state itself, which is exterior to and precedes society. The Brazilian state comes into being as an idea already realized and a model yet to be constructed, whose implementation and enactment depend on a divine leader. For Chauí, therefore, these theological ideas are not just the originating form of political power, they also function as the originating imaginary form of relating to political power.

As Chauí points out, the foundational myth has been a diffuse presence in Brazil, where it is unceasingly and compulsively repeated, finding new languages, values, and ideas. In this context Chauí's elaboration echoes much scholarship that has highlighted the ambivalent process of politics and state formation in Brazil, work that has focused largely on the modern period of the republic, highlighting the autocratic nature of the republic's beginnings in Brazil, which had little or no collective roots. Perhaps most well known to English-speaking readers is Roberto Schwarz's now-famous argument that European liberal ideas of democracy and citizenship were "out of place' when they were first imported to Brazil in the nineteenth century, when the country was still dependent on slave labor. For Schwarz, these ideas took on an ornamental guise that expressed the elite's aspiration to be modern, but had little or no connection to actual social relations.[3] In the period that followed the abolition of slavery (1888) and the establishment of the republican state (1889), modern liberal conceptions such as democracy and citizenship continued to be the privilege of a small minority who had access to civil, political, and social rights that were denied to others. Chauí's work can be interpreted as keying into such scholarship, revealing how Brazil's social structure was inherited from colonialism.

Instead of focusing on the foreign or out-of-place nature of Brazilian politics and the state, however, Chauí explores the internal determinations of Brazil's myth of origins and its rearticulation through a host of national intellectual and cultural debates that developed in the twentieth century. This entails explorations of the country's difficult history, witnessed in Chauí's essay "The Integralist Imaginary," which deals with the intellectual ideas of Brazil's protofascist Integralist Party that emerged in the 1920s and 1930s in the context of Getúlio Vargas's corporatist New State. It also includes new readings of well-worn concepts of Brazil's cultural history, evident in her work on popular culture. Popular culture has been a key concept in Brazil's intellectual thought arguably from the republic onward, when it was deployed as a source of national specificity and a promise of native regeneration in a secular world. Chauí returns specifically to the late 1950s and early 1960s and the deployment of the popular by left-wing intellectuals seeking to mobilize "the people" for a project of national transformation. In doing so she explores the ways in which popular culture became involved in the methods and language of the period's populism.

This involvement must be traced back to the decade before 1964, when Chauí was a student at the University of São Paulo. During these years the debate on Brazil's national identity was systematically taken up by a number of intellectuals that included distinguished sociologists, historians, and philosophers from the University of São Paulo. These intellectuals identified underdevelopment as the primary obstacle to Brazil's nationhood, since it involved appropriation by foreign imperial powers, as opposed to the realization of the nation's own essence. In this discourse the nation was thought of as transcending all internal conflicts, with the conflict between the periphery and the metropolis as primordial, and the people were enlisted in the progressive task of overcoming underdevelopment.

Popular culture became a central category in this debate, one of the nation's foundational myths, in which it operated both as an alibi of the identity between the state and Brazil and as a way of referring to the political potential of the people. As Chauí points out, an example of this populist cultural politics can be seen in the Popular Culture Centers (CPCs) that operated in Brazil between 1961 and 1964. For Chauí their use of the popular was highly ambiguous: on the one hand it was valued positively as a force of resistance and a potential source for political and social transformation, the political action of "the people"; on the other it was seen as negative, an example of conformity, as representative of a culture that has been usurped and infused with foreign dominant values and that is intellectually impoverished, a view that reflects "the people" themselves. Popular culture, therefore, emerges not as part of the subaltern classes' own conception of the world but as a political weapon for producing a national consciousness against the false metropolitan culture. Reducing a complex cultural field to two poles—conformity or resistance—this ambiguity, Chauí argues, produces an image *or idea of* popular culture (either in the sense of an idea to be realized or in the sense of a model to be followed) whose implementation depends upon the existence of a moral and intellectual leadership committed to the national project of enlightening the people. These intellectuals ignored the actual experiences of individual lives engaged in daily struggles and victories and opted instead for popular culture understood as an idea that was engaged in a cosmic battle against the evil forces of imperialism.

This form of paternalistic and pedagogical substitution is illustrative of the ways in which these ideas of popular culture were an example of what Chauí calls authoritarian thinking. Grounded in a transcendental and separated knowledge that was both exterior and previous to the existence of real social subjects, authoritarian thinking reduces the people to the condition of manipulable sociopolitical objects, whilst agency remains with the state and its intellectual bureaucrats. This authoritarian thinking is thus grounded in the kinds of exclusion and abstractions between the idea of the state and society that, according to Chauí, founded Brazil. However, if this idea of authoritarian thinking is linked to the particular context Chauí explores, it can also be related to the kind of representational thinking that has characterized Western metaphysics since Plato, reposing on a double identity: of the intellectual sovereign subject and the concepts it creates, concepts that have been at the service of the state.

In "Popular Culture and Authoritarianism," Chauí returns to the idea of popular culture and the binary of conformity or resistance, exploring its particular place in Brazil during the years of the dictatorship. Seeking to work beyond the exclusive dualisms of the past, she looks to wrench the popular away from its nationalist-populist contours and draws up a map of popular cultural practices in order to establish the terrain in which cultural transformation might take place. She seeks not to produce a static descriptive picture but to explore relations between dominant and subaltern forms in dynamic terms as they act upon each other in particular and located contexts. In doing so Chauí's work goes beyond the exclusive paradigms that previously subjected ideas of popular culture—as oppositional or dominated—and looks at it instead as a dispersed set of practices that develop inside a given social system.

This is well exemplified in the popular national housing project initiated "primarily as a means of controlling an urban population that had mushroomed due to internal migration." In the 1970s, in the midst of the military's economic miracle, state planners created housing projects for the people or the masses, producing uniform and homogeneous houses using low-grade material. Much to the planners' dismay these houses were "destroyed." Façades were repainted with bright colors by their occupants, sidewalks were transformed into communal gardens, and kitchens were turned into living rooms so that the faceless monotone and ordered residences became festively chaotic. Receiving the personal touches of the residences and the community, the houses were transformed into homes. As Chauí points out, residents did not oppose, reject, or critique these official programs of modernization. They resisted them through a process of creative appropriation and adaptation to their own everyday needs and desires.

This form of resistance is not disinterested or "universal"; it is linked to users' own particular needs and desires, and works through and in spite of dominant rationalizing projects, outwitting their ideal designs. There is a ludic element in this idea of the popular that owes much to the Brazilian notion of *malandragem (Malandroism)* or trickery elaborated in 1970 by literary critic Antonio Candido. For Candido *malandroism* represents a countercultural ethos of playfulness, the circumvention of social rules, and a defiance of discipline and order, which emerges as an immediate creative response to the needs of the present. Taking on the dialectical aspects of this "ethos," Chauí traces popular cultural practices to the dynamics of the workings of Brazil's society. In doing so she rethinks popular culture away from its populist and patriotic connotations, focusing on how users—previously assumed to be passive, guided by dominant rules and alienated—actively intervene in the field that attempts to regulate and control them. This emphasis on users marks a shift away from the idea of popular culture as a product that can be harnessed politically to its idea as a signifying practice.

All of this raises key questions regarding the place of politics in Brazil, questions that in the 1980s fed into the contemporary debates regarding the struggle for democracy. By illuminating everyday forms of resistance Chauí redefines the notion of democracy and political transformation away from the official politico-institutional realm to that of society as a whole. The demand for freedom, representation, and participation, she says, has defined the tenor of popular culture, in which the people have struggled to assert their own presence in public life and their own needs, desires, and rights in society. This bears close relations to the practices of the grassroots social movements and their demands for political representation and agency. Keying into everyday practices and struggles, Chauí provides us with an alternative analysis of cultural transformation, one that moves away from change as led by prophetic intellectuals and the state and that emerges from the ground.

In locating the popular as an everyday strategy, her work opens up a new methodological space that seeks to return to the things themselves. Rather than speaking for the people, Chauí's work adopts a historical anthropological approach that avoids essentialisms by attempting to listen to how subjects interpret their own lives. The approach is evident in her texts, which are replete with personal accounts, testimonies, and memories. These methodologies depart from the programmatic-pragmatic stance of authoritarian ideas regarding the popular in the past; they aim instead to confront that which has not yet been thought (the real being here and now) and attempt to understand the work of theory wherein form and content are not separate. Her work on popular culture can thus be read as a "thesis" or blueprint for a practical philosophy, one that is grounded in a more sustainable intellectual engagement with democracy. Given her active participation in the political process, this reinterpretation has profound significance for Chauí herself. Indeed, one of the hallmarks of Chauí's work is her insistence on bringing herself into the frame of her inquiries, reflecting on and representing her own position and methodology. Reading her essays, therefore, becomes a task of understanding her intellectual identity as an instantiation of the particular social, historical, and political narratives of Brazil she deals with and is part of.

Such engagement is central to her essay "Winds of Progress," which outlines a movement for popular educational reform at the University of São Paulo in the 1980s that Chauí was part of. The movement aimed to forge the space of the university and of learning as a democratic activity by changing the built in power structure between the professor and the students. This entailed moving beyond the notion of the university as a site of knowledge transfer and focusing instead on education as a dialogue that keys into the existing intellectual activity of students. These ideas correspond to a critical pedagogy and popular education as theorized and practiced by Paulo Freire that had been so influential in the years before the dictatorship. By taking up Freire's ideas, the movement presented a direct contestation of the political restructuring of education that took place in the late 1970s. It was then that Brazilian universities were modernized and opened their doors to the masses. This massification was by no means restricted to Brazil. The years following the student mobilizations of 1968 saw a number of educational reforms in Europe and the United States that also claimed to allow a broad populace to attend college. As a beginning and as a solution to the country's own student crisis, Brazil's democratizing reform of the university was impelled by the military regime and took place in the absence of the features of liberal democracy. In Brazil, this expansionist logic was part of the broader modernizing policies of the dictatorship that marked the years of the economic miracle. In line with these policies, education was to be faced as "a quantitative phenomenon to be resolved with maximum efficiency and minimum investment, devising a university system based on the administrative model of large companies, acting under a business management system" (4). The administration of the university was reformed in line with a more business-like approach to pedagogy. Students were transformed into statistics to be imparted with useful knowledge, or a technical knowhow, that could be applied practically to the bureaucratic world.

Chauí's essay offers a haunting Brazilian case study (for want of a better word) of the emergence of what Stanley Aronowitz calls "the knowledge factory" and others have variously referred to as "the corporate university," "digital diploma mills," and "academic capitalism."[4] Indeed, the expansion of the university that took place in Brazil involved the bureaucratizing trends highlighted by these scholars that also placed the sovereignty of administration above the purposes of faculty and students. If as elsewhere this administration of the university emerged in response to social and economic factors, that is, global capitalism, in Brazil it was also tied to the exigencies of the military, so that the reduced concept of learning was part of an authoritarian regime that aimed to replace cultural capital with an emphasis on producing a more efficient, disciplined, compliant, and less critical Brazilian workforce. The development of technical skills and regulation of teaching and research that underlay the Brazilian administered university took the place of an externally imposed discipline and went hand in hand with the economic demands of global capital, which, to use Chauí's words, fit the military like a glove.

Although Chauí's essay on the university is firmly grounded in the specific Brazilian context, it nevertheless has relevance to our own context today. Indeed, reading "The Winds of Progress" in England in 2010 is particularly poignant: the recent recession has served to justify and redouble efforts that began as openly political interventions by the neoliberalizing Thatcherite government (enthusiastically carried forward by Blair) to make the university more economically viable and sustainable. The contemporary downsizing and in many cases complete amputation of certain subjects—philosophy, literature, and modern languages[5]—is linked to a rational impetus that emphasizes the need for high student numbers, knowledge transfer, resource input, and profit margins. Research too has been subjected to restructuring with findings translated into intellectual property, a marketable commodity, economic development, and impact. Beyond the aim to produce a practical knowledge, shovel-ready for bureaucratic application, underlying the contemporary quantification of teaching and research is the desire to compare on a level plane every university, nationally as well as internationally.

One of the consequences of the emergence of the bureaucratic wage earner–producing university is the end of its autonomy. Of course, the university was never fully autonomous in Brazil. Under the populist and liberal states universities were privileged sites for manufacturing the intellectual fraction of the elite in charge of juridical and economic apparatuses. In this sense it was an ideological state apparatus par excellence, since it represented the epitome of a modern reflection of the state. But this function was never homogenous and the university was always the site where counterhegemonic movements evolved, 1968 being a case in point. The democratizing reforms that followed were in fact part of an authoritarian effort to make sure that this "crisis" never happened again. As Chauí notes, the autonomy of the university was a prime target since it was perceived as an "ideal venue for teaching material that could be prejudicial to the country's social order and to democracy." Given links between the university and the state however, the reforms Chauí describes must also be taken as an articulation of transformations in the role of the state, whose function from the 1970s onward was reduced to the workings of global capital.

In this context, the production of knowledge has become subsumed by the logic of the market. This situation, as Chauí points out, is damaging to the figure of the engaged intellectual, whose public discourse is silenced and threatened with extinction. However, Chauí's analysis of the contemporary silence of the engaged intellectual carries personal resonance. Since the PT assumed office in 2002, the mainstream press has repeatedly accused its intellectual adherents, Chauí included, of not taking part vocally in critiques against the government, of having lost or forsaken their autonomy and their oppositional stance. In her essay "The Engaged Intellectual" Chauí implicitly acknowledges these critics. She writes of the difficult situation faced by the intellectual who engages in left-wing party politics, that is, in opposition parties, which then become the ruling or governing party. If the intellectual always speaks in favor of this party, he becomes an ideologue; if he always speaks against it, he becomes a traitor. Yet the engaged intellectual's silence, she writes, is not the outcome of a refusal to formulate public discourses, but an inability to do so in a climate where knowledge has been made a slave to the demands of the market, thereby dissolving the grounds of autonomy central for critical reflection.

In the current climate, knowledge is increasingly bought and sold like a commodity and dependent on rapidly obsolete market trends. In this context, the voice of the engaged intellectual has been silenced, replaced by that of the competent specialist, a kind of free floating professional intelligentsia whose technical competency is on sale for anyone and whose critical activity is reduced to providing opinions and information. The emergence of these specialists can be linked to the often repeated charge that "grand narratives of emancipation and enlightenment" no longer have any currency and have been replaced by local situations in which intellectuals prize competence not universal values, like freedom and knowledge. For Chauí this situation is symptomatic of an oblivion of politics. In today's landscape, political action has been submitted to the methods of the society of the spectacle, reducing the citizen to the private figure of a consumer. Consequently, politics is expressed through private consumption rather than shared struggles and spaces, and citizenship has morphed into the twinned practices of accumulation and consumption.

Chauí's work touches on discussions beyond the Brazilian context that have likewise emphasized the dominance of private and specular forms of citizenship. This privatization of politics limits public space, preventing the development of counterhegemonic movements and controlling signifying practices. Yet as Chauí points out, in Brazil the constitution of public space has always been complex. It has been dominated by the private space, and forged by social relations configured by informal and patriarchal practices of favor and clientelism. Thus Chauí's work has relevance to broader discussions and highlights the ways in which the privatization of politics relates more specifically to Brazil, where the contemporary political landscape seems to replay the limitations that have marked the constitution of the country's public life.

Startlingly, absent from Chauí's recent analysis of the present and politics is an exploration of the kind of negotiations that marked her earlier essays on popular culture. Indeed reading these later essays leads to certain questions: does the society of the spectacle completely neutralize critical agency by conditioning an apolitical and atomized relationship to the media? Is it possible to see questions and demands for citizenship being answered in the private realm of consumption and the media? Chauí's contemporary work purposely shies away from this emphasis on everyday forms of reception in order to move beyond the festishization of the practice of culture and focus instead on the production of politics. At the heart of this is a renewed concern with questions of ideology and the new narratives by which it is reproduced. If this concern marks a return to the concerns of the past, it now emerges in a political and social landscape that has been radically reconstituted. The whirlwind of deregulation, privatization, and restructuring under Fernando Henrique Cardoso in the 1990s—and with it the dissolution of the industrial working class—has torn up all established relations between economy and politics, classes and representation, a process that has been overdetermined by the intense exposure to the relations of global capital. This new indeterminate era has given rise to a new form of subjectivity, corroding the prospect of class solidarity and collective identification and inculcating instead values of individual competition—all of which have been reasserted by the privatized form of politics.

Perhaps it is not surprising that in this age of indeterminacy, a number of myths from the past have been symbolically recuperated. Most significant here is Brazil's foundational myth itself. The 1990s saw an emphasis on "Brazil" in a way that reunited politics and culture. This return to the past culminated in the year 2000, the year of the country's quincentenary. The 500th anniversary of the discovery of Brazil saw the commemoration of the nation in a number of official celebrations elaborately prepared by the government of Fernando Henrique Cardoso. High profile discourses on national identity were also disseminated in the mass media, especially in the media conglomerate the Globo Network, which proliferated its hegemonic industrialized version of the national-popular. This electronic simulacra thus recycled Brazil's well-worn political imagery, packaging and marketing it as an image, both nationally and internationally.

If this myth returned with force, it was also accompanied by the dissemination of a dystopian imagery. Images of violence have proliferated the country's press and TV since the 1990s, with accounts of murders, kidnappings, and assaults gaining widespread circulation through the media. This proliferation has undoubtedly been influenced by the real increase in social violence, fueled by social inequality, poor governance, and conflict wrought by the drug trade. Real cases of violence have saturated the media with daily reports of urban crimes appearing on the television and in newspapers and becoming a marked feature of the country's cinematic production and its literature. This media saturation of violence contradicts a key image of Brazil's foundational myth, one that is still perpetuated on a daily basis: that of its non-violence. This aspect of the myth rests on "the image of an ordered and peaceful people, who are happy and cordial, racially mixed and incapable of ethnic, religious or social discriminations; who are friendly towards foreigners, generous with the needy, proud of our regional differences and destined for a great future." How is it possible for this myth of Brazil's non-violence to exist in the face of the dissemination of real-life violence, asks Chauí. For her the widespread circulation of a violent Brazil goes hand in hand with the myth of Brazil's essential non-violence. This new imagery, she argues, produces interpretations that depict violence not as the outcome of internal social inequalities or demands for justice by individuals or groups otherwise excluded from social and political life, but rather as criminal disruptions emerging from "foreign" elements that threaten Brazil's idyllic cohesion. Images of violence thus produce new patterns of exclusion and segregation within public life, in ways that actually reaffirm Brazil's foundational myth precisely in an age of indeterminacy.

Published in 2000, Chauí's book and essay of the same title, "Brazil. The Foundational Myth" is dedicated to demystifying this contemporary return to nation, exposing its theological-political roots. This testifies to the ways in which Chauí's work and her insights are closely imbricated in and engage with Brazil's sociopolitical scene. This engagement, however, is also mediated by a number of key thinkers and philosophers: Antonio Gramsci, Maurice Merleau Ponty, and Baruch Spinoza. Though highly diverse, these thinkers are united in their critique of negativity, hatred of interiority, the denunciation of power and a defense of freedom. Most significant here is Spinoza. The subject of her doctoral thesis written in the 1960s, Chauí's engagement with Spinoza has been lifelong obsession and passion. She has published three books and numerous essays dedicated solely to his practical philosophy. Her writings on Spinoza departs from other contemporary reflections of the philosopher's works, most notably Michael Hardt and Antonio Negri, which tend to focus on and deploy Spinozan concepts, such as the multitude, in a way that may extract them from Spinoza's particular theories of the state and democracy, This small collection reproduces one of Chauí's Spinozan essays, "Power and Freedom. Politics in Spinoza."

Its reading of Spinoza's principal works (*Ethics* and *Theologico-Political Treatise*) allows us to see how Chauí's explorations of Brazilian politics, culture, and society draw on his own examination on politics and democracy. Crucial here is Spinoza's demonstration of the religious or theological roots of political regimes, which for him formed the ideological basis and persistence of their power, becoming key obstacles to the formation of democracy.

These ideas are, of course, key to Chauí's formulation of Brazil's foundational myth and the ways in which it has been perpetuated by the invention of the country as a vision of paradise, free of conflicts. Like Spinoza, Chauí works to demythify this foundation of Brazilian politics, revealing its effects and the laws of its production, and also pointing to ways in which everyday needs and desires can form the basis of a true or absolute politics of democracy. Situating the foundations of Spinoza's politics in his ontology, this essay not only outlines his ideas concerning democracy; it also highlights an alternative conception of the political subject, power, and freedom, in which democracy emerges as the most natural of all regimes. The essay highlights how Chauí's dialogue with Spinoza has shaped her broader discussions and concerns regarding modern politics, culture, and society in Brazil. It also reveals how Brazil's own political history and its contradictory relationship with democracy have in turn shaped Chauí's own engagement with Spinoza.

The essays included in this collection are the first English translations of Chauí's work. The predominant focus here is Brazil, though collectively the essays speak to the association between culture, politics, and the state, including an examination of the complex link between intellectual ideas and state power. Underpinning this volume, therefore, is a belief that the value of Chauí's interventions extends beyond just Brazil and Latin America. The collection aims to provide English readers with a bold, original, and creative contribution to contemporary critical theory and cultural history, one that whilst emerging from a particular location, speaks across time and space.

In closing this introductory essay, it is worth stressing that editing and translating are inevitably and unavoidably difficult processes. The process of bringing Chauí's work into representation in English is marked by exclusions and absences. This collection of essays offers only a fleetingly partial glimpse at Chauí's sustained critique and engagement with Brazil and with philosophical thought more generally over the past forty years.

The Engaged Intellectual:
A Figure Facing Extinction?

Knowledge has no light but that shed on the world by redemption.
—Adorno, *Minima Moralia*

I.

Since the Dreyfus Affair, we have seen the emergence of a figure that Zola summoned to the public scene: *the intellectual*, whose speech and action are rooted in the affirmation of their autonomy and in their two fundamental characteristics: the defense of *universal causes*, namely those separate from personal interests, and the *transgression* of the dominant order. Therefore, by definition, the intellectual is always someone socially and politically engaged. Today, intellectuals seem to be publically invisible and silent. Is the engaged intellectual a figure facing extinction?

In his interpretation of the historical project of modernity, Boaventura de Sousa Santos writes that the project was based on two pillars: the pillar of regulation and the pillar of emancipation. The pillar of regulation was supported by three principles: the state (an indivisible sovereignty, which established a politics of vertical integration among citizens), the market (which established a horizontal individualist and antagonistic political obligation), and the community (horizontal political obligation and solidarity among its members).[1] The pillar of emancipation was constituted by three principles of rational autonomy: the expressive rationality of the arts, the cognitive and instrumental rationality of science and technology, and the practical rationality of ethics and rights. The project of modernity was underwritten by a belief in the possibility of a harmonious development between regulation and emancipation and the complete rationalization of individual and collective life. The abstract nature of the principles of each of its pillars, however, led to the tendency to maximize one over the other; moreover, the relationship between the modern project and the emergence of capitalism secured the victory of regulation at the expense of emancipation.

Using Boaventura de Sousa Santos' terminology, we can state that the pillar of emancipation or logic of the principle of the rational autonomy of the arts, sciences, technology, ethics, and rights determined the emergence of the figure of the modern thinker and the artist, independent from ecclesiastical, state, and academic institutions. The modern rational autonomy of actions (arts, ethics, rights, and techniques) and of thought (science and philosophy) provided these figures with more than independence: it provided them with the theoretical and practical *authority* to critique religious, political, and academic institutions, as the French Enlightenment *philosophes* did, and in the nineteenth century to critique the economy, social relations, and values, as the utopian socialists, anarchists, and marxists did. It will be useful here to cite an extract from Pierre Bourdieu's essay on the role of the intellectual in the modern world:

> Intellectuals have come about historically in and by their overcoming the opposition between pure culture and engagement. Thus they are *bi-dimensional* beings. To claim the title of intellectual, cultural producers must fulfill two conditions: on the one hand, they must belong to an intellectually autonomous field, one independent of religious, political, economic or other powers, and they must respect that field's particular laws; on the other, they must deploy their specific expertise and authority in their particular intellectual domain in a political activity outside it. They must remain full-time cultural producers without becoming politicians. Despite their antinomy between autonomy and engagement, it is possible to extend both simultaneously. The greater the intellectuals' independence from mundane interests because of their specific expertise (e.g. the scientific authority of an Oppenheimer or the authority of a Sartre), the greater their inclination to assert this independence by criticizing the powers that be and the greater the symbolic effectiveness of whatever political positions they might take.[2]

Tracing the historical trajectory of intellectuals, Bourdieu refers to the "paradoxical situation" and the "difficult synthesis" between pure culture and engagement, since intellectuals oscillate between retreat and public engagement, between silence and public intervention, an oscillation that emerges from particular circumstances in which the demand for rational autonomy is either respected or threatened by institutional powers.

Nothing illustrates the difficulty of this synthesis better than the debate between Jean-Paul Sartre and Maurice Merleau-Ponty concerning the figure of the *engaged intellectual* that emerged in postwar France and whose visible manifestation was the creation of their journal *Les Temps Modernes*, which was dedicated to political and cultural intervention. The debate took place in 1953 and was linked to the defense of the French Communist Party undertaken by Sartre, who until then had been an anticommunist.

On April 28, 1953, the French Communist Party summoned workers to a demonstration against the Korean War. It then called for a general strike on May 4 to protest against the imprisonment of the party's general secretary Jacques Duclos, which had taken place during the preceding month's demonstration. Neither of these actions received mass support from the French workers.

Sartre published his first article for the series *The Communist and Peace* in *Les Temps Modernes* in which he spoke out against Duclos' imprisonment, anticommunism, and the workers' weak response to the French Communist Party. With regard to anticommunism, Sartre stated that, when attacked, the communist party must be unconditionally defended by the left. With regard to the workers' response to the French Communist Party, Sartre's critique based itself in Marx's declaration in the *Communist Manifesto* that the proletariat must organize itself into a revolutionary party, concluding that, without the Communist Party, workers would not exist as a class—they would simply be a passive alienated mass.

Merleau-Ponty responded to and challenged Sartre's position. He published an article, in the journal, about the relationship between philosophy and politics and the contemporary crisis of the idea of revolution, in which Marx's idea of the development of class-consciousness had been substituted with the Bolshevik idea of "the interests of the party." So, in a Bolshevik manner, Sartre had identified the history of the proletariat with the action of the communist parties, overlooking the long and difficult history of the *workers' movements* to focus on the revolutionary self-image of a bureaucratic party that identified itself as the sole representative of the working class. Merleau-Ponty emphasized the difference between Marx and the communist parties: while the former demanded a praxis that was woven into the mediations between a proletarian subjectivity and the objectivity of historical material conditions, the latter undertook a Bolshevik identification between both, with no mediation.

Linked to the figure of the engaged intellectual, the debate highlights one of the key themes that Sartre and Merleau-Ponty developed in their work: the relationship between philosophy and politics, or what Merleau-Ponty calls "the difficult relationship between the philosopher and the City" and Sartre refers to as "a philosopher who is interested in real people, their labor and their suffering." With the impact of Marxism and the proletariat revolution, both men conceived of philosophy as a refusal of thought disconnected from the world, marking a departure from traditional French philosophy with its spiritualist and idealist foundations; but they also conceived of it as a critique of the philosophy of history elaborated by the French Communist Party that had been weakened by the division between idealist theory and an empirical praxis, linked to Stalinism and the bureaucratic idea of thought and action. In *Search for a Method*, Sartre writes:

> This Proletariat, far off, invisible, inaccessible, but conscious and acting, furnished the proof—obscurely for most of us—that not all conflicts had been resolved. We had been brought up in bourgeois humanism, and this optimistic humanism was shattered when we vaguely perceived around our town the immense crowd of "sub-men conscious of their subhumanity." But we sensed this shattering in a way that was still idealist and individualist. At about that time, the writers whom we loved explained to us that existence is a *scandal*. What interested us however, were real men with their labors and their troubles. We cried out for a philosophy that would account for everything, and we did not perceive that it existed already and that it was precisely this philosophy that provoked in us this demand.[3]

Similarly in *The War Has Taken Place*, Merleau-Ponty describes the disintegration of the French university's humanist optimism and good faith following the war, which had highlighted the brutal and inexcusable weight of history and the opacity of social relations, since these are not immediate relations between consciousnesses, but relations mediated by things and institutions.[4] In the summer of 1939, the war took the French by surprise because "we were not guided by facts" and had "secretly resolved to ignore violence and unhappiness as elements of history." At university, professors had been teaching that war was born from misunderstandings that can be resolved, or from events that can be reconciled by patience and courage. Intellectuals in the French Communist Party, convinced of possessing the master key to history and class struggle, saw Nazi-fascism as a capitalist crisis and the war simply as an event that would not affect the international solidarity of the proletariat. They, therefore, elaborated an ideology of war and class struggle that, based on a mechanical application of the relation between capital and labor, allowed them to avoid a materialist and historical analysis.

At the heart of Sartre's first philosophical work *Being and Nothingness* is the difference of essence between the world of things (Being) and consciousness (Nothingness). Being is resistant, opaque, and viscous, it is the *in-itself* (*en soi*), brutal and naked objectivity. Nothingness, on the other hand, is a consciousness that is insubstantial, pure activity, and spontaneity; it is the *for-itself* (*pour soi*), subjectivity. Here, the others, while presumed to be humans, are the world, and, therefore, beings or things. Hence the celebrated expression from his play, *No Exit (Huis Clos)*: "hell is other people," since each of them, consciousness or subject, reduces others to the condition of things and is reduced by others to the condition of a thing. Although situated in the world, consciousness, as Nothingness, is not conditioned by it and cannot be determined by things or facts; on the contrary, it has the power to negate them, making them exist as ideas, images, sentiments, and actions. Free from all ties, consciousness is pure freedom. Hence the well-known Sartrean adage: "man is condemned to be free." For Sartre, freedom provides engagement with meaning.

For Merleau-Ponty, Sartrean Nothingness is a new idealist version of a reflexive consciousness as sovereign, therefore, foundational, that constitutes the very meaning of Being. Merleau-Ponty's philosophy, on the contrary, accentuates the prereflexive world in which we live and from which we emerge as intercorporeal and intersubjective, as tied to the fabric of the world and of the others, without the power to constitute them. Merleau-Ponty's philosophy defines itself against intellectualism, that is, the supposition of the sovereignty of the consciousness as the creator of meaning and of the foundation of the world as meaning.

Against this intellectualist tradition, Merleau-Ponty emphasizes consciousness as embodied in a cognizant and reflexive body endowed with feeling and interiority, relating to other things as bodies that are also endowed with interiority and feeling, and with others, that are not things or parts of the landscape, but our own likeness. If consciousness is not a pure disembodied and sovereign spontaneity, then the philosopher cannot separate and detach himself from the world because we are not *in* the world (according to Sartre's emphasis on the *situation*); rather we are *of* and *with* the world. For Merleau-Ponty, engagement provides freedom with meaning.

We are involved in the world and with others in an inextricable tangle. The idea of situation rules out absolute freedom at the source of our commitments, and equally, indeed, at their terminus. No commitment, not even commitment in the Hegelian state, can make me leave behind all differences and free me for anything (...). I am a psychological and historical structure (...). All my actions and my thoughts stand in a relationship with this structure, and even a philosopher's thought is merely a way of making explicit his hold on the world, and what he is. The fact remains that I am free, not in spite of, or on the hither side of these motivations, but by means of them. For this significant life, this certain significance of nature and history which I am, does not limit my access to the world, but on the contrary is my means of entering into communication with it.[5]

What are the political consequences of these two different conceptions of philosophy? For Sartre, because consciousness is light and insubstantial, the philosopher can accept the call from all facts and all events, without being impregnated by them, therefore, conserving his sovereignty. For Merleau-Ponty, because consciousness is embodied and situated in an intercorporeality and intersubjectivity, the philosopher cannot, to use his own expression from *In Praise of Philosophy*, "assent to the thing itself, without restriction." This means, as he states, "one must be able to withdraw and gain distance in order to become truly engaged, which is also always an engagement with truth."

Sartre, however, claims that Merleau-Ponty possesses an idea of philosophy that would apparently allow him only to reconcile philosophy with politics, and that, in reality, both are incompatible. Politics, he writes, is an action founded in an objective choice based on available facts and events. If philosophy is, as Merleau-Ponty ascertains, the need to place oneself, prior to choice, at a point that allows for the complete apprehension of partial totalities, rather than the isolated facts that form our everyday experiences, then, Sartre writes, "today's philosopher cannot adopt a political attitude."

What was Merleau-Ponty's intention in July 1953? "One must know what the Soviet regime is in order to choose." For Sartre this intention seems merely empirical; it is the need to possess more facts, and is, therefore, fundamentally problematic since we never possess total knowledge of all historical conditions. We always make choices in the absence of full knowledge and, moreover, we cannot invoke philosophical reflexion when we are called to react to what is urgent and immediate. Sartre concludes that Merleau-Ponty's conception is wrong because, with it, one renounces politics. However, Merleau-Ponty replies that he does not renounce politics; he simply renounces the idea of engagement as conceived by Sartre.

What is Sartre's conception of engagement? The engaged intellectual is a writer who provides opinions on and intervenes in all relevant events as they take place. Engagement is a state of constant vigilance. Merleau-Ponty refutes this form of engagement for two reasons. First, by commenting on each event, the intellectual enables his readers to understand individual occurrences only in isolation. This approach does not impel readers to see the wider picture and it may allow readers to dismiss isolated occurrences as exceptional, whereas a comprehensive perspective may lead them to a fuller understanding. This type of engaged vigilance is then an example of *bad faith*. It does not inform, analyze, or reflect; rather it flows and changes in keeping with events, so much so that if a reader were to one day collect all of the manifestoes and articles written by this kind of engaged intellectual or political commentator, he would be able to comprehend the incoherence, levity, and irresponsibility of their author.

Merleau-Ponty's second reason initially seems paradoxical. Indeed, following his first reason, it would be easy to interpret Merleau-Ponty as attacking Sartre for acting blindly, commenting on all events taking place everywhere without comprehending the totality, or at least the lines of force and vectors of these events and their full significance. Merleau-Ponty's argument, however, takes the opposite approach. Thanks to the sovereignty of the consciousness over the Being, Sartre constructs a fixed future, both in thought and in the imaginary, one that is secret and that secretly regulates the course of events. Whatever may happen, Sartre possesses the future and history *in thought and in the imaginary*, making it easy for him to comment on everything and to take a position on everything. In other words, events are merely the surface of a secret history whose significance is known only to the philosopher, who can consequently comment politically in a sovereign manner. An absolute, sovereign, and transcendent spectator, the philosopher believes he holds the secret of time, history, and the world. Beneath the apparent modesty of the person who, as Sartre had stated, knows that the human condition is choosing blindly and in the face of ignorance and ambiguity, is the presumption of an Absolute Spirit. If the philosopher believes that he can assess the importance of events, it is because he believes he possesses the master key to history. His irresponsibility is based on the presupposition of a completed history (one that has already been realized in thought), which will erase the empirical steps it has produced from memory by absorbing them into a one-way street, making them and the fact that they were produced irrelevant. It is for this very reason that, in July 1953, Sartre could write that "every anticommunist is a swine, nothing will make me change my mind";

and just three years later, after the Soviet invasion of Budapest, did not hesitate to say: "It is and will be impossible to reestablish any sort of contact with the men who are currently at the head of the French Communist Party. Each sentence they utter, each action they take is the culmination of 30 years of lies and sclerosis."

With Sartre and Merleau-Ponty, two different ideas of philosophy and intellectual engagement come into conflict. We are faced with an opposition between the idea of philosophy as a clandestine sovereign consciousness that manipulates political opinions and positions (knowing, beforehand, that they are not decisive or important because the course of history takes place secretly without them), and the idea of philosophy that perceives consciousness as immersed within the world, constructing itself in its relationship with it and that, therefore, does not possess the master key to history and politics. History is not the logic of absolute necessity and politics is not the algebra of history: the revolutionary as Merleau-Ponty writes in *Adventures of the Dialectic* "navigates without a map." Every act, every gesture, every word, and every thought is, therefore, important in shaping the path of history and of politics, and it is our responsibility to understand the subjective and objective mediations that orient the course of events. To comment, have an opinion, and take a position on everything, to change one's position at the drop of a hat, abandon one's previous views, dismiss one's previous ideas and rethink one's position, is not freedom, it is irresponsibility. This means that true engagement often asks us to remain silent and to not give in to society's blind demands. The relationship between the philosopher and the City is difficult, Merleau-Ponty tells us, because the City requires something the philosopher cannot offer: immediate complicity, with no wider reflexion.

The difference between Sartre's and Merleau-Ponty's concepts presents us with the impasses and *aporias* of rational autonomy. Sartre regards Merleau-Ponty's defense of rational autonomy as an alibi that allows the impotent philosopher to accept weak forms of engagement. Merleau-Ponty regards Sartre's provisional suspension of rational autonomy as an alibi that allows the instrumental use of engagement by the omnipotent philosopher.

II.

With the power of the capitalist mode of production, the modern project of harmony between the idea of regulation and the idea of emancipation fails. The victory of regulation over that of emancipation confers hegemony to the identity between the dominant order and rationality, which is no longer autonomous but repressive and instrumental, to use the Frankfurt School's expression.

As soon as the failure of the project of modernity emerges from the form of insertion of rationality in the capitalist mode of production, it becomes essential to conceive of rational autonomy in other ways. We can recall that the victory of regulation over emancipation, or of order over transformation, was given a very specific name by Marx: it is bourgeois ideology. In other words, the rational autonomy of the arts, sciences, technology, philosophy, ethics, and law could not escape being determined by the historical form of the social division of classes, with the particular form of the separation between manual and intellectual labor in the capitalist mode of production. This separation led to the concealment of the material determination of reality, inverting the real relationship between the socioeconomic materiality and the spiritual, and because of this, it bestowed the latter with the power to produce reality and the march of history. Painfully conquered by modern rationality, independence was transformed into a powerful specter, the belief that ideas determine the movement of history or are the motor of history.

Concealing the historical determination of knowledge, the social division of classes, economic exploitation, and political control, ideas become abstract representations, images that the dominant class possesses of itself and that are extended to all social classes in all epochs. Ideology, therefore, assimilates the logic of class struggle for the benefit of the dominant class. This means, as Gramsci explained, that the dominant class possesses "organic intellectuals."

Marx stated that modern professionals, meaning artists and intellectuals, are paid wage earners who "find work only so long as their labor increases capital." They are peculiar kinds of workers and commodities: they "must sell themselves piecemeal," and are consequently subject to the vicissitudes, fluctuations, and competition of the market. They will construct objects of art and thought only if they are remunerated by capital and in return they are asked to help increase capital:

> In selling themselves piecemeal they are selling not merely their physical energy but their minds, their sensibilities, their deepest feelings, their visionary and imaginative powers, virtually the whole of themselves. Goethe's Faust gave us the modern archetype of a modern intellectual forced to sell himself in order to make a difference in the world (...). They are driven not only by a need to live, which they share with all men,

but by a desire to communicate, to engage in dialogue with their fellow men. But the cultural commodity market offers the only media in which dialogue on a public scale can take place.[6]

The desire for the rational autonomy of the arts and thought, therefore, tends to become entangled in contradictions and ambiguities, traps that intellectuals try to find ways out by inventing revolutionary ideas, which spring from their personal desires and needs:

> But the social conditions that inspire their radicalism also serve to frustrate it. We saw that even the most subversive ideas must manifest themselves through the media of the market (. . .). There is every reason to think that it will generate a market for radical ideas. This system requires constant revolutionizing, disturbance, agitation; it needs to be perpetually pushed and pressed in order to maintain its elasticity and resilience, to appropriate and assimilate new energies (. . .). Bourgeois society, through its insatiable drive for destruction and development, (. . .) inevitably produces radical ideas and movements that aim to destroy it. But its very capacity for development enables it to negate its own inner negations: to nourish itself and thrive on opposition.[7]

If conformity and radicalism together are Siamese twins in the life of the modern intellectual, absorbed by the logic of the destruction and development of capital, then the rational autonomy of the arts and of thought, understood as the autonomy of intellectuals and their public intervention, can be affirmed only if it is founded on the grounds of a negation that cannot be incorporated by the same movement of the negation/affirmation of the capitalist system. In other words, only if it is supported by the stance of taking a position within class struggle against the dominant classes, and in the redefinition of universals, comprehended as concrete universals.

This emphasis on position-taking is exactly what the notion of *engagement* or of the intellectual as a figure that critically intervenes in the public sphere seeks to express, including not just a transgression (as Bourdieu puts it) and critique of the existing order (according to the Frankfurt School), but also a critique of the mode of its own insertion in the capitalist means of production and, therefore, a critique of the form and content of its very activity, in other words of the arts, sciences, technology, philosophy, and law.

Conceived of in this way, the notion of engagement is inseparable from an understanding of the arts and knowledge as *social institutions* in the strong sense of this term, namely, not simply because they are determined by the social conditions that historically define their production, circulation, and maintenance, but above all because they express the social, political, and cultural relations in which they are produced, distributed, and preserved. Rooted in their time, it is this expressive dimension of the arts and of thought that allows one to speak of their autonomy, understood as the labor of transforming *given* experiences into experiences that are *comprehended*. Autonomous works are those that transfigure and surpass immediate experience because they fulfill a *work*, that is, they negate the immediate facts of experience through its mediation by a new meaning, one that was concealed or dissimulated by immediate experience.

The notion of engagement understood as taking a position within class struggle, as an internal negation of forms of exploitation and the dominant order in favor of freedom and autonomy in all spheres of economic, social, and cultural life, allows us to differentiate the intellectual from the ideologue. Inserted in the market, the ideologue speaks in favor of the dominant order, justifying and legitimizing it. The intellectual speaks against it. This highlights the problem faced by the intellectual who engages in left-wing political parties, that is, in opposition parties that then become the dominant or governing party. If the intellectual *always* speaks in favor of this party, he will be an ideologue; if he *always* speaks against it, he will be rejected as a traitor.

III.

If the difference between the intellectual and artists, scientists, technicians, philosophers, lawyers, lies in the fact that the intellectual is an artist, scientist, technician, philosopher, lawyer, when he intervenes critically in public space and speaks in public, then the expression "the silence of the intellectuals" may seem contradictory. Artists or thinkers cease to be intellectuals when they are silent. If they are silent, however, it may be useful to ask what caused their silence in the first place. I refer only to those causes that seem most relevant to my discussion here, that is, whether the engaged intellectual is indeed a figure facing extinction.

The first cause is undoubtedly the "embittered abandonment of revolutionary utopias," the rejection of politics, and "a disenchanted skepticism."[8] This situation is a corollary of the totalitarianism of the so-called communist countries, the failure of the Soviet Union's *glasnost*, the decline of social democracy, and the adoption of the so-called third way that marries "capitalism to socialist values," a form of politics defended by Britain's New Labor Party. Here the historical horizon of the future disappears. The present, deprived of all negative force, closes in on itself, the ruling order appears self-legitimized and justified because nothing seems to contradict or oppose it and ideologues can delight in speaking of the end of history or celebrating capitalism as the end point of mankind's evolution. The decline of the engaged intellectual, or the silence of the intellectual, is, therefore, a symptom of something that is more profound: the absence of a way of thinking that is capable of exposing and interpreting contemporary contradictions. What we are dealing with is not a refusal of public discourse but the impossibility of formulating it.

The second cause is the decline of public space and the growth of private space, impelled by the imperatives of a new form of capital accumulation, known as neoliberalism. One of the effects of this situation is the transformation of economic and social rights into services defined by the logic of the market, and the transformation of the citizen into a consumer. Democracy establishes citizenship and participation in political struggles as a form of social counterpower for the creation and guarantee of rights, thanks to the participation in social struggles. If rights, conquered through battles over public space and class struggles, are privatized, transformed into services that can be bought and sold like commodities, then the seed of democracy is mortally wounded and the depolitization of society is a necessary outcome. In this context of depoliticization and declining citizenship, the engaged intellectual is replaced by the figure of the *competent specialist* whose alleged knowledge bestows him with the power to instruct others what they should think, feel, act, and expect in all spheres of social life. The critique of contemporary life is silenced by the ideological proliferation of these advocates of good living.

The third cause is the new form of the insertion of knowledge and technology in the mode of capitalist production: these have become productive forces; they have ceased to be mere supports for capital to become agents of its accumulation. Consequently, the ways in which thinkers and technicians are inserted into society have changed because they have become direct economic agents, and capitalist power is now in the monopoly of knowledge and information:

> What characterizes the current technological revolution is not the centrality of knowledge and information, but the application of such knowledge and information to knowledge generation and information processing/communication devices, in a cumulative feedback loop between innovation and uses of innovation (. . .). New information technologies are not

simply tools to be applied, but processes to be developed (...). There is therefore a close relationship between the social processes of creating and manipulating symbols (the culture of society) and the capacity to produce and distribute goods and services (the productive forces). For the first time in history, the human mind is a direct force, not just a decisive element of the productive system.[9]

The expression "the knowledge society" seeks to indicate that contemporary society is founded on science and information, thanks to the competitive use of knowledge, technological innovations and information in the productive processes. "Intellectual capital" is even referred to and is considered by many as a key and active principle in business.[10]

Productivity and competitiveness in informational production are based on the generation of knowledge and information processing. Knowledge generation and technological capacity are key tools for competition between firms, organizations of all kinds and ultimately, countries (...). Economic development and competitive performance are not predicated on basic research, but on the connection between basic and applied research (the R & D system) and their diffusion throughout organizations and individuals. Advanced academic research and a good educational system are necessary but not sufficient conditions for countries, firms and individuals to enter the information paradigm (...). Global technological development needs the connection between science, technology and the business sector, as well as with national and international policies.[11]

It is stated that today knowledge is no longer defined by specific disciplines but by problems and their application in the business sector. Research is viewed as a strategy of intervention and control of the means or instruments for achieving certain objectives. In other words it is a *survey* of problems, difficulties, and obstacles in order to fulfill an objective, and it is a calculation of methods of partial and local solutions for local obstacles and problems. It employs extensive use of communication networks to produce itself; it transforms itself into a technology and submits itself to quality controls, according to which it must demonstrate its social relevance by displaying its economic efficacy. The expression "the explosion of learning" refers to the vertiginous growth of knowledge, when in fact it indicates the mode of the economic determination of knowledge, since in the strategic game of market competition a research organization is established and preserved only if it is capable of proposing new problems, difficulties, and obstacles.[12] Contemporary knowledge is characterized by accelerated growth and by the tendency of rapid obsolescence.

How can we speak of rational autonomy in this new context? If the arts have already been devoured by the culture industry, science and technology now too find themselves subject to the logic of business. It is not just that research has been transformed into a *survey* and object of possession for intervening and controlling something, but also that it depends directly on financial investments that are determined by the strategic game of market competition. Researchers are funded only if they are capable of proposing new problems, difficulties, and obstacles, which involves the fragmentation of old problems into new microproblems, whose control is increasingly greater. Producers of knowledge and technologies absorb the logic of business competition and also support it, thereby negating the rational autonomy that bestowed authority to the intellectual's critical intervention.

This phenomenon is not restricted to the so-called hard or applied sciences; it also affects the human sciences. Until recently economists, social scientists, and psychologists entered the world of business through departments of Human Resources, that is, as salaried workers. Today they are encouraged to create their own consulting firms, advising large businesses and public institutions.[13]

In addition to university and research centers' dependency on economic power, it is important to bear in mind that this power is based on the private property of knowledge and information, so that these become secret and constitute an unprecedented field of economic and military competition. In other words, as soon as the knowledge of specialists is the "intellectual capital" of business and industry and as soon as the strategic game of economic and military competition imposes the acceleration and vertiginous obsolescence of knowledge, the production as well as the circulation of information are submitted to imperatives that escape the control of the producers of knowledge, and moreover citizens' social and political control. On the contrary, the social and the political are controlled by a knowledge, or competency, whose full meaning escapes them entirely. In contradicting one of the most important principles of democracy, that is, the political competency of all citizens, then not only the economy but also politics are considered matters for specialists whose decisions seem to have a technical nature that is secret or, when they are published are written in a language that is incomprehensible to the majority of citizens.

Rational autonomy used to be the independence of scientific rationality to define objects, methods, results, and application, according to criteria relating to its own knowledge. The new situation of knowledge as a productive force determines the heteronomy of science and technology, which in turn becomes determined by imperatives external to knowledge, much like the heteronomy of scientists and technicians, whose research depends on business investments. Rational autonomy used to be the condition of both the quality of knowledge and the authority of the engaged intellectual. Once this autonomy disappears, what else is there, but silence?

IV.

If intellectuals today are silent, then ideologues are by contrast talkative. Their talkative-ness has been linked to so-called postmodernism, defined by Frederic Jameson as "the cultural logic of late capitalism."

In its contemporary form, capitalist society is characterized by the fragmentation of all spheres of social life, from the fragmentation of production, the temporal and spatial dispersal of work and structural unemployment, to the destruction of references for class identity and the nature of class struggle. Society now appears to be a network made up of mobile, unstable, and ephemeral organizations defined by particular strategies and programs that compete with each other. It appears to be a dangerous "environment," one that threatens and is constantly under threat, one that should be programmed, planned, and controlled by strategies of technological intervention and games of power.[14]

The economic and social materiality of the new form of capital is inseparable from unprecedented transformations taking place in the experience of time and space, which David Harvey calls "time-space compression."[15] In other words, the fragmentation and globalization of economic production engender two simultaneous and contradictory phenomena: on the one hand, spatial and temporal fragmentation and dispersal and, on the other, with the effects of electronic information and technologies, the compression of space—everything happens here, in a space that has no distances, differences, or frontiers—and the compression of time—everything happens now, in a time that has no past and no future. In reality, the fragmentation and dispersal of time and space conditions their reconciliation in an undifferentiated space and an ephemeral time, or in a space that is reduced to a superficial plane of images and in a time that has lost its depth and is reduced to the movement of rapid and fleeting images.

The naturalization and positive valorization of socioeconomic fragmentation and dispersal stimulates the aggressive form of individualism and the search for success at any cost. It also gives way to a form of living that is determined by insecurity and violence, and that is institutionalized by the volatility of the market. Insecurity and fear lead to a desire for intimacy, to old institutions, especially the family and kinships seen as spaces of refuge against a hostile world and to the return of mystical, authoritarian, or fundamentalist forms of religion, that are supported by the image of a strong, authoritarian, or despotic police force.

If, in the imperatives of the society of consumption and of the spectacle the arts were subsumed by the logic of the culture industry, now that those imperatives have been buttressed by the ever stronger personalized figure of the leader, politics has become a political industry. Marketing has been assigned the task of selling an image of the politician and of turning the citizen into a private consumer. In order to create an identification between the consumer and the product, marketing produces the image of the politician as a private person: their physical traits, sexual, food, literary, sport preferences, daily habits, family life, and favorite pets. The privatization of the political figure and of the citizen consequently privatizes public space. As a result, the ethical evaluation of governments possesses few criteria proper to public ethics and focuses instead on evaluating leaders' virtues and vices; and corruption is attributed to politicians' bad character, not to public institutions.

From the point of view of contemporary cognitive experience, Paul Virilio refers to *atopia* and *acronia*, or to the disappearance of the perceptive experience of the body, space, and time with the rise of the electronic and information revolution.[16] We live in an age of telepresence and teleobservation that problematizes the difference between appearance and reality, the virtual and the real, since everything is immediately present to us in a form of temporal and spatial transparency, which are put forward as evidence. Our experience and our thoughts are shaped by a dangerous rupture between the sensible and the intelligible; the experience of the body as one's own body is disavowed by the experience of an absence of distances and horizons and we are invited into a world of sedentary thought and forgetfulness.

Our experience is unaware of any sense of continuity and it exhausts itself in a present that is lived as a fleeting instance. This situation, far from stimulating an interrogation of the present and the future, leads to the abandonment of all connection with the possible and to the celebration of contingency and its essential uncertainty. The contingent is not perceived as an indeterminacy that can be determined by human action, but rather as the mode of existence of people, objects, and events, leading to discontinuity, for by losing temporal difference, we lose not only a sense of the past, but also a sense of the future as a possibility inscribed in human action, as the power to shape the indeterminate and overcome given situations, understanding and transforming their very meaning.

This new form of experience corresponds to the ideological formulation of postmodernism, an enthusiastic celebration of the fragmentation and dispersal of time and space, and the impossibility of distinguishing between appearance and experience, image and reality. In other words, this ideology sees social and economic fragmentation as a positive and final fact; it sees the absence of a sense of time as a celebration of contingency and chance.

In his 1996 book *The End of Certainty. Time, Chaos and the New Laws of Nature*, the physical chemist Ilya Prigogine presents the premises and results of various decades of research in the natural sciences, which questioned classical mechanics and reformulated quantum mechanics. Fundamentally, the new science of nature, he argues, abandons, on the one hand, the classical idea of a necessary causality or determinism in favor of using concepts of probability and symmetry; and, on the other hand, the idea of temporal reversibility (in which time is reduced to a geometrically conceived notion of space) has led to the concept of the arrow of time or temporal irreversibility, which has consequently provided new meanings for the notion of entropy, thereby responding to Prigogine's key question: What is the role of time, as a vector of irreversibility, in physics? These changes, or the abandonment of deterministic ideas, make it possible to conceive of a seemingly inconceivable idea: that of the historicity of nature, or as Prigogine puts it, "the evolutionary character of our universe."

> Mankind is at a turning point, the beginning of a new rationality in which science is no longer identified as certitude and probability with ignorance (...). Today we are no longer afraid of the "indeterministic hypothesis." It is the natural outcome of the modern theory of instability and chaos (...). This requires a new formulation of the laws of nature that is no longer based on certitudes, but rather possibilities. In accepting that the future is not determined, we come to the end of certainty.[17]

Examining the conceptual transformation of the natural sciences in 1979, Jean François Lyotard extended this transformation to the social sciences and to philosophy, comparing early modern thought (which emerged in the seventeenth century) to these transformations, which constituted what he then termed the *postmodern condition*.[18] Postmodern ideology is, therefore, born from the migration of categories from the natural sciences to the human sciences, the arts and philosophy.

This migration allowed Lyotard to state that society is not an organic reality (as positivist sociologists had maintained), nor is it a field of conflicts (according to Marxists); it is a network of linguistic communications, a language made up of a multiplicity of games whose rules are incommensurable, each game entering into a form of competition or agonistic relationship with others. Science, politics, philosophy, and the arts are language games and contesting "narratives."

Postmodernism, therefore, celebrates what Lyotard calls "the end of the grand narratives," that is, the foundations of modern thought. It relegates concepts that founded and oriented modernity—ideas of truth, rationality, universality, the contrast between necessity and contingency, problems between subjectivity and objectivity, the immanence of history, and difference between nature and culture—to the condition of totalitarian Eurocentric myths. In its place postmodernism affirms fragmentation as the mode of reality, making notions of difference (against identity and contradiction), singularity (against totality), and nomadism (against determination) the central source of the meaning of reality; and it values the superficiality of social appearance or images and their temporal and spatial speed.

> The current concepts of rationality and knowledge emphasize historical and cultural variability, fallibility, the impossibility of going beyond language and reaching reality, the fragmentary and the particular nature of all understanding, the penetrating corruption of knowledge by power and domination, the futility of all search for firm foundations and the need for a pragmatic approach to tackle these questions.[19]

In the landscape of virtual technology, postmodern ideology praises the *simulacrum* whose peculiarity, in contemporary society, resides in the fact that there is nothing that it cannot simulate or dissimulate, apart from another image, other simulacra. It evokes a taste and desire for the ephemeral and for images. This takes place together with the transformation in the circulation of commodities and in consumption, where a new type of publicity and marketing prevails. Commodities or "things" are no longer sold and bought, their simulacrum, that is, images (of health, beauty, youth, success, well-being, security, and happiness) are now bought and sold and, being ephemeral and disposable, they must be quickly replaced. In this way, the paradigm of consumption has become the fashion market, rapid, ephemeral, and disposable, which leads to individual preferences that are also ephemeral and disposable.

From the political point of view, postmodernism identifies rationalism, capitalism, and socialism: modern reason as the exercise of power or the modern ideal of knowledge as the control of nature and of society; capitalism is the realization of this ideal achieved through the market and socialism is the realization of this ideal through the planned economy. This entails combating rationalism, capitalism, and socialism, by unraveling and struggling against the network of micropowers that normalizes or normatizes all of society, by placing itself against the territoriality of organic identities that suffocate the nomadism of singularities, or yet, finally, by combating the libidinal investments imposed by capitalism and by socialism, that is, by changing the content, form, and direction of desire.[20] Postmodern "politics" thus carries out three great inversions: it substitutes the logic of production for the logic of circulation (micropowers and the nomadism of singularities), and because of this it substitutes the logic of labor for that of information (reality as narrative and language games); and consequently, it substitutes class struggle for the satisfaction-dissatisfaction of desire.[21]

Faced with this situation and with the paralysis of socialist thought (mentioned above), the left-wing's current fascination with the political ideas of an ideologue like Carl Schmitt is not surprising, in particular his idea of "decisionism" or his concept of sovereignty as the power of decision *ex nihilio* in situations of exception (i.e., war and crisis). A sovereign decision is exceptional—as a miracle in which God interrupts the ordinary progress of events with an extraordinary event. It is, therefore, unconditional, or rather, it does not depend on any condition (economic, social, judicial, cultural, and historical) and it is not subsumed by any condition. It is consequently, instantaneous, stripped of all temporal support; it is an absolute beginning, with no ties to the past and no projection into the future. The postmodern tendency to nomadic singularities or deterritorialization also finds resonance in this ideologue's work, in which the political sphere is autonomous, meaning that it is determined neither by the economy nor by ethics or rights, but by the aleatory emergence of antagonistic groups in the form of the friend-enemy opposition. Politically, the friend is whoever shares our way of life; the enemy is the "other," the stranger who threatens our way of life and, therefore, our existence. Politics is an operation of differences and inequalities and a confrontation of forces.

For Schmitt modernity (in this case, the French Revolution) is also a catastrophe that must be overcome. Why is political modernity a catastrophe? First, because by introducing the idea of the Constitutional

State of right, it gives precedence to the judicial over the political and embodies this in the institution of the state; second, because it destroys the defining nucleus of sovereignty by prohibiting the sovereign's intervention in the judicial order; third, because it destroys the idea of hierarchical order and thus paves the way for the greater catastrophe that unites egalitarian individualism and apolitical economic liberalism with democracy.

This is catastrophic because it mixes the economic dichotomy with the political dichotomy, eliminating the autonomy of both. In effect, democracy, like politics, maintains—though in a vague and fluid way—the friend-enemy distinction since it admits only the equality of citizens whose similarity derives from the linguistic, moral, and religious identity and, therefore, excludes the other or the different. In other words, democratic logic requires the exclusion of the slave, the foreigner and the barbarian, the latter because of possible impiety or atheism. On the contrary, liberalism introduces universal equality without discrimination because it is apolitical, since politics is an operation of distinctions and inequalities. Through the mediation of democracy, liberalism became a clandestine politics, hidden under a mask of justice, law, rights, truth, universality, and rationality. And Marxism was a theoretical and practical misconception for understanding reality from the economicism that intrinsically characterizes liberalism.

V.

In 1980, in the midst of the so-called process of Brazilian redemocratizaiton, I participated in a seminar about Brazil that took place in the United States. At the event, I mentioned the strong presence of intellectuals in Brazil's political debates, emphasizing my concern and discomfort with the fact that their discourses *about* Brazilian society could silence discourses *from* Brazilian society. Dominating the field of public opinion, the language of intellectuals could silence other social actors, a highly serious situation at a time when Brazil's social and political practices were undergoing unprecedented transformation with the emergence of new historical agents—the new social movements struggling to create rights and define citizenship. Always silenced and sociologically defined as "subaltern classes," the popular classes—more specifically, the working class, was emerging as a political subject.

During the discussion, a North American anthropologist told me: "Don't worry. As soon as there is democracy in Brazil, intellectuals will stop having much importance." This comment can be interpreted in two ways: First, it contains the idea that democracy, by instituting equality to citizens, provides everyone with the right to express themselves in the public sphere and to participate in forming public opinion. Second, it may have been influenced by recent historical experiences in the United States, a country whose intellectuals had a strong presence in the anti–Vietnam War movement and who returned to their natural habitat of the university once the war was over. Just as American intellectuals had occupied public space during a time of opposition to the existing system, Brazilian intellectuals would return to the silence of their academic work once the struggle against the dictatorship was over.

At that same discussion, an English historian asked me whether the public presence of Brazilian intellectuals reflected the influence of French culture in our *intelligentsia*.

Coming from the São Paulo Faculty of Philosophy, Science and Letters, whose foundation bore the strong and decisive influence of French culture, I was tempted to answer yes. Indeed, the French Enlightenment inspired Brazil's first attempt at independence, the movement of the *Inconfidência Mineira;* during the Second Empire, Brazilian painters were sent to Paris; Auguste Comte's positivism inspired the Republicans of Brazil's Military School and thinkers like Sílvio Romero; French literary romanticism had a significant impact on our romanticist movement; Zola left his mark not only on our naturalist literature, but his novel *Germinal* also influenced our anarchist writers; De Maistre and De Bonald were key references for Brazil's conservative and reactionary Catholic thought; Sartre's left-wing ideals shook our universities; Althusserian Marxism and Regis Debray's *foquismo* were influential for Brazil's left wing in the 1960s and 1970s, giving way only when Michel Foucault began to win hearts and minds.

My reply, however, was negative. I outlined the hierarchical and authoritarian Iberian tradition, in which lettered elites—or *letrados*—had three functions: the formulation of power, as theologians and lawyers; the exercise of power, as members of a vast state bureaucracy and university hierarchy; and benefactors of the favors of power, as graduates and prestigious writers. In Brazil, this tradition was linked to the idea of culture as an ornament and a sign of superiority, reinforcing *mandonismo* and authoritarianism, and also as an instrument of social mobility, reinforcing inequalities and exclusions. I, therefore, outlined the authoritarianism of our society and gave an overview of the *letrado* as one of its expressions. But what has happened to the *letrado*? Why did I bring this back when speaking of intellectuals in contemporary Brazil?

With the economic and social transformation of capitalism in Brazil, or industrialization, some intellectuals became part of the left. Influenced by Bolshevism, intellectuals tended to see themselves as an enlightened vanguard whose task was to raise the class consciousness of the alienated masses, overlooking the history of labor movements and their anarchist and socialist traditions, as well as the forms of action and organization of Brazilian workers. With the institution of the fordist and taylorist industrial models, or "scientific management," with urbanization, the growth of universities and scientific research, the establishment of the culture industry or of mass culture through communication and publicity, the traditional figure of the *letrado* was enhanced by that of the specialist and became a bearer of *the competent discourse*, according to which those who possess knowledge have the natural right to instruct and lead others in all spheres of social life. The social division of classes was thus overdetermined by the division between competent specialists, meaning that those who lead, and everyone else, namely the incompetents, who carry out instructions or accept the outcomes of the specialists' actions.

It was this figure of the Brazilian intellectual, that is, a *lettered* elite imbued with prestige, an individual linked to state bureaucracy, a political vanguard, and a competent specialist, that was the cause of my apprehension and discomfort in the 1980s. Many of us at that time asked ourselves whether we would be capable of understanding the country's new social and political actors and if we would be able to hear their social discourse without substituting it with a competent discourse *about* and *for* society and politics. Would we be able to not see politics as a technique of specialists or as the administration of professionals who understand "political engineering," but rather to practice it as the construction of citizenship?

In fact, in the 1980s, it was possible to outline a sort of "typology" of Brazilian intellectuals between the 1950s and the 1970s: between 1956 and 1963, intellectuals (generally linked to the Brazilian Communist Party) gave themselves the role of the advanced conscience of the masses (or the people, to use the word from that era) as well as the producers of political, economic, and governmental plans for the state, both roles possessing a vision of the demiurgic role of the state to solve class struggle; between 1964 and 1969, in the context of the dictatorship and state terror, intellectuals stopped placing themselves as the proletariat's theoretical conscience and began to see themselves as its supplementary and armed support, with everyone walking together hand in hand. The guerilla movement, however, isolated intellectuals from the working class and from society, leading in general to the construction of small self-centered and self-referencing groups, which were decimated by the state repression of the early 1970s. Between 1974 and 1980 two new "types" emerged. On the one hand, there were those who realigned themselves with ideas that had dominated before 1964, introducing the notion of the "modern party of the masses." Here the intellectual was seen as part of a theoretical vanguard, without directing its process; he or she should come from its political direction and its base. On the other, there were the intellectuals who finally discovered that the dominated can think, that they do know, and that they are aware of exploitation and domination, that they are not victims of a false consciousness but of the Brazilian state's systematic repression, which continuously destroys the possibility of transforming the knowledge they possess into political and historical practice.

History has demonstrated that the actions of these two types of intellectuals were effective in Brazilian politics in the years between 1980 and 1990. Why, therefore, do we accept the silence or the extinction of the figure of the engaged intellectual?

First, because the figure of the Brazilian intellectual as a lettered-specialist found a new place for itself, the mass media, that, as with the old figure of the lettered-bureaucrat, tends to erect obstacles in the construction of the sphere of public opinion, imposes its own opinions. Second, because the true silence of the intellectuals does not have its origins (as the North American anthropologist assumed) in the strengthening of citizenship and participation, but rather in the transformation of the form of the insertion of the arts and knowledge in the capitalist mode of production as well as the ebb and tide of left-wing thinking or the revolutionary idea of the emancipation of mankind. Knowledge and the arts as a critique of the present and an expression of the new, politics as an action that invents itself, and history as a field of the possible are all stifled by conformity.

Merleau-Ponty once wrote that everyone wants the philosopher to be a rebel. Rebellion pleases everyone. Indeed, it is always comforting to hear that things are going badly. Once this has been heard, people's consciences are calmed, silence reigns, and everyone can return to their duties, satisfied. The outline I have provided here can be taken as a call for rebellion. As an engaged intellectual, however, I want to make my final words those of Merleau-Ponty: "Evil is not created by us or by others; it is born in this web that we have spun about us and that is suffocating us. What sufficiently tough new men will be patient enough to really reweave it? The remedy we seek does not lie in rebellion, but in unremitting *virtù*."

On the Present and on Politics

There has been much talk recently of the "oblivion of politics."[1] A number of events have produced this oblivion, and here I mention those that have led to the privatization and destruction of public space:

- The decline of public space and the expansion of the private sphere in the context of the economic and political activities of so-called neoliberal governments, defined by the elimination of economic, social, and political rights guaranteed by public power, and benefiting the private interests of the ruling classes, that is, capital.
- The end of the sphere of public opinion. This has ceased to be a field for the expression of different opinions concerning economic, social, cultural, and political life. Public opinion was, from its inception, a space for the public manifestation of the ideas of different groups and classes concerned with defending their interests, which determined political decisions and actions linked to the collective. Public opinion has now become the public manifestation of individual tastes, preferences, and sentiments that previously belonged to the sphere of private life.
- The end of public discussions and debates of government programs and projects as well as laws. This is an outcome of the emergence of political marketing and an effect of postmodern ideology that submits politics to the methods of a consumer society and a society of the spectacle. Political marketing sells the image of the politician, reducing the citizen to the private figure of the consumer. In order to consolidate a form of identification between the consumer and the product, marketing produces an image of the politician as a private person: physical characteristics, sexual, dietary or literary preferences, favorite sports, habits, and pets, and family life. This privatization of politicians and citizens effectively privatizes public space.

- The ideology of competence. Society is divided between the competent, meaning those who possess scientific and technical knowledge and, therefore, have the right to rule and govern, and everyone else, who, lacking such knowledge, is seen as incompetent and obliged to obey. As a consequence of this ideology of competence, politics is regarded as a technical matter that must be dealt with by competent experts. Citizens have no choice but to acknowledge their own incompetence, to trust in the competence of the experts and limit their political participation to voting in elections.
- The role of the mass media. In the context of the ideology of competence, radio and television stations have increasingly become spaces for the discourse of experts who teach the public how to live and offer suggestions and advice on love, sex, diet, health, gynecology, cooking, physical exercise, cosmetics, fashion, medicines, gardening, carpentry, art, literature, and housekeeping. As Christopher Lasch points out in his book *The Culture of Narcissism*, the increasing power of the media has made the very ideas of fact and fiction inconsequential, replacing them with notions of credibility, plausibility, and reliability. For something to be accepted as real, it must only seem credible or plausible, or it must be put forward by someone reliable. Facts are replaced by statements offered by "authorized personalities" and "opinion makers" who provide not information but rather preferences that are immediately turned into propaganda. The basis for "credibility" and "reliability" lies in an appeal to intimacy, personality, and to private life as a mechanism that can support and guarantee public order.

However, to talk of the forgetfulness of politics presumes that we know what the object of oblivion was, that is, politics.

II.

You citizens of Athens, you judges at the first trial ever held for murder, hear what I decree. Now and forever this court of judges will be set up here to serve Aegeus' people, (...) Mount of Ares. From this hill Reverence and Terror, two kindred rulers of my citizens will guarantee they don't commit injustice, by day or night, unless the citizens pollute the laws with evil innovations. Once limpid waters are stained with mud, you'll never find a drink. My people, avoid both anarchy and tyranny. I urge you to uphold this principle. Show it due reverence. As for terror, don't banish it completely from the city. (...) So here I now establish this tribunal, incorruptible, magnificent, swift in punishment—it stands above you, your country's guardian as you lie asleep.

The above words are spoken by the goddess Athena at the end of the *Oresteia* trilogy. With them she announces the "birth" of politics, created by the Greeks.

Similarly, in Euripides' *The Suppliants*, the Athenians declare, "it is this that holds men's states together, strict observance of the laws." In the same spirit in *The Republic,* the Roman Cicero writes, "this public thing, the *Res Publica*, belongs to the people. But the people does not mean a human gathering congregating in any manner as a flock, but a numerous assembly brought together by legal consent and community of interests."Moses Finley describes the birth of politics, or the invention of politics as he calls it, as an event that distinguished Greece and Rome from the ancient empires. Why does he use the word invention? Because the Greeks and Romans had no previous models. They had to invent their own way of dealing with conflicts and social divisions.

The invention of politics went hand in hand with the emergence of a form of public power. This entailed the invention of the law (i.e., the institution of tribunals) and the creation of public institutions for decisions and deliberations (assembly and senates). This was possible only because political power was separated from the three traditional authorities that had previously defined the exercise of power: the authority of the private or economic power of the head of the family, on whom the life or death of family members depended; the authority of the military leader and the authority of the religious leader. In the ancient empires these figures were united around a single leader—the King. Politics was, therefore, born when the private sphere of the economy and personal will, warfare, and the sphere of the sacred or of knowledge were separated and when political power was no longer identified with the mystical body of the leader as father, commander, and priest, the human representative of divine and transcendent powers.

In *The Suppliants*, a messenger arrives in Athens and asks: who are the *tyrannós* of this city? Theseus replies: "Sir stranger, thou hast made a false beginning to thy speech, in seeking here a *tyrannós*. For this city is not ruled by one man, but is free. The *démos* rule in succession year by year, allowing no preference to wealth, but the poor man shares equally with the rich."

The Greeks invented democracy. All adults born in the *pólis* were citizens with *isonomia* and *isegoria*. They were members of the assemblies and tribunals and participants in the military force, created as a popular militia. They were armed citizens.

Following Theseus' reply in *The Suppliants*, the messenger, somewhat surprised, asks: "How shall the demos, if it cannot form true judgments, be able rightly to direct the city?"

Thus, although the messenger questions the people's ability to rule, he does not question the principle of the rule of law; neither "anarchy nor tyranny" as the goddess Athena states. There were, of course, a number of debates concerning who had the right to formulate and issue laws. These debates highlighted differences between the Greek cities, and between Greece and Rome.

Rome invented the Republic. The *Res Publica* or "public thing" was the land of Rome. It was distributed among the founding families of the *civitas*, the founding fathers or *patres*, from whom the patricians descended, who possessed the right to citizenship. The republic was oligarchic: male adults of the patrician families were citizens, meaning that they were members of the senate, the judiciary, and were also military leaders. The populace or the plebians, the *plebs*, excluded from citizenship or direct participation in government, were represented by the plebian tribune—a patrician elected by them. Through the plebiscite they demonstrated whether they were for or against a decision of the Senate or they made proposals. They also served in the military.

III.

Ancient philosophers, especially Plato and Aristotle, define politics as a superior form of life. According to Plato, politics is the just life; for Aristotle, it is the good and noble life. Both philosophers believe that justice defines politics, although each deals with the idea of justice differently. Plato claims that politics is just when the wise man (the philosopher king) governs the city, the courageous men protect it, and the concupiscent men produce the material means to preserve the community. In other words, the just form of politics is that commanded by reason, to which military force and economic power are subordinated. Aristotle's notion of justice, however, begins with the existence of a social division between the rich and the poor. He believes that just politics functions to diminish this inequality; or to put it more specifically, politics is the art of providing equality to those who are unequal. Aristotle identifies two kinds of justice: first, distributive or partible justice, which refers to the public distribution of goods in order to reduce the divisions between the rich and the poor; second, participatory justice, that is, a justice that emerges from something that cannot be divided or distributed, and that can, therefore, be only participated in. It is political power in which all citizens may participate.

During the Middle Ages the idea of politics as the realization of justice was maintained thanks to a curious mixture of Plato and Aristotle and Christian theology, specifically the work of Saint Paul. Preserving the Hebrew idea central to the Old Testament, Saint Paul stated that "all power comes from on High"; in other words, political power is a grace or divine favor that is invested in the figure of the ruler. Politics became political theology. As a representative of God on earth, the ruler is consecrated and crowned by the Pope, who confirms the ruler's divine status and pledges that he is the Son of justice and the Father of the law, and that he keeps the law in his heart, so that the will of the ruler is law—"what pleases the prince has the force of law." As a representative of God on earth, the just ruler must be virtuous and must serve as a mirror to the governed. This means that politics is just when the ruler is morally virtuous and that it is unjust when the ruler is morally corrupt. Justice was conceived of in two ways: first, as the hierarchical order of the world that was instituted by God, that is to say, the natural order is a juridical one established by divine decree; and second, as a hierarchical social order that was instituted by the ruler according to his divine will. From this perspective, politics is just only if it respects these two hierarchical orders.

In fact, we may say that medieval political-theology is "pre-political" if by politics we understand the Greek and Roman invention of public power as no longer identified with the ruler as father, commander, and priest, the human representative of divine and transcendent powers.

We can thus appreciate the significance of the Machiavellian rupture. Niccolò Machiavelli broke with and subverted these ideas. Distancing himself from the ancient philosophers and from political theology, Machiavelli states that politics has nothing to do with justice or divine grace; rather he claims that it is linked to the exercise of power. Every society is traversed by a fundamental division; it is divided between the desire of the Mighty (*i Grandi*) to oppress and command; and the desire of the People (*il Popolo*) who do not want to be oppressed and commanded. The Mighty are motivated by the desire for goods; the People are motivated by the desire for freedom and security. It is this idea of social division, rather than the classical idea of the community, that is the starting point for Machiavelli's notion of politics. For him, politics is the exercise of power, in terms of taming, restraining, and containing the desire of the Mighty and concretizing the desire of the People, that is, their desire for freedom and security. The originality of Machiavelli's work lies not only in its refusal of the classical idea of the undivided community, nor in its emphasis on power rather than justice as a guarantee of popular freedom and security. It also lies in his idea of the virtuous ruler. Far from asserting the figure of the prince as a mirror of moral virtues, Machiavelli defines the prince's *virtù* as his capacity to give his attention to the *verità effetualle delle cose*, that is, to the course of events. The virtuous prince changes his mind, sentiments, and actions as fortune, that is, contingent circumstances dictate. This means that he will never be their victim and will always be their master.

The Machiavellian definition of politics as the exercise of power introduces the modern concept of political power as sovereignty. It was Jean Bodin who first defined sovereignty: the sovereign is someone who has the power to make a decision, someone who issues and abolishes laws, and who has the power to decide the life and death of his subjects. This definition of sovereignty is initially applied to the figure of the absolute monarch and defines state sovereignty. Hence, politics refers to the exercise of sovereign power by the state. This idea was subsequently developed by Thomas Hobbes and then by theorists of the Enlightenment as well as North American Independence and the French Revolution. For all of these theorists sovereignty has a social origin, that is, the social contract. In spite of their differences, these theorists see the social pact as the moment of the institution of sovereignty, that is, a voluntary agreement to institute a sovereign and submit to him, since he guarantees life, private property or goods, and freedom of the ruled.

It not by chance that Antonio Gramsci has written *The Modern Prince* and defines politics using Machiavelli's key ideas: social division, freedom, and security of the people. He does so in order to develop Marx's critique of the social contract as the foundation of sovereignty. Like Machiavelli, Marx's idea of politics starts from social division, specifically, the division of classes, and he sees the modern state as the exercise of power because it realizes, in Machiavellian terms, the desire of the Mighty to command and oppress, or in Marxian terms, the desire of private owners of the social means of production. Gramsci in turn theorizes the proletariat revolution as the renaissance of politics against domination, or the revolutionary party as the Modern Prince.

From contractualists to liberals and from liberals to Marxists, much has been written about and achieved in politics. However, the idea of social division remains constant; be it in a liberal manner to conceal the state and the nation as an indivisible imaginary unit, or in a revolutionary manner to reinvent politics as a politics without and against the state. Within this the key point of modernity has also persisted, that is, the Machiavellian idea of politics as the exercise of power.

It is well known that, according to Max Weber, power is the ability to command obedience through the law, and it is the legal use of violence. This can be carried out in a personalized manner, when it is charismatic, or in an impersonal manner, when it is realized by the state and its legal mechanisms.

It is also well known that Hannah Arendt emphasizes distinctions between force, authority, and power. Force, she says, is the direct and immediate exercise of coercion and repression, and its foundation is fear. Authority is coercion by a tradition that is internalized and remembered by society though the use of symbols; its foundation is obedience and the respect for hierarchy. Power is coercion mediated by the law. This can be the source of freedom or domination and it fosters consent. When consent is voluntary, power leads to freedom; when it is obtained through force it becomes domination and oppression. Force operates through violence and functions to eliminate differences. Authority operates by constructing a sense of community, in which differences are secondary. When it is not transformed into domination, power operates in order to legitimize differences.

No less well known are the ideas of Michel Foucault. Opposing the Weberian and Marxist notion of power as essentially repressive, Foucault approaches the subject from a different angle. Analyzing changes in the penal and prison system in *Discipline and Punish*, Foucault refers to power as the production of docile bodies: power is disciplinary and is dispersed throughout society, penetrating its social institutions. In his lectures at the *Collège de France*, Foucault draws on Aristotle's difference between natural life and the good or ethicopolitical life to analyze the use of power from the start of the nineteenth century as the control of men's natural life, demonstrated by the development of demography, hygiene, and public health, a process Foucault defines as *biopower*, that is, a power exercised over the life of individuals and societies. He believes that racism, Nazi ideas of racial eugenics, and the concentration camp as the "final solution," are clear manifestations of these changes in the form of power. In fact, Foucault explores the end of the idea of sovereignty as the definition of power. Foucault highlights one aspect of sovereignty that culminates in biopower. From the sixteenth century onward, beginning with Jean Bodin, sovereignty has been defined as the power to produce, promote, and execute the law and as the power to decide the life and death of citizens. Indeed, this idea appeared in Weber's concept of power. For Foucault, however, it is obvious that no power can give life and thus sovereign power is not defined by the ability to give life, but rather by the ability to take it. In other words, sovereignty is the power to take someone's life away from them or to allow them to live. The uniqueness of biopower, therefore, consists of crossing the limits imposed on sovereignty, since demography, hygiene, public health, and individual identities defined by nationality or citizenship are the means by which power is exercised over life and over the giving of life. Foucault refers to biopolitics or the growing implications of the natural life of mankind in the calculations and mechanisms of power, implications expressed in the 1948 Universal Declaration of Human Rights life, which not by accident began with the affirmation of life as a basic human right.

In spite of his rich and exciting analysis, Foucault does not highlight the material conditions of these two forms of power—discipline and biopower. In fact there is no mention in *Discipline and Punish* of the moment that the capitalist mode of production requires salaried labor and, therefore, docile bodies or discipline. From its inception capitalism finds its ideological expressions in the protestant ethic of labor as a vocation and duty; therefore, economy and ideology institute the duty to work and repress desire and pleasure, imposing an iron discipline on bodies. In the same manner, in his lectures on biopower at the *Collège de France*, Foucault never mentions the emergence of industrial society and mass society. Neither does he talk about the terrifying presence of a large and frightening working class, living in squalid conditions in urban centers, a class whose reproduction as a workforce necessitates a politics of hygiene and public health. And he does not mention contemporary politics, which actually stimulates pleasure, desire, and enjoyment, evidenced in the politics of mass culture, which has effectively destroyed the repressive morality of early capitalism.

Nevertheless, Foucault's analyses return to classical ideas of politics, crucially returning to the idea of a nonidentification between politics and the state apparatus. In thinking of power as an activity and operation that is present in all social institutions, Foucault's work reveals surprising affinities with that of Hannah Arendt and Claude Lefort. Like them, he questions the point of view of political science.

These philosophers effectively conceive of politics as a public space in which actions related to the collective are debated and decided. Politics, therefore, determines forms of sociability and of societies according to the form of power and the exercise of government. This perspective is opposed to that of political science.

In political science the existence of a political sphere and of political facts is different from all other spheres and social facts. Politics is equated with the state or state institutions, government, the existence of political parties, and the presence or absence of elections. Politics is, therefore, a circumscribed fact rather than a sociohistorical mode of existence.

Arendt, Lefort, and Foucault, on the contrary, consider social formations are instituted by political action. Politics is the creation of multiple social institutions where society represents itself to itself, where it recognizes or disavows itself, where it produces and works on itself and where it transforms itself. Politics is, therefore, not just the institution of the social; it is also historical action.

However, the similarity between Arendt, Foucault, and Lefort ends there. For Arendt, political power is the result of public consensus. For Foucault, power is a collection of operations, mechanisms, and institutions that are spread throughout society. For Lefort, political power is symbolic; it is not scattered through society nor circumscribed to the state but a point of reference in which a class divided society seeks to reunite itself, working through the conflicts that divide it. In other words, like Machiavelli's and Marx's, Lefort's concept of power stems from the idea of social divisions and, therefore, from conflict, not consensus. This is why Lefort praises democracy for being the only political regime that acknowledges the legitimacy of conflict, and its centrality for the existence of democratic society.

IV.

At the start of this essay, I mentioned some aspects of contemporary society that lead to the "oblivion of politics." I also mentioned the invention of democracy as the historical beginning of politics. If there is an "oblivion of politics," then we should ask what is happening to democracy. Therefore, I now focus on some key aspects that are currently attacking democracy everywhere:

1. *The organizational form of economic, social, and political practices.*
   By this I mean the predominance of management and administrative ideas, seen as instrumental practices in functioning according to norms, rules, and criteria applicable to all spheres of social existence (workplace, school, hospital, culture, trade unions, political parties, the army, the state, etc.). In other words, the uniformity of all human, economic, political, and cultural practices. An organization now refers to particular practices for obtaining particular objectives. It no longer refers to actions that articulate external or internal notions of recognition nor to internal or external legitimacy. Instead it is linked to operations, defined as strategies, which are supported by ideas of efficacy and success in reaching the particular objectives that define a particular business. It is

governed by ideas such as planning, forecasts, control, and outcome. This organization is, therefore, different from the idea of the social institution, which is the nucleus of democracy. The institution aspires to universality (the essential trait of rights), whereas the efficacy and success of an organization depends on its particularity. Society is the key principle for the institution, as well as its normative and valorative reference. The only reference for the organization, however, is itself, and it competes with other organizations that share its particular objectives. The institution is inserted in the social and political division of classes and it attempts to define a universality that allows it to respond to the contradictions this division creates. The organization, on the contrary, generates its own particular time and space, and accepts as a general fact its participation in the process of social division. Its goal is not to respond to social contradictions, but rather to defeat the competition from its supposed equals.

2. *Inverse political problems caused by social democracy and neoliberalism*:
    (a) *The case of social democracy.* The appearance of popular struggles, which brought mass workers onto the scene of politics, and the creation of the economic and social rights of workers, through the implementation of indirect salaries (free education, healthcare, minimum wage, unemployment benefit, holiday pay, social security), have meant that the state must broaden its bureaucratic and administrative apparatus to cater to demands and needs. As previously stated, the predominance of administrative ways of thinking has impeded democracy. In addition, it is necessary to understand bureaucracy not as a form that guarantees the functional operation of work in the public sphere, but rather as a form of power, since it operates as an authority without mandate, one that has the power to determine the life (and death) of citizens. This authority is achieved via three principles that are incompatible with democracy: (1) the hierarchy of roles and functions, anathema to the idea of democratic equality; (2) the secrecy of roles and functions, which goes against the right to information; (3) routine, which goes against social and political innovation that are at the heart of democracy.
    (b) *The case of neoliberalism.* Social democracy or the Welfare State began to collapse because it could not fully achieve its goal of

directing public funds in two simultaneous directions: first, toward the financial needs and social rights of workers, and secondly, toward capital. Neoliberalism has responded to this collapse by proposing: (1) a strong state that can break the power of trade unions' and workers' movements, in order to control public spending and make drastic tax cuts; (2) a state whose principal goal is monetary stability. This entails restricting social spending and creating unemployment growth that effectively produces a surplus workforce capable of breaking the power of the trade unions. For the first time in the history of capitalism, unemployment became structural; (3) a state that carries out fiscal reforms to encourage private investment, reduce tax on capital and wealth, and increase tax on individual income and, therefore, on jobs, consumption, and commerce; (4) a state that no longer regulates the economy but that leaves this instead to a market whose "rationality" is deregulation. To put it another way, the elimination of state investments in production, the elimination of state control of financial flows, the implementation of drastic legislation to clamp down on strikes and a vast program of privatization. The ideological nucleus of neoliberalism is that the market is the bearer of all sociopolitical rationality and the principal agent of the Republic's well-being. This idea places social rights (health, education, social security, culture) within a service sector defined by the market. To summarize, neoliberalism *reduces the public democratic space of rights and increases the private space of market interests.*

3. *Change in the locus of decision-making.* Economic, social, and political decisions are made by supranational organizations (the World Bank, the IMF, etc.). These now possess global power, and states contract public debts with them so that citizens effectively pay for their governments to fulfill the needs of these organizations (the majority of which are private). These global organizations function secretly, interfering in the decisions of elected governments. Governments, therefore, no longer represent citizens; they manage the secret will of these global organizations, restoring the principle of the "Reason of the State," which prohibits the Republic as democracy because it increases private space and decreases public space.

4. *Technical-scientific developments or the emergence of a knowledge society.* I refer here only to two antidemocratic effects that have resulted from these technological advances:

   a). The vertiginous obsolescence of qualifications as a result of the incessant increase of new technologies. Automation and the high turnover of labor lead to structural unemployment, as well as social, economic, and political exclusion. Economic and social inequality have now reached new levels. Divisions between the rich countries of the center and the poorer peripheral countries are still in place; as are internal divisions within countries, with pockets of extreme wealth and pockets of extreme poverty.

   b) The *ideology of competence* that expresses the appearance of a new social division that begins in the economic sphere of production and penetrates all spheres of human existence: the division between the "competent," meaning those who possess scientific and technological knowledge and are, therefore, able to rule, and the "incompetent", who do not possess this knowledge and are, therefore, obliged to obey. When this division occurs in the political sphere, politics becomes a technical matter that is best dealt with by competent specialists, so that it excludes citizens from discussions, debates, and decision-making processes. Citizens' participation is reduced to voting in elections, a process that is determined by another antidemocratic element: political marketing.

5. *The emergence of a political industry or the marketing of politics.* This operates by submitting politics to the procedures of a consumer society or the society of the spectacle. Political marketing sells an image of the politician and reduces the citizen to the figure of the private consumer. In order to forge an identification between the consumer and the product, marketing produces an image of the politician as a private person: physical characteristics, sexual, dietary, or literary preferences, favorite sports, habits, and pets and family life. The privatization of politicians and of citizens privatizes public space.

6. *The economic and ideological power of the mass media.* The economic power of the mass media is akin to a monopoly and total control of information and whose ideological power is exercised by the culture industry that regards culture as an instrument of indoctrination, intimidation, and manipulation of information.

This destroys the public sphere of opinion that is central to democracy.

V.

In the case of Brazil, we must add some other aspects to those mentioned above. First, the difficulty of implementing democracy in Brazil, and, second, the Brazilian authoritarian imaginary concerning the state.

Democracy is a form of social existence. Therefore, only a democratic *society* can forge a democratic *political* regime. As a social institution, democracy defines citizenship through the idea of social, civil, economic, and cultural rights; and as political institution, democracy exists through the creation of new rights and the protection of former and new rights. Now, Brazilian society is polarized between privilege and poverty, and, therefore, the difficulty of implementing democracy in Brazil stems from the social absence of the dimension of rights.[2]

It also stems from the image of the state in Brazilian society. Indeed, taking into account the role of society in the creation of politics, it is evident that Brazilian society is authoritarian, and authoritarianism leads us to conceive of the state as the only political and historical agent. In other words, social classes, social groups, and social institutions are not perceived as political and historical actors, and as a consequence in the Brazilian imaginary it is clear that Brazil's political and historical protagonist is not society but rather the state. In Brazil the state has always been regarded as preceding society. In the colonial period the legal existence of the colony depended on ordinances from the metropolitan state, which existed before and beyond its establishment. Following the proclamation of the Republic, the state continued to be seen as an agent that preceded the nation and established it.

During the colonial period Brazil was created by laws and regulations, that is, by decrees, licenses, royal orders, determined by the administrative order of the metropolis. Colonial society was established by the metropolitan state, which preceded and was exterior to it. This image of the state did not disappear with the proclamation of the Republic. Although it was preceded and followed by the declarations of various political parties as an event that corresponded to, or conflicted with, social desires, liberals, and conservatives saw the proclamation of the Republic simply as a reform of the state, carried out by the state itself. Therefore, while the Republic may have expressed real and concrete social and economic struggles, as well as new arrangements in the power of the dominant class (the end of slavery, the decline of the sugar plantations, state subsidies for immigration promoted by a new coffee planter class, urbanization, the international conjunction of industrialization, etc.), it was not perceived in this way and it did not appear as an outcome of these struggles. The state did not emerge as an institution founded by society or engendered by social struggles. It emerged as a reform of the existing state, one that was carried out by the state itself, which as we have already seen was founded by decrees, licenses, and Portuguese orders.

How can we explain this curious phenomenon? It was the result of various social agents' expectations of the state. Liberals were not interested in the idea of the state as something that is produced by society because they wanted to preserve the separation between state and society in order to hinder the state's intervention in the market. Conservatives were not interested in the state as an institution established by society because they believed that the state's exteriority and superiority in relation to society gave them the power to intervene in the social sphere. Both sides, therefore, regarded the state as the Portuguese had: as separate from and external to society. This produced the image of the state as the only historical subject, so that historical and political changes and social transformations are forged by the state.[3]

High school textbooks dealing with the history of Brazil highlight how our history is periodically configured according to changes in the state, making the state the only protagonist of Brazilian history: the captaincy general, the General Government, The United Kingdom of Portugal, Brazil and the Algarve, The First Empire, The Regency, The Second Empire, The Republic, The Old Republic, The New State, and so on.

Clearly, the Brazilian state is founded by Brazilian society, that is, by class struggle and social pacts devised by the ruling class in order to maintain power. For example, the so-called Old Republic was linked to the power of the landed gentry, the New Republic, to the emerging industrial bourgeoisie of the supposed revolution of 1930; the New State was an outcome of a pact between agrarian forces and industrialists who controlled the working class by labor laws; the coup of 1964 emerged from the struggle between a new powerful bourgeoisie associated with international finance, and the national bourgeoisie, and so on. The Brazilian state is undoubtedly a guardian of the interests and powers of the ruling elite that founded it, a fact that is evidenced by (1) national legislations that curtail and repress trade unions and popular social movements, that is, the ideology of the defense of order and security; (2) financial infrastructures and building projects (railway lines, ports, highways, hydroelectric plants, etc.) that were always state initiatives, highlighting the ways in which the country's ruling class used the state for its own private interests.[4] Raymundo Faoro's expression, *os donos do poder* meaning the owners of power, refers the state as patrimonial, that is, the ruling class owns the national territory. This explains, on the one hand, the difficulty (not to mention the impossibility) of achieving real agrarian reform in Brazil, and on the other, the hostility to the privatization of state industries in the context of neoliberalism.

This perception of the state is also at play in the myth of non-violence. The state's real class origins (its foundation by the ruling class) are hidden beneath a social imaginary, which sees it as a self-instituted power. Concerning this imaginary, the key question is what is the origin of political power in Brazil?

It is important to remember that Brazil's colonial political culture consecrated a religious conception of power or a theology of power. This was present in the Iberian Peninsula and although it has undergone numerous transformations, it is still prevalent today. There are two key points to this theological conception of power.

The first is the belief that because of mortal sin, man lost all of his rights, including the right to power. This right belongs exclusively to God because, as the Bible states, "All power comes from on high / Kings rule and princes govern on my behalf." God concedes power through a mysterious decision or a divine grace. The origin of human power, therefore, lies in a divine favor bestowed upon the person who represents God. The ruler, therefore, does not represent the ruled; he represents a transcendent power, God. To rule and govern is to carry out and distribute favors (an imitation of divine grace). Those "on high" (the ruling class) concede powers and rights to their subjects through decrees and laws. This is evidenced in Brazilian politics (both in the past and present). Here representatives do not see themselves as bearers of a mandate given to them by those they represent, but as representatives of state power, maintaining instead a relationship based on favor or *clientelism* with those they represent.

The second point is linked to the first because it explains why the ruler represents God. He represents God because he possesses a nature that is similar to Jesus Christ. The ruler possesses two bodies: a physical, mortal, and human body, and a mystical, political, eternal, immortal, and divine body. When the physical body receives the mystical or political body, the ruler receives the very imprint of power: absolute personal will. Therefore, the ruler is imbued with absolute will, hence the saying "if it pleases the King, it is law." Sovereignty is not popular power or the power of citizens, but absolute power over citizens. God uses the ruler's power as an instrument of His will, and although they may exercise the right to vote, the people are not regarded as having their own will, rather they are seen as instruments of a divine will or God's plan—*vox populim, vox Dei*, the voice of the people is the voice of God. Although he is elected, a Brazilian politician does not represent the people but God. Leaders are dubbed "Fathers of the People," exemplifying a relationship of tutelage, not of representation.

This highlights why the state appears as a distinct and separate force from society, as a transcendent power that can interfere in the social sphere; it also explains the popular tendency to relate to rulers as holy figures, to saviors, or to gods.

Our present and past political imaginary contains an image of power that is formed from on high, develops from on high, and rules all of society from on high. It is present in all aspects of everyday life; for instance, in the public notary that produces an authenticated photocopy of identity (an aberration, of course, since how can a copy be authentic?), bureaucratic agents act as mediators between the citizen and the power of the state. It is also, and above all, present in two aspects that are remnants from the Iberian state: bureaucratic power and the juridification of power.

I have already referred to bureaucracy as a power, not as a form of the functional organization of work in the public sphere, because it operates as an authority without mandate and has the power to determine the life (and death) of citizens. It is an authority legitimized by those on high, that is, by the state itself.

The juridification of politics is the transformation of a social, economic, or political conflict into a legal problem to be resolved by judiciary power as the highest authority or as the law itself. Educational or labor conflicts are not resolved in their own sphere; they are transferred to judiciary power. Parliamentary conflicts too are not worked out politically in their own space; they are transferred to the judiciary. A recent example of this would be Parliamentary inquiries, which began in the legislative domain and are eventually transferred to the judiciary. The state functions by blocking the key defining feature of democracy: conflicts.

In Brazil, we live in a vertical and hierarchical society (although we may not perceive this) in which social relations always take on the form of a complicity (when social subjects acknowledge each other as equal), or order and obedience between a superior and an inferior (when social subjects see themselves as different, difference is not perceived of as symmetry but inequality). In this context, political democracy based on ideas of citizenship and representation is impossible. It is substituted by ideas of favor, clientelism, tutelage, co-optation, and intellectual pedagogy.

Here, political parties are private clubs for local oligarchies. They consolidate the middle class with an authoritarian imaginary (order) and maintain three types of relations with electorates: co-optation, favor, and clientelism, tutelage, and the messianic promise of redemption. For the ruling classes politics has a theocratic perspective, that is, rulers are the bearers of a divine power. For the popular classes, the political imaginary is messianic. This means that politics operates with religious images for both the ruling and the popular classes. Politics is not configured as a field of social struggles. It takes place within the realm of theological representation, oscillating between the sanctification and adoration of a good ruler and the desecration and demonization of a bad ruler.

The state is perceived by society only within the executive power and judiciary power, while legislative power is dismissed as corrupt. The state in turn perceives civil society as a dangerous enemy, and blocks and represses democratic attempts made by social and popular movements as well as by trade unions.

Religious Fundamentalism: The Return of Political Theology

I.

It is well known that religions make use of mass and spectacular cultures—this is a phenomenon that pervades and permeates all societies, since religions cannot exist without rituals and ceremonies. It should, therefore, not surprise us that, throughout the world, they have easily adapted to the vagaries of time, which has witnessed the emergence of mass culture and the culture industry.

In Brazil, the presence of religion in the mass media is comparable to that in the United States. In fact, a survey of public telecommunication concessions (not counting radio stations) highlights the television channels in Brazil, which includes public, commercial, free, and cable stations. Of these, at least a dozen is religious. The mid-1980s saw a startling diffusion of evangelical Protestantism in Brazil's major cities. As a reaction to this, the Catholic Church established the "charismatic church." Consequently, religious television channels are largely split between evangelical and charismatic religions, with a varied programming that includes *telecults, telecourses* dealing with biblical exegesis and *teleadvice* featuring personal accounts of conversion and even adverts selling personal religious material, all interspersed with song and dance, as well as educational videos. Evangelical churches have mushroomed in Brazilian cities, where they are located in old cinemas, theaters, factories, and shopping centers. At the other end of the spectrum, football stadiums are periodically transformed into cathedrals for prayer, song, and the activities of charismatic Catholics.

As I have stated, this should not surprise us. Nevertheless, it does. However, our surprise stems not from the presence of religion in the media and its increasing visibility in city squares and streets; neither is it related to its increasing manifestation in peoples' clothes, behavior, and lifestyle. It stems rather from the incredible ability of religion to politically and militarily mobilize millions of people around the world. After all, we cannot forget Ronald Reagan's unprecedented arms race at the end of the cold war that proclaimed to prepare the "free world" for victory in the cosmic battle of Armageddon. Neither can we forget the Sabra and Shatila massacre, the civil wars in Ulster and Belfast, Tehran and Kabul, the genocide in Sarajevo and Kosovo, and the war in Gaza, Jerusalem, and Baghdad. These battles were perpetrated as religious struggles and they culminated in suicides carried out as acts of sacrifice—all in the name of God.

Such events compel us to ask whether (and if so, why) today's dominant cultural politics is ultimately founded on religious values. In other words, we know that throughout history there has never been a war based on religion and that no one can attribute contemporary conflicts to religious causes—their causes are economic, social, and political. And yet, these wars adopt religious expressions. It is precisely this fact that surprises us.

Why?

In the search to define a single and indivisible sovereign figure, Western modernity needed to separate itself from the ecclesiastical power that impeded this unity and indivisibility. Consequently, public expressions of religion were placed under the control of rulers (the adage *cujus regio, eius religio* stems from the treaty at Westphalia) and intimate expressions were relegated to the private realm. Religion was displaced from public space (which it had occupied during the Middle Ages) to private space. This task was broadly supported by the Protestant Reformation, which combated the exteriority and automatism of rites, as well as priests' mediatory presence between God and the faithful, situating religiosity within the individual conscience. From the Enlightenment onward, and the defense of civil and religious liberty (or tolerance), religion began to be seen as an archaic tradition that would be overcome by the march of reason or science. This view disregarded the specific needs religion responds to and its significance. Religion came to be viewed from a civilized point of view as something linked to rural, primitive, and backward populations. There was also the belief that, in more progressive and civilized societies, the market would respond to requirements formerly satisfied by religious life. That is, Protestantism was seen as an ethic not a religion, and the Protestant ethic of work and production would fulfil the Christian promise of redemption.

Marx's assertion that "religion is the opiate of the masses" is characteristically cited in Western modernity, yet what tends to be ignored is the fact that Marx preceded this statement with an analysis of religiosity as the "heart of a heartless world" (a promise of redemption in a future world for the wretched and the poor, like the working class), "its encyclopaedic compendium, its logic in popular form" (a coherent and systematic explanation of nature and human life, of natural events and human actions, understood by all). In other words, Marx expected the political action of the proletariat to be born from another logic, one that did not entail the immediate suppression of religiosity, but its dialectical comprehension and overcoming, a process imbricated with necessary mediations.

On the contrary, the belief that the light of reason would immediately suppress religion means that modernity has been unable to account for the religious avalanche that smothers contemporary societies. The return to religion can be analogized with what psychoanalysis refers to as "*the return of the repressed*," the repetition of what was suppressed by culture, because, not having known how to deal with it, this suppressed object simply prepared for its return. Before attempting to understand this phenomenon, it is necessary to outline the religious changes that took place between 1960 and 2000.

II.

In *The Revenge of God*, Gilles Kepel notes that between 1960 and 1976, the "three religions of the Book"—Judaism, Christianity, and Islam— were forced to deal with the effects of the Second World War and the Cold War.[1] On the one hand, the political spheres' decisive conquest of autonomy, a process that began with the Enlightenment, and on the other, the construction of socialism in the East, and the Welfare State and the society of consumption in the West. Political autonomy discredited the idea that religion organizes social life, leaving little space to seek from the divine an explanation of the social order. The cold war in turn imposed an alternative beyond which there could be no salvation; everyone was obliged to struggle for the victory of their side, and faith was gradually subordinated to the realization of earthly ideas. This led to the emergence of Marxist and socialist tendencies in Latin America, the Caribbean, and countries in the Middle East that were linked to Soviet interests.

Optimism pervaded the modern world and religious discourse was regarded as an instrument of political support that spoke of justice, rights, development, progress, and freedom, in a language understood by social classes that could not comprehend modern categories and rhetoric. Many advocates supported the libertarian movements that emerged in 1968, in Europe, the United States, and the Third World.

This situation changed in 1975: Christianity began to speak of "reevangelizing Europe" and "saving America"; Judaism dismissed the legal State of Israel and emphasized instead the biblical notion of the *land* of Israel (justifying the occupation of Palestinian territories); Islam no longer referred to modernizing Islam but of "Islamicizing modernity." A new religious militancy emerged. Its members did not emerge from the popular classes or the rural world, they were young university students, science and technology graduates, who critiqued the absence of a common project they could adhere to. In Europe, they began to question society and its secular foundations. In the United States and in Muslim countries they started to challenge the organization of society and its secular itinerary. They appropriated the language of the social sciences and of Marxism to invent a conceptual syntax that reaffirmed religion as the foundation of the social system.

According to Gilles Kepel, in the 1960s and the early 1970s, these militants were unable to express themselves in political space and they, therefore, sought a return to Christianity, Judaism, and Islam, acting "from below." In other words, they sought to make religion intervene powerfully in private life and in customs, creating believers (through community and aid organizations) and producing profound cultural transformations.

At the end of the 1970s, however, these militants began to enter the political field. Blaming dominant classes and leaders for economic, social, and political failures, they sought to reinvigorate religion from above, either by symbolic acts of terror or by taking over the state (elections or coups). These actions from above intended to change the nature of the state by reclaiming its religious foundations.

It was at this moment that Islam became Islamism. It affirmed *al-Ummah al-islamiah* or "the community of all believers" (which corresponds to what the West calls Christianity) as the source of Arab unity; it critiqued the secular foundations of modernity (or Western imperialism); military groups gained power—such as the Muslim Brotherhood and Hamas, the latter contrasting its religious standpoint to the secularism that characterized El Fatah and the PLO—and the internal disputes between the Shiites and the Sunnis developed.

At the same time in Judaism, the Gush Emunin movement, which spoke in the name of *Am Israel*—the people of Israel—and *Eretz Israel*—the Land of Israel—(extended to all territories situated between Israel and Jordan), emerged. This proposed an aggressive politics of occupation by colonization, and it affirmed the enduring and sustained divergence between political Zionists and religious Zionists, between those who defended the nation-state—legally defined and inclined to recognize the Palestinian state—and the integralists, who, having emigrated to the new State of Israel in the 1940s, refused its creation and attributed to the political Zionists the extermination of Jews by the Nazis (they referred to the genocide using the religious term "the holocaust" meaning that God, using the Nazis, sacrificed people for having succumbed to idolatry by desiring a nation-state).

There are some emblematic dates that mark religion's passage from private to public space: 1977, when for the first time in its history, the Workers' Party of Israel—largely lay and socialist—lost the legislative elections and Menahem Begin became prime minister; 1978, when the Polish Cardinal Karol Woytila was elected Pope John Paul II, with the support of conservative North Americans who cornered the Catholic left; 1979, when the Ayatollah Khomeini returned to Iran and the Islamic republic was proclaimed, at the same time that an armed group attacked the Grand Mosque in Mecca as a protest against the Saudi dynasty's control of religious places; 1979, when North American evangelists formed the politicoreligious organization the Moral Majority, which aimed to save the United States by restoring moral Christian values (ranging from including prayer at schools to outlawing abortion) and helped to elect Ronald Reagan the following year. The early 1980s, with the start of the civil war in Lebanon, a conflict that involved Maronite Christians, Lebanese, and Palestinian Muslims, and Israel. The mid-1980s, when the Iran-Iraq war erupted, involving Sunni and Shiite Muslims, along with the socialist Ba'ath party and religious leaders. The civil war in Afghanistan also started then, with the Taliban and local powers subordinated to the Soviet Union.

In each of these cases, these events were determined by local and regional history. In Israel, the victory in the Six Day War (in 1967), the defeat in the Yom Kippur War (in 1973), and Sephardic voters' support of right-wing military parties, in response to the living and working conditions that have always made them economically subject to and politically excluded by the Ashkenazi elite. In Catholicism, the uncertainty that accompanied increasing secular power and the emergence of Liberation Theology in the Third World after the Second Vatican council. In Iran, the petrol crisis and the final overthrow of the Shah (or the idea that modernity is responsible for despotism, corruption, and poverty). In North America, double digit inflation, the petrol crisis (which led to the "friendly" occupation of Saudi Arabia, the arming of Sadam

Hussein against Iran, and of the Taliban against the Soviet Union), and the demoralization of the military following the hostage crisis at the Tehranian embassy. In the United States these events fostered a need to reaffirm imperial power externally (which had suffered a severe blow with Vietnam), and to legitimize morality and religion internally. In Lebanon, the dispute between the six political minorities—Alowite, Maronite, Sunni, Coptic, Palestinian, and Zionist—that reclaimed not just the struggle between Muslims and Christians, but also the invasion of Syria by Palestine and Israel. And, finally, in Afghanistan, mass poverty, political corruption, the struggle between the tribal worlds ruled by religious chiefs and the secular state, and the territory's strategic position, in terms of oil, led to a geopolitical contest between the United States and the former Soviet Union.

However, these events cannot be solely attributed to local and regional history, especially in the context of internationalization and globalization. Indeed, it is important to remember that the end of the 1970s were marked by the fiscal crisis of the state, the end of the Welfare State and the fall of the Soviet Union with *glasnost* and *perestroika*. These years constituted the beginnings of neoliberal capitalism and its state, of Thatcherism and Reaganism.

III.

What caused the crisis that led to neoliberalism?

The Welfare State is characterized by two simultaneous directions given to public funds:[2] on the one hand, financing the accumulation of capital;[3] on the other, financing the reproduction of the work force, which encompassed the entire population by means of social spending achieved through indirect wages.[4] The latter increased social classes' consumption, especially the middle and working classes; in other words, it led to mass consumption.

This process of guaranteeing the accumulation and reproduction of capital and the work force threw the state into debt, beginning a process of public debts known as fiscal deficit or the "fiscal crisis of the state." This crisis worsened with the internationalization of production since multinational oligopolies do not send overseas profits to their own country, and consequently do not nurture the nation's public funds, which continue to finance capital and the work force.

Why do those who defend neoliberalism critique social rights, or public spending using indirect wages? The direct wage has always been the nexus that links capital to the work force, so that each technical innovation in capital has always been a reaction to struggles for higher wages. The indirect wage undid the knot that linked capital to the work force and freed capital for practically unlimited technological innovations, fostering an increase in investments and an increase in productive forces, with ample liquidity but with insufficient profit to realize all the technological possibilities. Capital, therefore, started to exact public money, and began to use public funds to finance technological investments.[5] As we see, neoliberalism is by no means a belief in the rationality of the market, the decline of the state, and the disappearance of public funds. It is a decision to stop using public funds to finance indirect wages, or public services and social rights, and to employ them instead in investments demanded by capital whose profits cannot cover all the technological possibilities it created. Neoliberalism, therefore, operates through two distinct forms of privatization: first, it uses public funds for the private interests of capital (or the market); second, it transforms social rights (education, health, housing, etc.) into private services that are acquired by the market. Neoliberalism increases private space and decreases public space.

IV.

The economic and social aspects of this new form of capital are inseparable from an unprecedented transformation in the experience of time and space, described by David Harvey as "time-space compression."[6] Fragmentation and the globalization of economic production have created two contradictory and simultaneous phenomena: the diffusion and fragmentation of time and space, and conversely, the compression of space—everything takes place here, there are no distances, differences, or frontiers—and time—everything takes place now, there is no past and no future, thanks to electronic and information technologies. In reality, however, fragmented and diffused space and time are reunited in an undifferentiated and ephemeral space, a space that is reduced to a superficial plane of images, in which time loses its profundity to become a movement of rapid and fleeting images.

Paul Virilio's work echoes this description. For Virilio, the rise of the electronic and information revolution has produced what he calls nonplaces or atopia, and nontimes or acronia or the disappearance of sensory units in the space and time of perception.[7] The extension of time and its power to differentiate is dissolved by the primacy of the instant. The depth of field that defines space also disappears and is replaced by nonplaces and technologies of flight. We live in an age of telepresence and teleobservation, which obliterate the difference between appearance and sensibility, the virtual and the real, since everything is instantly present in a kind of temporal and spatial transparency that becomes evidence of our reality. A dangerous rupture between the sensible and the intelligible shapes our experiences and thoughts. The experience of the body as one's own body is disavowed by the space marked by an absence of distances, and we are invited into a world of sedentary thought and forgetfulness.

Ephemeral and volatile, there is no sense of continuity in contemporary experience, and individuals exist in a present that is lived as a fleeting instance. This situation blocks any interrogation of the present and the future as well as any connection with the possible. It fosters a celebration of contingency and uncertainty. The contingent is understood as a mode of experience rather than something that can be shaped by human action. So-called deconstructionism or the crisis of the narrative are part of this discontinuity and contingency. With the loss of temporal differences we rely on what Virilio calls an "immediate memory," or an absence of the extension of the past, and all sense of the future as a possibility that is inscribed in human action as the ability to determine the indeterminate and overcome situations by understanding and transforming their very meaning.[8]

The religious imaginary of a *sacred space* renounces the compression of space. Against the homogenous space of the state (territory) and the atopic space of satellite, missile, and Internet (virtual) technology defended by the topological space of guerrilla and resistance movements (deterritorialization), sacred space offers itself up as the holy land, a symbolic, absolute, and communitarian space, the creator of a complete identity.

The religious imaginary, therefore, renounces the contingent, the ephemeral, and the here-now, the perception of a fleeting present that has no ties with the past or the future. This renunciation goes hand in hand with the reappearance of sacred time—the idea of the holy war as a collective mission (in Muslim faith), the return to a promised land as the realization of a messianic promise (in Judaism), as well as charismatic enthusiasm and celestial apparitions (especially those of the Virgin Mary) that condemn the present and call upon individuals to become one with a sacred time in order to find the road to salvation (in Christianity). These ideas express an attempt to capture time and infuse it with transcendent meaning.

The unity of sacred time and space defines the present as a space of exile: the present is defined as a distance, absence, or interdiction that shapes all ways of relating with sacred space. As the realization of a return to a sacred land, sacred time is linked to the notion of a mission, and the belief that the holy war is an obligation.

V.

The project of modernity was based on two pillars: regulation and emancipation.[9] The pillar of regulation was supported by three principles: the state (an indivisible sovereignty that established a politics of vertical integration among citizens), the market (that established a horizontal individualist and antagonistic political obligation), and the community (horizontal political obligation and solidarity among its members).[10] The pillar of emancipation was constituted by three logics of rational autonomy: the expressive rationality of the arts, the cognitive and instrumental rationality of science and technology, and the practical rationality of ethics and rights. The project of modernity was underwritten by a belief in the possibility of a harmonious development between regulation and emancipation and the complete rationalization of individual and collective life. However, the abstract nature of the principles of each of its pillars led to the tendency to maximize one over the other, and the relationship between the modern project and the emergence of capitalism secured the victory of regulation at the expense of emancipation.

We now find that today's critique of regulation has also led to a critique of the modern idea of emancipation, since postmodern thought claims that modern reason is incapable of leading to emancipation, considering it instead to be a construct that impedes emancipation. While modern thinkers believed that religion was an obstacle to emancipation achieved through reason, postmodern thinkers argue that reason is itself such an obstacle, since the rational foundation of ideas of identity, causality, totality, finality, progress, and truth is itself a perverse simulacrum that conceals difference, singularity, alterity, temporal discontinuity, meaning, and the essential contingency of the world.

Modern thought (which placed religion in private space and expected reason and science to eliminate religion), the neoliberal market (that operates by exclusion and destruction and by virtue of a mystical phantasmagoria of virtual wealth), the neoliberal state (characterized by expansion of the private space of interests and the decline of the public space of rights), postmodern thought (supported by the fracturing of space and time and a refusal of rational tradition), and finally, the postmodern condition of insecurity generated by the compression of time and space (in which the ephemeral leads to the search for the eternal), provides us with some useful insights for understanding the reappearance of religious fundamentalism, not just as a personal expression but also as the interpretation of political action—that is, the return of *political theology*.

The key feature of politics, which manifests itself in democracy, is the legitimacy of conflict, realized through actions. These actions are social counterpowers that create the political powers and rights to legitimize and guarantee them. Are the great monotheistic religions capable of coexisting with conflict, of working with it, and providing it with a legitimate form of expression?

The three great monotheistic religions, Judaism, Christianity, and Islam, as religions that produce theologies or explanations about God and the world from divine revelation, are religions that from the point of view of knowledge must deal with philosophical and scientific explanations of reality.[11] They must also deal with the plurality of rival religions and secular morality as determined by a profane state. This means that each of these religions views philosophy, science, and other religions through the prism of rivalry and reciprocal exclusion. This is a peculiar opposition that cannot be expressed in a democratic public space, since there can be no debate, confrontation, or reciprocal transformation in religions whose truth resides in divine revelation and whose divine precepts are dogmas. Because they imagine themselves to be in immediate contact with the absolute, and because they believe themselves to be bearers of an eternal and universal truth, these religions exclude conflict and difference and they produce the Other as demonic and heretic, impious and impure, depraved and ignorant, bad and false.

Seen in this light, today's return of religious fundamentalism presents us with some incredible risks. First, because modernity relegated religion in the private sphere, the contemporary reduction of public space and increase of private space may reinforce religions' role of organizing society and providing social cohesion. Second, history has already shown us the effects of the organization and cohesion provided by religion, that is, in the bloody struggles fought as holy wars.

VI.

It may seem surprising to talk of a *return* of political theology.

Indeed, we know that the birth of politics—or "the invention of politics" as Moses Finley wrote—was something that distinguished Greece from Rome and from other great ancient empires. Politics was born or invented when public power, as the invention of rights and the law (tribunals) and the creation of collective institutions of deliberation and decision making (assemblies and senates), was separated from three traditional authorities: that of the private or economic power of the head of the family, that of the military leader, and that of the religious leader (figures that in ancient empires were consolidated in one figure, the King or Emperor). Politics was, therefore, born when the private spheres of the economy, of warfare, and of the sacred or knowledge were separated and when political power was no longer identified with the mystical body of the ruler as father, commander, and priest, a human representative of transcendent and divine powers.

In this case, can there be a *political* theology? Strictly speaking, the problem of political theology cannot be limited to the fact of its reappearance at a time when politics appears to have become a completely rational activity dominated by specialists. Rather it forces us to ask how a *political* theology is possible, since the invention of politics took place precisely because of its separation from the sacred and from religion. The problem then is not the existence of a religious authority and a theological power. Indeed, the problem emerges only when this authority and this power is deemed *political*.

Now, as the chapter title highlights, this essay deals not only with this paradox but also with another opposing conundrum. How can we speak of the return of political theology if, according to Carl Schmitt, Western culture has always been and remains theological, in other words, the mere secularization of religion?

> All significant concepts of the modern theory of the state are secularized theological concepts not only because of their historical development—in which they were transformed from theology to the theory of the state, whereby, for example, the omnipotent God became the omnipotent lawgiver—but also because of their systematic structure, the recognition of which is necessary for a sociological consideration of these concepts.[12]

I refer to a return for two reasons. First, because I agree with Hans Blumenberg's critique of Schmitt's use of the term "secularized" as vague, imprecise, and often inadequate, because he employs it in isolation of the juridical context (the canonical right of the Roman Church) that provides it with meaning—to secularize is to expropriate ecclesiastical goods—and also because his use of the term introduces a continuity without ruptures in political history (modern politics is a secularized medieval politics), which leads to the belief in the existence of a substance (politics) whose identity is preserved beneath the surface of temporal changes.[13] Second, and importantly, because Schmitt's conception differs from Spinoza's.

Indeed, for Schmitt all politics is theological. However, for Spinoza all theology is political so that according to Spinoza, it is possible to conceive of and practice a nontheological politics. Or more precisely, because of the specificity of politics, it is possible to understand the conditions in which politics may stifle by theological-political power.

At the start of this essay, I outlined some of the social, political, and psychological effects produced by the contemporary experience of contingency, the aleatory, and the ephemeral: insecurity, solitude, exclusion, and violence. Fear, in its various guises, pervades everyday personal experience, social and political relations, and it fosters the reemergence of religious fundamentalism not just in the private sphere of morality, but also in the public sphere of politics. It is precisely the experience of contingency and fear that are key to Spinozan thought and its attempt to understand the origin and form of political-theological power.

At the start of *Theological Political Treatise* Spinoza writes:

> Men would never be superstitious, if they could govern all their circumstances by set rules, or if they were always favoured by Fortune. But being frequently driven into straits where rules are use-less, and being often kept fluctuating pitiably between hope and fear by the uncertainty of fortune's greedily coveted favours, they are consequently, for the most part, very prone to credulity. (...). They it is, who (especially when they are in danger, and cannot help themselves) are wont with Prayers and womanish tears to implore help from God: upbraiding Reason as blind because she cannot show a sure path to the shadows they pursue, and rejecting human wisdom as vain; but believing the phantoms of imagination, dreams, and other childish absurdities, to be the very oracles of Heaven. As though God had turned away from the wise, and written His decrees, not in the mind of man but in the entrails of beasts, or left them to be proclaimed by the inspiration and instinct of fools, mad-men, and birds. Such is the unreason to which terror can drive mankind! Superstition then, is engendered, preserved, and fostered by fear, (...) only while under the dominion of fear do men fall a prey to superstition; and lastly, that prophets have most power among the people, and are most formidable to rulers, precisely at those times when the state is in most peril.[14]

Fear is the cause that gives rise to and feeds superstition, and men allow themselves to be dominated by superstition only when they are afraid. But where does this fear come from?

If men had complete control of their lives, says Spinoza, they would not be at the mercy of fortune, that is, an order of the world imagined as a series of fortuitous encounters between things, people, and events. Subject to the whims of fortune because they have no power over the conditions of their lives and are motivated by desires for independently existing goods, men are naturally assailed by two passions: fear and hope. They fear that bad things will happen to them and that good things will not happen to them; they hope that good things will happen to them and that bad things will not. Since these good and bad things are entirely dependent on fortune or chance rather than men themselves, and since events are ephemeral, men's fear and hope is eternal. Indeed, just as good and bad things occur without men knowing why or how, they also disappear without men knowing the reasons for their disappearance.

Superstition, therefore, has its origins in the experience of contingency and chance, or what classical philosophers called fortune. The imponderable relationship with a time whose trajectory is uncertain, in which the present seems to have no continuity with the past or the future, generates a sense of ephemerality and discontinuity, of the uncertain and unforeseeable nature of all things. All of this produces a desire to overcome uncertainty and insecurity by seeking signs of the predictability of things and events, signs that may allow men to foresee good and bad things happening to them. This search generates a belief in and a search for premonitions. It leads to a belief in supernatural powers that can inexplicably produce good and bad things for men.

Religion is born from this belief in mysterious transcendent powers. Because they are uncertain of the real causes of events, and because they are uncertain of the necessary order and connection of all things and the real cause of their feelings and actions, human beings imagine that everything depends on an omnipotent will that creates and governs everything according to designs beyond the reach of human reason. They, therefore, relinquish reason as the possibility of achieving knowledge of reality and hope that religion will not just provide this knowledge, but will also remove their fear and increase their hope.

Spinoza, however, continues: if fear is the source of superstition, then three conclusions can be drawn from this. The first is that all men are naturally subject to superstition, not because they have a confused idea of the deity, but on the contrary they have such an idea because they are superstitious—superstition is the source not the effect of ignorance. The second is that superstition must be extremely variable and inconstant. If the circumstances that cause fear or hope change, the reactions of each individual to these circumstances will also change, and so will the contents of what is feared or hoped for. The third is that superstition can be maintained or can persist only if a stronger passion allows it to exist, such as hatred, anger, and deceit. Men easily fall prey to all kinds of superstition. And they rarely persist with only one.

Spinoza notes that the most effective means of controlling men is to maintain their fear and hope. However, the most effective means of making men seditious and inconstant is to change the source of their fear and hope. Consequently, those who strive to control men must stabilize the sources, forms, and contents of fear and hope. This stabilization is performed by religion.

Cult officials, masters of the morality of believers and of rulers, and authorized interpreters of divine revelations, priests set out to fix the fleeting forms and uncertain contents of the images of good and bad things and the passions of fear and hope. This act of fixing forms and contents is most effective if followers believe that God's will is revealed to a few men through decrees, commandments, and laws. In other words, it is easier to control superstition if the content of fear and hope is seen as emanating from revelations of the will and the power of a transcendent deity. This means that revealed religions are more potent and stabilizing than others. The most powerful religions are those that unite the different powers that govern the world in a single omnipotent figure—so that monotheistic religions are more powerful than polytheistic religions. Religions are powerful too if followers believe that theirs is the only true god and that they have been chosen to carry out his will. In other words, monotheistic religions are more powerful if its followers believe they have been elected by the true god, who promised them earthly goods, revenge against their enemies, and salvation in another eternal life. And, finally, these religions will have even greater power if their followers believe that their god reveals himself, that is, if he speaks to the faithful, telling them of his will—the monotheistic religion of an elect people and a revealed god is, therefore, the most powerful religion of all.

The will of a revealed god will have even greater force if the revelation is not an everyday event within everyone's grasp, but something mysterious and directed to a chosen few—the prophets. At the core of monotheistic revealed religions is the prophet, who fixes the contents of fear and hope. This is achieved by commandments or divine laws that determine both liturgy, that is, ceremonies and cults, as well as customs, habits, ways of living, and behavior. Revelation, therefore, determines relations between men and god, as well as among men themselves.

Prophecy is also a revelation of a divine will that governs men: god decrees laws of social and political life and determines who should rule, which is chosen by the god himself. Revealed monotheistic religions or prophetic religions establish theocratic regimes in which rulers govern by the will of god.

Nevertheless, even though prophecies are consigned to inviolable sacred texts—indeed the monotheistic revealed religions described here are the three "religions of the Book," Judaism, Christianity, and Islam—the fact that these texts are the source of theocratic power transforms them into an object of constant dispute and war. These disputes and wars are pursued according to the interpretation of the sacred text, in keeping either with the person who has the right to interpret them or with the contents of the text itself. It is during these disputes and wars of interpretations that the figure of the theologian emerges. Theology, therefore, is not a theoretical or speculative knowledge about the essence of god, the world, and man. It is the power to interpret the power of god, consigned to texts.

For Jewish and Christian traditions theology is supranatural or supernatural, because its source is the divine revelation registered in sacred scriptures. Now, for Spinoza philosophy is knowledge of the essence and power of God, that is, the rational knowledge of the idea of the absolute infinite being and his necessary action; and on the contrary, Spinoza also considers that sacred texts do not provide (they never claim to) a rational speculative knowledge of the essence and power of the absolute. They provide a number of simple rules for religious and moral life. These can be summarized as loving God and loving one's neighbor (justice and charity). There are no speculative mysteries in sacred texts, neither is there a philosophical knowledge of God's essence and power, or of the nature of man because, Spinoza claims, a revelation is a form of knowledge using images and signs, and it is from these images and signs that our imagination creates a divine figure and relates to it through belief. The Judeo-Christian Bible, or the Old Testament, is a historical document of a specific people and their state, the Hebrew theocracy that has now disappeared; the New Testament is a historical account of the coming of a savior, relating his life, deeds, death, and his promises to those who want to follow him.

Because sacred texts do not aspire to an intellectual and conceptual knowledge of the absolute, they do not provide a theoretical basis for the formulation of a theology understood as a rational or speculative interpretation of divine revelations. In fact, appearing to offer images of a rational foundation that may allow believers to conceive of the divine and their relationship with him, the theologian invokes reason in order to "ratify his own interpretation of revelations," yet he finds grounds to cast doubt on reason, challenging and condemning it. Theologians, Spinoza explains, carefully found out how to extort their own fictions and ambivalences from sacred texts, and so "they unscrupulously and recklessly interpret scriptures." The only thing that unsettles them is any opposition to their interpretation, which is contested by others who challenge their very right to interpret these texts.

Theology is thus not a system of ideas but of images that, on the one hand, acknowledges the authority of the theologian (not the intrinsic truth of his interpretation), and, on the other, the subjection of those who listen to him, something that is more effective if gained by consent. The theologian aims to create in the faithful a desire to obey and serve. Useless for faith—because this is reduced to simple rules of justice and charity—and dangerous for reason—which operates according to autonomous internal necessity—theology is detrimental to politics because it blocks the processes of social conflicts that strive for peace, security, and freedom for all citizens.

Let us examine the origins of theology and its operations more closely in order to evaluate the extent of its danger. To do so, we must return to the first effect of the essential inconstancy of superstition and the ephemeral duration of beliefs that stem from it, which consequently destroy the preservation of power. To make power constant, a few individuals (exploiting the misery of others) must present themselves as intermediaries between men and unfathomable powers: in rites and ceremonies, for instance, priests and kings initially present themselves as mediators and then as representatives of the powers that govern the world. But, a further effect is also necessary, allowing religion to become a fixed doctrine, crystallizing the form and content of fear and hope and making them permanent. Thus, in addition to the effective mediation provided by rites and ceremonies, theology, that is, a supposed knowledge about the divine, is also necessary. This is why priests and theologians surround religion with cults and ceremonies that impact public opinion and elicit greater respect, and why they do not hesitate to censure, capture, torture, and kill those who, using free thought and action, dare to question it.

However, the stabilization of superstition through rites and doctrines alone cannot guarantee the permanence of political power. Indeed, the visibility of politics seems to place it in the realm of men and within their reach, whereas religion is more distant as it seems to exist in the realm of the gods, aspiring to invisibility. This is why those who seek to dominate the masses through superstition deify politics, inducing the masses "under a cloak of piety to adore kings as gods or to abhor them as the plague of mankind." This deification of political power is carried out by theology, which contains the secrets of politics. Captivated by the seduction of theology, rulers adhere to the deification of political authority, using ceremonies, secret, laws and censorship, armies and fortresses, and the torture and murder of objectors.

So from superstition are born two new and powerful fears: fear of God in religion (according to the Bible, fear of the Lord is the birth of wisdom); and fear of the ruler in politics (the state conceals the real source of power from citizens, reducing them to the condition of vassals). Moreover, in an endless game, fear of god, whether visible or invisible, inspires a fear of the theologian in the religious imagination of believers, as well as creating a fear of heterodoxy and other religions in the imagination of the theologian. Fear of men in a context marked by social and political divisions creates a fear of rulers in the political imagination of the dominated, and a fear of the masses in the imagination of the rulers.

So, in order to be free from the vicissitudes of fortune, men subject themselves to the mercy of powers whose form, content, and action provide them with security if they and their representatives are directly obeyed. Religion rationalizes (in the psychoanalytic sense) fear and hope; the submission to political power, as the power of a secret sovereign will situated above the individual will of rulers, rationalizes the lawful and the unlawful. This double rationalization is extremely marked in revealed monotheistic religions that are directed to people who believe they were elected by god. The power of this political-religious rationalization is even greater if experts or specialists claim the exclusive right and power to interpret revelations (and, therefore, divine will), deciding the content of what is good and evil, just and unjust, true and false, permitted and prohibited, possible and impossible, as well as who has the right to political power in terms of legal forms of civil obedience.

This domination is religious and political—it is *theological-political*. Whoever exercises it, as a competent specialist, evokes knowledge of the divine will and controls the body and spirit of believers, of rulers and the ruled—he is a *political-theologian*.

Born of and through fear, superstition delegates to religion, which in turn delegates to theology, the delirious task of finding an imaginary unity, capable of recovering and reconciling a reality that is perceived as fragmented in time and space, made of multiple and contradictory forms, a unity that appears to provide events with continuity and that seems to control an irascible nature, pacify irate leaders, offer hope, and conjure up terror.

This unity cannot, of course, belong to the same dimension as the fragmented and disjointed world; it must transcend it, in order to provide its isolated and contradictory forms with some sense of cohesion. This cohesion can be obtained only by the extraordinary power of a desire and a gaze capable of sweeping away the totality of time and space, the visible and invisible. The distressing experience of fragmentation flows into the imaginary unity of the providential will of a divine sovereign. Thanks to his power, which transcends the fragmentation of nature and the divisions of society, the trajectory of the world seems secure and the destiny of each individual is safeguarded.

This safeguarding, however, is precarious. Because this power is imaginary it remains uncertain and surrounded by mysteries and is deprived of necessary intelligibility. Consequently, the image of God becomes an incomprehensible amalgam, since the omnipotence of his will, where the necessity of his action lies, means that he does everything he pleases so that he too is arbitrary and contingent. His reasons are secret. His omniscience is mysterious. He has become the new figure of fortune. Thus, in order to be perceived as omnipotent, divine power must be understood as unfathomable and it must not have a fixed place, thereby duplicating the mystery of the world that requires it. From the moment that the arbitrary nature of divine power is interpreted as proof of omnipotence, human beings are obliged to devise a threat. Finding mechanisms that provide divine favor with a sense of constancy (hence the proliferation of rituals and the art of prophecy) become crucial or, conversely, blindly abandoning oneself to the inscrutable designs of providence, without daring to interfere in its trajectory, trusting in a sovereign will that foresees everything.

This representation of higher powers, or of the powers of the High, appears to descend from heaven to earth. Hence, the same desire to subject oneself to a single and sovereign power that transcends social and political divisions produces a relation between men that ultimately leads them to subject themselves to the mysterious powers of rulers. Spinoza states that from the *arcane imperii* onward—the secrets of power or the reason of the state—human beings accept servitude as though it were their salvation.

In reality, however, and Spinoza never tires of repeating this point, *this representation did not descend from heaven to earth but ascended from earth to heaven—politics is not secularized religion or theology; on the contrary, religion and theology are sacralized politics.*

Immersed in a fear of being overcome by the uncontrollable power of external forces, either nature or social relations, the uncertain trajectory of events or the presence of an alterity, men weave an imaginary web of relations whose origin and meaning depend on an absolute authority, the ruler of nature, and society. In devising contingency or fortune, human beings imagine a power whose decrees provide all things and events with a necessary itinerary; but, because this power is imagined as a free will (i.e., as the absolute power of decision and choice), the necessity depends on an even greater contingency, that of the desire of the divine sovereign who imposes an order on the world and who can suspend it with extraordinary actions, such as miracles. It should not surprise us, then, that this image is precisely the image of sovereignty conceived by Carl Schmitt, as we shall see in Part VII of this essay.

The Spinozan critique of theological-political power aims to untie the knot that binds contingency, the feeling of fear and the imaginary of a transcendent power to a single fabric. Politics is the immanent activity of a society that has established itself by the activities of human beings in specific natural and historic conditions. While the imaginary of transcendence asserts theocracy as a regime of power established outside and beyond society by divine will, the rational knowledge of immanence conceives democracy as established by human desire and the superior form of politics.

Since the origin of political power is immanent to the social actions of men, and since the political actor is a collective agent (or the multitude), and since the constituents of the collective subject decide to act, but not to think, collectively, it is possible to understand why theological-political power is violent: first, because it aims to deprive men of the knowledge of the origins of their social and political actions, projecting them as the realization of the transcendent order of an incomprehensible or secret divine will, the foundation of the "reason of the state"; second, because divine laws are revealed and decreed as political and civil laws, they hinder the exercise of freedom, because they are not, as they should be, the regulations of external behavior and lifestyles, but of language and thought, seeking to control bodies and spirits; third, because this power instrumentalizes religious faith, ensuring obedience and making it honorable to die or kill others to satisfy the ambitions of the few, it also arouses voluntary servitude—a desire to serve superiors in order to, in turn, be served by inferiors. This submission is in fact the desire for tyranny.

VII.

We can now deal with some of Carl Schmitt's ideas, which are contrary to those that have been discussed so far.

The objective here is not to examine Schmitt's theories, but simply to highlight some key aspects of his work that relate to the subject of the contemporary return to theological-political power.

For Schmitt, as we have seen, modern politics is secularized theology. This secularization appeared in its most perfect form only at a particular historical moment: during the absolutist monarchy, the heyday of European civilization that was followed by the decadence brought on by the French Revolution, that is, the emergence of the republic and of democracy.

According to Schmitt, under absolutism the origin of the state was made completely visible, because it is born of the sovereign's pure will founded not on reason, debate, or norms, but rather on the absolute power of the decision of the sovereign to create the state. Like God, the sovereign creates ex nihilio and has no obligation to be rational or just. Just as God proves Himself to be omnipotent through his creation of the world, the will of the sovereign is proved to be omnipotent when it creates the state. Just as God is not bound by divine laws, the sovereign is also above the law, *legibus solutus*. Just as God suspends his own laws and interferes in the universe in extraordinary ways at moments of danger, that is, miracles, the action of the sovereign is also unrestricted by laws and at moments of danger responds to exception with an exceptional act or the "reason of the state."

The exception of jurisprudence is analogous to the miracle in theology.[15]

Demiurgy and exception constitute sovereignty as the monopoly of decision making.

The sovereign is he who decides on the exception.[16]

A reflection and expression of the cosmos—order, hierarchy, discipline, and strength—absolutism became the perfect embodiment of the state.

> In its literal sense and in its historical appearance the state is a specific entity of a people. Vis-à-vis the many conceivable kinds of entities, it is in the decisive case the ultimate authority.[17]

By highlighting the absolute essence of the sovereign and the state, absolutism makes politics visible as autonomous, independent of reason and knowledge, morality and religion, law and the economy. Each realm of human existence is polarized by a constitutive distinction: in the moral realm good and evil, in the aesthetic beauty and ugliness, and in the economic the profitable and unprofitable. The political realm is constituted by the friend-enemy distinction. Political autonomy means that this distinction is independent of the criteria that define other distinctions. In other words the friend-enemy distinction cannot be thought of in ethical, aesthetic, religious, or economic terms. Politically, a friend is someone who shares our way of life; an enemy is someone who is other, or stranger who threatens our way of life, and consequently our existence. The enemy is, therefore, always a public enemy and only the sovereign or the state has the power to define him as such.

> The specific political distinction to which political actions and motives can be reduced is that between friend and enemy. This provides a definition in the sense of a criterion and not as an exhaustive definition of one indicative of substantial content. Insofar as it is not derived from other criteria (...), it is independent, not in the sense of a distinct new domain, but in that it can be neither be based on any one antithesis of any combination of other antithesis, nor can it be traced to these.[18]

The friend-enemy distinction expresses unity-disunity, association-antagonism. Conflicts with the enemy can never be resolved using pre-established rules or impartial arbitration. The enemy's existence is a threat to our existence, and it necessitates war, that is, conquest or submission, and in extreme cases, physical elimination.

However, since true politics establishes power over life and death, and since absolute power is single and indivisible, anyone who attempts to share or divide sovereign power is an enemy. This means that the enemy can be internal; the other can exist within our own state. They must be removed, punished, and crushed.

The state must, therefore, define the enemy, because it can exist only if this figure is individualized and because moral, religious, and economic antagonisms are transformed into political antagonisms when they organize men into friends and enemies. Religious wars are, therefore, political events, in the same way that class struggle is political when it adopts a revolutionary form.

Accordingly, politics does not refer to a way of life that involves different spheres of human existence nor to a specific activity. It refers to the intensification of associations and disassociations for economic, religious, moral, or other reasons leading to a test of force; and it is the sovereign who decides the underlying conflict in order to reestablish unity. All wars, that is, all states of exception, depend, on the one hand, on the intensity of distinctions that originate in other spheres of human life, and, on the other, on the identification of the enemy by the state and its finality is the "existential negation of the enemy." Negation does not necessarily mean annihilation; it may entail subjecting the other to our way of life (colonization) and annihilating them only if this is not possible.

There is an apparent paradox in Schmitt's work. Seeking to uphold the autonomy of politics, he rejects the idea of politics as a way of life (as with the Greeks for instance) or as a professional activity (in line with the contemporary definition of politics). For Schmitt politics is an event that depends on the intensity of conflicts that are born in nonpolitical spheres and sovereignty is an action or the power that determines the trajectory and conclusion of these conflicts. What is the paradox here? If politics is an event that depends on the intensification of antagonisms in different realms of human life, then political autonomy is not absolute but relative and the demiurgy of the sovereign is comparable to the demiurge of Plato's Timaeus, who works with preexisting matter (as in Schmitt's notion of the sovereign who works with conflicts that emerge in other realms), rather than to God from the Book of Genesis who acts ex nihilio.

Schmitt, however, manages to resolve this paradox: by reconfiguring friends and enemies for a test of force, the emergence of politics is always a state of exception that, on the one hand, depends on the absolute will of the sovereign, and, on the other, this exceptional reconfiguration highlights *politics as a kind of war*. The famous proverb claims that war is the continuation of politics by other means. Nevertheless by distinguishing between politics (the friend-enemy distinction) and the state (the public institution), and between politics as a sovereign action and public institutions as inert matter, and by stating that politics is born when social divisions are expressed by the friend-enemy distinction, Schmitt states that *there is no difference between politics and war*. As a state of exception war defines sovereignty—or rather—without war there is no sovereignty and without sovereignty there is no politics, because there can be no enemy without the sovereign. Furthermore, as the culmination of the tension of the friend-enemy distinction, war is the most perfect embodiment of politics, which, is after all, *the logic of force*.

So, it is not by chance that like Joseph de Maistre and Juan Donoso Cortés (men of theological-political power) Schmitt believes that absolutism or imperial power, a secularized theocratic power, is the culmination of politics, nor that he attributes its decline to the French Revolution.

> The idea of the modern constitutional state triumphed together with deism, a theology and metaphysics that banished the miracle from the world. This theology and metaphysics rejected not only the transgression of the laws of nature through an exception brought about by direct intervention, as is found in the ides of the miracle, but also the sovereign's direct intervention in a valid legal order.[19]

Modernity, that is, the French Revolution, is a disaster. First, by introducing the idea of the constitutional state it provides politics with a juridical anteriority embodied by the state. Second, by prohibiting his intervention in the juridical order it destroys the very identity of the sovereign. Third, it destroys the idea of the cosmos (or hierarchical order) and in doing so paves way for an even greater disaster, the union of egalitarian individualism and apolitical economic liberalism with democracy.

This union is disastrous because it mixes the specific dichotomy of economy (profitable-useless) with that of politics (friend-enemy) and denies the autonomy of both politics and economy. In fact, the politics of democracy preserves the friend-enemy distinction, albeit fluid and vague, because it acknowledges citizens' equality, but only in terms of their linguistic, moral, and religious identity, and excludes the other who is different. In other words, the democratic logic depends on the exclusion of the slave, the stranger, or the barbarian who can be evil or atheist. However, once politics is the manifestation of differences and inequalities, liberalism, because it is apolitical, introduces the idea of universal equality. Mediated by democracy, liberalism becomes a clandestine politics, hidden beneath a cloak of rights, justice, the law, truth, universality, and rationality. Following in the slipstream of Donoso Cortés, Schmitt claims that the ideal place for liberal hypocrisy is the parliament, whose interminable discussions exemplify its inability to make decisions.

This brief overview of Carl Schmitt's work takes as its point of departure the outline of Spinozan thought I have given above. Nevertheless, another reason may now clarify our choice of examining some features of Schmitt's work, that is, the affinity between Schmitt's ideas and the work of Leo Strauss and, therefore, indicating an affinity with recent North American politics.

VIII.

Leo Strauss' works on the Greeks and Romans, Machiavelli, Hobbes, and Spinoza, and his writings on natural right, political philosophy, and North American philosophy, do not seem to authorize the idea of a common ground with Schmitt's work (which was in fact criticized by his student Strauss). This is so notwithstanding their similar critiques of modernity, the French Revolution, liberalism, liberal democracy, Marxism, and communism and their emphasis on the disaster of the Weimar Republic as proof of the correctness of their political ideas. A closer reading, however, highlights similarities that may initially have been invisible, to the extent that it does not surprise us to find Schmitt's friend-enemy distinction reformulated in Strauss as an us-them dichotomy, and his definition of justice as aiding one's friends and hurting one's enemies, that is, those who are different from us.

A more precise example will highlight how what initially seems to be differences in their work are in fact similarities. Instead of departing, as Schmitt does, from an assertion of politics' autonomy from morality and religion, Strauss claims that in every society public orthodoxy must define good and evil, just and unjust, noble and ignoble, true and false. The unity and cohesion of society depends on the interiorization of this orthodoxy by all of its members, which can be achieved only if mediated by an official religion. Why religion? Because religion links the political order to truth, or, an ultimate reality, providing this order with a sacredness or sanctity that citizens will then fight, kill, or die for. Religion thus imbues politics with something that is absolutely necessary: transcendence of the origin of power. *The theologization of power is the only possible alternative to modernity.* It is precisely this observation of Strauss' work that echoes Schmitt's.

Indeed, for Schmitt, as we have seen, the origin of the state is the absolute decision of the sovereign who, like God, creates ex nihilio. For Strauss, too, the foundation of politics is always the work of a great ruler whose genius lies in providing people with a myth of origin, one that is capable of inspiring respect, devotion, and fear. Hence Strauss' critique of modernity, and especially, Machiavelli, Hobbes, and Spinoza.

Why are religion and myth necessary for the foundation and preservation of politics? Because there is an overwhelming conflict between individual interest and common good. Neither reason and institutions nor laws and power are able to overcome this conflict, which can be resolved only by the majesty and transcendence attributed to the origin of power. This means that each society and each state must have just one religion—*the plurality of religions is a political threat.*

If we focus on the relationship between morality and politics, we can see how initial differences between both thinkers become similarities. At first glance the differences are stark: Strauss does not acknowledge the autonomy of politics vis-à-vis morality (hence his critique of Schmitt's work). If politics is to recover a sense of dignity and morality, against modernity, it must take up the question of what is good and evil, true and false. However, this is only a small aspect of Schmitt's argument. In fact, just as Schmitt's decisionism presupposes the figure of an omnipotent sovereign, Strauss too develops the idea that only populism, or the figure of a strong and charismatic leader, can liberate politics from the threat of modernity. This theory is linked to the idea of the formation or political education of an elite in charge of an antimodernist mission (which is antirationalist, antisecularist, and not nihilist).

The starting point consists in separating a small elite and educating them so that they may indirectly rule society on behalf of those who rule it directly. What this points to is the establishment of a body of counsellors. To this elite are opened the secrets of power and the knowledge of the terrible and sombre features of reality (that is, Schmitt's concept of the political), with the condition that this is kept secret even from rulers. According to Schmitt's conception of politics, this elite group must make society (including its future rulers) aware of the destructive effects of modern education, one that is receptive to the light of reason in its social and political critiques, and replace it by another form of education that is capable of producing the internalization of social values as absolute and inviolable. Ignorant of the secrets of power and reality, educated to defend the sacred values of his society and imbued with the majesty of a power that stems from his forefathers (which for him is real and not mythical), the ruler will be a strong and convincing leader, while his counsellors will secretly exercise politics as defined by Schmitt, that is, both as an absolute power of decision and as war.

Leo Strauss dedicated his academic career to this task. Between 1950 and 1970, he taught more than a hundred intellectuals at the University of Chicago. These intellectuals became allies of the Christian right—the Moral Majority, which as we have already seen was a movement that promised to "Save America." They saw Ronald Reagan and then George W. Bush as leaders who could take the United States in the right political direction. This elite gave the enemy a religious identity and defined war as the struggle of good against evil. It was this elite who produced the theological-political charade of the geopolitical war of occupying all of the territories from Afghanistan and Iraq, perhaps a strange and unexpected fate for ideas arising from the crises of the Weimar Republic. It is time to rethink Spinoza.

Power and Freedom: Politics in Spinoza

Necessity and Freedom

The theological-metaphysical tradition proposed a series of distinctions by means of which it intended to oppose freedom and necessity. It claimed that all things that occur "by necessity" are "by nature" and, on the contrary, all things that occur "by freedom" are produced by "free will." A necessary operation or natural necessity was the result of an efficient cause, while a free or voluntary action was the result of the articulation between the formal cause (the rational essence of the agent) and the final cause (the *télos* of the action), so that freedom was constituted in relation to the ends or final outcomes. Identifying the natural and the necessary, on the one hand, and the free and voluntary, on the other, this tradition declared that, being omnipotent and omniscient, God could not act out of necessity but only of freedom and, therefore, free will. Created in the image and likeness of God, man too was conceived as a free agent because he was endowed with free will. To act with a view to ends or final outcomes presupposes intelligence or reason; therefore, voluntary action was understood as rational or intelligent action, and natural or necessary operation was understood as blind and raw automatism. These distinctions led to defining human actions in terms of one precise question: what is and what is not in our power? The answer was: whatever occurs by natural necessity or the intervention of fortune or chance is not in our power; whatever occurs by a deliberate choice between contrary alternatives or contrary ends, that is the possible, is within our power. Only God has power over the necessary, the possible, and the contingent and it was from the absolutely free decision of His will, that is, a contingent decision, that the world was created out of nothing. Or as John Duns Scotus asserts, an intelligent agent acts voluntarily and an omnipotent voluntary agent acts contingently.

If the world is contingent, because it is the outcome of God's contingent choice, then the laws of nature and truth (such as those of mathematics) are themselves contingent and they become necessary only by a divine decree that makes them immutable. Natural necessity was, therefore, defined as the divine act of decreeing laws, in other words, necessity is nothing more than the authority of God, who arbitrarily decides, as he so wishes, that 2 plus 2 are 4, that the sum of the internal angles of a triangle are equal to two right angles, that heavy objects fall, that the planets elliptically orbit the sun, and so on. Or, as Descartes stated, God contingently willed eternal truths and natural laws to be necessary. By His Providence, God can make certain things always identical—necessary for us, but contingent in themselves—just as he can also reveal the omnipotence of his freedom by altering them, in the case of miracles. It is, therefore, possible to understand why freedom and necessity have traditionally been considered as opposed and contrary, for the former was imagined as a contingent choice between possible alternatives, whereas the latter as the decree of an absolute authority.

Politically, this theological-metaphysical tradition focused on the formulation of two master theories of natural right, in which the relation between natural right and free will was developed in two directions. The first is that of the *objective natural right*, according to which the will of God creates nature as a primordial juridical order, decreeing an originative justice that fixes the hierarchy of beings according to degrees of perfection and power, and determines order and obedience, authorizing certain actions and prohibiting others, so that we are all born with a natural sense of what is just and unjust. There is, therefore, a natural juridical order that precedes a positive, or juridical-political law whose quality or perfection is evaluated according to its approximation to or distance from the natural order: the "good regime" and the "politically corrupt regime" are evaluations determined by their relation to the natural juridical order. The second theory is that of *subjective natural right*, according to which reason and will distinguish man from mere things, making him a person whose natural right is a dictate of reason, and teaching him which acts conform to and which go against his rational nature. It is the idea of a universal human nature that provides the criteria to assess whether a political order conforms to the laws of nature or not, that is, conforms to the rational nature of man. The theory of objective natural right is founded on divine will, while the theory of subjective natural right is founded on the rational will of man.

The theological-metaphysical tradition was based on the image of God, and it fabricated the divinity as a transcendent person (i.e., separate from the world) endowed with omnipotent will and omniscient knowledge, the creator of all things from nothing (with God imagined as an artisan), the legislator and monarch of the universe, one who can, like a prince who rules according to his own whims, interrupt natural acts by the extraordinary acts of his will (miracles) and punish or reward men who are created by Him in his own image and likeness, who are endowed with free will and are the preferred objects of all the divine work of creation. This image makes God a superman who creates and rules all beings according to the secret designs of His will, which correspond to outcomes that are beyond our full comprehension. Incomprehensible, God is presented as having supreme human qualities: He is good, just, merciful, wrathful, loving, vengeful. Unfathomable, he is presented through images of nature, taken as divine artifact or a harmonious beautiful and good creature, destined to provide all human necessities and desires and who governs according to laws that are determined by a natural juridical order. This tradition, which sustains Christian political philosophy, is undermined by the work of Spinoza.

Spinoza begins with a very precise concept, that of substance: a being that exists in and through itself, that can be conceived in and through itself and without which nothing exists or can be conceived. Every substance is substance because it is the cause of itself (cause of its essence, of its existence, and of the intelligibility of both) and, as the cause of itself, the cause of the existence and the essence of all beings in the universe. The cause of itself, the substance exists and acts by the absolute infinite power of its own nature and because of this it is unconditional. Or, as Spinoza demonstrates, it is the absolutely infinite being, because the infinite is not an existence without beginning and without end (negative infinite), rather it is what causes itself and produces itself unconditionally (positive infinite).

Cause of itself, and intelligible to and by itself, the essence of the absolute substance is constituted by infinite attributes, infinite in their own genre, that is, by infinite simultaneous orders of reality; it is, therefore, an essence that is infinitely complex and internally differentiated into infinite real structures. Existing in and through itself, an absolutely complex essence, the absolute substance is the absolute power of self-production and of the production of all things. The existence and the essence of the substance are identical to its power or infinite force to exist in and through itself, to be internally complex and make all things exist. Now, if a substance is that which exists in and through itself by the force of its own power, which is identical to its essence, and if this is an infinite complexity of infinite orders of infinite realities, then it is clear that there can be only one substance, otherwise it would be necessary to acknowledge an absolute infinite being limited by another absolute infinite being, which would be absurd. There is, therefore, a unique and absolutely infinite substance that constitutes the entire universe, and this substance is eternal not because it has no beginning and no end, but because within it, being, and acting are one and the same. *This substance is God.*

In causing himself and in producing His own essence, God brings into existence all singular things that express Him because they are effects of His infinite power. In other words, the existence of the absolutely infinite substance is, simultaneously, the existence of everything that its power produces, for, as Spinoza shows, in the same sense that God is His own cause, He is also the cause of all things. Therefore, one can conclude that there never was, nor could there ever have been, a contingent creation of the world. The world is eternal because it expresses the eternal causality of God, even though things in it may be temporary, constantly emerging and disappearing or rather, continuously changing from one thing into another.

Spinoza demonstrates that God is not the transitive efficient cause of all things, that is, not a cause that separates itself from effects after having produced them, rather He is the *immanent efficient cause* of its effects; he does not separate Himself from them but expresses Himself in them and they express Him.

There are, therefore, two forms of being and of existing: that of the substance and its attributes (existence in and through itself), and that of the effects that are immanent to the substance (existence in and through another). Spinoza calls this second form of existing *modes of the substance.* The modes or modifications are necessary immanent effects produced by the power of the attributes of the substance. Spinoza calls the substance and its attributes as an infinite activity that produces the totality of the real, *natura naturans* (nature naturing). He calls the totality of the modes produced by the attributes *natura naturata (nature natured).* Thanks to the immanent causality, the totality constituted by nature naturing and by nature natured is an infinitely eternal unit called God. Immanence is summed up by the well-known phrase *Deus sive natura*—"God, or nature."

From immanence, it follows that God's force or power is indistinguishable from the force or power of nature. The natural order is not a juridical order decreed by God, but an order and necessary connection of causes and effects produced by the immanent power of the substance.

Thus, what we call the "laws of nature" are not divine decrees, but specific expressions of the absolute causal power of the substance. In the *Theological-Political Treatise*, Spinoza states that there is nothing to stop us from referring to these natural laws as natural divine laws or natural rights, since we understand that natural laws are divine laws because they are inseparable from the power of the substance. If they are natural rights, then it is necessary to conclude that *right and power are identical*, or as Spinoza writes, *jus sive potentia*—"right, or power."

Of the infinite attributes of the absolute substance, we know only two: Thought and Extension. The activity of the power of the attribute of Thought produces an immediately infinite modification, the intellect of God or the necessary and true connection of all ideas, and it also produces finite modifications or finite modes, that is, ideas and one specific kind of idea, that is, minds (or what is commonly called souls). The activity of the power of the attribute of Extension produces an immediately infinite modification, the material universe, that is, the physical laws of nature as specific dimensions of motion and rest; it also produces the finite modifications or finite modes, bodies. Ideas and bodies, or minds and bodies, are finite modes immanent to the absolute substance, expressing it in a specific manner, according to the order and necessary connection that governs all beings in the universe. Everything that exists, therefore, possesses a determined and necessary cause to exist and to be as it is: it is of the essence of the attributes to necessarily cause the essences and powers of all of the modes; it is of the essence of the infinite modes to connect the universal causal laws that regulate the existence and the operations of the finite modes. And all finite modes, because they express the universal power of the substance, are also causes that produce necessary effects. This means that, on the one hand, everything that exists is a power or cause that produces effects, and on the other, that there is nothing contingent in the universe, since everything is causally necessary.

In *Ethics*, Spinoza demonstrates that everything that exists has a necessary cause and everything that does not possess a determined cause does not exist. Everything that exists does so by the necessary essence and power of God's attributes and modes. For this reason, everything that exists is doubly determined, by existence and essence, that is, the finite modes are determined to exist and to be by the necessary activity of the divine attributes and by the necessary order and connection of the causes and effects of nature natured. Nothing in the universe is undetermined, since the substance determines itself by its own essence and other beings are determined by the power of the modified substance.

Therefore, what is the possible and what is the contingent? A thing is said to be possible, Spinoza explains, when we understand that it will occur, but we do not know the true and necessary causes of its production. The possible is our ignorance regarding the cause of a thing. A thing is said to be contingent, the philosopher explains, when its nature is such that we believe it could either be or not be, for we do not know the essence of the thing and we do not know if it could be or not be. The contingent is our ignorance regarding the essence of a thing. The possible and the contingent are images and with them we forge the imaginary field of freedom.

We are thus able to understand why, instead of the traditional distinctions between "nature/freewill" and "necessity/ freedom" the only real distinction that Spinoza acknowledges is that which exists within necessity itself: the necessary in respect to its essence and the necessary in respect to its cause. There is a necessary being in respect to its own nature or its own essence—God—and there are necessary beings in respect to their cause—the singular beings, immanent effects of the necessary power of God. Necessity and freedom are not opposed, but concurrent and complementary, because liberty is not the indetermination that precedes a contingent choice, nor the indetermination of that choice. Freedom is the spontaneous and necessary manifestation of the internal force or power of the essence of the substance (in the case of God) and of the internal power of the essence of finite modes (in the case of humans).

We say human beings are free when, in respect to the internal necessity of their essence and power, they identify their manner of existing, being, and acting. Freedom then is not the voluntary choice nor the absence of a cause (or an action without a cause), and necessity is not the order, law, or external decree that would force beings to exist and behave in a manner contrary to their essence. This means that only a politics that corresponds to human nature can be a politics that is reconciled with freedom. This provides us with secure criteria to evaluate political regimes, depending on whether they fulfill or prevent the exercise of freedom.

Conatus: Right Is Power

All things that exist express, in a *certain* (meaning no other) and *determined* manner (i.e., through this connection of causes only), the essence of the substance. Because the essence and the power of the substance are identical, all things that exist express in a certain and determined manner the power of the substance. The substantial power is the force to produce itself and, simultaneously, to necessarily produce all things. If these are specific and determined expressions of the substantial power, then they are also powers or forces that produce necessary effects. Therefore, the finite modifications of the absolutely infinite being are the powers to act or to produce necessary effects. Spinoza calls this singular and finite power *conatus*, a striving for self-preservation in existence. The human being is a *conatus* and it is through the *conatus* that he is part of nature or a finite part of the absolutely infinite power of the substance.

The union of body and mind, human beings are not created substances but rather finite modes of the substance constituted by modifications of Thought and Extension, that is, they are immanent effects of the activity of substantial attributes. Or, as Spinoza argues, man is part of nature and expresses in a certain and determined manner the essence and power of the substantial attributes. In a *certain* manner, a human being is a singularity that possesses a singular form and not another or other form. In a *determined* manner, the singular form of a human being is produced by the necessary causal action of the *natura naturans* (the substantial attributes) and by the necessary operations of the infinite modes of the attributes, that is, by the laws of *natura naturata* (the world).

So, what is the human body? A finite mode of the attribute of Extension constituted by the union of a plurality of hard, soft, and fluid corpuscles that relate to each other by the harmony and equilibrium of their proportions of motion and rest. This union of bodies or *unio corporum* is a singularity, that is, a structured unit: it is not an amalgamation of parts, nor is it an automaton of motions, but rather an *organism*, or a unit of aggregates, and an equilibrium of internal actions linked together by organs. It is an *individual*, because as Spinoza explains, when an aggregate of interlinked parts acts together and simultaneously as single cause to produce a determined effect, this unity of action constitutes an individual. Above all, it is a dynamic individual, because the internal equilibrium is achieved by continuous internal changes and by continuous external relations, forming a system of centripetal and centrifugal actions and reactions, so that the body is, by essence, relational: it is constituted by the internal relations of its organs, by its external relations with other bodies or *affections*, that is, the ability to affect other bodies and to be affected by them without being destroyed, regenerating oneself through them and regenerating them. The body, a complex structure of actions and reactions, presupposes that *intercorporeality* is present from the beginning. And it does so because of two aspects: on the one hand, because it is, albeit a singular individual, a union of bodies; on the other, because its life is realized by the coexistence with other external bodies. In fact, not only is the body exposed to the action of all of the other external bodies that surround it and which it needs to conserve, regenerate, and transform itself, but it is itself necessary for the conservation, regeneration, and transformation of other bodies. A human body is stronger, more powerful, and more capable of conservation, regeneration, and transformation, if its relations with other bodies are richer and more complex, in other words, if the system of corporeal affections is broader and more complex.

So, what is a human mind? It is a mode of the attribute of Thought and, therefore, a thinking force or an *act* of thinking. As a mode of Thought, the mind is an *idea* (all finite modes of the attribute of Thought are ideas) and an idea is an act of thought. To think is to understand or to imagine, rationalize, desire, and reflect. The human mind is, therefore, a *thinking activity* that is realized as a form of perception or imagination, reason, desire, reflection. What is it to think, then, in these various forms? It is to affirm or negate something, to be conscious of it (in perception, imagination, or reason), to be conscious of that consciousness (in reflection). This means that the mind, as an idea or thinking power, *is* an idea that *has* ideas (ideas that the mind has had are the content that it has thought). In other words, because it is a thinking being, the mind is naturally and essentially focused on the objects that constitute its content or the significance of its ideas. It is by nature internally linked to its object (or *ideatum*) because it is no more than the activity of thinking it. Spinoza demonstrates that the first object that constitutes the thinking activity of the human mind is its body and so the mind is no more than the *idea of the body*. And because the mind is the power of reflection, conscious of being conscious of its body, it is also the idea of its idea of the body, or rather, the idea of itself, or the *idea of the idea*. If the human body is the union of bodies, the human mind is the connection of ideas (*conexio idearum*), or rather, it is the causal activity of a singularity whose being is an idea that produces ideas. In other words, the mind-body union and connection are the activities that constitute a singular human being.

The human mind is not an independent and finite substance, a soul that is simply lodged in a body that guides, directs, and controls it. The human mind is not lodged in a piece of flesh but it is united to its living body. As a finite mode of thinking, it is a thinking activity defined as the knowledge of its own body and of exterior bodies by means of its own body (since it knows them from the way they affect its body and from the ways it affects them), and as knowledge of itself. This means that the richer and more complex the bodily experience is (or the system of bodily affections), then the richer and more complex the mental experience will be, or the more the mind will be capable of perceiving and understanding a plurality of things, since as Spinoza highlights, nothing occurs in the body that the mind has not formed an image or an idea of (even if they are confused, partial or distorted). The richer the mental experience, the richer and more complex the reflection will be, that is, the knowledge that the mind will have of itself. Because they are different expressions of two different attributes of the substance, the body clearly does not produce thoughts in the mind; neither does the mind produce actions in the body: it perceives and interprets things that take place in its body and in itself. So, bodily affections do not cause affects, feelings, or ideas in the mind. United, the body and the mind constitute a human being as a complex singularity in relation with all others. *Intersubjectivity* is, therefore, originary.

Singular individuals are *conatus*, that is, they are an internal force that unites all operations and actions to persevere in existence, meaning, not simply to persevere in its own state (as a stone does, for instance), but to continuously regenerate, transform, and produce itself (animals and vegetables, for instance). In Part III of *Ethics*, Spinoza defines the *conatus* as the actual essence of the body and of the mind.

What does it mean to define the *conatus* as *actual essence*? First, it does not mean that the human being is the particular product of a universal essence or of "human nature," but rather that it is an individual singularity by virtue of its own essence. Second, that the *conatus* is not an inclination or virtual tendency or power, but a force that is always active. Third, and consequently, it means that the essence of a singular being is its activity, that is, the operations and actions that preserve its existence, and that these operations and actions are logically anterior to its definition as rational or irrational, right or wrong, good or evil. Fourth, and most importantly, the idea that the *conatus* is the actual essence of a singular being allows us to understand the appetites (of the body) and volitions (of the mind) that constitute human desires not as inclinations or tendencies that take place when they find their final outcome, but as active aspects of the *conatus*. They are, therefore, efficient causes determined by other efficient causes, rather than by ends or outcomes. The *conatus,* therefore, leads to the Spinozan definition of the essence of man:

> Desire (*cupiditas*) is is the very essence or nature of each man insofar it is conceived to be determined, by whatever constitution he has, to do something.[1]

Or as it is presented in the Definition of the Affects at the end of Part III of *Ethics,*

> Desire (*cupiditas*) is man's very essence, insofar as it is conceived to be determined, from any given affection of it, to do something.[2]

If desire is the essence of man in *so far as it is conceived as determined to a particular action,* then not only is essence a cause that produces effects, but also that *being determined to a thing* does not equate to an absence of freedom, unless this is imagined as a power to do or not do something by an *indeterminate* power. As Spinoza explains,

> Man can be called free only in so far as he preserves the power of existing and operating according to the laws of human nature (...). That does not confound freedom with contingency (...). For liberty is a virtue, or excellence. Whatever, therefore, convicts a man of weakness cannot be ascribed to his liberty. And so man can by no means be called free, because he is able not to exist or not to use his reason (...) As then he exists by the necessity of his own nature, by the necessity of his own nature also he acts, that is, he acts with absolute freedom (...) For freedom, as we showed above, does not take away the necessity of acting, but supposes it.[3]

In order to highlight Spinoza's political ideas, it will be useful to take up the following aspects of the theory of the *conatus*:

- A singular individual is a complex and dynamic structure of operations and actions that conserve, regenerate, and transform it, ensuring its preservation in existence; it is not the particular realization of a universal essence;

- The complexity of the individual body leads to two fundamental consequences: first, because the individual is constituted by individuals, it follows that nature can be defined as an extremely complex individual, composed of infinite modes of the finite attributes of Thought and Extension, composed by infinite individual causalities, preserving itself by the proportional preservation of its composites; second, a decisive outcome for politics, just as the individual is *unio corporum* (the body) and *conexio idearum* (the mind) and just as nature is an immense and complex individual, the *uniones corporum* and the *conexiones idearum* can constitute a new complex individual through common action: the *multitude*, which, as outlined in both *Theological-Political Treatise* and *Political Treatise*, constitutes the political subject, without the need to fall back on the concept of the social contract;

- If the *conatus* defines an actual singular essence, the universal aspects of a thing cannot constitute its essence, they are merely properties that it shares with others. These universal and common properties are what Spinoza calls the concept of the *common notion*, defined as that which is common to all parts of a whole and is present equally in it and in each one of them. A system of necessary relations of internal and necessary coherence among the parts of a whole, the common notion expresses intrinsic relations of agreement or convenience among those individuals who, because they possess common determinations, form part of the same system. Thus, to define a human being as *part of nature* means, on the one hand, being an actual essence that has the power to exist and to behave because such a power defines nature itself; and on the other, possessing a quality, property, or common aspect with others that participate in the same system. If, therefore, the theory of *conatus* as a complex individual allows us to understand the origins of the *multitude* as a political body, the theory of common notions allows us to understand how and why the *multitude* is formed;

- The *conatus* is the internal power that defines this singular individual and this power is a force that can rise or decrease, depending on how each individual relates to others in carrying out its task of self-preservation. The intensity of the force of the *conatus* decreases if the singular individual is affected by others in such a way that it becomes entirely dependent on them; it increases if the singular individual does not lose its independence and autonomy as it is affected by others and in turn affects them;

- The increase or decrease of the force of the *conatus* indicates that desire (*cupiditas*) can be achieved adequately or inadequately. It is inadequate when the individual *conatus* is simply a partial cause of the body and mind's operations because it is determined by the power of external causes that impel it in particular directions, controlling it and decreasing its force. It is adequate when the *conatus* increases its force because it is a total and complete cause of actions that are achieved through a relationship with external forces, which do not constrain, direct, or control it;

- Inadequate ideas are called *Passions* (passivity with regard to external forces); adequate ideas are called *Actions* (autonomous activity that coexists with external forces without submitting to them). Spinoza is emphatic when he demonstrates that the *conatus* is always at work both in the inadequate-passion and the adequate-action equation, so that human beings are always striving for self-preservation, either passively or actively. The cause of inadequacy or passion is the imagination, that is, sensorial knowledge or knowledge through the perception of the images of things and other human beings, a knowledge by means of confused, partial, and distorted images, which, maintaining our ignorance of the true causes of things and their actions, leads us to invent explanations, causal links, and interpretations that do not correspond to reality. The cause of adequacy or action is rational and reflexive knowledge, which leads us to knowledge of the necessary origins of things, their order, necessary connections, essences, and their true meaning. With Passions, in which desire is determined by external causes, men's relations are conflictive, because everyone imagines that their lives depend on external things, and also that this is exclusive, even though this produces conflicts with other men who challenge the right to our possessions. With Actions, in which desire is self-determined and does not depend on the possession of external things, men are aware of the common notions, that is, they acknowledge what they possess in common with others, and discover that they agree and be useful to each other, and they understand that they can live together in peace, security and freedom.

Spinoza is a rationalist—reality is completely intelligible and can be completely and fully known by human reason. However, Spinoza is not a an intellectualist—he does not believe that it is sufficient to have a true idea of something to lead us from inadequate-passion to adequate-action, in other words to transform the quality of our desire (in Part IV of *Ethics* he writes that we do not desire a thing because it is good, neither do we dislike it because it is bad, rather it is good because we desire it and bad because we dislike it). In addition, Spinoza does not believe that our transition from passion to action is achieved by the mind's control of the body—we are passive in terms of our bodies and minds, or we are active in terms of our bodies and minds, a passive body corresponds to a passive mind, and an active body corresponds to an active mind. Neither is our transition from inadequate-passion to adequate-action achieved by reason's control of desire, since, as he argues in *Ethics*, a passion can only be conquered by another stronger and contrary passion, not by a true idea.

The transition from inadequate-passion to adequate-action depends on the affective game and the force of desire. Images and ideas are interpretations of our bodily and mental life and of the world that surrounds us. We experience everything that happens in our body—affections—as affects (happiness, sadness, love, hatred, fear, hope, anger, indignation, jealousy, wonder). Because of this there is no image or idea that does not possess affective content or that that is not a form of desire. It is these affects, or the affective-desire dimension of images and ideas, that increase or decrease the intensity of the *conatus*. This means that full knowledge can occur only following a transformation in the quality of affect, not vice versa, and because of this an affect can be conquered only by another stronger and contrary affect, not by a true idea. An image-affect, or an idea-affect, is a passion when its cause is an external force; it is an action when its cause is us, ourselves, or more specifically, when we are aware that there is no external cause for desire, that there are only internal causes for desire.

Not all affects and desires possess the same force or intensity: some are weak or weakened forms of the *conatus*, while others are strong or strengthened forms of the *conatus*. According to Spinoza, there are only three originative affects: joy, sorrow, and desire. All affects that originate from sorrow are weak, since Spinoza defines sorrow as the feeling that our power to exist and act decreases because of an external cause. Affects are strong when they originate from joy, which is the feeling that our power to exist and act increases because of an external cause. The force of the *conatus*, therefore, increases when sad passions become joyful passions and it is within joyful passions that the transition to action can take place, that is, the feeling that an increase in the power to exist and act depends only on oneself as the internal cause. The first moment in the transition to truth and to action is when rational and reflexive knowledge are experienced as the greatest joy. Since the mind is an idea of the body, it too will be active or passive. In other words, passivity or passion is not the power of the body over the mind, nor is activity or action the power of the mind over its body (as philosophical tradition has always said), but mind and body are passive or active together. This means that freedom, as an activity whose cause is the autonomous force of the *conatus*, refers not just to the mind but also to the body and is defined as the joint capacity of the body and the mind toward simultaneous plurality. In other words, freedom is the complexity and richness of affections, affects, and simultaneous ideas that have the very body and the mind as their necessary efficient cause.

Ethics and politics take place in this affective space of *conatus cupiditas*, upon which, on the one hand, passion and the imaginary, and, on the other hand, true knowledge depend.

Conatus is what Spinozan political philosophy calls *natural right*:

> And so by natural right I understand the very laws or rules of Nature, in accordance with which everything takes place, in other words, the power of Nature itself. And so the natural right of universal nature, and consequently of every individual thing, extends as far as its power: and accordingly, whatever any man does after the laws of his nature, he does by the highest natural right, and he has as much right over Nature as he has power. (PT II: 4)

Deus sive nature and *jus sive potentia* are the foundations of Spinozian political thought.

Politics

From the political point of view, the Spinozian theory of the *conatus* highlights two problems to be resolved, pointing to their possible solution as well as upholding the formulation of Spinoza's key political ideas.

The first problem is this: if the *conatus* is the desire for self-preservation, if natural right is individual power, inasmuch as it emerges from the power of nature, if this power is natural freedom that can be extended to wherever possible without prohibiting or limiting its action, then how can we explain the fact that men can live in servitude? Moreover, if the *conatus* is desire, how can we explain that men desire servitude and that they mistake it for freedom? The first problem that political thought must deal with, therefore, relates to the origins of submission and domination.

However, the second problem that is highlighted is exactly the opposite of the first one. In fact, the *conatus* of the human mind is the desire to know and its force increases in its transition from imaginative knowledge—or a system of beliefs and preconceptions that have no basis in reality—to rational knowledge of the laws of nature and to a reflexive understanding of the self and one's body as parts of nature. Spinoza shows that one of the most important effects of passion is that it turns men against each other, because the objects of their desire are imagined as possessions or property, and each person imagines that they can become stronger if they are able to weaken others and deprive them of their desires. The state of nature is, therefore, a perpetual state of a war of all against all, because it is natural and necessary for each person to believe that in order to strengthen their own *conatus* they must increase their own strength and power by weakening the power of others. If passion and the imagination function this way, then, Spinoza states, within action and reason, men do not fight against each other, because knowing the common notions (or as we have seen the common properties and qualities of all the parts of the same whole), they know that the unity and peace of each person will increase the strength of their own *conatus* and their own freedom. In other words, reason reveals that it is necessary to strengthen men's common possessions or what they naturally share without conflict, since this leads to a greater freedom for all. Spinoza adds that if all men were led by reason, there would be no need for politics in order to live in peace and freedom.

The *conatus* can, therefore, generate two opposite effects: servitude, which is the price of living together; or the isolation of rational men, which is the price of freedom. In the former, politics is a burden; in the latter it is useless.

However, this formulation is misleading. Spinoza never states that politics is instituted by reason—which would make servitude incomprehensible. On the contrary, he believes that oppression is as natural as freedom, stating that "there is no singular thing in nature than which there is not another more powerful and stronger. Whatever one is given, there is another more powerful by which the first can be destroyed."[4] Nevertheless, he does not state that politics is founded against reason—this would make rational men useless and even dangerous. On the contrary, not only does he claim, in both *Ethics* and the *Political Treatise* that rational man desires the company of other beings, but he also notes that only in political life can man live a truly human life. These problems highlight something that is also indicated in the opening pages of the *Political Treatise:* the need to look for the origins of politics not in reason but in *conatus-cupiditas*—whether rational or passionate:

> As all men everywhere, whether barbarous or civilized, frame customs, and form some kind of civil state, we must not, therefore, look to proofs

of reason for the causes and natural bases of dominion, but derive them from the general nature or condition of mankind. (PT I: 7)

"From the general nature or condition of mankind" must be understood as the natural foundations of power (*fundamenta natural imperii*). In *Ethics* and *Theological-Political Treatise* Spinoza writes that men are not by nature adverse to conflict, hate, anger, jealousy, ambition, or revenge. Nothing from the *cupiditas* is contrary to Nature and, it is natural that everyone wants to rule and that no one wants to be ruled. So, experience has shown that all men "whether barbarous or civilized" frame customs and some kind of civil state and do so not because reason determines it, but because *cupiditas* so desires it. What must now be examined is whether reason can find the causes and foundations of what experience has revealed. Can reason determine how and why men are capable of social and political life?

The answer to this question presupposes first, abandoning the juridical rationalism that characterizes the theories of natural rights, and second, the effect of these theories, that is the distance between theory and practice. In fact, juridical rationalism developed from the idea of a rational human nature capable of controlling appetites and desires. At the start of *Political Treatise,* Spinoza writes:

> Philosophers conceive of the passions that harass us as vices into which men fall by their own fault, and, therefore, generally deride, bewail, or blame them, or execrate them, if they wish to seem unusually pious. And so they think they are doing something wonderful, and reaching the pinnacle of learning, when they are clever enough to bestow manifold praise on such human nature, as is nowhere to be found, and to make verbal attacks on that which, in fact, exists. For they conceive of men, not as they are, but as they themselves would like them to be. (PT I: 1)

This image of a nonexistent human nature that would be the foundation of politics produces an immediate effect:

> Whence it has come to pass that, instead of ethics, they have generally written satire, and that they have never conceived a theory of politics, which could be turned to use, but such as might be taken for a chimera, or might have been formed in Utopia, or in that golden age of the poets when, to be sure, there was least need of it. Accordingly, as in all sciences, which have a useful application, so especially in that of politics, theory is supposed to be at variance with practice; and no men are esteemed less fit to direct public affairs than theorists or philosophers. (PT I: 1)

Spinoza's subversion does not end here. If the origins of politics are not to be found in reason, the stability and security of a political regime are also not to be found in morals.

> A state then, whose well-being depends on any man's good faith, and whose affairs cannot be properly administered, unless those who are engaged in them will act honestly, will be very unstable. (...) Neither does it matter to the security of a state, in what spirit men are led to rightly administer its affairs. For liberality of spirit, or courage, is a private virtue; but the virtue of a state is its security. (PT 1: 6)

In a tone that is somewhat reminiscent of Machiavelli, Spinoza claims that peace, stability, and political freedom do not depend on the moral virtues of its rulers, but on the quality of its public institutions, which obliges them to act for the state rather than against it, independent of whether or not men are dominated by passion or guided by reason.

If the origins of political life are not to be found in God, nor in the reason and virtue of men, and if natural right is the power to exist and to act independent of what is considered good and evil, just and unjust, then where can we locate the cause of politics? This cause is natural right itself.

In fact, the *conatus* is independent of values and in the state of nature nothing prohibits men from quarrelling with each other or from being angry, vengeful, jealous, or even being murderers. However, the *conatus* is subject to one natural law, which is always determined by utility. Although the imagination of passionate men may be unaware of true utility (known by rational men), the principle of utility nevertheless determines their actions, once the useful is not just an experience but also an aid to self-preservation. In the state of nature, the useful produces two forms of knowledge in men: first, the knowledge that the war of all against all strengthens no one and weakens everyone, because living in reciprocal fear no one is their own master and free; second, that in order to survive, each person needs things that they alone cannot obtain, but that they can obtain by cooperating with others. Therefore, utility teaches the *conatus* that freedom from fear is positive, as is acquiring security and cooperating, so that men may preserve their natural right to exist and act, without harming themselves or others. Or as Spinoza said, men make the transition from the state of nature to the civil state when they discover that it is useful for them to exchange all of their fears for one single fear, that which is inspired by the law.

If political life is born so that men can enjoy their natural right, we can conclude not only that natural right is the cause of politics but also that it is an immanent efficient cause of civil right that cannot be suppressed by it or suppress it because, as we have seen, an immanent cause does not exist before and external to its effects nor does it exist separate from them once they have been produced – the effects express their cause. One of the indelible characteristics of natural right is that all men want to rule and no man wants to be ruled. If civil right is born to make natural right more effective, then the political life in which civil right can best realize natural right would be that in which the desire to rule and not to be ruled can be achieved. This kind of political form is democracy and it is for this reason that Spinoza distances himself from traditional political philosophy, which always believed the monarchy to be the first form of politics, by stating quite clearly that "democracy is the most natural political regime" or *absolutum imperium*, absolute power.

Natural right is, therefore, the immanent efficient cause of civil right and this is the natural collective right or the natural right of the *multitude*, that is, of the masses as political agent:

> For the right of the state is determined by the power of the multitude, which is led, as it were, by one mind. But this unity of mind can in no way be conceived, unless the state pursues chiefly the very end, which sound reason teaches is to the interest of all men. (PT III: 7)

The founding of the state is apparently a convention and in distinct states similar acts are judged differently according to the law. In other words, civil right and civil duties are products of an arbitrary convention or of a norm established by men according to criteria of common utility. Spinoza's texts initially seem to point to this interpretation. However, we know that Spinoza differentiated his work from that of Hobbes', by emphasizing natural right as existing within civil right, which means that civil right is the natural right of the multitude and that political life is natural life in another dimension. What is at stake here are the millennial theories concerning the foundation of politics, whether these are determined by nature or produced by a convention – *phýsis* or *nomos*. The determination of the just and unjust, of crime and common good occurs only following the institution of the law and, therefore, these values cannot be natural. Yet, saying that the convention of the law defines the very subject of the law would entail mistaking the cause for the effect. It is the latter that institutes politics by founding itself on human nature, defined as part of nature and as natural power or desire.

The debate concerning the origins of the social and the political is not related to questions concerning the distribution and redistribution of goods or the regulation of natural equality or inequality—this regulating moment of the redistribution of goods is subsequent to the advent of the law and is, moreover, determined by it, for that, for instance, a monarchical regime can, in an effort of preservation, nationalize land and commercial goods, while the aristocratic form will aim to protect private property. The debate deals more specifically with *participation in power* and the *distribution of collective power within society.* Individual power is natural and the law provides it with a new meaning by making it not just part of nature, but also part of a political community. The law determines the distribution of goods because it determines the form of participating in power.

the right of the supreme authorities is nothing else than simple natural right, limited, indeed, by the power, not of every individual, but of the multitude, which is guided, as it were, by one mind—that is, as each individual in the state of nature, so the body and mind of a dominion have as much right as they have power. And thus each single citizen or subject has the less right, the more the state exceeds him in power, and each citizen consequently does and has nothing, but what he may by the general decree of the state defend. If the state grant to any man the right, and therewith the authority, to live after his own mind, by that very act it abandons its own right, and transfers the same to him, to whom it has given such authority. But if it has given this authority to two or more, I mean authority to live each after his own mind, by that very act it has divided the dominion, and if, lastly, it has given this same authority to every citizen, it has thereby destroyed itself, and there remains no more a state, but everything returns to the state of nature; all of which is very manifest from what goes before. And thus it follows, that it can by no means be conceived, that every citizen should by the ordinance of the state live after his own mind, and accordingly this natural right of being one's own judge ceases in the civil state. I say expressly "by the ordinance of the state," for, if we weigh the matter aright, the natural right of every man does not cease in the civil state. For man, alike in the natural and in the civil state, acts according to the laws of his own nature, and consults his own interest. Man, I say, in each state is led by fear or hope to do or leave undone this or that; but the main difference between the two states is this, that in the civil state all fear the same things, and all have the same ground of security, and manner of life; and this certainly does not do away with the individual's faculty of judgment. For he that is minded to obey all the state's orders, whether through fear of its power or through love of quiet, certainly consults after his own heart his own safety and interest. (PT III: 2/3)

This long extract determines the equivalence between the right and the power of sovereignty, each one extending itself to wherever the other is. Moreover, if sovereign power and the right of sovereignty are defined as collective power, even if the latter is confused with the sum of individual powers, power is not understood arithmetically but geometrically. In other words, the geometric proportionality defines the form of the political regime because it defines the form of the exercise of power, from the way in which sovereignty is instituted to the relations it establishes among members of the political body. Hence, the power of sovereignty is measured by its incommensurability with the sum of individual powers. There is an inverse proportional relationship between civil power and individual power, meaning that, when the state is more powerful the more its power is compared to that of isolated individuals and when it is less powerful the less its power is compared to that of its citizens, for there is no greater danger for the state than the idea that some of its individuals, as individuals, can become defenders of the law.

The state is founded from an unprecedented power and Spinoza anticipates the deduction of political forms: the transference of sovereignty to an individual identifies the state with a single being in whom the state becomes concentrated, with all other citizens being reduced to a position of impotence. This is the monarchy in which proportionality is virtually absent. The transference of sovereignty to certain individuals divides the state, since it is limited to only a part of the social body, depriving others of power. This is aristocracy. Ultimately, if sovereignty is transferred to each individual there is no state, but a regression to a state of nature—a state of the war and the self-destruction of political life. Reading between the lines, we can comprehend the peculiarity of democracy and its proportionality—sovereignty is transferred to no one and is embodied by no one; it is instead distributed throughout the social and political body so that everyone participates in it, without it being redistributed or divided up among its members. Hence, it is not in the difference between the monarchy and the aristocracy, but in the opposition to the process of the state's self-destruction that democracy can best be understood, since it is here that sovereignty is not redistributed but participated in. Democracy maintains the founding principle of politics, that is, sovereign power is greater if the individual power of its members is reduced and, above all if, as argued in the *Theological-Political Treatise*, political life occurs in a space where citizens decide to act in conformity or together, but without abdicating their natural right to think and to judge independently.

Yet, if the law is founded on nature and if natural power determines the proportionality of the law, then Spinoza paradoxically seems to overturn his argument, stating that the law is the foundation of natural right itself. For this reason the previous extract *simultaneously* guaranteed the disappearance of natural right with civil right *and* that the latter would not suppress the former. In order to make sense of this *volte-face* in Spinoza's work we need to understand that we are now faced with a new question, thanks to which we will be able to understand not just the question of proportionality, but also its role in transforming experience into political experience. This new question concerns the phenomenon of oppression:

> But inasmuch as in the state of nature each is so long independent, as he can guard against oppression by another, and it is in vain for one man alone to try and guard against all, it follows hence that so long as the natural right of man is determined by the power of every individual, and belongs to everyone, so long it is a nonentity, existing in opinion rather than fact, as there is no assurance of making it good. And it is certain that the greater cause of fear every individual has, the less power, and consequently the less right, he possesses (...); natural right, which is special to the human race, can hardly be conceived, except where men have general rights, and combine to defend the possession of the lands they inhabit and cultivate, to protect themselves, to repel all violence, and to live according to the general judgment of all. For the more there are that combine together, the more right they collectively possess (...). Where men have general rights, and are all guided, as it were, by one mind, it is certain, that every individual has the less right the more the rest collectively exceed him in power; that is, he has, in fact, no right over nature but that which the common law allows him. But whatever he is ordered by the general consent, he is bound to execute, or may rightfully be compelled thereto. (PT II: 15)

Once it is defined in negative terms, natural right—not being the master of itself—is something that does not exist or that exists only as opinion. It is an abstraction. This explains the statement in *Political Treatise* that it is only within the state that men can live a truly or concretely human life. A right or power really exists only when it can be preserved or exercised, because Spinoza does not define power as virtual but as actual power. Now, in the *state of nature*, there is no *right* of nature. This distinction between the state of nature and the right of nature is key. The state of nature is real—man is a part of a nature caused by others and interacts with others. Nevertheless, this "part of nature" is something abstract, since it does not tell us what a *human part* of nature is. As a part of nature, man is *conatus* like any other, but his power is nonexistent because he has no means of preserving it, for, as Spinoza argues in *Ethics,* man is a part of nature whose force is infinitely less than that of other things that surround him and that act upon him. On the other hand, the *Political Treatise* takes up the statement made in *Ethics* that, as passionate beings, men are divided and have nothing in common apart from the desire to oppress others, making them live according to the passions of their rulers. This state of war is, therefore, universal and it is defined by the desire for the other to be an *alter ego* and by the consequent need to exercise the reciprocity of oppression.

Oppression is defined simultaneously as the state of nature and its limit. Natural right is present wherever the power of each individual exists and it is, therefore, unlimited. All desire that is fulfilled defines the reach of natural power. Now this desire, unlimited in principle, is concretely limited. And, moreover, it engenders a reciprocal form of oppression so that the fear of personal destruction replaces all other affects. Fear, as Spinoza shows in *Ethics,* is a sad and hateful passion that impedes, weakens, and annihilates individual power. This is why natural right, being separate from that which allows its full realization, gives rise to a phantasmagoric form of equality that is achieved in the real context of absolute inequality: because everyone fears everyone (everyone is equal in this regard), and each person aspires to oppress others (attempting to impose inequalities).

Natural right in the state of nature is an abstraction in the Spinozian sense, that is, whatever is separate from the originative cause that provides it with meaning and reality. In the state of nature, natural right (power of preservation) is separate from its vital power. Natural right, defined as the power of the whole of nature, is a concrete reality. It is defined as the power of each part of nature that is also concrete, since its positivity emerges from that which everyone possess. However, because the power of nature is not the same as the laws of reason and human will, this power is not yet sufficiently determined to define natural human right. Here, natural right in the state of nature has a reality (man is part of nature), but this reality is abstract (natural right defines a desire of power that is consumed in impotence). The situation of natural right in the state of nature is exactly that in which each person, desiring all of the power, oppresses those who inevitably appear to be enemies, that is, the cause of fear and hatred, and, therefore, the cause of sorrow and of the weakening of the *conatus*. Yet, conversely, since no one can achieve full power, they become victims of their own appetite. It is in this sense that natural right is offered up as an abstract reality, determined by imaginary operations of exercising power and, which are, in reality, manifestations of impotence. Moved by the fear of others and by the hope of harming them, the state of nature reveals the precariousness and nonexistence of natural right when, precariously, power is exercised as violence.

The state of nature and natural right, however, do not presuppose isolation but rather *solitude*, embedded in an intersubjectivity that is founded on reciprocal fear and annihilation. The fact that Spinoza uses the terms solitude, servitude, and barbarism synonymously allows us to understand the specific character of abstraction of a power that can be achieved only by the death of another. And, furthermore, Spinoza's decisive argument, if *real* inequality engendered by natural right were not an *imaginary* form of equality, civil right would be impossible. We can also understand why the law does not stem from the regulation of possession or property, but rather that it precedes it, for the former would legitimize violence and would never lead to power.

In the state of nature the undetermined situation of the parts, which are all equal and do not manage to become determined singularities, means that everything is common to all and, therefore, that everything can be equally coveted and envied by everyone. Thus, undetermined or abstract equality produces absolute inequality, so that the founding of the state will correspond to the moment when the determination of the singularity of one of the parts is acknowledged equally by all, precisely because the social and political foundation defines what is truly common and remains ignored in the natural indetermination.

Civil right, a social acknowledgment of individual power, is concrete and positive, and natural right is abstract and negative. This is why the law, ultimately, establishes natural right at the same time that it establishes civil right, for the first can be established only via the latter.

For Spinoza, however, it is precisely because the law preserves natural right by transforming it that the question of politics becomes a question of proportionality. The law can, effectively, undo what it establishes. This means that the law that is capable of preserving itself is that which can delimit the boundaries of natural right and civil right and stop civil right from falling back on the precariousness of natural right. This conclusion leads to three further points: first, that the act of establishing the state is inscribed in an indeterminate natural necessity that is determined by the law, endowing it with a reality it did not previously possess; second, that the law is possible only because it takes up that which already existed in human nature, that is, passion and conflicts. This is possible, however, only because the law provides reality with an operant reason, which acts in the real, without the imagination realizing it, and which defines the useful as something that favors self-preservation, impeded, in fact, by oppression, for as Spinoza writes in Chapter 9 of *Political Treatise,* "he who seeks equality between unequals, seeks an absurdity." Third, because natural right is achieved by civil right, the social is constantly threatened by the possibility of the first usurping the second, in other words, that individual power may take the place of sovereignty, something that is perfectly comprehensible given that political life is not established by reason but by a rationality that operates within passions. Natural right is not contrary to strife, hatred, anger, and lust because these are "suggested by desire," for "nature is not bounded by the laws of human reason, which aim only at man's true benefit and preservation." In other words, the advent of social and political life is not the advent of the human "good reason," which will control passions, condemn vices, eliminate conflicts, and establish once and for all peace and cooperation among men.

These conclusions lead to another: that the state never ceases to establish itself. The state is effectively inhabited by a conflict between collective power and individual power, which, as with all conflicts, according to *Ethics,* can be resolved only if one of these has the power to satisfy and to delimit the other, for passion is never conquered by reason or by an idea, but by another and stronger passion. Therefore, the law must be reaffirmed, so that the desire to oppress, which defined natural right, may reappear within civil right:

> every individual wishes the rest to live after his own mind, and to approve what he approves, and reject what he rejects. And so it comes to pass, that, as all are equally eager to be first, they fall to strife, and do their utmost mutually to oppress one another; and he who comes out conqueror is more proud of the harm he has done to the other, than of the good he has done to himself. (PT I: 5)

This explains why Spinoza argues that the political enemy is always internal, and only seldom external, because the enemy is simply the natural right of someone or some individuals, who aim to achieve power in order to take the place of the sovereign. This risk depends not on the good or bad faith of the state—all states possess this risk—but on a sovereign's ability to control the origins and source of his power.

Politics does not create or eliminate conflicts, just as it does not transform the passionate human nature. It simply produces new ways of dealing with them and the difference between political regimes stems from their ability or inability to satisfy the desire that all men have to rule and not be ruled.

Just as the law offers a reality for natural right by providing it with a political statute—yet also finds in natural right a point of origin for the foundation of politics—natural right operates as guarantee of the law with respect to the possibility of its destruction. Because sovereign power is, effectively, measured by an inverse proportion of the power of citizens, the law is destroyed if one or some of these citizens are invested with enough power to take control of sovereignty. However, because sovereign power is also measured by the proportional power that it bestows to each one of its citizens, when they, in the name of upholding the law, are able to stop the appropriation of sovereign power, then the natural right of citizens is powerful enough to defend the law. In either situation, natural power is always the same with reference to the power of the people. When such power is deprived of natural right as a result of the excessive power of an individual (or a group of individuals) that has taken over sovereign power, then the result is tyranny. When people are invested of all natural right by the proportionality that is established between them and the power of the sovereign, the result is democracy. Clearly, therefore, the number of rulers, either in an electoral or representative regime, does not determine a political body. This is determined, exclusively, by the proportion of power between the sovereign and the people.

Once right is measured by power and once freedom is defined as being one's own master, the degree of right, power, and freedom allows us to perceive the political form in terms of the proportional distribution that constitutes it. It is only then that we can know if a state is the best, superior, and free. Generally, a political form is better the less chance of tyranny there is in the transition from the sovereign right to the natural right of one or a number of men. And a political regime is superior to another when it requires fewer institutions to prohibit the risk of a dictatorship. And a political body is freer than another when its citizens have little chance of oppression because their autonomy is greater if the power of their state is greater. Consequently, the freer a state is, the less risk of oppression there will be.

This means, for example, that a monarchical political regime is the most likely to be taken over by another since its subjects are already accustomed to being ruled by one individual, so that switching obedience to another ruler makes little difference to them. With democracy, however, individual autonomy is clearly established in the collective autonomy, each and every person is prepared to fight to the death to avoid the threat of internal power struggles as well as external invasions. In spite of Spinoza's argument that every political body may possess in different degrees the good, the superior, and the free, it is clear that the underlying criteria for these is political democracy, because it is only in democracy that the universal cause of political life (proportional distribution of power) coincides with the singular cause of the establishment of democracy, and because it is in democracy too that the question of preservation changes.

Indeed, when Spinoza deals with the monarchy, a key question takes over his deductive trajectory: which institutions are necessary in order to limit the power of the King and ensure that he never rules alone? In his examination of the aristocracy, the key question that shapes his argument is since the aristocracy is characterized by the visibility of class difference and by the fact that only one class holds power, which institutions are necessary to avoid the oligarchy and bureaucracy? With regard to democracy, Spinoza simply claims that this is a collective sovereignty, which is crucial for individual freedom. Citizens must make sure that positions of authority are not occupied by people who have personal ties or relations of dependency with others, since this would lead to a form of favor in public institutions.

If democracy highlights the meaning of political life, tyranny conversely is the manifestation of political experience gone astray.

At the start of *The Political Treatise*, Spinoza states that passion imagines freedom as an "empire within another empire." An incessant form of privation, passion produces images of something that could satisfy it, replacing privation with the possession of another object, and, the most desired object to possess is that of another human being. In this manner, being free is imagined as being the master of another and freedom is defined not in terms of an opposition to slavery but in terms of the possession of slaves. Reason, however, often advises men to live in peace, for without this their desires will be satisfied only in an extremely precarious manner. However, the rationality that advises men to live in peace is not nonpassionate: an operant rationality, it guides passionate individuals toward the lesser of two evils. Between the risk of being dependent on another's power or being dependent on collective power, this second alternative imposes itself. The initial movement toward freedom consists in establishing the state, since it is there that freedom is determined as the capacity for not being subjected to the power of another person.

The freest and the most powerful state, that is, the most autonomous, is that whose citizens allow themselves to be ruled because they respect and fear its power, or because they respect civil life.

In a first moment, Spinoza determines the power of the state by defining its limits, namely, that which is necessarily beyond its power. Hence, everything that the state cannot demand of its citizens, either by threat or promise, is beyond its control. What is beyond the power of the state? Everything that is heinous to human nature, and that, if it were imposed, would unleash popular anger and indignation. In short, everything that makes the state hated by its citizens, meaning everything that can weaken and destroy power. Hatred is the most destructive passion and, therefore, Spinoza initially writes simply that the state cannot be hateful nor can it be hated. If it were, it would destroy itself, that is, it would lose power because it desired an impossible power. Patricide, matricide, fratricide, infanticide, false witness, love of hateful things, a hatred of all things that are loved, renunciation of the right to judge and to express oneself—the state cannot demand these things. However, history reveals that these demands are in fact made of citizens, and that they constitute the dictates of tyrannical laws. For Spinoza, the concept of the impossible, in addition to defining that which in essence cannot exist (an absolute negative), also defines that which, coming into existence in a determined way causes its own destruction (a negative reality). We can, therefore, interpret tyranny as the impossible, not because it cannot exist—since it does in fact exist—but because it corresponds to the death of political life, even though tyrants, and those who are ruled by them, may have the illusion of existing politically.

The insane reality of tyranny allows us to understand the first political necessity of proportionality. The excess of tyrannical power highlights that

> those things are not so much within the state's right, which cause indignation in the majority. For it is certain, that by the guidance of Nature men conspire together, either through common fear, or with the desire to avenge some common hurt; and as the right of the commonwealth is determined by the common power of the multitude, it is certain that the power and right of the state are so far diminished, as it gives occasion for many to conspire together. There are certainly some subjects of fear for a state, and as every separate citizen or in the state of nature every man, so a state is the less independent, the greater reason it has to fear. (PT IV: 9)

If the state must fear its enemies, it must establish itself in such a way that it can prevent them from finding the means of emerging and justifying themselves. This means that the state must be respected and feared by its citizens, however, this can occur only if its demands are proportionate to what the multitude are able to respect and fear without becoming angry. Sovereignty can exist only in the specific context of not being hated because it is not hateful. If the state demands more or less than it should, it ceases to be a political body:

> when we say, that a man can do what he will with his own, this authority must be limited not only by the power of the agent, but by the capacity of the object. If, for instance, I say that I can rightfully do what I will with this table, I do not certainly mean, that I have the right to make it eat grass. So, too, though we say, that men depend not on themselves, but on the state, we do not mean, that men lose their human nature and put on another (...). But it is implied, that there are certain intervening circumstances, which supposed, one likewise supposes the reverence and fear of the subjects towards the state, and which abstracted, one makes abstraction likewise of that fear and reverence, and therewith of the state itself. The state, then, to maintain its independence, is bound to preserve the causes of fear and reverence, otherwise it ceases to be a state. (PT IV: 4)

The foundation of politics is not, therefore, a change in human nature from one form to another that is foreign to it. There can be many interpretations of the above extract. On the one hand, it takes up a number of observations made at the start of *The Political Treatise* that refuses a utopian politics, aimed at making men something that they possibly cannot be. On the other, if it is only within the state that men can live a completely human life, the extract also contains a critique of tyranny, which reduces men to fearful barbarism and to the condition of a passive flock. It also includes a refusal to interpret the state as destroying natural right, because this is the first determination of human nature as the power to act.

It is precisely because political life is not a change in human nature, but its concretization that natural right will give the causes for fear and respect to the state; these can, therefore, never be seen as the result of civil legislation, because this is an effect of the institution of the state. To say that natural right provides the first measure of political power means that the state cannot become its own enemy and that there can be conflicts only among citizens subject to the law, not conflicts of citizens against the law. If the state were capable of blocking individuals from usurping the law, without this involving the suppression of social conflicts, it will have determined its own autonomy and power. Therefore, fearing and respecting the state must never be confused with fear and hatred, because he who hates lacks fear, and he who fears lacks respect:

> For a civil state, which has not done away with the causes of seditions, where war is a perpetual object of fear, and where, lastly, the laws are often broken, differs but little from the mere state of nature (...). But as the vices and inordinate license and contumacy of subjects must be imputed to the state, so, on the other hand, their virtue and constant obedience to the laws are to be ascribed in the main to the virtue and perfect right of the commonwealth (...). *Of a state, whose subjects are but hindered by terror from taking arms, it should rather be said, that it is free from war, than that it has peace. For peace is not mere absence of war, but is a virtue that springs from force of character: for obedience is the constant will to execute what, by the general decree of the state ought to be done.* (PT: 2, 3, 4)

The *Theological-Political Treatise* stated that obedience diminishes freedom, without however, denoting slavery. This is because the slave is someone who acts for the benefit of another person who orders his actions, while the agent carries out an order that nevertheless fulfills his own desire meaning that he cannot, therefore, be seen as a slave. Nevertheless as both of Spinoza's *Treatises* highlight, in democracy (unlike other political forms), obedience merely expresses the uninterrupted recreation of the state, since in it citizens obey a law that was instituted at the very foundation of the state by all political agents, that is, by the multitude as the political agent, so that by obeying it, these agents are in turn obeying themselves as citizens. The element of obedience is merely the repetition or reiteration, in the imaginary dimension, of the foundational act of the state, since in this symbolic act, the creation of collective power produces an incommensurability between sovereignty and the individuals who are subject to it. Obedience is, therefore, a second or derived act, and for this very reason, it expresses the virtues of the state rather than that of citizens, for it is only the state that fulfills the desires of the political agents that are obeyed. In transferring both citizens' vice and virtue onto sovereignty, Spinoza seeks to distinguish slavery from freedom in the state itself, rather than in its individual members. If a state's founding principle cannot suppress sedition, understood not as conflicts among citizens but as struggles against the law, then the state has not been properly instituted because it lacks its essential characteristic: the power of sovereignty to be acknowledged as sovereign.

Civil war is thus an indicator of injustice within the state and of the need to destroy it so that a new and true state can be founded. This is why there is more injustice in states where citizens are too afraid to take up arms, than in states where there are frequent revolts. It is the state, not men, that is good or bad, virtuous or sinful, for "sin is not imputed when there is no law." A population that lives in peace because of fear or even inertia does not live in the state, it lives in isolation, and this kind of state is not inhabited by people, but by a solitary herd. Whence the second rule for establishing political proportionality: in the foundation of the state the agent must constitute *a single political subject*. This is because the foundational moment of the political body, whatever it may be, has the *multitude* as the political subject.

Distinguishing the state "established by a free multitude (*libera multitudo*)" from that "established by the conquest of a defeated people," Spinoza does not differentiate them by civil right, because the philosopher states that at this level they are identical. This means that the differences between them do not stem from classic ideas of the legitimacy and illegitimacy of power. The difference between them is the difference between a state "which has the cult of life" and is established by hope and another regime that is established by fear. The former is free; the latter enslaved. The state that confronts the risk of death imposed by natural right, and that is victorious over this supreme danger by hope in political life, is free. The state that accepts survival without confronting the risk of death is enslaved.

The difference between a free state or an enslaved state is not, therefore, civil right, but the meaning of the collective life that they establish, because they differ in terms of the institutional apparatus of their preservation and the principles of their foundation. So, the second rule of proportionality is not just a question of the agreement between the law and human nature: it is a question of the *convenientia* between power and freedom.[5]

For Spinoza, freedom, as we have seen, means autonomy, that is, one's power to give to oneself the norms and rules of one's own action. Thus as individual freedom is the active power of *conatus* to be the internal and total cause of its ideas, feelings, and actions, political freedom is the active power of the multitude when self-determined or sovereign.

Brazil: The Foundational Myth

The French philosopher Maurice Merleau-Ponty once compared the appearance of new philosophical ideas—in this case, the idea of subjectivity in modern thought—to the discovery of America. This comparison led him to state that a new idea cannot be *discovered*, since it is never "there" waiting for someone to find it. An idea is invented or constructed in order to explain or interpret new events and situations created by mankind. An idea, he wrote, does not wait for us, just as America was not waiting for Columbus.

The philosopher was mistaken.

America was not waiting for Columbus, just as Brazil was not waiting for Cabral. These lands are not "discoveries" or to use the sixteenth-century word, "finds." They are historical inventions and cultural constructions. Of course, a land that has not yet been seen or visited still exists. But *Brazil* (like *America*) was a European creation. *Brazil* was founded as a Portuguese colony and invented as a "land blessed by God" and, to cite Pero Vaz de Caminha, the author of the well-known letter to King of Portugal on the arrival to the New Land, "He, who brought us here did not do so without purpose." Four centuries later, the historian and poet Afonso Celso echoed Caminha's words: "if God has endowed Brazil in such magnanimous ways, it is because he reserved a higher destiny for it."[1] This construction is what I term the foundational myth.[2]

A number of key elements emerged during the conquest and the colonization of America and Brazil to construct this foundational myth. The first is, to use the historian Sérgio Buarque de Holanda's classic expression, the "vision of paradise," which I refer to here as the mythical elaboration of the symbol of the "Orient."[3] The second is present, on the one hand, in the theological providential history elaborated by orthodox Christian theology, and, on the other, in the prophetic history of Christian Heresy, that is, in Joachim of Flora's millenarianism. The third comes from the juridical-theocratic idea of the ruler as a King by the grace of God, which developed from the medieval doctrine of objective natural right and subjective natural right and was reinterpreted by theologians and jurists in Coimbra in order to establish the foundations for Iberia's absolute monarchies.

In the sixteenth and seventeenth centuries these three components appeared in the form of three divine operations that, in the foundational myth, were responsible for Brazil. These were: the work of God, or Nature; the word of God, or History; and the will of God, or the State.

The foundational myth is, therefore, constructed from a particular perspective that the Dutch-Jewish philosopher Baruch Spinoza calls *theological-political power*.

The Sacralization of Nature

From a historical or economic, social, and political point of view, all of us know why the great voyages of discovery, conquest, and colonization took place, that is, we know that they were a constituent part of mercantile capitalism: Modern European colonization initially took place as part of a purely commercial expansion. The opening of new markets for European mercantilism went hand in hand with the discovery of new American territories.

From a symbolic point of view, however, the great voyages were seen as extending the frontiers of the visible world and displacing the frontiers of the invisible world, in order to venture to regions that tradition had been deemed impossible (the antipodes) or dangerous (the torrid zones). Maps dating from the initial period of exploration are cartographies of the real and the imaginary, and the first voyages produced not just new commodities and knowledge, but also new semaphores: exotic lands (India, China, and Japan) and a New World, believed to be the Earthly Paradise referred to in the Bible and Medieval scriptures. In this way, the voyages of discovery and conquest—by extending the boundaries of the visible world and binding it to an invisible originary of the Garden of Eden—produced the New World as a semaphore.[4]

But they did more than this.

Medieval writers consecrated a powerful myth: the so-called Fortunate Islands, holy places, where spring and youth reign eternal, and where men and animals live together in peace and harmony.

According to Phoenician and Irish traditions, these islands were located in the Western parts of the known world. The Phoenicians called this place *Braaz* and the Irish monks termed it *Hy Brazil*. Between 1325 and 1482 maps included the *Insulla de Brazil* or *Isola de Brazil* to the west of Ireland and below the Azores and Pero Vaz de Caminha described this place, the Fortunate Islands, in his letter of the discovery written to the Portuguese King.

This myth became the name of our land as well the name of its first commodity: *Pau and do-Brasil, Pau-Brasil* (wood from Brazil, Brazil wood). Brazil was discovered.

When we read explorers' accounts and chronicles, as well as letters, essays, and texts written by missionaries, especially Franciscan and Jesuit friars, we can see that the word *Orient* is a symbol because it signifies more than a place or region. This symbol has two meanings.

On the one hand the word *Orient* refers to Japan, China, and India, therefore, to empires with which the West sought economic and diplomatic relations and above all military and political domination. But on the other hand the *Orient* is also the symbol of the Garden of Eden.

The Book of Genesis states that an earthly paradise, a land of milk and honey, divided by four rivers, is located in the Orient. Departing from this biblical account, the great prophecies, especially those of Isaiah, described the Orient-paradise in profuse details, as a land divided by rivers whose banks are made of gold, silver, sapphire, and rubies, where milk and honey flow and mountains are filled with precious stones; a land inhabited by people who are beautiful, docile, sweet, and innocent, just as on the day of Creation; a land of eternal joy and redemption. On the basis of these prophetic texts, as well as Classical Latin texts, particularly those by Ovid, Virgil, and Pliny the Elder, medieval Christianity produced a body of literature whose theme was the location and description of the Earthly Paradise. This literature was enthusiastically adopted during the Renaissance, in the context of the strong impact of millenarian and prophetic thought. According to the Renaissance's search for the rebirth of man and for world's primeval perfection, the word Orient, therefore, signifies the reencounter with a lost origin and the return to it.

What is the Earthly Paradise? It is above all a perfect garden: with luxurious and beautiful vegetation (perennial fruit and flowers), docile and friendly animals (in unequaled abundance), an agreeable climate ("never too cold and never too hot" as the literature from this period tells us), and an eternal spring, which contrasts greatly with the "autumnal world" spoken of at the end of the Middle Ages when referring to the decline of the old world and the hope of restituting the origins of the world. These ideas were vigorously adopted during the Renaissance, especially by Hermetic Neo-Platonists, such as Campanella, who elaborated utopian cities that were perfectly guided by the Sun and the "seven planets"—like Campanella's golden *City of the Sun*—foundations for the future image of Brazil as El Dorado. In the account of his third voyage and in a letter written to the Catholic Kings in 1501, Columbus claims to have reached this Earthly Paradise, describing it as though glimpsed from afar (in an account that replays the imaginary descriptions elaborated throughout the Middle Ages, in which Paradise is protected by a wall of mountains and raging rivers).[5]

Explorers' texts are replete with these images. In them, the absence of precious stones and metals is not an indication that the land discovered is not the gateway to heaven. The newcomers did not venture inland and, therefore, could not testify to the presence of riches there; furthermore, when the natives presented them with gold and silver objects gesturing toward the interior of the land, it seemed entirely appropriate for the Europeans to interpret this as a sign that precious metals were to be found there. But the explorers' texts also contain the visible presence of three signs of paradise, which would have been immediately familiar to sixteenth- and seventeenth-century readers: reference to the abundance and good quality of the water (implying that land discovered is divided by the rivers referred to in the book of Genesis); the agreeable climate (suggesting an eternal spring); and the characteristics of the people, described as beautiful, noble, simple, and innocent (just like those described by the prophet Isaiah).

Travelers' letters and diaries are impressive because they describe the world discovered as new and other. However, this newness and otherness differs from our contemporary understanding. The world is not new because it has never been seen and it is not other because it is different from Europe. It is *new* because it is a return to the perfection of the origins, to the world's spring or the "newness of the world," as opposed to the autumnal or decadent old world. It is *other* because it is originary, anterior to the fall of man. Hence the descriptions of the new people as innocent, simple, and ready to be evangelized.

This vision of paradise, that is, the *topos* of the Orient as the Garden of Eden, the *Insulla de Brazil* or *Isola de Brazil*, are constitutive of the production of Brazil's foundational and mythical image. We reencounter it in the works of nineteenth-century writers, such as the historian Rocha Pita who explicitly states that Brazil is an Earthly Paradise, or in the civic poems of Afonso Celso, or in the nativist poetry of romanticist movement, and, of course, in the words of the national anthem, and in pedagogical texts as well as civic poetry produced by the celebrated Parnassian poet Olavo Bilac, for instance. This explains the mythical colors of Brazil's flag. From the French Revolution onward, revolutionary flags have tended to be tricolor, emblems of the political struggles for liberty, equality, and fraternity. The Brazilian flag, however, has four colors and it does not express politics or relate to the country's history. It is a symbol of nature. It is Brazil as garden, Brazil-paradise. Any Brazilian child knows very well that the green represents our forests, the yellow our mineral wealth, the blue the perfection of our sky, the white the kindness of our good natured hearts.

This mythical production of the nation-garden throws us into the bosom of nature and, in doing so, it throws us out of the world of history. And, since it deals with nature as paradise, it hinders any understanding of the state of nature as described in the seventeenth century by the English philosopher Thomas Hobbes, in which the war of all against all and the fear of death would foster the appearance of social life, the social pact, and the rise of political power. The state of paradisiacal nature in which we find ourselves contains only us—a peaceful and ordered people—and God who, looking after us, has given us the best fruits of his labor and the best of his will.

What are the real effects of this production of Brazil as nature? I briefly outline some effects that date from the colonial period, whose concealment was decisive in constructing the foundational myth.

From the start of colonization, slavery was imposed as an economic necessity:

> Producing for the European market in the context of a colonial commerce accustomed to promoting the primitive accumulation of capital in European economies required compulsory forms of labor, for their absence would result either in non production for the European market (. . .) or, if there were to be an export production created by merchants who would produce salaried labor, costs would be so high that colonial exploitation would be hindered (. . .), so catering to the requirements of the development of capitalism, meant adapting the colonial system (. . .) through various forms of compulsory labor—at its extreme slavery—and colonial exploitation ultimately meant the exploitation of slave labor.[6]

How can slavery be justified in paradise? If we live in a state of nature, in terms of modern and capitalist concepts, that is, as the war of all against all, or what one historian termed "possessive individualism," it can be justified. But if the state of nature is a state of pure innocence, it cannot have any justification at all, except, of course, if the state of nature is conceived according to theories inspired by the ideas of objective and subjective natural right, which were developed by theologians of the counterreformation based at the University of Coimbra.[7]

The theory of objective natural right comes from the idea of God as the supreme legislator and claims that there is a natural juridical order created by Him. This order organizes beings in a hierarchy according to their perfection and degree of power and it determines relations of command and obedience according to these degrees. The superior naturally orders and subordinates the inferior being who in turn naturally obeys him. The theory of subjective natural right, in turn, states that man, being endowed with reason and will, naturally possesses a sense of good and bad, right and wrong, just and unjust, and that this sense is a natural right, the foundation of natural sociability, since man is, by nature, a social being.

In these theories, the state of nature, as related by the Bible, that is, as a state of the innocence of the first man and woman, is threatened by the risk (as a result of original sin) of degenerating into injustice and war. This is avoided because God, as ruler and legislator, sends the law and a representative of His will, who according to objective natural right, preserves the originary natural harmony, establishing the state of society. According to these theories, as a hierarchy of powers and perfections desired by God the natural juridical order reveals that nature is constituted by individuals who naturally subordinate each other. This explains why, after having described the innocence of the natives to the Portuguese King, Pero Vaz de Caminha states that they possess no faith, thereby situating them on the scale below the Christians and suggests, "The best profit which can be derived, it seems to me, will be to save these people. And this should be the chief seed you should sow here."

So, in keeping with theories of objective natural right and subjective natural right, the subordination and enslavement of the Indians were considered a spontaneous act of nature. In fact, according to the theory of a natural juridical order, the natives were juridically inferior and needed to be ruled by their natural superior, the conquistador-colonizer. However, according to the theory of the subjective right of nature, someone is the subject of right when they are in full possession of the will, reason, and material goods necessary for life—their body, property, and freedom. In its modernized form, this subjective natural right endorses the idea of unconditional or absolute private property, as defined by ancient Roman law. In other words, a life, body, and freedom are conceived as natural properties that belong to the subject of rational and voluntary right. Theorists thus claimed that because of their barbaric (or savage, since they displayed no reason) state, the Indians could not be considered to be subjects of right and they were, therefore, natural slaves.

The Indians' natural inferiority would have been immediately understood by people in the sixteenth and seventeenth century by the simple fact that the word used to refer to them was "nation." This word (up until the mid-nineteenth century) referred to a group of people who had a common background, but did not possess civil or legal status. Explorers and colonizers stated that the Indians were "without faith, reason and a King," which made them *naturally* subordinate and subject to the power of the conquistador.

If this theory appeared excessively cruel at the time, then it could be reframed using the concept of *voluntary servitude.*

According to the theory of subjective natural right, the freedom that characterizes the subject of right is the freedom of the will to choose between possible alternatives. This choice means that will is an *ability* (*aptitudo*, in Latin) and that its use depends on the rationality of the subject of right. An ability is a *faculty* (*facultas*, in Latin), that is, something that may be used or practiced or not be used or practiced according to a choice made by a rational and voluntary agent. In other words, a person may freely choose not to use his/her freedom. Those who choose not to exercise the faculty of freedom choose, either spontaneously or by free will, servitude, which is thus voluntary servitude. The objective inferiority of the natives in the natural hierarchy of beings justified their subjective choice of voluntary servitude and their legal and legitimate status as natural slaves.

But, how could situations such as the following one described by Pero de Magalhães Gandavo be explained?

The inhabitants of this the coast of Brazil all hold lands in fee (*sesmarias*), granted and guaranteed by the Captain of the land; and the first thing which they will seek to obtain are slaves to work the land and till their plantations and ranches because without them they cannot maintain themselves in the country; and one of the reasons why Brazil does not flourish much more is that the slaves revolt and flee to their own land

and run away every day and if these Indians were not so fickle and given to flight, the wealth of Brazil would be incomparable.[8]

Everything here indicates that the Indians decided to use the faculty of will to refuse voluntary servitude. Nature, therefore, needed to offer a new solution.

What was consequently emphasized was the Indians' *natural disposition* to labor, as well as blacks' *natural affection* for it. Nature reappeared in the guise of objective natural right—which legalizes and legitimizes the subordination of the inferior black man to the superior white man—and subjective natural right, although this was no longer couched in the idea of voluntary servitude, but rather in the natural right to possess those who have been defeated in war. It was claimed that those who had been defeated in the wars between different African tribes and between the Africans and Europeans were natural slaves and could be used according to their masters' will. Because of blacks' "natural affection" for labor, it was also deemed natural that those who had been defeated in these wars were natural slaves who could be used for working the land. This naturalization of African slavery (their affection for labor and the natural right of their victors) clearly obscured the principle: that the *African slave trade* "opened up a new and important sector for colonial commerce."[9]

The enslavement of Indians and Blacks shows us that God and the Devil do battle in the Land of the Sun. It could be no different, since the serpent inhabited paradise.

This leads us to another effect of the image of Brazil-Nature. The cosmic battle between God and the Devil that appears at the start of the colonial period and refers not to social divisions, but to divisions of and in nature itself: the New World is divided between the coast and the backlands (*sertão*).

The division in nature between the coast, where the word of God initially bears fruit, and the arid backlands, a place of evil ruled by the devil who is always ready to strike, first appears in poems and plays by the young Jesuit Anchieta. "Evil is spreading in the backlands or hiding in caves and swamps, from which it comes out at night in the species of a snake, rat, bat and leech. But the mortal danger is when these external forces penetrate the souls of men."[10]

In order to understand the battle between God and the Devil that was central to the events in Canudos at the end of the nineteenth century and the beginning of the twentieth century, Euclides da Cunha, possessed by what Walnice Galvão beautifully describes as a "Cain complex," set out to describe the backlands.[11]

Substituting God and the Devil for science, that is, a study of the climate, geology, and geography, Euclides' description is impressive for two reasons; first, because of the literary force of the text, and second, because it can be interpreted as an epic and dramatic reversal of the idyllic descriptions offered by Pero Vaz de Caminha, whose letter of discovery merely speculates as to the nature of the backlands, which remains invisible.

What are the backlands of *The Backlands*?

> It is an impressive bit of country. The structural conditions of the earth combine with a maximum of violence on the part of the external agents in the carving of stupendous sculptural reliefs. The torrential rainfalls characteristic of such a climate of altering flood and drought, coming of a sudden after protracted dry periods and beating down upon these slopes, carrying away all the loose rock mantle, have left largely exposed the older geologic series (. . .) forming pictures which give the landscape here its impinging and tormented aspect. (. . .) In the depressions, in the dismantling of the hills, the winding of the river beds of intermittent streams, the construction of the defiles, and the almost compulsive appearance of a deciduous flora lost in a maze of undergrowth—is in a manner of speaking, the martyrdom of the earth, brutally lashed by variable elements (. . .). The forces that work upon the earth attack both its inner contexture and its surface, with no letup in the process of demolition, one following the other with unvarying cadence in the course of only two seasons that the region knows. The scorching summers loosen the rocks and the torrential winter rains crumble them.[12]

Euclides describes a land tortured by the fury of the elements. He describes a rape. Feminized, the land is assaulted, tormented; its intimate texture is martyred, beaten by the heat and degraded by the rain. Yet, this tragic vision of a tortured nature is counterposed with epic descriptions of its inhabitant—the *sertanejo* or man of the backlands, establishing a contrast between the land's feminine pain with his courageous masculine force. Euclides warns us not to be fooled by the backlander's rachitic appearance, lazy walk, and speech, for beneath this appearance lurks a man who battles the elements. The "debilitating, rachitic tendencies of the neurasthenic *mestiços* of the coast" are contrasted with "the *sertanejo* or man of the backlands who is above all else a strong individual."[13]

Brazil's natural division between the coast and the backlands gives rise to a theory that has long persisted, that of "two Brazils." This gave rise to a theory was forcefully reasserted by the Brazilian fascists, the Integralists in the 1920s and 1930s who contrasted coastal Brazil, seen as formal, bourgeois, enlightened, European and liberal, with the backlands of Brazil, seen as real, impoverished, illiterate, and uncivilized. Plínio Salgado, the leader of the Integralist party, stated that the backlands was a way of thinking, a spirit, and that *Brasilidade* was a sentiment emerging from the land itself.

This same contrast resurfaces in images of the "west" and the "center" formulated politically during the New State present in Getúlio Vargas's 1939 speech, in which he calls upon the nation to march into the backlands: "Let us march in unity, toward the center, guided not by the force of prejudiced doctrines, but by the predestination of our racial identity!"[14]

The "predestination of our racial identity," which turned the backlands or the center into the place of our natural destiny, receives ideological impetus in the work of modernist writer Cassiano Ricardo, where he formulates the image of the *sertanista* (frontiersman) and the *bandeirante* (pioneer) as the essence and destiny of *Brasilidade* and constructs the backlands as a natural protective barrier that defends the origins of the nation from the dangers of the coast—the importer of liberalism, communism, and fascism:

> Pioneers in the appeal to Brazil's origins; the defense of our spiritual frontiers against foreign and debilitating ideologies; the sum of authority conferred to our national chief and commander; the march inland becomes synonymous with Brazil's internal imperialism, defined in its own terms, that is, in the dynamic sentiment of the state.[15]

As the historian Alcir Lenharo observes, a geography of power is at play here, in which a "unified physical space constitutes an empirical ballast for other constitutive parts of the nation to lean on."[16] Brazil is the national soil and it possesses a primordial foundational quality, a color that taints the sky, the flora, the fauna, and the races; or as Cassiano Ricardo says, "it is as though God spilled ink everywhere." So, "the Nation rediscovers its tropical colors, it own natural quality, which is a vivid creative force and a divine work of art that man has not corrupted."[17]

The extensive construction of the mythical backlands, beginning with Anchieta's plays, witnessed in Euclides da Cunha's deterministic work, in the Integralist ideology and in the discourses of the New State, culminates in *Grande Sertão: Veredas* (*Devil to Play in the Backlands*) that takes up the Jesuit formulation of the battle between two cosmic forces. Guimarães Rosas writes that in the backlands "only strong and wise men lead. God himself, if he comes here, needs to be armed. And we all know that the Devil is both strong and wise."

For this reason, in the battle against the Devil the way in which the millenarian hope of Canudos was expressed is as important as the attempt to turn the world upside down, which is key to all popular revolts. Hence Antônio Conselheiro's prediction that "the backlands will become the sea and the sea will become the backlands (...). There shall be a great rain of stars and that will be the end of the world."[18]

"The backlands will become the sea and the sea will become the backlands." These words reappear in the poetic lyrics of Brazilian popular music in the 1960s. The prediction highlights how, intoxicated by nature, we entered history. Or as Euclides da Cunha writes, "breaking through the teachings of the religious messiah, came those of the racial messiah," with "the same casting down of the mighty, the same trampling of the profane world, the same millennium and its delights." And he finally asks, "Is there not, to tell the truth, a trace of a higher Judaism in all this?"[19]

The Sacralization of History

If the first element in the production of Brazil's foundational myth places us outside of history, the second element places us in it. However, this is a theological or providential history; it is a history that fulfills God's plan or divine will.

Cosmic time was conceived in antiquity—both oriental and occidental—as a cycle of perennial return, whereas the time of mankind was conceived as a finite straight line, delimited by birth and death. In the former, time is characterized by repetition and a kind of eternity; in the latter it is the natural state of becoming of all things, including empires and cities. Although it is linear and finite, the time of mankind is measured by the cyclical time of things, because eternal repetition is the "metron" of all discernible things: the movement of the planets, the changing seasons, the germination and growth of plants. Because it is based on repetition, cyclical time excludes the idea of history as the appearance of the new; the linear time of mankind introduces the notion of history as memory. The first will be placed under the sign of the capricious goddess, *Fortuna*, whose wheel allows for the inexorable rise of the fallen and the fall of the victorious. The second, placed under the protection of the goddess *Memoria*, guarantees immortality to mortals who have carried out deeds worthy of being commemorated, making them memorable and examples to be imitated. The eternity of the past is guaranteed by its repetition in the present and the future as an imitation of great deeds. The time of ancient history is epic. It narrates the deeds of great men and cities whose duration was finite and whose preservation is achieved through commemoration.

As Erich Auerbach demonstrates, unlike cosmic (natural) and epic (historical) time, biblical time is dramatic, since the history it narrates is not just sacred, but also the drama of man's separation from God and the hope of a reconciliation between God and man. An account of distance and proximity between God and man, time expresses neither the cycles of nature, nor the deeds of men, but rather the will of God and the relation of man with God: Jewish time is the expression of the divine will that submits it to one plan whose fulfillment depends on man's separation from and reconciliation with God by virtue of His will.[20]

This time and plan can be deciphered and God bestows some individuals with the gift of temporal decipherment, otherwise known as prophecy. Time is, therefore, prophetic time, which produces two key outcomes that can be immediately perceived. First, the present can receive divine signs allowing mankind to decipher the meaning of the past and the future; second, time is always the fulfillment of a divine promise and, because of this, it is completed and messianic. Time is not repetition (cosmic), nor is it simply linear (human); it is the passage to an end that *provides* it with meaning, that orients *its* meaning and its direction.

It is this dramatic character of Jewish time that will give form and meaning to the Christian notion of history, whose drama reunites man with God, both because man is the culmination of the start of time, that is, the Creation, and because man is the form chosen by God to fulfill his Promise of salvation, that is, the Incarnation.

In the Judeo-Christian world, therefore, history is the work of God in time. Because of this, it is (1) providential, unitary, and continuous because it is the manifestation of the will of God in time, which is endowed with meaning and an end thanks to the fulfillment of the divine plan; (2) theophanic, that is, the continuous, increasing and progressive revelation of the essence of God in time; (3) epiphanic, that is, the continuous, increasing, and progressive revelation of the truth in time; (4) prophetic, not just as a rememoration of the Law and the Promise, but also as an expectation of the future. As the Jesuit Father Antônio Vieira states, prophecy is the "History of the Future."[21] Prophecy reveals a knowledge of things beyond human observation—both things that are distant in time—a sense of the past and the future—as well as things that are distant in space—present events that are not directly experienced by the prophet. Prophecy offers mankind the possibility of knowing the secret structure of time and of historical events, of having access to the divine plan; (5) salvationary or soteriological, because what is revealed in time is the promise of redemption and salvation as the work of God himself; (6) apocalyptical (from the Greek word which means a direct and divine revelation) and eschatological (from the Greek *tà schaton*, meaning final events and the end), this means that it refers to the start of time and above all to the end of time, or the time of the end, which, according to the prophet Isaiah, will mark the Day of the Lord whose ire and judgment precede the final redemption when the Promise will be fulfilled; (7) universal; there is no history of a specific empire or people, but a history of God's people, for He created man and will save the chosen few; (8) complete, because it will end when the Promise has been fulfilled. For those who believe in the advent of the Messiah, this has already taken place. For others, specifically for millenarianists, it will take place with the Second Coming of Christ, or the End Times. Whether messianic or millenarian, history will be completed and time will end.

The expression End Times comes from the *Book of Revelation* by the prophet Daniel, where it is preceded by the abominations and the fulfillment of the promise of resurrection and salvation for those who are "inscribed in the Book" of God. The prophet describes this End Times as one of increased learning when "men will divide up the earth and knowledge will multiply" because only then shall "the book of secrets" be opened. It is an appointed time: "it shall be for a time, times, and a half," and it will begin after "1260 days" of abomination and will last "1335 days," after which the just will be saved.

The completion of universal history (referred to by Jews and Christians as the plenitude of time and by twentieth-century ideologues as the end of history) was, from the start of Christianity, the subject of much debate and controversy, and consequently, heresy and orthodoxy. In fact Christianity was born of two successive movements: in the first, the Old Testament was interpreted as a prophecy of the advent of the Messiah; in the second (in which, historically, the world did not end after the resurrection of Christ and the Final Judgment was delayed while evil spread throughout the world), the New Testament was interpreted as a prophecy of the Second Coming, that is, the Second Advent of the Messiah at the end of times, when history will finally be completely consummated.

In order to decipher the signs of the coming of the end of the world, Christians turned to texts by the Prophets Daniel and Isaiah, to the so-called little apocalypses of the Gospel of Matthew, Mark, and Luke, as well as, of course, the Great Apocalypse by John. The image of the Day of Wrath and the Day of the Lord, when the Final Judgment will take place, comes from Isaiah. The idea that temporal succession goes hand in hand with the rise and fall of four monarchies or unjust kingdoms, and the emergence of a final kingdom, the Fifth monarchy or Fifth Empire (Daniel believed this to be Israel), is taken from Daniel and his interpretation of Nebuchadnezzar's dreams. The signs of abomination that announce the coming of the end of times (the four horsemen of the apocalypse—war, famine, pestilence, and death), the kingdom of the anti-Christ or Babylon, the final battle between Christ and the anti-Christ, the 1,000-year kingdom of abundance and happiness, which precede the Final Judgment that initiates the end of time and the advent of the blessed and saints into eternity, are all taken from John.

The institutional consolidation of the Church during the fall and the end of the Roman Empire led to the condemnation of millenarian hope, because it afforded little importance to the ecclesiastical institution and had little reason to submit itself to the power of the Church, which was fleeting and ephemeral. As a reaction and in order to affirm its power, the ecclesiastical institution, or the "Church of just and good," proclaimed the 1,000-year kingdom or the celestial city of Jerusalem, stating that the revelation had been completed with the Incarnation of Jesus and that universal history had been concluded with the Gospel. Everything in the world has been concluded and so, even if the world does not end today but only when God decides, there is nothing more that can occur in the world, apart from a soul's individual progress to God and the Church's diffusion throughout the world. All of this introduces a new distinction between the century (the *saeculum*, in Latin) or profane time, and eternity or sacred time: the sacred order of eternity has been concluded and the profane order of the century is irrelevant in universal terms—it is relevant only for the individual soul, a pilgrim in this world whose itinerary is directed toward God.

Perfect and completed time is divided into seven days (the Cosmic Week: the Creation, the Fall, the Flood, the Age of the Patriarchs, Salvation through Moses, the Incarnation, and the Last Judgment) and three ages corresponding to the Holy Trinity: the time before the law or the time of the Father, which begins with Adam and ends with Moses; the time of the Law, or the time of the Father and the Son, from Moses until Jesus; the time of grace, or the time of the Son and the Holy Spirit, the final moment of universal history and of sacred time, the time of Christianity or the Kingdom of God on the Earth.

This chronology responds to an age-old question that is constantly posed as a problem: what occurs in the interval between the time of the first and the second coming, when "there was silence in heaven for about half an hour" between the opening of the sixth and the seventh seal mentioned in the Apocalypse? What occurs in the interval between the coming of the Son of Perdition (the anti-Christ) and the Final Judgment? These intervals unite profane time with sacred time and form the center of the millenarian history, because they contain revelation, innovation, events, and preparation for the end of time.

There is disorder in the world. Disorder is an event that weighs heavily on Christianity and must be deciphered. This decipherment reopens temporality and becomes a search for the knowledge of the secret structure of time and its meaning in an apocalyptical-eschatological interpretation of prophetic and providential history, whose most important interpretation is found on the work of the twelfth-century Calabrian Abbot, Joachim of Flora.

In Joachim of Flora's work time is the order of a successive and progressive expression of the Holy Trinity, but sacred time is divided into three ages that do not exactly reconcile with the official ecclesiastical sequence: the age of the Father is the age of the Law (the Old Testament), the age of the Son is the Time of Grace (that of the Gospel), and the age of the Holy Spirit is the age of Science or the Plenitude of knowledge (The eternal Gospel). The cosmic week maintains the seven ages or days, but between the sixth and the seventh day the anti-Christ will be imprisoned by a representative of Christ, leading to the establishment of the 1,000-year kingdom of peace and happiness, after which Christ will free the anti-Christ, fight and defeat him. The seventh age or the Final Judgment will then begin and the eighth day will be eternal Jubilation.

Sacred time is imbricated with profane time. This imbrication is *the order of time*, structured by the threads of three progressive times directed to the apotheosis, thanks to the figurative or symbolic ordering of the events that are narrated or proclaimed by the Bible. The 1,000-year kingdom of happiness that precedes the final battle between Christ and the anti-Christ is the work of a special envoy, an envoy of Judgment Day. This envoy is Flora's own contribution to explaining the order of time and it is divided into two personages: first, the Angelic Pope, later interpreted by the Joachimites as the Last World Emperor; and second, the spiritual men—these are two new monastic orders concerned with preparing for the End of Time—the order of active prayer and the order of spiritual contemplation (Umberto Eco's novel, the *Name of the Rose* deals with this spiritual monastic order). The plentitude of time will be highlighted, as Daniel prophesied, by the increase of spirituality or learning in the world and the institution of the Fifth Empire or Celestial Jerusalem when "all the kingdoms shall unite under one scepter, all heads shall obey one Supreme Being and all the crowns shall be united under one diadem." "One flock, one shepherd," as Isaiah prophesized, is the condition for the fulfillment of the future.

What now remains to be explored is how the Judeo-Christian construction of history, either the providential version of the ecclesiastical institution or the prophetic Joachimite version, becomes linked to the discovery of Brazil?

If Brazil is "a land blessed by God" and a paradise found, then it is the source of the world because it is the originary and original world. And if this country is "eternally lain on a splendid cradle" (as noted in Brazil's National Anthem) it is because it is part of God's providential plan. Pero Vaz de Caminha believed that God did not bring us here "without purpose" and Afonso Celso wrote that "there is an immanent logic: so many premises of greatness can only lead to a great conclusion, as God would not provide us with such precious gifts to sterilely waste them (...). If He endowed Brazil in such magnanimous ways, it is because He reserved a higher destiny for it."

Our past secures our future in a temporal *continuum* that dates from the origins to our destiny. If Brazil is, as we often say "a country of the future," it is because God provided us with the signs to know our future: the constellation of the Southern Cross, which protects and orients us, and Nature-Paradise, the gentle mother.

However, during the period of conquest and colonization, explorers and missionaries did not adopt the providential ecclesiastical history. They adopted the prophetic millenarian history of Joachim of Flora.

This is why, in his letters to the Catholic Kings, Columbus explains that he had no use for maps and compasses; the only things he needed, he says, are the prophecies of Isaiah and the abbot Joachim of Flora. The Franciscans and Jesuits also promoted these ideas because they believed they were the two religious orders Flora predicted would exist in the new millennium or the time of the Holy Spirit (the order of active prayers, and the order of contemplation).

What were the signs that Joachim of Flora's millennial prophecies were being fulfilled? The first sign was the voyages themselves and the discovery of the New World, proof that Isaiah's prophecies were being fulfilled, that is, that God's people would be scattered to the four winds, that "the unity of tongues and nations would be restored" by God and that new lands and new people would be seen because God would create "new heavens and a new earth." They are proof too of Daniel's prophecies of explorations throughout the earth at the end of time.

What did Isaiah write? "Surely you will summon nations you know not, and nations that do not know you will hasten to you."

What did Daniel write? "But you, Daniel, shut up the words, and seal the book until the time of the end; many shall run to and fro, and knowledge shall increase."

If these prophecies were fulfilled, then they could be taken as a sign that Isaiah's most important prophecy would also be fulfilled: "I will gather all nations and tongues; and they shall come and see my glory (. . .). For as the new heavens and the new earth, which I will make, shall remain before me, saith the Lord, so shall your seed and your name remain."

God shall turn to the nations and languages and they shall turn to Him: the evangelization of new heavens and new lands was prophesied and so they were effectively created. Why was the evangelization prophesied? Because the prophet referred to "nations" that would be created by God, meaning a people without faith, without King, and without Law, who would become God's people through the work of the evangelists. The nations will come to God and God will come to them: this divine reunion, the restoration of Zion described by the prophet, will be the work of reuniting all of nations and languages, so that the world will come together under one single power, that is, one scepter and one crown, the Fifth Empire that Daniel referred to.

In the seventeenth century, Father Antonio Vieira vigorously defended this outlook in his book *History of the Future of the World, or the Fifth Empire of the World and Hopes for Portugal*.

In his intricate interpretation of the work of the great prophets, especially Daniel and Isaiah, Father Vieira argues that Portugal would fulfill Daniel's prophecies and the work of the millennium by instituting the Fifth Empire of the world led by *O Encoberto* or The Hidden One, a final embodiment of the Portuguese monarch Dom Sebastian who was supposed not have died in the battle of Alcacerquibir.

What did Isaiah say that provided Vieira with such hope? The prophet asked, "Who are these that fly as a cloud, and as the doves to their windows?" The Jesuit in turn responded: "the clouds that flock to these lands to fertilize them are the Portuguese preachers of the Bible, taken by the wind like clouds, they are also called doves because they take these clouds to the baptismal waters upon which the Holy Spirit appeared in the shape of a dove."

For Father Vieira, Daniel's prophecies, together with Isaiah's, contained signs that the conditions for the Fifth monarchy or Empire and the 1,000-year kingdom were being fulfilled: the appearance of an "unknown nation" or the New World, the dispersal of the Elect People (the Church) "scattered to the four winds" and the discovery of a "new people" waiting for "swift angels."

To prove that Portugal was the subject and object of these great prophecies, Vieira had to highlight Brazil's role in God's plan. He did so by proving that Isaiah had prophesied Brazil as a Portuguese deed:

Woe to the land shadowing with wings, which is beyond the rivers of Ethiopia. That sends ambassadors by the sea, even in vessels of bulrushes on the waters, saying, go, you swift messengers, to a nation scattered and peeled, to a people terrible from their beginning till now; a nation meted out and trodden down, whose land the rivers have spoiled!

Father Vieira reinterpreted this passage in the following way:

The ancient interpreters worked hard to find an explanation for this text but they could not guess it correctly, because they had no knowledge of the land, nor of the people that the prophet spoke of [...] that Isaiah spoke of America and the New World can be easily and clearly proven. The land that the prophet describes is situated beyond Ethiopia and is a land beyond which there is nothing. These two descriptions are clear manifestations of America [...] yet because Isaiah here includes so many particular signs and many individual differences, it is clear that he is not speaking of all of America or the New World in general, rather he is referring to a particular province—I mean to say that Isaiah's text refers to Brazil.[22]

Two conclusions can be drawn from this: the first is that the reinterpretation of Isaiah's texts highlights that the prophet "can be found among the chroniclers of Portugal, as he speaks many times of the spiritual conquest of the Portuguese and those people and nations who were converted to Christianity by these preachers."[23] The second is that the time is right for the fulfillment of these words because "there are prophecies that are more than prophetic," such as the following prophecy by John the Baptist, which refers to the promise of the future and the revelation of the present:

> And so I hope that it will be with my future hope and that as our future happiness has been promised, so will our present be revealed. When this takes place, our History shall gloriously disappear. It shall no longer be the history of the future but the History of the Present. But if the hoped for empire I refer to in my title, is that of the world, then these hopes shall also belong to the world and not only to Portugal? The reasons being: the best part of the advantageous and glorious future that is expected shall not just belong to Portugal; it shall be uniquely and singularly Portuguese. The nations, enemies and adversaries shall suffer pain, and envy, its friends and associates pleasure and for all of you, glory and moreover hope.[24]

The Inquisition accused Father Vieira of Judaism. Euclides da Cunha referred to Antônio Conselheiro as a superior form of Judaism. What is the significance of these accusations of Judaism against the Jesuit priest and the messianic leader? Christians referred to the belief that the Kingdom of God exists in this world, not the next one as "Jewish" or "Judaism," a belief the Church called "carnal."

Brazil, a Portuguese discovery, entered history through the gates of paradise. This idea will become the dominant class' version of this country, according to which our history has already been written and merely requires an agent to concretize and complete it in time. This vision is present in the very opening lines of our National Anthem, in which an absent subject who hears "the resounding cry of a heroic people," which "at that very moment" makes "the sun of liberty shine in the skies of the homeland." It is "at that very moment," therefore, that the heroic people emerge; they are significantly created by the heir of the Portuguese crown, who in an act of sovereign will, divides time, founds the nation, and completes history.

But, Brazil also entered history through the gates of a millenarianism that would gradually be the trajectory adopted by the popular classes. Antônio Conselheiro promises that "the backlands will become the sea and the sea will become the backlands (. . .) and that will be the end of the world." In prophetic time, our history has been promised but it is still to be realized and will be the work of a community of the saints and the righteous, an auxiliary army that will assist the Messiah in the final battle against the anti-Christ, that is, against darkness, evil, and injustice. Canudos, Pedra Bonita, Contestado, Muckers, Liberation

Theology—these are just some of the events of this long history that is to be fulfilled.

However, in this prophetic trajectory just as in the providential itinerary, we are agents of the will of God, and our time is that of the sacralization of time. History is part of theology.

The Sacralization of the Ruler

One flock, one shepherd. One mind, one scepter, and one diadem. The theological image of political power is upheld because it finds expression in profane time: the absolute monarchy by the divine right of Kings.

Historians have demonstrated that overseas expansion and the establishment of colonial empires were contemporary with absolutism in the political sphere, and with the persistence of a stratified society founded on juridical privileges in the social sphere. Mercantile capitalism, which began to dismantle the feudal structure, was, therefore, simultaneous to the "Absolutist State, with the extreme centralization of royal power that, to a certain extent, unified and disciplined a society into 'orders' and implemented mercantilistic politics that fostered the development of a market economy, both internally and externally."[25] Mercantilism is favored by a centralized state that establishes and guarantees it, and in which the King functions as

> an active economic agent (forcing feudal masters to take part in overseas commercial ventures), seeing navigation and its respective traffic, as well as new industrial activities, as a means of generating income no longer provided internally by the land in the context of new needs stipulated by the economic contract.[26]

Only a unified and centralized state can initiate and organize internal and external resources. Portugal was able to embark on its overseas voyages and build its empire, precisely because it already had a centralized state, which had started to focus on mercantilism as a solution to the feudal crisis.

From the outset, the absolute monarchy was established to solve the crisis of feudalism and guaranteed the preservation of aristocratic privileges that were threatened by the disappearance of servitude (i.e., by an economy founded not just on slave or indentured labor but also the Lord's arbitrary power over the life and death of his serfs) and by growing peasant uprisings occurring all over Europe. Local authorities no longer had the power to counter these two key events. The result was

A displacement of politico-legal coercion upwards towards a centralized militarized summit—the Absolutist State (. . .). A reinforced apparatus of royal power, whose permanent political function was the repression of the peasant and plebian masses at the foot of the social hierarchy.[27]

The function of the absolute monarchy, however, was not restricted to preserving the power of the nobility over the rural masses. It was also responsible for adjusting aristocratic power and the interests of the mercantile bourgeoisie that had developed in medieval cities. The emergence of the absolute monarchy was, therefore, determined by the feudal regroupment against the peasantry, and overdetermined by the rise of an urban bourgeoisie or the pressures of mercantile capital.

While overseas expansion and the colonial system are the Iberian monarchy's response to the antagonistic economic pressures that threaten it, from a political and social point of view this monarchy also made use of other instruments. The first of these was Roman law, the second was professional bureaucracy, and the third was the Divine Right of Kings.

Roman law possessed two categories: civil right, which was relative to absolute and unconditional private property and governed all individual relations; and public right, which governed political relations between the state and its citizens. In Roman terminology, the former was *jus* (which dealt with the object of litigation and arbitration) and the latter was *lex* (which defined the *imperium*, the power of command legally established and recognized). The adoption of Roman law by the modern monarchy, from the sixteenth century onward, facilitated the slow, gradual, and definite break away from a feudal system based on vassalage (i.e., power founded on personal relations of loyalty and fidelity to feudal masters, according to a hierarchy of intermediary powers leading up to the King) and the acknowledgment of the only and single authority of the monarch. To ensure that the intensification of private property, at the base of society, would not come into conflict with the public authority, at the top of society, the absolute monarchy invoked the doctrine elaborated by Roman jurist Ulpian: "what pleases the prince has the force of law," as well as its complementary maxim, which declares that the King, as the originating force of the law, cannot be bound to the law and is, therefore, *legibus solutus* (hence the regime becomes known as an absolute monarchy). Existing above the law and not bound to the law, the King is judged by no one, *a nemine judicatur*.

Territorial unification, undertaken in keeping with the Roman doctrine that public space (the land) was the King's *dominium* and *patrimonium*, and royal authority, as the very foundation for the law and, therefore, not bound to it, determined the physiognomy of the absolutist state, which was created by bureaucrats and state administrators well versed in Roman jurisprudence: the *letrados* in Portugal and Spain, the *maître des requêtes* in France, and the *doctores* in Germany.

A professional class, or *estamento* (state), at the service of monarchical interests, bureaucrats, or administrators were responsible for enforcing the law and for the functioning of the civil and fiscal system. Their services were *offices*, which could be obtained by the King's favor or purchased (the cost of purchasing an *office* could be recouped by licensed privileges and corruption). The "growth of the sale of offices was, of course, one of the most striking by-products of the increased monetarization of the early modern economies and of relative ascent of the mercantile and manufacturing bourgeoisie within them."[28]

Fiscal policies meant that the nobility and the clergy were not taxed and thanks to their offices the bourgeoisie and professional classes were also exempt from taxation; the overwhelming weight of taxation, therefore, fell on the poor masses. Consequently, it was not uncommon for tax collectors to be accompanied by fusiliers and for popular uprisings to erupt everywhere. However, because the juridical principle declared "that which affects all as individuals must be approved by all," monarchs were forced to summon the professional classes or "orders"—nobility, clergy, and bourgeoisie—or the "royal council" (the Portuguese and Spanish Courts) to establish fiscal policies and the business of the Kingdom. Rarely summoned, the courts soon became disputed spaces among the nobility, the clergy, and bourgeoisie, forming rival networks of patronage within the state apparatus. This professional class, as Raimundo Faoro notes, constituted a closed group of people whose ascent was based on social inequality and who sought exclusive material and spiritual advantages, preserving privileges and ordering, directing, orienting, and defining uses, customs and manners, as well as social and moral conventions that promoted social distinctions and political power. This professional class defined the entire style of life.[29]

In order to exercise complete control over this intricate network of privileges and powers, this web of favors, clientelism, corruption, and venality, the absolute monarchy required a theory of sovereignty that could free the monarch from the intermediary powers that came between him and his very power. This theory was that of the Divine Right of Kings, which allows political power to preserve its professional classes (the nobility and the clergy) and produce new ones (the bourgeoisie's *letrados* and professionals), but at the same time limits them by redefining them as instances that give rise to and situate themselves above the law because they obey only the Divine law, represented by the King—who is its *only* representative.

The modern theory of the Divine Right of Kings is founded on the new theory of sovereignty as a single, unique, and indivisible power. However, we can only fully comprehend the persuasive force of this theory if we link it to the theory of objective natural right as the natural divine juridical order, which provides the foundations for the theocratic idea of political power, that is, an idea that political power comes directly from God. The formulation of theocratic power depends on two different yet complementary medieval formulations. The first states that, because of original sin, man lost all rights, including the right to power. This right belongs exclusively to God. As the Bible states, "All power comes from on High/ By me kings reign and princes decree justice." According to these ideas, someone possesses power because they have received it from God, who, for some mysterious and incomprehensible reason has bestowed it onto them as a special grace or favor. Human power, therefore, has its origins in a divine favor bestowed to someone who represents the source of all power—God. This involves a very precise idea of *political representation*: the ruler does not represent the people; he represents God, the transcendent source of all power. As God's representative, the ruler acts as His supreme delegate and ruling is a form of fulfilling or distributing favors. Men, therefore, have power because of the King's grace or favor, which transforms them into His representatives.

The second formulation of the theocratic power, without abandoning the notion of divine favor, introduces the idea that the ruler represents God because he possesses a nature that is linked to that of Jesus Christ. Just as Christ possessed both a mortal human nature and an eternal and everlasting divine nature, the ruler possesses two bodies: the natural physical body and the political body—or the mystical, eternal, immortal, and divine body. The King receives the political or mystical body during coronation, when he receives the insignias of power: the scepter (which symbolizes the power to rule), the crown (which symbolizes the power to make decisions), the mantle (which symbolizes the divine protection that the King will bestow onto his subjects), the sword (which symbolizes war and peace), and the ring (which symbolizes the King's marriage to his heritage, that is, to the land).

Chosen by God to be the shepherd of His flock and to look after it as a father (or master), the ruler receives the signs of power at the moment he receives the political body: the absolute personal will with which he represents divine will. This theological thesis perfectly adapts Ulpian's juridical doctrine that "what pleases the prince has the force of law," as well as its complementary idea, that is, having received God's and not men's power, the King is above the law and can be judged only by God. The theory of the mystical political body also adapts the juridical idea of public space (the land) as royal dominion and heritage: the land (all of the territories conquered or inherited by the King as well as all of their products) is transformed into the body of the ruler that can be transferred or distributed to descendents CHECK through the system of favor. This inherited land is, strictly speaking, the *pátria* or homeland (defined above) and it is this land that the King's army swears to defend when it promises to "die for the country." The idea of the homeland is perfectly adjusted to the idea of the Crown's exclusive monopoly over all of the products of its metropolitan and colonial territories, a monopoly that is one of the pillars of the absolutist monarchy during the mercantilistic period.

How is the theocratic power of the absolute monarchy implemented in Brazil? Here it is important to remember that the theory of favor is the juridical basis of the distribution of colonial land by the King in the form of hereditary captaincies, distributions that preserve the King as the absolute master of these lands. Captaincies are *endowments* from the King and their owners are *beneficiaries*.

An integral part of the mercantile capitalist system, colonial society was stratified politically, as well as in terms of customs. Social classes (landowners and slaves) operated within an economic realm of production and commerce, but it was the professional class that ruled. This rule depended on three sources: the noble origins of the ruler (his status as an aristocrat or nobleman); the purchase of a title of nobility (which allowed a commoner to become an aristocrat, thereby gaining the nobility required to rule); or the purchase of an *office* within the state bureaucracy (which allowed the *letrado* to become an intermediary between the colony and the metropolis, developing its laws and procedures, opening up new procedures or legal avenues and blocking others, using and abusing his privilege, distributing favors and obstructing rights). Royal power thus appears in two forms: on the one hand, as a collector of taxes and an enforcer of the law; and on the other, as the final adjudicator of litigation when its solution was encumbered by the web of local powers, that is, the economic power of landowning classes, the social power of the professional classes, and the political power of noblemen and the bureaucracy.

Society is entirely vertical or hierarchical. The fundamental social division between masters and slaves was overdetermined by the intraclass horizontality and the interclass verticality. This forges an intricate network of relations that the black population learned to make use of. In doing so they avoided being reduced to the condition of victim and constructed themselves as agents in social relations, in a society that, as Laura de Mello Souza points out, poor free men, mulattos and *mestiços*, had no mobility because they had no place in it, other than being used to signify vagrancy in a way that concealed the foundations of social hierarchy and made their visible presence within society merely negative.[30] This gave rise to social relations that were subject to favor and a system of command-obedience, obscuring divisions between the public and the private, divisions that were already structurally vague because of the endowment, leasing, and purchase of land provided by the Crown to the landed gentry that operated in the public or administrative realm.

How was monarchical power seen in the colony? Monarchical centralization was seen through the lens of the ideology of objective natural right and was, therefore, deemed necessary and natural. All powers were perceived as forms of privilege and favors that emanated directly from the will of the Crown, a will that had the force of the law.

In practice, however, as Caio Prado Jr. observes, the metropolis' juridical or legal apparatus were far removed from the reality of the colony, which invented its own activities within the itineraries, intervals, and silences of the legal and juridical apparatus. The dispersal of property throughout the territory, the fragmentation of local interests and powers, the burden of the Crown's economic monopoly, conflicts between masters and slaves and between masters and poor freemen, along with divisions between the religious and lettered classes, produced two seemingly contrasting effects: on the one hand, monarchical centralization and the monarch by the Divine Right appeared to be the only means capable of unifying the interests and privileges of the wealthy and bureaucratic classes; on the other hand, the metropolitan reference seemed inefficient and untenable in the context of the colony's real social fragmentation, revealing the fact that it had been constructed from the mere threads of Royal decrees, charters, and ordinances.

From an ideological point of view, which is our key focus here, this duality should not be taken as an obstacle to understanding the political imaginary. On the contrary, it reinforces the image of a power perceived as transcendent, but that, because it is distant, is also seen as a vicarious space composed of multiple networks of local order and privilege, each one imitating and reproducing the two principles of the consecration of power: the will of the ruler as a law above the law and the natural right to power, according to the hierarchy of objective natural right.

Since my intention here is not to trace the historical formation of Brazilian politics, I do not (nor would I be able to) explore transformations that occurred in the passage from the colony to the Empire and from the Empire to the Republic, that is, the reception of liberal, Jacobin, positivist, fascist, and socialist ideas, forms of class struggles and Brazilian *mandonismo* or bossism. I highlight, however, a few examples that reveal the lasting effects of the sacralization of power.

The first effect can be clearly and easily seen: the symbol chosen to represent the recently proclaimed Republic was Tiradentes, "a civic Christ" (to use José Murilho de Carvalho's expression) a Christ-like figure.[31] The symbol fell not on the possible political action of Tiradentes but rather his martyrdom at the altar of the nation. There was little opposition or debate concerning the contradiction between this image and the historical reality of the group of rebels that under the influence of the American Independence and of the French Revolution fought for Brazilian independence, as well as its inadequacy for representing the new Republic as a supposedly secular power, when the so-called religious question or *Padroado* (i.e., the separation between church and state) was key to Republican propaganda.[32]

Another effect can be perceived if we unite the sacralization of history with the sacralization of the ruler. In doing so we can see that Brazil's foundational myth functions in a socially differentiated manner: for the dominant, it functions through the production of a vision of a natural right to power, legitimized through networks of favor and *clientelism*, patriotism or *ufanismo* and the ideologies of developmentalism and modernization, all of which are secular expressions of the theology of providential history and ruling by the grace of God; for the dominated, it operates through a millenarian vision of the ruler as a savior and the sacralization-demonization of politics. In other words, the myth sows the seeds of a messianic vision of politics that has as its parameter the millenarian nucleus of the final cosmic struggle between light and darkness, good and evil, in which the ruler is either a sacred figure (light and goodness) or a demonic figure (darkness and evil).

An additional effect of the sacralization of the ruler is the way in which political representation takes place in Brazil. In fact, as we have seen, the king represents God, not the people; and those who receive the royal favor represent the King, not his subjects. This conception appears in Brazilian politics where, even though they are elected, representatives are not perceived as representatives of the people but as representatives of the state against the people, leading them to solicit favors or receive privileges. It is precisely because the democratic practice of representation does not take place that the relationship between the representative and the people is one of favor, clientelism, and tutelage. It is this effect that is expressed in the power of populism in Brazilian politics.

What is populism? It is

1. A power that is actively achieved without recourse to institutional political mediations (parties, the tripartite structure of republican powers, etc.), seeking a direct relation between the ruler and the people through a network of personal mediations.

2. A power formulated and achieved in a context of tutelage and favor, in which the ruler presents himself as the only individual who possesses power, knowledge of society, and the meaning of the law. As the exclusive guardian of power and knowledge, he considers those who are ruled to be without action and politics and is thus able to tutor them. This tutelage is achieved within a kind of canonical relationship between the ruler and the ruled: clientelism.

3. A power that operates through transcendence and immanence, that is, in which the ruler exists outside of and above society, transcending it to the extent that he is the guardian of power, knowledge, and the law. At the same time, however, he can fulfill his role only if he also forms part of the social, since he operates without institutional mediations. It is precisely this position that the ruler by God's grace occupies, the ruler who transcends society, producing it through the law that expresses his will, yet who nevertheless remains immanent in relation to it because he is the father of the people.

4. The place of power and its occupier are indiscernible (Weber calls this indistinction "charismatic authority" and Kantorowicz defines it as the embodiment of power), because the place of power is completely occupied and filled by the ruler, who fills it with his person. The populist ruler embodies and personifies a power that, because it is founded by his knowledge and favor rather than public institutions or sociopolitical mediations, is not separate or distinct from him.

5. A type of autocratic power. The ability of the ruler to be an autocrat clearly depends on a number of conditions, but the exercise

of power and the form of government will be autocratic. Today, this aspect is favored by a neoliberal ideology, which functions via an "industrial politics" or "marketing politics" that emphasizes the personal, the narcissistic, and the intimate, presenting a politician's private life as his public persona.

Authoritarian Thought: The Integralist Imaginary

Approaching texts in which authoritarian thought in Brazil is expressed is always a thankless task. Even for readers who are rarely surprised, inevitable questions arise: how can a thought whose theoretical weakness is so striking be counterbalanced by its practical efficacy? Or, how can efficient domination give rise to such incoherent theoretical expressions? However, if we do not want to reduce Brazil's authoritarian discourses to the status of "a bad rhetoric" born of the idiosyncrasies of its *intelligentsia* or the injustice of its power holders, it is worth considering these questions seriously. An initial clue in dealing with them may be discerned from observing that one of the most pronounced characteristics of this ideology consists in asserting a coincidence between the idea of truth (of thought) and the idea of efficacy (of action), which entails reducing social and political praxis to a set of techniques of action supposedly appropriate for obtaining specific ends. It is, therefore, not peculiar but necessary that authoritarian thought's theoretical weakness go hand in hand with its practical efficacy.

For the interpreter of historical and social scientific texts, Brazilian authoritarianism becomes more coherent if the historical roots of its influence as well as the nature of its more flagrant conjunctural manifestations are clarified. Nevertheless, on another level, the enigma of Brazilian authoritarianism remains, that is, the question remains: how does its theoretical weakness and its practical efficacy relate?

This question may incline the interpreter to immediately disqualify the authoritarian discourse. This occurs in Sérgio Buarque de Holanda's *Raízes do Brasil (Roots of Brazil)*, which considers Integralism as a product of the lucubrations of "neurasthenic intellectuals," eager to "seal the *nihil obstat* of civil authority."[1]

The same inclination leads Dante Moreira Leite to write the following of Oliveira Vianna, one of the fathers of Brazilian authoritarian thought: "Despite criticism (and fortunately there were already those in Brazil who perceived the nonsense of his affirmations, an absence of their historical basis) there were numerous editions of his books, which were cited seriously as though they represented more than the unhealthy imagination of a man who must have been deeply unhappy. In spite of everything, for sociologists and psychologists, his work demonstrates the cruelty of one group being ruled by another: the dominated group ends up seeing itself through the eyes of the dominant group, disdaining and hating in itself signs that the other considers inferior."[2] However, besides this reference to the social origin of alienation and resentment, Dante Moreira Leite seeks to contain his inclination to immediately disqualify Oliveira Vianna, noting that "The success of his work would be incomprehensible had it resulted from scientific qualities or virtues. Its success and prestige, even among intellectuals, is easier to explain when we bear in mind that his books slightly preceded or were contemporary with various European fascist movements. As would occur with Gilberto Freyre, Oliveira Vianna's work satisfied the dreams of rural nobility held by a part of the Brazilian population."[3] The reception of Vianna's work then can be explained, on the one hand, by the success of European fascism, and on the other, by the choice of the landed class as its intended audience. Maria Stella Bresciani and Evaldo Amaro Vieira have put forward similar interpretations. The former highlights links between Vianna's ideas and Brazil's internationally successful Statism; the latter emphasizes his work's conservative audience.[4]

The need to contain the inclination to immediately disqualify the production of our authoritarian ideologues in order to historically understand them can, however, lead us to attempt a realist interpretation, that is, to confront the texts with the historical reality they are part of in order to verify their reciprocal adequacy or inadequacy.

The problem with this form of interpretation is the authority it confers upon historical reality, which serves as a beacon for evaluating discourses rather than seeing reality (when past) as also textual. By no means do I mean to imply that confronting authoritarian texts with other documents would be arbitrary merely because historical reality possesses the same discursive dimension as the object of investigation. On the contrary, I seek to point out that the confrontation cannot have "realist" pretensions, that is, it cannot pretend to a definitive encounter with facts that serve as parameters for its interpretation and value. For the points that follow, it will be more enriching to take not the adequacy or inadequacy between the text and the real as criterion, but rather the representation of the real conveyed by the text and, then, to interpret differences and conflicts between the documents according to their representation of the social, the political, and the historical, as well as, consequently, according to their intended public. In short, to take as beacon the question: to what class is the discourse intended? After all, it is men who make their own history, even if they do not know it. But because they do so under certain circumstances, the most pronounced trace of our authoritarian ideologues reveals itself in the construction of discourses where these circumstances cannot appear. They are, as Spinoza would say, texts where conclusions are given in the complete absence of premises. Such absence engenders theoretical weakness as well as its counterpart, that is, practical efficacy, since when premises are absent, discourse becomes normative and programmatic-pragmatic, the ought occupying the place of being, techniques of action occupying the place of acting. It is not surprising that, among us, the formulation of a government project always appears to be the only way of making politics and history.

In dealing with the question of theoretical weakness through this internal prism, I would like to contribute to the debate surrounding the question of the "out of place ideas," that is, of the importation of ideas. It has been frequently affirmed that one of the sources of the theoretical weakness of Brazilian thought and, more specifically, of ideology in Brazil, stems from the tendency to import ideas. These possess their reason for being in the place where they are originally produced, so that when transplanted to Brazil they become false and a grotesque ornament. It is this importation that makes our philosophers, to use the words of Cruz Costa, mere glossers of ideas; it is furthermore this transplantation that explains the contradictions in the discourses of Sílvio Romero, Euclides da Cunha, or Nina Rodrigues who made "use of a wrong theory to give an account of a reality that European theory negated."[5] Or, finally, it is the importation of ideas that forms the basis of second-degree ideological formulations, as was the case with our liberal ideas that "do not describe reality, not even falsely, and do not move according to a law of their own (. . .). Their law is other, different from that which they name; it relates to the order of social prestige, rather than relating to its objective meaning and to the system."[6]

This is not the place to discuss the significance of historical necessities for the importation of ideas "where every once in a while a constellation is repeated in which the hegemonic ideology of the West cuts the derisory figure of a mania among manias."[7] There is no doubt that importation is determined internally by the necessary rhythm of Brazilian capitalism to adjust itself to the tempo of international music.

Nor is it the case that importation is not indiscriminate and collects in toto metropolitan ideological constellations. As a contribution to the debate I would like to suggest that in the specific case of authoritarian thought, the importation of ideas possesses a particular meaning.

We know that a certain representation of the economy was part of the ideology of the First Republic (1889–1930), during which the question of industrialization was avoided thanks to the use of the dichotomy natural industry versus artificial industry. This representation of the economic sphere was repeated in the representation of the political nation through the dichotomy between the real country versus the legal country.[8] These two representations, in turn, reappeared in the representation of intellectual activity as a dichotomy between national ideas versus imported ideas. A means of dealing with the problem of imperialism without, however, running the risk of reflecting on it in order to understand it, this ideological constellation functions to support the ideas of our authoritarians where the series "artificial," "legitimate," and "foreign" forms an opposing unit to the "natural," "real," and "national" series. In this context, it would be positive if our authoritarians were *not* importers of ideas.

They certainly presented themselves as original thinkers: didn't they discover that we are a result of "ethnic tempering?" That our backwardness comes from *mestiçagem*, which weakens traditions? That we are heirs of the fearless *bandeirante* and of the strong *sertanejo*?[9] Didn't they return to the *tupi-guarany* origins of our people? Didn't they propose economic models for our essentially agrarian country, which because of its solid agrarianism distinguishes itself from all other nations? Mounted on mythical images, nationalism gives our authoritarians the illusion of being related to historical conditions transfigured in allegorical mist. Confusing native images with the movement of history, they believe that the substitution of myths of European origin by others is a theoretical operation that can sufficiently liberate national thought from foreign "influences." So that when the *bandeirante*, the *tupi*, the *gaúcho*, the *sertanejo*, the *mestiço*, the forest, the virgin territory, the vast landscape, and the psychology of the people enter on to the scene, they function as bewitching words: they have the miraculous gift of allowing, through lexical change, the application of European theoretical projects without the need to be ashamed of them. Reduced to an empty form, European thought can then be used nationally once it is filled with local contents. What is of interest, for now, is understanding why this procedure makes one of the peculiar traces of authoritarian thought legible.

I believe that it is because of authoritarian thought that there is an importation of ideas and not that because there is an importation of ideas that Brazilian thought becomes mimetically authoritarian. In making this claim I am stating that I believe there is an authoritarian way of thinking and not just thoughts that are born of authoritarian ways of acting. Although one does exist without the other, I believe it is possible to ascertain certain determinations that constitute a thought as authoritarian thought.[10]

Authoritarian thinking is peculiar in its need to employ certainties decreed before and outside of its elaboration in order to enter into activity. It would be misleading to assume that authoritarian thought leads to a need for obedience, since this is its very starting point: it requires prior certainties in order to take hold and it searches for them in "facts" and "theories." Moreover, it is the very manner of manipulating facts or of securing itself with a theory that signals the need to subject itself in order to then effectively subject. Facts are reduced to examples and tests, while theory is reduced to a formal scheme or, as is often stated, a model. Providing reality with the task of mere empirical example and bestowing on theory the role of an empty framework for changeable contents, authoritarian thought frees itself from the disturbing need to confront that which has not yet been thought (the real thus being the here and now) and of understanding the work of a theory wherein form and content are not separate, since in it the opacity of a new and not yet conceived of experience is made intelligible. Authoritarian thinking, a field of conclusions without premises, needs to locate a set of obligatory affirmations in some external, previous, and fixed point thanks to which it enters thought. It supports itself in the already seen (exemplary fact), in the already thought (previous theory), in the already enunciated (authorized discourse); it fears the new and the unknown and it endeavors to displace them to the borders of the already known. Incapable of thinking difference, in space as well as in time, it needs to feel itself authorized before imposing itself: it lives under the sign of repetition. We need only read the opening pages of *The Eighteenth Brumaire* to understand the origins of the need for repetition.

If we acknowledge that the need to find an already realized "knowledge" on which it can support itself is constitutive of the logic of authoritarian thought, as well as the need to manipulate facts in which it can exemplify itself and, thanks to such procedures, prevent the risk of the elaboration of knowledge, then the theoretical weakness and the need to import ideas already consecrated elsewhere become clear. There is importation in "time" (the sacred image of tradition) as well as in "space" (the auratic image of European superiority). Paraphrasing Sérgio Buarque de Holanda, it can be said that our authoritarian thought asks for the seal, the *nihil obstat* of "theoretical" authority and of political authority. Importation of ideas and privilege conferred to state power as origin, middle, and end of society constitute the same ideological context and are foundations of the same practice.[11]

*　*　*

By interlacing theoretical weakness and practical efficacy, the trajectory of these observations may appear untenable, since Integralism is one of the historical failures of authoritarianism in Brazil. And it may be of little help, or none at all, to refer to the existence of the programmatic points of the Brazilian Integralist Action (BIA) subsequently put into practice by the New State, since other authoritarian sources contributed to the consolidation of that state. To simply invalidate this interpretative trajectory, however, would be to incur *post-festum* reasoning, taking the future failure of BIA as a given already apprehended by its militants and leaders in the years between 1932 and 1938. It is exactly the contrary that we are dealing with here. The causes of the failure are undoubtedly of concern, but there is, above all, a need to understand how and why Integralism became a political proposition capable of converting BIA into a successful social and political agent at a specific moment of Brazil's history. It is important to understand why militants and leaders accepted the doctrine as a solid theory of Brazilian reality, capable of proposing a line of action considered fair. The key concern, therefore, is Integralism as interpreted by its militants and Brazilian society as interpreted by the Integralist vanguard, as well as the interpretations of those who had opposed BIA. It is important to understand why, at a given moment in this country, part of society believed that it would seize power with the cries of "Anauê," "Anauê," "Anauê."[12]

Integralist discourse has the distinctive characteristic of operating with images instead of concepts. This operation gives texts, even those with theoretical pretensions, a bombastic tone that, in principle, seems incompatible with Plínio Salgado's assertion that the "Brazilian Integralist movement is a cultural movement that includes—a) a general revision of dominant philosophies up to the start of the century and, consequently, of the social, economic, and political sciences; b) the creation of a new thought, based in part on the synthesis of the knowledge bequeathed to us during the last century."[13] Before asking why the doctrine is built on images, it will be useful to highlight the way in which this imaginary functions.

The Integralist discourse operates, grosso modo, in three ways: by a simple juxtaposition of images, by the transformation of a concept into an image, and finally, by a free association of images.

An example of the first operation, where an image juxtaposes itself to others with no immediate connection, can be seen in the following text: "The Brazilian race and, more generally, the South American, has a cosmic value originating from ethnic sources. This origin linked to the land presents us as an inversion of history, transcribing the primitive ages for the century of the machine. The Stone Age coexists with the age of the radio. The ultra modern luxury of Copacabana is contemporary with savage Indian huts and villages."[14] Or as in the following passage, "Germany feeds the powerful dream of race; Italy, the wonderful dream of empire; England extends its gaze over the vastness of markets and conquests; North America is committed to a powerful organization that aims for the rule of man over machine; Russia cloaks itself in proletarian sacrifice; and France is already moving to reaffirm its higher values. And Brazil? Brazil has an unknown quality: the ideal. We have lived without ideal in passive admiration of the splendor of our nature (. . .) the greatness of Integralism consists in having revived the old ideal of the Nation, exalting new *bandeirantes* for the conquest of the land and of ourselves. Spiritual force will give the world a new type of tropical civilization, full of ethereal and Christian spirituality."[15] If the intention here is to produce an epic effect by invoking "new *bandeirantes*" who will revive the national ideal in the tropics, making a *tabula rasa* of the historical *bandeirantes* thanks to a mythical one that is equal to European heroes and capable of uniting all social agents, there is also another mode to the juxtaposition of images where the epic yields its place to the dramatic: "In this phase of the disorganization of society, man transforms himself into a cruel machine. He no longer has a heart. Intimate life disappears. The club supersedes the home. And there is no deep affection in the home either, as there are no true friendships in clubs. Everyone revolves around interests. Men do not love each other: they tolerate each other so as to not to make life completely unbearable."[16] The arrangement of the images here allows for the construction of another: the image of "universal suffering" or "universal malaise," which proposes revolution as essential and also universal.

The image of revolution, in turn, illustrates the other mode of the function of images, that is, free association: "Revolution is not a revolt by mutinous soldiers; it is not a rebellion by peasants and proletarians;

it is not an armed movement by the oligarchic bourgeoisie; it is not a movement of troops from provincial governments; it is not a military blow; it is not a conspiracy of parties; it is not a generalized civil war. Revolution is a cultural and spiritual movement (. . .). It is not an offensive against a government, against a class: it is an offensive against civilization."[17] Salgado associates the Brazilian events of 1924, 1927, 1930, and 1932 to these negative images of revolution and establishes a link between these events and those of 1917, in Russia, and 1935, in Brazil. By associating distinct images of social mobilization or political movement without differentiating the historical processes in which they were carried out, he can produce a critique of what revolution lacks and, in this way, define the spiritual and civilizing place of the Integralist revolution.

Finally, let's move on to the third and most frequent operation of the discourse, that which reduces a concept to the condition of an image. Here, for instance, historical materialism is "translated" into hedonism and evolutionism. In order for this translation to take place, the discourse initially establishes a separation between the terms so that materialism connotes lifeless industry, hedonism, a rampant search for carnal pleasures (according to a strange combination of Marx and the epistles of Saint Paul), and the historical connotes "a biological type of deterministic evolutionism." It then becomes possible to claim that Marxism opposes the freedom of men. Doubly immoral, the concept of historical materialism is undone thanks to the association of images that, on the one hand, link together substances, machines, and "the carnal," and, on the other, associate history with blind evolution. Once we arrive at this point, where historical materialism becomes synonymous with naturalism, the discourse can pronounce: "Thus was Marxism. It brought about the brutality of the Darwinian "struggle for survival," the violence of the Hegelian conflict of ideas; it imagined human beings only under the economic aspect of reproduction. Yet by borrowing Hegel's dynamics of the dialectic, Marxism applied it to the action of the masses in history and unleashed the material revolution (. . .). Marxism unleashed hatred on the Earth; it accepted the principles of absorbent capitalism, sparked the struggle between classes; it provoked riots, revolts, bloody wars and eclipsed humanity in confusion, desperation and madness."[18]

The concept of social class undergoes similar metamorphosis. In the context of the critique of liberalism, the discourse affirms that class struggle was invented by liberal democracy wherein the weakened state allows for the appearance of "the panic of Capital" and the "misery of labor."[19] Viewed from a different angle, in the context of the critique of

Marxism, it appears responsible for causing class conflict—or a conflict between classes—at the same time as, in the context of the critique of liberalism, there is an attempt to use Marxist analysis, always clearly translated into Integralist images. In relation to the political project of the integral reorganization of society, the existence of class as something real tends to be denied, and Salgado can thus write: "Marxism functioned to show us that there are no classes. 'Military class,' 'religious class,' 'bourgeois class,' 'proletarian class, these concepts are inconceivable today.' The error of Marxism was its formal conception of class and its creation of a 'bourgeois class' and a 'proletarian class.' More modern than Marxists, 'we Integralists do not even accept the dualism of Capital and Work.' "[20]

Such affirmations, however, do not prevent the 1932 *Manifesto* from stating that "Brazil cannot achieve the perfect union of its children while (. . .) there are still classes struggling against classes, isolated individuals exerting personal actions in government decisions, that is, while there are all kinds of divisions among the Brazilian people. The nation therefore needs to organize itself into professional classes. Each Brazilian will register their own class."[21] Translating the concept of social class into the empirical basis of the professional class, the imagination performs the same function it carried out in the case of historical materialism, that is, it overshadows the explanatory force of the concept through its dilution into easily recognized images of daily experience. However, this operation now has a specific purpose that exceeds the simple attempt to prove the fallacy of Marxism, as occurred in the previous case. Translating class into profession, the discourse advances a central point of the Integralist political project: the corporatist organization of Brazilian society as a subsequent project of its own social experience. If the dilution of the concept of historical materialism delineates the counterrevolutionary profile of Integralism, the redefinition of class as profession in order to abolish social divisions by means of corporations leaves no doubt as to the devices that will be set in motion by the BIA to stop revolutionary whims. In this regard, what occurs to the concept of superstructure when clothed in Integralist images is suggestive. "Losing control of the nation, the liberal state was changed into superstructure, to use Marxist terminology, a luxury of bourgeois and capitalist civilization, a strange superficiality considering the organic imperatives of the people."[22] By moving from the concept of superstructure to the image of superfluity, the discourse lays the ground for the defense of something else: the strong, not "superstructural," state.

The aforementioned operations (juxtaposition, free association, translation) are in reality but one and the same operation, upon which the very image of integrated or integrating thought is based. Let us say that *it is the very image of Integralism that guides the operations of discourse in which the work of synthesis is substituted by the syncretism of imaginary juxtaposition or association.* Miguel Reale writes: "We synthesize, so to speak, the medieval spirit and the modern spirit. The Middle Ages knew the corporations, but it did not know the state; the Modern Age, which developed from the Renaissance and the Reformation until the Great War, passing through the landmarks of the English and French Revolutions, created the state, but after purifying the corporations, outlawed them. The Integralist doctrine does not understand the state without corporations. It is the natural march of History."[23] This style (common to all Integralist leaders) is illuminating: the way of enumerating, of establishing orders and sequences, of quickly grouping together all historical events according to similarity and of separating them according to dissimilarity, thereby establishing thought via analogies, not only economizes reflections concerning historical processes, but also assures the public of a presumed knowledge that convinces it that Integralism is the "natural march of History." Here the paradox of a movement intending to be a cultural revolution and a doctrine concerning civilization, but expressing itself in pamphleteering texts—clotted with words written in capital letters—is clarified, at least in part.

The use of images fulfills certain purposes that will be useful to outline, since they help to explain my previous statement regarding the authoritarian way of thinking.

The first effect of the use of images is epistemological: the images are an enhanced and luminous reflection of immediate experience, endowed with the capacity of unifying what appears to be fragmentary. By uniting the dispersed, the image—a mirror of immediate facts—prevents thought and contemplation and its ordering aspect simultaneously creates an illusion of knowledge. This procedure also has a psychological effect. It functions both to calm the public, by providing an order for its experience, and also to frighten them, by highlighting the disorder of the world. This psychological aspect, however, is merely the surface of something deeper and more obscure: the metaphysical need to guarantee and preserve identity against the disintegrating risk of contradiction. This need comes to light when nationalistic images enter the scene, simultaneously guaranteeing identity to the subject (the Brazilian) and to the object (the Brazilian nation) above and beyond contradictions, thereby making the subject and the object what they really are: abstractions, that is, images. Once the use of images, besides providing an order for reality without upsetting appearances, besides preventing the work of thought that would undermine immediate evidence, and besides counting on the support of confirming "facts," grants identity to its public, it starts to have a persuasive and even constraining force. We can now understand the political meaning of the use of images.

By analyzing authoritarianism discourse from its own exclusively theoretical or internal prism, we understand its intrinsic political meaning and style. An authoritarian way of thinking does not anticipate an authoritarian form of acting: this is ingrained in it. Abolishing the distance between the world and the discourse, images weld together the real and the word so that the former organizes its parameters in accordance with the latter, which then organizes reality and action. When dealing specifically with the latter, the role of images is clear: they foster a feeling in the public of the need to act and to act in a specific way; they also convince the public that those who pronounce the discourse can also guide the actions. The Integralist's imaginary goes hand in hand with the Enlightenment expressed in many of Plínio Salgado's texts, which demands an "enlightening" attitude from its vanguard, for whom the ignorance of the masses demands leaders to be *Aufklären*.

In his book Portuguese title O Integralismo Perante a Nação (*Integralism Faces the Nation*) Salgado asserts that "Integralism exerted its action in Brazil in three ways: 1) By developing intense cultural endeavors, courses, conferences, centers of research, and the study of national and human problems; 2) By organizing itself in the direction of greater efficiency in the moral and civic teaching of its youth and in the social ministry providing ample assistance to the popular classes; 3) By *teaching the Brazilian people what they should know of* their tradition, their realities, their possibilities, their future, through periodicals, magazines, urban assemblies, and the presence of lecturers in the fields and small cities of the interior."[24] The movement's educational nature finds its reason for being in the situation of the Brazilian people: "We cannot court the popular masses. They are unconscious and dull savages. On the contrary, we must irritate the savage so that it attacks us. We must provoke violent aggressions in order to exert decisive action. The people have already enslaved themselves to their exploiters for a long time. We should not praise the slave but save him from captivity, not with affability, but by imposing new forms of mentality."[25] This magisterial authoritarian doctrine accomplishes through images what the party will accomplish through acts, with no discontinuity between them.

Ethics and Violence in Brazil: A Difficult Democracy

The words *ta ethé* and *mores* have similar meanings, both signifying customs and ways of acting in society. In its singular form the word *ethos* refers to an individual character or temperament educated according to social values, while *ta ethiké* is a part of philosophy that deals with all forms of social character and conduct of individuals and that is dedicated to understanding a given society's intrinsic values, investigating, as a result, individual and collective human actions, exploring their meaning, origins, principles, and purposes.

All morals are normative, since their task is to impart social norms, customs, and values to individuals. Not all ethics however, are normative (Spinoza's ethics, for instance, is not). Normative ethics is an ethics of duties and obligations (Kantian ethics, for example). Nonnormative ethics is devoted to actions and passions directed toward the pursuit of happiness, and it takes as its criteria the relations between reason and free will in the exercise of freedom, understood as an expression of the singular nature of the ethical individual who aspires to happiness.

Nevertheless, whether normative or nonnormative, ethics as a philosophical investigation cannot exist without a theory that constructs ideas of the ethical agent, ethical action, and ethical values. From this general perspective, we can say that ethics seeks, above all, to define the figure of the ethical agent and their actions, as well as the set of notions (or values), that delimit the field of action that is considered ethical. The ethical agent is conceived as an ethical subject, in other words, as a *rational* and conscious individual fully aware of their own actions, as a *free* individual who decides and chooses their own actions, and as a responsible individual who responds for their own actions. The ethical action is supported by ideas of good and evil, just and unjust, virtue and vice, that is, by values whose content may vary from one society to another, or even within the history of a single society, but that always propose an intrinsic difference between forms of behavior based on what is good, just, and virtuous and those based on what is evil, unjust, and vicious. Therefore, an action is ethical only if it is conscious, free, and responsible, and it is virtuous only if it is realized according to what is good and just. The ethical action is virtuous only if it is free, and it can be free only if it is autonomous, that is, if it results from a decision intrinsic to the agent, not from obedience to an external order, command, or force. As the word itself suggests, autonomy (from the Greek *autos,* oneself, and *nomos,* rule or law) refers to a person who has the capacity of assigning to him or herself the norms and rules of their own action.

Evidently, this leads to the belief that there is a conflict between the autonomy of the ethical agent and the heteronomy of the moral values of his or her society: these values effectively constitute a set of duties and aims that, from outside, oblige the agent to perform in a determined manner and because of this operate as an external force that compel him or her to act according to something that was not self-directed. In other words, the agent does not act according to him or herself but rather according to something that is external to him or her, something that constitutes the moral of their society. This conflict can be resolved only if the agent recognizes the moral values of his or her society as though they had been self-instituted, as though he himself or herself had authored the values or moral norms of their very society. In this case, he or she would have provided themselves with the norms and rules of their own actions, thereby making it possible for them to be considered autonomous. For this reason, different philosophical ethics tend to resolve the conflict between the autonomy of the agent and the heteronomy of values and objectives by proposing the figure of the rational free and universal agent, a figure that every individual agent is in accordance with and that everyone recognizes as the institutor of moral norms and values. Thus, action is ethical only if it realizes the rational, free, and responsible nature of the agent, and if the agent respects the rationality, freedom, and responsibility of other agents, so that ethical subjectivity is intersubjective. Ethical subjectivity and intersubjectivity are actions, and ethics is that which exists through and in the actions of individual and social subjects, defined by ties and forms of sociability that are also created by human actions in historically determined conditions.

The word violence comes from the Latin word *vis,* force, and means (1) everything that acts by using force against the nature of a being (to denaturalize); (2) all acts of force against someone's spontaneity, will, and freedom (to coerce, constrain, torture, brutalize); (3) all acts that violate the nature of someone or something that is valued positively in society (to violate); (4) all acts of transgression against things and actions that someone or a society defines as just and as a right; (5) consequently, violence is an act of cruelty, brutality, and of physical and/or psychic abuse against someone, and it characterizes intersubjective and social relations that are defined by oppression, intimidation, fear, and terror.

Violence is opposed to ethics because it treats rational and conscious beings, endowed with language and freedom, as though they were objects or things, as though they were irrational, unconscious, silent, inert, or passive. Insofar as ethics is inseparable from the figure of the rational, free, and responsible subject, to treat someone as devoid of reason, freedom, and responsibility is to treat them not as a human being but as a thing, subjecting them to the five meanings of the word violence outlined above.

There is much discussion these days concerning "a return to ethics" or "a need for ethics." A crisis of values is mentioned, as is the need to return to ethics, as though ethics were something that is always ready and available, something that is periodically misplaced or lost and that must periodically be recovered. The implication here is that ethics is something that is acquired, possessed, lost, and found rather than a conscious, free, and intersubjective action that is achieved by our actions and that exists because of and through our actions. How can we explain this emphasis on the "return to ethics?" We can explain it by the following:

- the weakening of social and political movements fighting for emancipation has created a vacuum that, faced with no opposition, neoliberal ideology now occupies on its own terms;

- today's expanded accumulation of capital, known as flexible accumulation, has led to a dispersal and fragmentation of social groups and classes, destroying old forms of identity and action and problematizing the formation of new social ties, so that fragmentation and dispersion appear natural and are offered up as positive values;

- the naturalization and positive valorization of socioeconomic fragmentation and dispersal appears, on the one hand, in the neoliberal emphasis on competitive individualism and on success at all costs; and on the other, as the redemption from an egotism through the production of communitarian sentiments by all forms of

religious fundamentalism. The emphasis on aggressive individualism and the search for religious orthodoxy destroy the fields of
intersubjective action and sociopolitics as fields of an opening up
and a collective realization of the possible in time, that is, of historical creation.

- technological changes: from the moment that technique ceases to
be an applied science to become a science that is crystallized in
objects of human intervention in nature and society, technology is
transformed not only into a form of power but also a productive
force and an integral part of capital. This transformation occurs
exclusively within the logic of the market. It involves its transformation into a logic of power as a decision concerning life and death
at a global scale.

- the media society and the consumption of ephemeral, perishable,
and disposable goods generate a new type of subjectivity, that of
the narcissistic subject who surrenders to the cult of his or her own
image as the only available reality, which precisely because it is
narcissistic demands that which the media and mass consumption
ceaselessly offer, that is, the immediate satisfaction of desires and
the unlimited promise of youth, health, beauty, success, and happiness. These are offered through fetishes, or promises, that can,
however, never be fulfilled and, therefore, lead to frustration and
nihilism.

In this context the phrase "return to ethics" emerges as a general
elixir. But how is this "ethics" that is to be "returned to" conceived?

First, it is conceived as a reform of customs (and, therefore, morality)
and as a restoration of values, not as an analysis of the present conditions of an ethical action.

Second, it is conceived as a dispersal of ethics (political, social, domestic, professional, scholarly, entrepreneurial, medical, and academic)
devoid of any universality because it reflects, without criticizing or analyzing, socioeconomic diffusion and fragmentation. Ethics is confused
with the organization and division of functions and responsibilities in
firms and bureaucracies, and, therefore, as a code of actions defined
according to the functional objectives of these institutions. More than
ideological, this plurality of "ethics" is the expression of the contemporary form of alienation, of a society that is so dispersed and fragmented
that it is even unable to construct for itself an image of unity, one that
would give meaning to its own dispersal. Fragmented into smaller local

forms, what has ethics been reduced to? It is now understood as the specific expertise of specialists (ethical commissions) who define local rules, norms, and objectives and judge the actions of others according to these localized parameters, which frequently contradict other local patterns since capitalist society is forged from internal contradictions.

Third, it is understood as the humanitarian defense of human rights against violence, both as an indignant comment on politics, science, technology, the media, the police, and the army, and as a demand for medical, military, and nutritional aid for the poor. It is at this moment that NGOs cease being seen and understood as part of broader social movements linked to citizenship, and are reduced to being social assistance organizations that the image of the victims imposes on the guilty consciences of the privileged.

Conceived in this way ethics is transformed into ideology pure and simple, and as such, it is useful for the exercise of violence. Why does this occur?

First, it occurs because the ethical subject, or the subject of rights, is splintered into two: on the one hand, the ethical subject as a victim, who suffers passively; on the other, the ethical subject, as a virtuous and compassionate person, who identifies the suffering of others and acts to allay it. This victimization means that acting is concentrated in the hands of the "nonsufferers," of the nonvictims, who should provide, from the outside, justice to those who do not have it. The victims thus lose their condition as ethical subjects to become objects of our compassion. This means that in order for nonsufferers to be conceived as ethical, two forms of violence are necessary. The first, in fact, is the existence of victims; the second is the treatment of another as a passive and inert victim. This explains the fear caused by Brazil's Landless Workers' Movement, which refuses to assume the condition of the passive, silent, and inert victim, refuses compassion and, in a typical inverted ideology, is considered a nonethical subject and an agent of violence.[1]

Second, it occurs because, as Alain Badiou has clearly observed in his essay *On the Understanding of Evil,* while in ethics it is the idea of the good, the just, and of happiness that determines the ethical subject's self-construction, in ethical ideology, it is the image of evil that determines the image of the good, that is, the good simply becomes the absence of evil (not being offended, not being mistreated in body and spirit is the good). The good becomes the mere privation of evil; it is not something affirmative or positive, it is purely reactive. This is why ethics as an ideology highlights and underscores individual and collective suffering, political and police corruption, since these images offer visible facts that sustain its discourse and attempt to obtain a popular consensus: we all oppose evil; however, don't ask us about what is good because opinion concerning this is divided and, as we all know, "modernity" is fundamentally consensual.

Third, it occurs because the images of evil and of the victims possess considerable appeal in the media: they are powerful images presenting a spectacle for our indignation and compassion, intending to appease our guilty consciences. We need images of violence to conceive of ourselves as ethical subjects.

Instead of uniting people around positive ideas and practices of freedom and happiness, ethics as ideology unites them by the consensus regarding evil. Ethics as ideology is, therefore, doubly perverse. On the one hand, it seeks to base itself in an image of the present, one that is ostensibly eternal and also independent, one that does not result from human actions and has no roots in the past or links to the future; in other words, it reduces the present to the immediate instant, with no memory and no future. On the other hand, ethics as ideology seeks to show that any positive idea of good, happiness, and freedom, of justice and human emancipation is evil. In other words, it considers as responsible for the present evil modern ideas of rationality, of the meaning of history, of the objectivity, and subjectivity, and the notion that human action can open temporal possibilities. It ultimately treats them as totalitarian mystifications. Ethics as ideology is perverse because it treats the present as inevitable fate and annuls the essential characteristic of the ethical subject and of the ethical action, which is freedom.

* * *

There is a powerful myth in Brazil, that of Brazil's non-violence, that is, the image of a generous, cheerful, sensual, and supportive people, who are untouched by racism, sexism, and *machismo*, who respect ethnic, religious, and political differences and do not discriminate against people on the basis of sexual preference, and so on. Why do I use the word "myth" and not the concept of ideology to refer to the way in which non-violence is imagined in Brazil? I use the word "myth" because of its following characteristics:

1. As the Greek word *mythos* indicates, myth is a narrative of origins, which is reiterated in numerous stories, which repeat an initial narrative pattern that is itself a variant of a narrative of origins

that have been lost. In short, myth is a narrative of origins without an original narrative;

2. The myth operates through antinomies, tensions, and contradictions that cannot be resolved without a profound transformation of society and because of this are transferred to a symbolic and imaginary solution that justifies and supports reality. Myth thus denies reality at the same time that it justifies it;

3. The myth is crystallized in beliefs that are interiorized to the extent that they are not perceived as beliefs but rather are seen not only as an explanation of reality but also as reality itself. The myth, therefore, replaces reality with a belief in the reality it narrates, making the existing reality invisible;

4. The myth is the result of social actions and it produces, in turn, other social actions that corroborate it. This means that the myth generates values, ideas, and ways of behaving in society that function to reiterate it in and through the actions of the very members of society. The myth, therefore, is not just a way of thinking, but a form of action.

5. The myth has an appeasing and repetitive function, ensuring society's self-preservation throughout historical transformations. This means that the myth is the basis of ideologies: it fabricates them in order to simultaneously confront and negate historical transformations, since each ideological form is charged with maintaining the initial myth of origins. To summarize, ideology is the temporal expression of a foundational myth that society narrates to itself.

I, therefore, use the word myth in the anthropological sense, that is, as an imaginary solution for tensions, conflicts, and contradictions that cannot be resolved neither in the realm of the symbolic nor in reality. I speak of a foundational myth because, as with all foundations, it constructs an internal link with the past as origin, that is, with a past that does not cease, does not permit the work of historical difference and maintains itself perennially present. I, therefore, use the word myth also in the psychoanalytic sense, that is, as the impulse to repetition, because of the impossibility of symbolization and, above all, as a blockage in the passage toward reality. A foundational myth never ceases to find new ways of expressing itself, new languages, new values, and ideas, so that, the more it seems to be something else, the more it is a repetition of itself. In our case, the foundational myth is the essential non-violence of Brazilian society, whose elaboration dates back to the period of the discovery and the conquest of Brazil. The great myth that nourishes Brazil's social imaginary is, therefore, that of non-violence. Our self-image is one of an ordered and peaceful people, who are happy and cordial, racially mixed and incapable of ethnic, religious, or social discriminations; who are friendly to foreigners, generous with the needy, proud of our regional differences, blessed by nature and destined by God for a great future.

Many will ask themselves how the myth of non-violence is able to persist in the context of real, everyday violence that is so familiar in Brazil and that has recently been amplified by its dissemination in the media. Yet, it is precisely in the way that violence is represented that the myth finds its means of self-preservation. The myth of non-violence persists because it acknowledges the real empirical existence of violence, while at the same time fabricating explanations that negate it at the very moment that it appears. I am referring here to the recent production of the image of violence produced by various figures of violence that function to conceal real violence. This concealment is striking because it takes place precisely at the very moment that the media exposes and exhibits acts of violence.

If we focus on the language employed by the press, radio, and television, we can see that the terms they use are distributed in a systematic manner:

- the words *slaughter* and *massacre* are used to refer to the mass murder of defenseless people, such as street children, *favelados*, prisoners, the landless;

- the words' *lack of distinction between crime and police action* are used when referring to the participation of police forces in organized crime, especially illegal gambling, drug trafficking, and kidnapping;

- references to an *undeclared civil war* are used when speaking of the Landless Workers' Movement and to confrontations between the *garimpeiros*[2] and Indians, the police and drug traffickers, to large- and small-scale homicides and robberies; as well as to the increasing number of unemployed workers and street dwellers, to the looting of stores and supermarkets and road accidents;

- *weakness of civil society* is used to refer to the lack of social institutions and organizations that articulate critiques and call for investigations into public institutions;

- *weakness of political institutions* refers to corruption in the powers of the Republic, delays in justice, and absence of political modernization;
- the words *ethical crisis* are used to refer to unmotivated crimes, to illicit links between the bourgeoisie and public powers in order to obtain public resources for private objectives, to the lack of political decorum, to the impunity of the awful treatment of consumers by industry and commerce and the impunity of malpractice cases.

These images function to offer a unified image of violence that appears to be their nucleus. Murder, massacre, an undeclared civil war, the lack of a distinction between police action and crime contend to be *the place where* violence is situated and realized. The weakness of civil society, the weakness of political institutions and the ethical crisis are presented as *impotent in combating* a violence that is, therefore, seemingly located elsewhere.

The images of violence point to a division between two groups: on the one hand are the *bearers* of violence, and on the other those who are *impotent* in combating it. It is precisely this division that allows us to talk of an ideology of ethics or of ethics as an ideology. Otherwise, how can we explain the fact that the continuous exhibition of violence, during at least the last twenty years, has not affected the myth of Brazil's non-violence and has, moreover, given rise to the call for the "return to ethics"? In order to answer this, we must examine the ideological mechanisms that preserve the myth.

The first mechanism is that of *exclusion*. The idea of Brazil as a non-violent nation is constantly reaffirmed; when there is violence, it is caused by people who do not belong to the nation (even thought they were born or live here). The mechanism of exclusion produces a difference between us, the non-violent Brazilians and them, the violent non-Brazilians. *They* are not part of *us*.

The second mechanism is that of *distinction*. The essential is distinguished from the accidental. Brazilians are, essentially, non-violent, and violence is, therefore, accidental, a fleeting occurrence, an "epidemic" or an "outbreak" that emerges on the surface at a particular time and in a defined space, one that can be overcome, leaving our essential non-violent nature intact.

The third mechanism is *judicial*. Violence is circumscribed to the field of delinquency and criminality, in which crime is defined as an attack on private property (theft, burglary, and robbery). This strategy facilitates the identification of the "violent agents" (generally the poor) and it legitimizes police action (which is violent) against the poor, black, street children, and the *favelados*. Police action may, at times, be considered violent, and is referred to as *slaughter* or *massacre* when it appears to have been unjustified or when the number of victims is very high. Mostly, however, police action is considered normal and natural when it is concerned with protecting *us* against *them*.

The fourth mechanism is *sociological*. The "epidemic" of violence is attributed to a particularly defined moment in time that takes place during the "transition to modernity" undertaken by populations who migrated from rural areas to the city and from the country's poorer regions (the North and Northeast) to its richer areas (the South and Southeast). Migration, according to some Brazilian sociologists, must cause the temporary phenomenon of *anomie*, in which the loss of old forms of sociability have not yet been substituted by new ones, causing many poor migrants to carry out isolated acts of violence that will disappear once they have completed their "transition." Here, violence is not only ascribed exclusively to the poor and "unadapted;" it is also consecrated as something that is temporary and episodic.

The final mechanism is that of the *inversion of reality,* thanks to the production of masks that disguise violent ideas, values, and behavior as non-violent. Sexism, for instance, appears as a logical form of protection against women's natural weakness and includes the idea that women need to be protected from themselves, since, as is well known, rape is the outcome of feminine actions of provocation and seduction. White paternalism is considered an act of helping naturally inferior blacks. The repression of homosexuality is viewed as a defense of the sacred values of the family and the well-being of all humans now threatened by AIDS caused by these "degenerates." Environmental destruction is proudly seen as a sign of civilization and progress.

To summarize, violence is not perceived where it actually originates and where it becomes violence, that is, as all practices and ideas that reduce a person to the condition of a thing, actions that internally or externally violate someone's being and that perpetuate social relations based on profound social, cultural, and economic inequalities. Moreover, society does not perceive that the very explanations it offers are themselves violent because it is blind to the place that effectively produces violence, that is, the structure of Brazilian society. As a result, economic and political inequalities and exclusions, institutional corruption, racism, sexism, and religious, sexual, and political intolerance, are not considered forms of violence. Brazilian society is not perceived as structurally violent and violence thus appears as a sporadic and superficial fact. The myth and its ideological procedures mean that the violence that structures and organizes Brazil's social relations remains unacknowledged and, therefore, naturalized. Its naturalization allows for the myth of non-violence to be preserved, giving rise to the call for a "return to ethics."

This originary myth is preserved because it is periodically revised with notions that correspond to the historical present. In other words, the mythology is preserved thanks to ideologies. These, in turn, find a real material basis in order to construct themselves as imaginary expressions in Brazilian society: social authoritarianism. In other words, the country's social structure and organization reiterates, nourishes, and repeats the myth because it is one of the foundations of the very form of our society.

Preserving traces of its colonial slave-holding past, Brazilian society is marked by the predominance of private space over public space, and with the family order as its center, it is strongly hierarchical in all aspects: social and intersubjective relations are invariably characterized by a superior who gives orders and by an inferior who obeys them. Differences and asymmetrical relations are transformed into inequalities that reinforce these relations of order and obedience. The "other" is never acknowledged as a subject with rights, a subjectivity, or alterity. Relations among those who are considered equals are based on kinship, that is, they are relations of complicity and those among people who are considered unequal are based on the practice of favor, a form of clientelism, tutelage, or co-optation, and when inequalities are extreme, they take on the form of oppression. Micropowers are thus propagated throughout society and the authoritarianism of Brazil's familial structure extends to relations at work, school, the street, the media, as well as to personal relations, to the treatment of citizens by the state, the market's disregard for consumer's rights (at the heart of capitalist ideology) and the naturalization of police violence.

We can, therefore, summarize the principal traits of our social authoritarianism, in view of the fact that the following aspects characterize Brazilian society:

- Structured according to the model of the nuclear family, it imposes an implicit (at times explicit) negation of the liberal principle of formal equality, and inhibits struggles for the socialist principle of real equality: differences are posited as inequalities that stem from a natural inferiority (in the case of women, workers, blacks,

Indians, migrants, and the elderly) or an aberration (in the case of homosexuals).

- Structured in terms of family relations of order and obedience, it imposes an implicit (at times explicit) negation of acknowledging the liberal principle of judicial equality and inhibits the struggle against forms of social and economic oppression: for the elite, the law is a privilege, for the popular classes it is repression. The law should not and does not represent public power, it does not regulate conflicts, and has never defined the rights and duties of citizens, for the role of the law is to maintain privileges and exercise repression. Because of this, laws seem innocuous, useless, and incomprehensible. They are made to be transgressed, not transformed. Judicial power is perceived as something distant and secret. It represents the privileges of the oligarchy, and not the rights of society in general.

- The lack of distinction between public and private in Brazil is not a defect, nor is it a symptom of the country's backwardness; rather it is the outcome of society and politics: it is not just that politicians and parliamentarians practice corruption using public funds, but also that there is no notion of a public sphere of opinions, of a social collectivity, of the street as a shared space, just as there is no notion of the rights to privacy and intimacy. From the point of view of social rights there has been a restriction of the public sphere; from the point of view of economic interests, there has been an expansion of the private sphere. It is precisely because of this that the idea of the "strong state" has always been natural here and because of this too that liberalism fits us like a glove.

- A particular way of avoiding social, economic, and political conflicts and contradictions, once they negate the mythical image of the good society, a coherent, united, and peaceful commonwealth. It is not that conflicts and contradictions are ignored, but rather that they have a very precise meaning: they are seen as synonymous with danger, crisis, and disorder, for which there is only one response: political and military repression of the popular classes and a contempt of all opposition. A self-organizing society is, therefore, seen as dangerous for the state and for the "rational" functioning of the market.

- A particular way of blocking the sphere of public opinion as an expression of the interests and rights of different groups and social classes. This blocking is not an absence or void, it is a combination of certain actions that translate a specific way of dealing with the sphere of opinion: the mass media monopolizes information, and consensus becomes conflated with unanimity, so that dissent is posited as backwardness or ignorance.

- The naturalization of economic and social inequalities, as well as the naturalization of ethnic differences, which is put forward as racial inequalities between superiors and inferiors, the naturalization of religious and gender differences, as well as of visible and invisible forms of violence.

- The fascination with signs of prestige and power: the use of honorific titles that bear no relation to their designation, the most common being "doctor" used when referring to people deemed superior in social relations, in which the title "doctor" becomes an imaginary substitute for earlier titles of nobility; the employment of domestic servants whose number is seen as an indication of prestige and status, and so on.

Authoritarianism is, therefore, interiorized in the hearts and minds of a people who are able to use phrases such as "a black man with a white soul" and not be considered racist; who can assert that their maids are "great workers because they know their place" and not consider this as an example of class prejudice; can refer to workers as "trustworthy because they don't rob" and claim that there is no class struggle in Brazil; who can say that a woman is "perfect, because she has not given up her place in the home for the indignity of work" and believe that they are not sexist.

The disparity in wages between men and women, blacks and whites, the exploitation of children and of the elderly are considered normal. The existence of landless, homeless, and unemployed people is attributed to the ignorance, laziness, and incompetence of the "wretched." The existence of street children is interpreted as an outcome of "the poor's natural tendency to criminality." Accidents at work are attributed to workers' incompetence and ignorance. Women who work are potential prostitutes (unless they are teachers or social workers) and prostitutes are degenerate, perverse, and delinquent, albeit unfortunately indispensable for maintaining the sanctity of the family.

Brazilian society is oligarchic and is polarized between the absolute deprivation of its popular classes and the absolute privilege of its dominant and ruling classes.

The authoritarian ideology that "naturalizes" inequalities and socioeconomic exclusions is expressed by the way politics operates. The dominant class practices politics from a naturalist-theocratic point of view, that is, leaders occupy power by natural right and divine selection. For the popular classes, the political imaginary is messianic and millenarian, corresponding to the self-image of the ruling class. Consequently, politics is not configured as a field of social struggles; it functions at the level of theological representation, oscillating between socialization and the adulation of a good leader, and the demonization and denunciation of evil. The state is perceived only as an executive power; legislative and judicial powers are reduced to feelings that the latter is unjust and the former corrupt. The identification between the state and executive power, the absence of a reliable legislative power and fear of judicial power, along with the social authoritarian ideology and theological-political imaginary, create the permanent desire for a "strong state" that can lead everyone to "national salvation." For its part, the state transforms civil society into a dangerous enemy, blocking the initiatives of social, labor, and popular movements.

We live in a hierarchical and vertical society (although we may not perceive this) in which social relations function either as a form of complicity (when social subjects believe themselves to be equal) or as a form of order-obedience between a superior and inferior (when subjects are seen as different, difference not being considered as asymmetry but rather as inequality). We can, therefore, comprehend the difficulty of formulating a democratic politics, based on ideas of citizenship and representation. In Brazil, this has been substituted by favor, clientelism, tutelage, co-optation, by vanguard educationalists' pretentions. We can also comprehend why ideas of social justice, liberty, and happiness are placed in a utopian realm.

Two great neoliberal gifts can be added to this general situation: in the economic sphere, a form of accumulation that does not need to incorporate more people into labor and consumer markets because it operates with structural unemployment; in the political sphere, the privatization of the public, that is, not only the abandonment of social politics by the state, but also the strengthening of the historical structure of Brazilian society centered in the private sphere, has increased the impossibility of constructing a public sphere, since before the difference between the public and the private were forged here, the new form of capital instituted the lack of differentiation between the public and the private. Politics is reduced to a narcissistic marketing of private life, and the state is reduced to an apparatus that strengthens privileges (a Brazilian style "privatization" simply involves transferring state mechanisms of protection against the oligopoly to the oligopoly itself).

Politically and socially the neoliberal economy is a project of restricting public space and extending private space—hence its essentially anti-democratic character—and thus it fits Brazilian society like a glove. In the case of Brazil, this has led to extreme polarizations between the privileged and the poor, the sociopolitical exclusion of the popular classes, the disorganization of society as a mass of unemployed workers; it has involved solidifying and finding new reasons to justify the oligar-chic structure of politics, its social authoritarianism, and for blocking democracy.

Maurice Merleau-Ponty once wrote that ethics and politics are impossible if we believe either that everything is necessary or that everything is contingent. Against this rival dualism between necessity and contingency, he proposed the idea of the possible: the possible is not the probable, neither is it the not-impossible; the possible is the power of our freedom to give a real situation (necessary or contingent) new meaning acquired only through our action. Freedom is, therefore, the power to transcend the present in a new sense that transforms it into the future. If ethics is possible, it exists in this action that creates its own meaning, not in the undignified and compassionate reaction to evil. Merleau-Ponty also wrote that good and evil do not lie within ourselves, neither do they lie in other people or objects, but rather in the ties that we weave among ourselves and that either suffocate or liberate us. We should not counter this with suffering or compassion, he added, but with *virtù* and without resignation.

Popular Culture and Authoritarianism

An Authoritarian Society

Brazil is an authoritarian society, for, even on the verge of the twenty-first century, it has yet to fully realize the (300-year old) principles of liberalism and republicanism. It is a society in which there is no distinction between the public and the private, in which there is an inability to tolerate the formal and abstract principle of equality before the law, in which the dominant class contests the general ideas contained within the Declaration of the Rights of Man and of Citizens, in which social and popular forms of struggle and organization are repressed, in which racial, sexual, and class discrimination are pervasive. Brazilian society, while sporting the appearance of fluidity (for sociological categories suitable for describing European and North American societies seem to fall short of capturing Brazilian reality) is structured in a rigorously hierarchical manner; here, not only does the state appear as the founder of the very social, but also social relations are formed by notions of tutelage and favor (never rights), and legality is constituted as a fatal cycle of the arbitrary judgment (of the dominant) over the transgression (of the dominated).

Cultural scholars frequently attribute this authoritarianism to the Iberian origins of colonization. Roberto Schwarz's interpretation of the peculiarities of a society in which political liberalism is erected upon a slave society is the most useful in countering this perspective.[1]

The military coup of 1964, paradoxically dubbed a "revolution," undoubtedly reinforced the features of authoritarianism.

While calling itself a nationalism that was responsible (with no social and political movements), pragmatic (based on the economic model of foreign debt and the triumvirate of state, multinationals and national industries) and modern (technocratic), by the mid-1960s the coup instituted a form of power concentrated in the executive and based on laws of exception (Institutional and Complementary Acts), the militarization of everyday life, initially called a "permanent war on the internal enemy" that, following the eradication of subversive and guerilla groups, shifted the focus of its military-repressive apparatus to the daily behavior of the general population, concentrating especially on workers, both rural and urban (particularly the opposition's unionists), the unemployed, blacks, juvenile delinquents, prisoners, and other delinquents (including transvestites and prostitutes).

The "regime," the term employed for this governmental façade, is directed by the "system," that is, by the National Information Service and the so-called Information Community—that guaranteed the implementation of an inflationary monetary policy, based on reducing salaries and repressing workers' movements (the so-called Brazilian Miracle).[2] This policy exacerbated socioeconomic inequalities, produced an accelerated yet artificial economic growth through systems of credit and government subsidies, funded by internationally financed loans (the famous "foreign debt"), consolidating the state's intervention in the economy through state and mixed-venture companies.

This new regime—or the System—based itself on a geopolitical ideology inherited from the East-West division forged during the Cold War and manifested in the National Security Doctrine and had the intention of turning Brazil into a world power by the year 2000. This goal was to be met thanks to ideas of national development (the "economic miracle" i.e., the public debt), national integration (i.e., the centralization of sociopolitical decisions, considered mere technical questions), and national security (anticommunism). Under the auspices of the idea of planning, the regime and ideology became known as *Conservative Modernization* (an expression that was well received among Brazilian and North American political scientists and that led them to call the state a "new" authoritarianism, in order to distinguish it from an "older" more personal *caudilho* style).

The fact that this political situation coalesced shortly after João Goulart's populist government, which was marked by a popular presence in the public sphere, led to the formation of a curious historical memory. According to this memory, between the years 1946 (the end of the dictatorship of Getúlio Vargas known as the New State) and 1964 (the end of Goulart's populist government with the coup of April 1) Brazil had been a democracy. This memory is paradoxical because it is marked by a number of significant lapses. For instance, the fact that the Constitution of 1946 illegalized strikes, upheld the

Labor legislation authorized by the Vargas dictatorship (a literal repro-duction of Mussolini's *Carta del Lavoro*), prohibited voting rights for the illiterate (the majority of the population at this time), criminalized the Communist Party, conserved racial discrimination, and, finally, did not oppose discrimination against women consecrated in the Civil and Penal codes.

This curious memory, proclaimed the coup of '64 as a rupture in Brazil's democratic order (initially considered by theorists of develop-mentalism as an impossible rupture, once capitalism and democracy come together; and, then as inevitable by the dependency theorists, because the accumulation of capital and repression walk hand-in-hand), prioritizes the *re*-democratization of the country, undertaking the establishment of new links between civil society and the state, to use the terminology of progressives, or between the nation and the state, to use the terminology of conservatives.

From this perspective, 1975 is the year when the country embarked upon a process of "re"-democratization, when General Golbery's curi-ous political organ resulted in the "distention" of General Geisel's government and subsequently the process of *"abertura"* (opening) of General Figueiredo's government. *Abertura*, also known as the "liberal-ization of the regime," culminated in the following events: the suspen-sion of the Fifth Institutional Act[3] (really displaced only from a single *corpus* toward a plurality of laws and institutions deemed to be "safe-guarding" measures, with no suspension of the National Security Law or the regime's right arm, the National Information Service), amnesty for political prisoners and exiles, the return to a multiparty system, direct elections of state governors and the election of a civilian for the office of President of the Republic in 1985 (although this election was actually indirect as it was carried out by a coalition of opposing fac-tions and government forces, in the classically Brazilian *Conciliation from Above*, which obscured the social movement for direct elections). Having initiated the so-called Transition to Democracy, the economic model remained intact. To use less pompous terms, civil government was subject to a military veto.

Transmitted via this memory, the interpretation of Brazil's political reality has two fundamental characteristics: on the one hand, it visual-izes the changes taking place in Brazil privileging the actions of the state and giving little or no importance to the popular social movements that contributed to them (which is paradoxical when dealing with democ-ratization); on the other hand, it defines authoritarianism not only as "rupture" or "exception," but also largely and principally as a political regime, or rather as a form of government, overlooking the fundamental quality of Brazilian *society*, that it is authoritarian. Moreover, this memory, which privileges actions from above and minimizes practices of contestation and popular social resistance, is, in itself, authoritarian.

A more inclusive memory would seek to recall that, from the point of view of those governing, liberalization was seen as an instrument that could resolve problems created by the impasses of the economic model, thereby sharing the burden of this crisis with society. They also viewed liberalization as an acknowledgment or approval of the population's civil rights (or just civil rights). This does not, however, mean that these views were correct; nor does it mean that they were the only views possible. In fact, from 1974 (the MDB or the *Brazilian Democratic Movement's* victory in the proportional elections is the clearest indication of this) different sectors of the social classes challenged the regime, which was compelled to provide them with an answer.

We would undoubtedly be deceiving ourselves significantly if we imagined that all demands, challenges, and resistances stemming from society, which appeared to be social struggles for democratization, had the same origins, motivations, and contents.

For example, from 1976 onward, the business community viewed the struggle as the simple liberalization of the regime, which was always discussed as an opposition between statism and free initiative in the economic domain. These discussions invariably focused on reducing the degree of the state's interference in the economy. It was only gradually that business owners realized that liberalization would entail more significant political changes than initially desired, changes that could not be confined to the domain of economic decisions.

For the middle class, discussions revolved around amnesty for political prisoners and exiles (all predominantly from the middle class given the nature of guerrilla recruitment), freedom of the press (journalists too were largely from this class), the democratization of public services, particularly education (involving the student movement and professors of all ranks), healthcare (involving the doctors' and social workers' movement), an end to police and military violence—especially the torture of prisoners—and changes to the penal system, which included psychiatric hospitals. In short, there was a concentration of social movements that aimed to develop dialogue and open up the decision-making cores of public and private institutions.

For workers (principally industrial workers in the South and opposition unionists), the struggle involved the unions' freedom and autonomy from the state that controlled them through compulsory union membership; it sought the right to strike and to form factory commissions that could monitor production and prevent high job turnover and instability, as well as protect against violence in the work place; it fought for the minimum wage, equality for female workers, land distribution and ownership rights for squatters, the redistribution of wealth, workers' involvement in company budgets and finances, and the formation of a single workers' center that would override the corporatist divisions instituted by labor legislation.

Social movements formed by minorities, such as blacks and women, succeeded in joining ranks with these three other movements, thereby bringing together elements from different social classes as well as different political tendencies: these included the struggle for human rights (led principally by the Brazilian Bar Association and the Catholic Commission for Justice and Peace), the struggle against Immigration and National Security Laws and the demands for a free and sovereign Constitutional National Assembly, elected through universal suffrage.

* * *

In what ways is Brazilian society authoritarian?

It is a society that configured citizenship through an unprecedented figure: the citizen-lord, who upholds citizenship as a class privilege; a regulated and inconstant concession made to the other social classes, and one that may be retracted when deemed necessary (during dictatorships, for instance).

It is a society in which social and personal differences and asymmetries are directly transformed into inequalities and consequently, into relations of rank, command, and obedience (a situation that extends from the family to the state, that traverses public and private institutions and that permeates culture and interpersonal relationships). Individuals are immediately distinguished as superior or inferior, although someone who is superior in one particular situation may be inferior in another depending upon the codes of hierarchization that govern social and personal relations. All relations take the form of dependence, tutelage, concession, authority, and favor, transforming symbolic violence into the norm of social and cultural life. This violence is all the greater as it is masked by paternalism and clientelism, which are considered natural and are, at times, even exalted as positive traits of the "national character."

It is a society in which laws have always been the means of preserving privilege, as well as the best instruments for repression and oppression; they have never been the means of defining rights or responsibilities. Rights are always presented to the popular classes as a special dispensation and function, which authorizes the state's activities as they depend on the personal will or judgment of those governing. This situation is clearly recognized by workers who state that "justice only exists for the wealthy." It is also part of a more diffuse social awareness as conveyed in the well-known national expression: "for our friends, everything; for our enemies, the law." Consequently, it is a society in which laws have always been considered useless, innocuous, or made to be broken; they are never seen as something to be transformed or challenged. It is a society in which popular transgression is violently repressed and punished, while the transgression of the powerful always goes unpunished.

It is a society in which neither the idea nor the practice of political representation exists. Political parties always take the form of clientelism (a relation between inferiors and superiors mediated by favor), populism (a relation based on tutelage), and, in the case of the Left, vanguardism (a relation based on a pedagogical substitution, the "enlightened" vanguard taking the place of a universal "retrograde" class).

This situation profoundly shapes intellectual and artistic life—most of which originates from the urban middle classes and oscillate between the positions of the Enlightened (defining for themselves the "right to the public use of reason," i.e., to public opinion) and the Revolutionary Vanguard (defining for themselves the role of educators of the working class), who are always fascinated by power, which is identified with the state and with state tutelage, therefore, relegating themselves to the status of being, to use Hegel's expression, "civil servants of the universal" (bureaucracy, as Marx would put it), although they may desire the role of civil servants of "reason in history."

Consequently, it is a society in which the public sphere is never constituted as public. It is always defined according to the demands of private space, so that will and judgment are the defining features of the government and of "public institutions." This explains the fascination that theoreticians and agents of "modernization" have with technocratic models that they believe are imbued with the kind of impersonal nature that can define public space. It also explains political scientists' strange description of Brazilian authoritarianism (and Latin American in general) as the "new authoritarianism," simply because the figure of the charismatic ruler or *caudilho* is seemingly absent. In doing so, these scientists fail to observe that the *structure of the social and political fields are themselves determined by the indistinction between the public and the private*. It also explains the error of those who present the "new authoritarianism" as a separation between civil society and the state, without noting that *civil society itself is structured by relations of favor, tutelage, dependence, the immense reflection of the state, and vice-versa.*

It is a society, therefore, in which the struggle of classes[4] is perceived only at moments in which there is a direct confrontation between the classes—which becomes a "police issue"—and does not take into account its manifestation in daily life in the techniques of discipline, surveillance, and repression carried out by dominant institutions—it is at these moments when the struggle of classes becomes a "political issue."

It is a society in which disputes over the possession of farmed or arable land are resolved with armed struggles and clandestine assassinations; in which economic inequalities can be linked to genocide (the estimated deaths of more than 5 million people in the Northeast is due to malnutrition and hunger). It is a society in which blacks are seen as infantile and ignorant, an inferior and dangerous race. This is a race that is represented by lettered culture as the Harlequin. One that is characterized even more negatively in an inscription in São Paulo's Police Academy: "When standing still, a black man is suspicious, when running he is guilty." It is a society in which Indians are seen as irresponsible (i.e., incapable of citizenship), lazy (unable to adapt to the capitalist labor market), dangerous, and who need either to be exterminated or to be "civilized" (meaning turned over to the ravages of being bought and sold on the labor market, yet with little labor rights due to their "irresponsibility"), while lettered culture since Romanticism has presented the Indian as the heroic and epic founder of the "Brazilian race." It is a society in which rural and urban workers are seen as ignorant, backward, and dangerous; where the police are authorized to stop any of them in the streets, check their identification, and take them into custody if they don't have any (if they are black, the police are authorized to not only check their identification but also to examine their hands for "signs of work" and take them in if none are found). It is a society in which women who turn to the police when they are beaten or raped are subsequently violated in police stations where they are again beaten or raped by the "authorities." Not to mention the torture carried out in prisons on homosexuals, prostitutes, and petty criminals. In sum, these are the so-called subaltern classes, who are stigmatized by the constant burden of suspicion, guilt, and discrimination. This situation is all the more terrifying if we remember that instruments developed to torture political prisoners were transferred to the daily treatment of the working population, and that the reigning ideology attributes this violence to the misery of its victims, those "unfortunate" classes who are seen as potentially violent and criminal.

This prejudice profoundly affects the inhabitants of the *favelas* who are stigmatized by the middle and dominant classes, and by themselves as well. "Without a doubt, the organization of housing reflects the complex processes of segregation and discrimination of a society that is replete with harsh contrasts. In varying degrees, this process traverses all levels of the social pyramid in which the wealthy seek to differentiate themselves from the poorest. Yet, the rest of the city's residents severely stigmatize the *favela*, forging an image of it that condenses all of the ills of an excessive poverty that is defined as depraved and dangerous: the city looks upon the *favela* as a pathological reality, an illness, a plague, a cyst, a public calamity."[5]

Curiously, these situations are not identified by their real name, a *struggle of classes* (for this is a question of class domination via institutions and ideology—a struggle of classes guided by the dominant class). This is a significant reality of social authoritarianism, which identifies these situations as "natural" or, in the words of university students, as "anonymous." Just as significant is the fact that politicians and journalists use the expression "struggle of *classes*" in the singular, referring to the "struggle of *class*," indicative of the fact that when openly expressed the struggle, or conflict, is seen as the result of worker or popular violence.

It is a society in which the population of large cities is divided between the "center" and the "periphery," in which the "periphery" is used not only in a spatial-geographical sense, but also a social one, to refer to remote neighborhoods that lack basic services (electricity, water, sewage, sidewalks/pavements, public transportation, schools, medical services). This situation is also found in the "center," in its pockets of poverty and *favelas*. This is a population whose work day is fourteen or fifteen hours long, as well as commute time and, for many married women, housework and childcare. In these areas, public services—hospitals, retirement, childcare—when they exist, are considered favors and concessions of the state.

In a study of the reading habits of female workers, Ecléa Bosi found that the majority of married women would like to read, yet are unable to, because they have no time after work, because they are fatigued and fall asleep, because they suffer from poor eye sight caused by tiredness and the relentlessness of factory work, and because they lack the financial resources to buy books, magazines, and newspapers.

It is a society in which the organization of land and the implementation of agrobusiness has not only caused migration, it has also created new figures in the countryside: the landless, migrant workers, *bóias-frias*—day laborers with no contracts or with only minimal rights. These are workers whose shifts begin at around three in the morning, when they gather on the side of the road waiting for trucks to take them to work, and finish at around six in the evening, when they are dropped at the roadside to start their long walk home. These trucks are often in a very poor condition and fatal accidents are a constant reality, leading to the death of dozens of workers whose families never receive any type of compensation, though their labor is replaced by that of a family member—women or children. They are called *bóias-frias*, or cold lunches, because their only meal between three in the morning and seven at night consists of a portion of rice, egg, and banana, prepared at the beginning of the day and served cold. Many workers are not able to bring their cold lunches, and they hide from the others at lunch time, humiliated and ashamed.

Finally, it is a society that cannot tolerate the explicit expression of its own contradictions, and so displaces divisions and inequalities to the margins and does not allow them into the social except in the form of the routinization of "conflicts of interest" (in the manner of liberal democrats). It is a society in which the dominant class exorcizes the horror of these contradictions by producing an ideology of national indivisibility and unity, which is why popular culture tends to be appropriated and absorbed by the dominant class through the *national-popular*.

The horror of the reality of these contradictions is expressed by the ways in which the dominant class renders crisis.

A crisis is never understood as the result of latent contradictions that become manifest through historical processes that need to be politically and socially understood. It is always converted into the *specter of the crisis*, the inexplicable and sudden eruption of irrationality that threatens the social and political order. Chaos. Danger.

In response to "irrationality," the dominant class appeals to rationalizing techniques (the celebrated "modernization"), which envision technologies as having the fantastic power to reorder. In response to "danger," which is always represented as an explicit manifestation of the popular classes, the dominant class goes in search of "agents of subversion; they initiate a witch hunt for those who threaten 'national peace' and the 'unity of the Brazilian family.'" In response to "chaos," the dominant class invokes the necessity of "national salvation." The "unity of the Brazilian family" (an element of private space defined as though it were a central element of public space) and "national salvation" lead to "national conciliation," in other words to military coups and dictatorships (old or "new"). In sum, the preservation of what could be public and contradictory is negatively created through its reduction to the private (the "Brazilian family") and its indivisibility ("national conciliation"). As one may observe, political authoritarianism is organized in the very heart of this society, in its ideology; it is not an exception, nor a mere governmental regime, it is rather the norm and expression of social relations.

Nevertheless, it would be unjust and unfair not to consider the population's efforts to overcome authoritarianism. The failure of many social and political struggles does not invalidate these efforts. It does reveal, nevertheless, the ensemble of obstacles that complicate them. Before directly addressing Popular Culture and the ways it has resisted authoritarianism, it is important to end this discussion by recalling struggles for citizenship carried out in three distinct, yet coexisting, spheres.

First, this struggle took the form of a demand for establishing a democratic legal order in which citizens participate in political life through political parties, with a voice and with votes. This involves a limitation of Executive Power in favor of Legislative Power and the parliament. In this sense, citizenship refers to the right of political representation, a right to be represented as much as a right to be a representative.

Second, this struggle demanded the establishment of individual, social, economic, political, and cultural rights whose general scope defined a state of rights where agreements are respected and maintained and in which the right to form an opposition also exists. At this level, there is a primary emphasis on the defense and independence of the Power of the Judiciary. In this context, citizenship relates to civil rights and liberties.

Third, this struggle took the form of a demand for the establishment of a new economic model geared toward a more equal redistribution of the national revenue. The intention was to not only end/abolish the excessive concentration of wealth and change the state's social policy, but also to allow the working classes to defend their interests and rights through social movements, unions, the formation of public opinion, and direct participation in decisions concerning their life and working conditions. At this level, citizenship is formulated as a question of social and economic justice and as the sociopolitical emergence of workers (who were always excluded from decision-making processes in Brazil).

So, representation, liberty, and participation have defined the tenor of democratic demands, which have intensified the question of citizenship, moving it beyond the politicoinstitutional realm to that of society as a whole. By examining the broad spectrum of popular struggles of recent years, we can see that they have primarily taken on two new forms. First, politically: the struggle has been unable to achieve power in the sense of state power, and has instead forged the right to organize politically and to participate in the decision-making process, thereby breaking with the vertical hierarchies of authoritarian power. Second, socially: the struggle is not solely concentrated in defending or conserving certain rights; they are aimed at achieving the very right to citizenship and to the formation of social subjects, which is particularly visible in popular and workers' movements.

Resisting

It is in the interior of this society that I wish to examine certain aspects of Popular Culture as resistance. It is a resistance that can be diffused—as in the irreverence of the anonymous humor that runs through the streets, in popular sayings, in the graffiti spread upon walls throughout the city—or localized—in collective or group activities. I am not referring here to deliberate acts of resistance (which I address more generally at the end of the previous section), but rather to practices imbued with a logic that transforms them into acts of resistance.

During the years of the "economic miracle" and the uncontested reign of the geopolitics of Brazil as an Emerging Power, the state decided to modernize (the period's magic formula) primary education, focusing principally on child, adolescent, and adult literacy in order to meet new demands of the labor market. Prior to the ill-fated appearance of MOBRAL[6] there was SACI.[7] Through an agreement between Brazilian and North-American aerospace research centers, Stanford University, National Research Centers and multinationals, members developed a program of national education via satellite communications called the SACI Project.[8] Given the excessive cost of carrying out the project on a national scale, it was implemented only in the state of Rio Grande do Norte and was pompously named SACI/EXERN (Advanced Satellite of Interdisciplinary Communications/Experiment in the state of Rio Grande do Norte).

Why was the project implemented in Rio Grande do Norte, Brazil's poorest state, where schools generally lack the conditions needed to function, where a lack of materials force teachers to write lessons on the palms of their hands and students to copy them on the ground? Because it was there in the early 1960s that the Popular Education

Movement, which used Paulo Freire's methods, was extremely success-ful.[9] Therefore, the new project was intended to erase the local memory of the previous years' politicized education program. The choice of Rio Grande do Norte was politicoideological.

The program's implementation was not without technical problems: it lacked electricity needed to install televisions and radios, and it lacked roads and railways needed to transport equipment and batteries. Once these material difficulties were overcome, the actual failure of the SACI program began to be manifested.

Intrigued by systemic techniques, the program's designers called upon modern behaviorist learning techniques, the psychology of "moti-vation" and an audiovisual language modeled after *Sesame Street* and commercials, to develop broadcasts divided into "serious" and "comic" modules, the latter intended to reinforce the former. As Garcia dos Santos observes, the program designers were "very similar to market-ing professionals in charge of developing techniques for creating loyal customers." Since, from a systemic point of view, society is one-dimen-sional and undifferentiated, SACI developers tested the initial programs on children in São José dos Campos, an industrial city in São Paulo, certain that the children and adolescents of São José dos Campos were identical to those of Rio Grande do Norte, just as those of São José dos Campos were identical to those of Palo Alto, California.

Unfortunately, the "reinforcement" did not reinforce. What was the problem? Modernizers blamed the teachers. They were ignorant, not very "modern" ("traditional" in fact). They were incapable of "moti-vating" students. Violating the norms of the systemic approach, plan-ners decided to do something unheard of: they carried out research! Although they were convinced that problems were solely technical, programmers carried out quick evaluations to assess why lessons were not "reinforced." They were surprised to find that the notion of humor employed (developed in Stanford and tested in São José dos Campos) did not coincide with local norms and, moreover, that living conditions in the region were so tragic that laughter had acquired a very special meaning for its residents. Laughter was not easily elicited. Of course, understanding the population of Rio Grande do Norte was not the real concern, making them literate was, and so "comic" modules were elimi-nated and the level of the "serious" ones was lowered, thereby modify-ing the program for the area's "low intelligence."

Meanwhile, new problems awaited the program's designers. They found that they were unable to assess the results of the project at a pre-determined moment. The reasons they put forward for this were simply incredible: they suggested that it was impossible to assess questionnaires because "answers provided were not objective, and did not fit the questions made *because the respondents say what they think and give their opinions.*" The impossibility of assessment, therefore, stemmed from the fact that specialists had to confront the unexpected and the unforeseeable—the fact that poor workers in Rio Grande do Norte do *think and have opinions.* The simple fact that the population thinks, has opinions, and makes decisions according to its own standards could invalidate "scientific or objective assessment."

The final cancellation of the SACI project, however, was caused by the population's general attitude toward the use of radios and televisions. They would turn them on to see and hear the programs that interested them (sports, soap operas, variety, and talk shows), and used the local radio stations to transmit messages from one region to another. These other uses exhausted batteries regularly distributed to the population leaving no power for SACI's television and radio broadcasts.

This case serves as a quintessential example of a community's popular resistance. Aspects of this resistance are illustrative for the following reasons: first (as we shall see toward the end of this discussion), Brazil's working population significantly values scholastic or formal education. Those in Rio Grande do Norte did not reject education; rather they rejected a form of education imposed upon the population by the state. Second, the population did not criticize the project; it did not openly oppose it, nor did it propose another to replace it. The population was not "mobilized" (as political scientists like to say); it did not confront those that govern (an unequal confrontation that would have been very dangerous); the population simply *did not give* the state what the state asked for—support, recognition, and cooperation. Third, the population did not reject "modernity;" on the contrary, it took advantage of radios and television sets, integrating them into its own leisure activities, while deciding on its own what it wanted to see and hear.

Another case may serve here as an example of popular resistance. Under the aegis of "modernization," a national housing plan was initiated, primarily as a means of controlling an urban population that had mushroomed due to internal migration. Since this involved the issue of "popular housing," state planners created housing projects for the "people" or the "masses." Not only were low-quality materials employed, but also space was used in the poorest and least imaginative way according to assumptions regarding the residents' uniformity and homogeneity. This comes as no surprise in an authoritarian society, like Brazil, where individuality is a feature restricted to "the middle classes and those above them." "Below" these classes, there are no individuals; there are only the "masses."

Much to the planners' dismay (whose housing projects were "destroyed" by residents), inhabitants individualized their houses: façades were painted with bright colors—pink, blue, red, yellow, green—sidewalks were transformed into gardens, kitchens turned into living rooms, and living rooms made into extra bedrooms in order to accommodate the larger families. Interiors were also individually decorated with furniture, paintings, photos, and curios. Therefore, what was intended to be an immense, faceless, and monotonous collective residence became festively "chaotic" and received the personal touch of its residents.

Here again the population did not rebel against "popular housing," it simply did not accept it as envisioned from a modernizing perspective. It reinvented the house. It resisted.

The inhabitants of the "periphery" not only invented a home. They invented space. They created the *pedaço*. It is worthwhile citing Magnani's eloquent work at length here, for the way in which it describes and interprets the symbolic meaning of *pedaço*:

There are two constitutive elements of the "*pedaço*": one is a component of spatial order which corresponds to a certain network of social relations. Certain points of reference demarcate its center: the payphone, the bakery, a few bars, the stores, the fortunetellers, the *terreiro*, the church, the soccer field and some dancehalls. More than anything, bars are places to meet up at weekends or after a day's work before returning home (...); they are also places that prompt long discussions about the town's latest soccer game (...). The bakery, another meeting place, functions as a bar, supermarket, lunch counter, rotisserie, and confectioner; it is open to everyone—men, women, children. It is the place where people get information, make announcements (days and times of soccer matches, excursions to Aparecida do Norte and to Praia Grande, the upcoming circus (...). Certain basic services are located in the center of the *pedaço*—transportation, fuel, culture, entertainment, information—making it the essential meeting point. It is not enough to just live close to this key point or go there frequently: to be from the *pedaço* one has to be part of a particular network of relations that combine ties of kinship, proximity, and origin. Some categories describe the degree of involvement within this network: "*chegado*" can designate someone that is barely known and whose relation to others is merely superficial. To be a "*colega*" though requires more concrete ties—business, school, soccer—and, therefore, a greater knowledge of someone's work, sports allegiances, abilities, participation in neighborhood associations. The term "brother" can be a simple form of address as well as a deeper bond. "Uncle" and "aunt" are used to address adults and serve not only to bridge the distance implied by age or role but also to establish a preferred type of relation with them (...). The term *"pedaço"* designates that intermediate space between the private (the home) and the public, in which a basic sociability is developed, one that is more extensive than those forged through familial bonds, and yet more dense, meaningful and stable than individualized social relations imposed by society (...). In the metropolis the different institutions that cater to the requirements of leisure and knowledge are diversified and dispersed. High turnover in the job market displaces people from one job to another, complicating the creation of more permanent bonds. The same occurs in other urban service institutions, such as schools, certain leisure institutions, public agencies, etc. Consequentially, the place of residence concentrates people, permitting the establishment of more personalized and enduring relations that constitute the basis for the particular identity produced by the *pedaço*. Elsewhere, the individual is identified with respect to society and its institutions (...) by his/her official record, voter registration, work credentials (...). In the *pedaço*, however, that fact of someone's unemployment does not mean that he/she stops being so-and-so's son/daughter, so-and-so's brother/sister, or so-and-so's *colega*. Being part of the *pedaço* means being recognized under all circumstances, which entails meeting certain norms of loyalty (...). An example is the way in which the periphery of large urban centers does not constitute a continuous and undifferentiated reality. On the contrary, it is divided up into territorially and socially defined spaces by way of rules, markers and events, all of which acquire greater meaning due to the relations that constitute them. When one compares the periphery with neighborhoods occupied by other social classes, one can appreciate the *pedaço*'s importance for the lowest-income sectors of society. Unlike other social classes—or those in which predominantly professional bonds extend the restricted sociability of the nuclear family—the residents of the *pedaço* constitute a population that is subject to changes in the job market and precarious conditions of existence and a population that is more dependent upon the network formed by bonds of proximity, kinship and origin. This web of relations guarantees an essential cultural and vital base and in turn, survival. In the space formed by these relations, an associative life is developed, free-time is enjoyed, information is exchanged, and religious beliefs are held. It is, in sum, the place where the narrative of everyday life unfolds.[10]

Faced with formal global economic institutions, the difficulties of the long commute to work and back, the fear of being robbed, and the fear, especially, of an arbitrary police force, the abstract individualization of work and the constant humiliation of long lines at public service agencies, the threatening and hostile space of the large city and the privacy of home, the population of the "periphery" creates a space of its own in which symbols, norms, values, experiences, and situations permit the recognition of people, establish bonds of coexistence and solidarity, and recreate an identity that does not depend upon that produced by greater society.

It is in the *pedaço* that collective leisure takes place. Birthday parties, weddings, baptisms, football matches, music, or dance festivals. In the *pedaço*, the umbanda *terreiro*, the Pentecostal temple, the Catholic chapel, and the headquarters of the neighborhood association coexist.

It is in the *pedaço* that the *circo-teatro* or circus theater, sets up from time to time. With its brightly colored big top, raised with the help of the neighborhood kids, advertised by speakers perched upon cars roaming through the streets and posters placed in the bakery and the pharmacy, the *circo-teatro* is part of the *pedaço* and is offered "to the distinguished families of this distinguished neighborhood."

An heir to the *commedia dell'arte*, the *circo-teatro* is a popular manifestation. Not just because it is set up in the *pedaço* and is geared toward the "distinguished families of this distinguished neighborhood;" nor because many of its activities receive the local population's help and collaboration. It is a popular manifestation because both the artists and the public are of the same social class. What is unique too is the relation this establishes between the stage and the audience. Unlike the audience at shows in the "center," which is silent, passive, and distant from the stage, here the public actively engages with the show, even altering it as the actors perform. Yet this engagement obeys precise rules: a respect for the actors and an acceptance of the fictional character being represented.

For instance, during a performance by the *Circo-Teatro Bandeirantes*, the show was interrupted by a number of children making lots of noise. The director—also a clown and an actor—turned to the audience: "no one has to believe what they see on the stage. In real life Décio (the actor interpreting the villain in the piece), also has a mom whom he likes a lot and who did not die like the woman in the play. I also have my own mom. Here I am a clown. We make our living this way. *Circo-teatro Bandeirantes* has been entertaining families for ten years. We are respected because we respect. If we were to go to the homes of one of these noisy kids one day (those that were creating a distraction by howling at Décio), they would see what good manners are, something they are not showing us here. *This is our house.*"[11] As Magnani points out, the director of *Circo-Teatro Bandeirantes* does not criticize the public's engagement with the show, since this is common and is part of it. He also does not criticize the possibility of not believing the play, since everyone knows it is fiction. He criticizes the lack of respect for the actors, and the lack of consideration for their work—"we make a living this way"—and, moreover, good manners in the homes of others—"this here is our home." The director's discourse exhibits a code of sociability based upon mutual respect.

Although the circus may be a variety act and, within it, each person a factotum (artist, artisan, set designer, acrobat, gymnast, candy man, ticket salesman), the main attraction is the theater. The pieces always attempt to depict "what happens in people's lives," as one director has noted. For this reason, the diverse plots are not only realist; they also focus on family relations and work, a common theme being the amorous relations between a worker and the boss' daughter. The repertoire is simple and never changes (an actor can take up a part after at least one rehearsal). It is complemented by a set (which is also simple and varies between realism and expressionism) and by music (usually radio and television's biggest hits). They are often adaptations of well-known serialized novels, operas, famous songs from the radio or television and soap operas. In other words, their themes are always known by the public. The circus does not compete with mass media; it integrates it into its own structure and repertoire ("we have to present what people saw on television because they prefer it," one director noted). Occasionally, when there are funds available, television or radio stars are invited for a "special" presentation. Often they come to the circus on their own accord because they began their careers there. Yet, because it is a manifestation of popular culture, the plots adapted from radio or television or from song lyrics are changed according to their popular interpretation. The audience frequently demands these changes according to its interpretation of the content and characters.

Here the idea that Popular Culture restructures communication according to participants' practices and desires, and consequently thought, emerges. To do is to redo—or as the popular saying goes, "The story teller always adds something new to the story." This is why much of the research regarding popular art finds the underlying presence of storytelling within it. In other words, a given object results from successive transformations that frequently obfuscate its origins. Those familiar with the *marujada*, or the dramatic dance in Arembepe (in the state of Bahia) depicting the arrival of the Moors, will have noted how the sixteenth-century Portuguese sailors are represented as sailors and officers of the Brazilian navy, whose banner is not Portuguese, but rather the Brazilian flag. Yet curiously, the Moors remain Moors, and swords and scimitars are still used. A similar phenomenon occurs in the popular stories in the *literatura de cordel*, literally string literature,[12] in which the *Roman de la Rose* or *Charlemagne and the Twelve Peers of France* reappear in characters of the Brazilian backlands or in the *cangaço*, maintaining the archetypical features of agonistic communities—honor, nobility, and gallantry—while protesting or celebrating the present in the Brazilian Northeast.

The plays of the *circo-teatro* demonstrate two tendencies: melodrama and comedy (although the latter appears within a drama, either to "keep the public alive," as one author has noted, or to "correct" the solemnity of the dramatized issues and situations). With regard to this discussion, what is particularly interesting is the significance of this division between melodrama and comedy. Melodrama reproduces and reinforces dominant values and ideas regarding good and evil, vice and virtue, crime and punishment, the just and the unjust, right and wrong. It deals fundamentally with the family, conjugal and filial love, desires for social advancement, and crime and vengeance. It also reiterates stereotypical notions of masculinity and femininity. Melodrama's counterpart is comedy, which is a corrosive critique that is irreverent and disrespects all social institutions, family and work, and dominant values and ideas. Comedy's preferred target is, of course, sexuality, and its attacks are leveled primarily against authority figures—the priest, the judge, the police chief, the boss, the fat cat, the policeman, the bureaucrat, the politician. This is how comedy deconstructs melodrama and appears as reality's antagonistic exposé. If melodrama suggests conformism, comedy is a gesture of resistance.

According to Magnani, the *circo-teatro* is structured as an interplay between order and disorder, much like that examined by Antonio Candido in his "Dialectic of *Malandroism*."[13] For the purpose of this discussion, it is worthwhile noting a subtle detail of this interplay that is frequently overlooked by its interpreters. "Disorder" is not found on the "periphery" of a narrative, it is found in its "center." If the urban center of the city looks distrustfully upon the periphery and views it as dangerous, then comedy responds, showing that danger resides, after all, in the center. *Malandroism* is symbolic combat.

With regard to resistance, the situation of so-called popular religions is both delicate and ambiguous. Not only because the Sociology of Religion has defined them with reference to ideas such as syncretism, superstition, sectarianism, and irrationality, but also because populism attempted to convince us that popular religions, by virtue of their popularity, are essentially good—they are expressions of the heart of a combative people. Recent studies[14] have shown how popular religions—like umbanda in the South—have been co-opted by the military regime, authoritarian in its symbolic and social composition. Furthermore, the immediate classification of popular religiosity as a form of superstitious irrationality has been seriously critiqued in anthropological, sociological, and historical research.

As is already known, religiosity is frequently part of popular movements of political resistance (in Brazil and elsewhere), as was the case in the Canudos Rebellion and the Contestado War.[15] These Brazilian movements are frequently interpreted as products of the fanatacism of an isolated and dispossessed population. But, as research by Ralph della Cava,[16] Duglas Monteiro,[17] and Marli Auras[18] has highlighted, the popular religious movements of Canudos and the Contestado War were not the results of sociopolitico isolation brimming with fanaticism, but rather a concrete, religiously inflected response to political transformations in Brazilian society that were adverse to the weak and the unprotected.

This type of millenarian response was not due to alienation, as Christopher Hill[19] has shown with regard to similar responses in seventeenth-century England. Millenarian responses to social and political adversity possess peculiar characteristics, which are important to consider, or rather, they possess three qualities that disguise them as religiosity: first, they refer to the general world order (injustice) and not to isolated aspects of social life; second, they suggest a profound desire to change the reigning order in the here and now (for it is only when a millenarian movement is repressed that the focus shifts from the here and now to a remote future or a life beyond, which is perfectly understandable); third, they express the oppressed's feelings of weakness with respect to their oppressors and thus the feeling that they can alter the reigning order only through complete unity, forming a true, new, and indivisible community, a prototype of the world to come (in this regard, it is relevant to note the similarities between the community of the just, in Canudos and the Contestado, or in the European Anabaptist and Puritan Brotherhoods, and in the organization of the nineteenth-century utopian communities, as well as similarities between all of these and the organization of the vanguard and left-wing groups).

The millenarian sentiment manifests itself as a desire for totalization and the search for a totality, such as a cosmic vision or redemption. It also involves a conception of time as a referential history that bears

within it a premonition of the coming order's preparatory moment, a
time of universal conflagration or the moment of the "end of time" (or,
if we were to use a different term, the revolution and the end of prehis-
tory, which is more accessible to "modernity"). It is for this reason that
the millennium is anticipated by prophetic signs announcing the advent
of the new through the complete destruction of the old (the new does
not rise from the ashes of the old, but rather against the remains of
the old), a destruction imagined as arising from the universal collision
between old forces of injustice and new forces of justice.

It is precisely because millenarian desire possesses these characteristics that we are able to find them in other situations, which are
apparently disconnected from any immediately religious connotation,
where the perception of prolonged oppression and momentary power-
lessness of the oppressed prevails. In other words, just as millenarian
religiosity may become political, politics also may take on millenarian
sentiments.

This idea is present in numerous *political* (not religious) statements
collected by Teresa Caldeira[20] in her study of the political consciousness
of a neighborhood of São Paulo's "periphery," the *Jardim das Camélias*.
Indeed, it is because they are political statements that their diffuse
and invisible millenarian dimension, despite the careful analsis by the
author goes unnoticed. It is this dimension that is of particular interest
to me here.

Regina: *What is going to take place is war.* You can get ready for it because
it will be exactly that, and it will be hardcore too, because messing with
people like that is war. *Because there's going to be a time when we will all
fight back*; and if we fight back, its going to be old-school war, *there's
no doubt about it* (. . .). We're going to ask God to prevent war, *ask God
because it's Him we have to appeal to.*

João: . . . Do you know how all of this is going to end? *If there's a world
war*, that's it, it'll hit harder, do you understand, *it will make everything
better* because those that are left will improve a bit."

Maria: What could have happened? It could only have been a revolution
(. . .). A fight between the government and workers, I think it was meant
to be that (. . .) but I know it was a revolution, a strike, and then it
turned out to be like a revolution (. . .). The government agreed, because
if it didn't then *a world war would break out . . .*

Wilson: This can only be worked out by *everybody stopping, everybody
stopping* (. . .). It's too late to be trying all of that, listen: *Brazil, north,
south, east, west, everybody* that works is going to do this: nobody is going

to leave the house to work, everybody's going to stay home (...). A stay-at-home strike, nobody leaves home, everybody stays at home with their arms crossed, to see if the government doesn't react.

Moacir: Only if a revolution or something breaks out (...). *Revolution is everybody against the government*, so the revolution is to take down the government, *everybody goes there* and tries to take out the man. *First everybody is going to try to do it in theory*, through the courts, and then, if it doesn't go anywhere, they'll do it in practice. Manually (...). Hah! Justice...justice *never favors the poor, only the rich*.

Margarida:...*if everybody gets together, and we go there, with it written down, everybody together* to demand a solution for us here, because we are all suffering a lot (...). Everybody together demanding, *lots of fighting, lots of real fighting*, we would succeed (...). *You can't do anything alone.*

Fátima: *Only the people together* could change things (...). I think if *everyone* put in, it could really break down, if *everyone got together and had a strike, everybody* together, it would work out one way or another, *or balance out soon, or soon turn into a war* (...). They are going to find out that *the people are united, all fighting* for their own good, so *they are going to want to do it their way, and then we are going to see who is stronger* (...) the people had to do this.

Domingos: *There is a lack of justice in our country*, if we had a *court system to carry out* justice for the working class, according to us, everything would be worked out (...). I think that the *biggest problem in this country is the justice system* (...). If the justice system was right I wouldn't call out to anyone, only to the courts, if the justice system was right, but unfortunately, it isn't.

Although not explicitly expressing a religious dimension (with the exception of Regina's), in these statements world war, revolution, and general strikes are equated with a religious dimension because, through them, a new order is highlighted as possible, an order in which "justice is correct," and in which the poor are favored as much as the rich. But the millenarian sentiment comes through precisely because world wars, revolution, and general strike are made equivalent. They are the desire for a universal conflagration that would turn *the world upside down*, to use an expression used by seventeenth-century English revolutionaries.

Another millenarian sentiment is also present in these statements, that is, in the unity of all of the oppressed, of all of the weak—"all the people united," "everybody together," because it is apparent that "you can't do anything alone."

These statements also reveal a sense of "the end of time," which Walter Benjamin would call the "time of the Anti-Christ," and which the chronicler collects (to spite the schools of "objectivist" history). It comes into being *"because there's going to be a time when we are all going to fight back,"* a time in which something will have to be done "in response" (to power) and in which change will be radical. When they first "try to do it in theory, through the courts" and when this does not work, they will then try it "in practice, by hand/manually." One can also see how the moment of conflagration is a polarized one, in which *it is known* that all are divided, since *"they"* are going to want "to do it *their* way," but with all of the people together, and then it will be evident "who is the strongest."

It would be irrelevant here to discuss the differences between strike, revolution, and war, or to adopt, as the Left tends to do, a "delayed consciousness," regarding these events. What is essential though is the desire to change the entire world order, the search for justice, and the ideal of "everybody together." It is equally irrelevant to argue that the justice system does not favor the poor because in Brazilian society the courts are a privilege for the wealthy and obey the logic of a capitalist society. What is essential, however, is that each of these statements highlights the failure of the justice system that in turn prompts the imaginary rebellion. It is also important to take into account how these statements define the instrument of struggle—the paralyzing of work— the adversary—"revolution is everybody against the government"—and how they reveal class alliances—"they are going to want to do it their own way." They also establish the objectives of the struggle—justice.

The ideal of "everybody staying home" or of the "stay-at-home strike" is also not arbitrary. Brazilian workers know the weight of repression that falls upon them every time they challenge the system, as seen in the statement of one of the masons that constructed Brasilia, João, when he recalls some of the strikes of the early sixties: "Many of us disappeared, many, I don't know. They say they killed some around there, I don't know. Others say that they took some away to who knows where...." Frequently, the memory of this terror takes on features of the apocalypse or of the kingdom of the Anti-Christ, to use Benjamin's term. We hear this in the reflections of a São Paulo *bóia-fria* regarding events that were transmitted to him through the memory of older workers:

> I fear the coming of a greater power that takes everyone and destroys them. There was a time, back in my parents' day, that people said this. That children died of starvation, that it was really hard, there wasn't anything to eat. If they asked the government for help it was just for a little help, something small. They told them: everybody go up there

and wait. And everybody went there and waited. The little kids were all happy. They say that they sent a bomb that finished them all off. That it was the only thing that there was to give them. Was this a joke or the truth?[21]

When the adversary's power is perceived as omnipotent, even when its origin is known—since all of these interventions make it clear that the government's power comes from the power of the wealthy—it is necessary for the weak to get "together," and for their desires for change not to provoke a bloodbath and destruction. It is justice—not death—that is sought.

This search for justice is seen in most of the practices of Brazil's popular religions. These religions are offered not just as palliatives (the opiate of the masses) of the real misfortunes of an everyday life, seen as having no alternative, but also as a realistic and conscious elaboration of everyday adversities, so that they function as a form of resistance in a society in which the majority have been denied citizenship and where oppression defines the social existence of the popular classes (we shall return to this subject when we discuss the ambiguities of popular religiosity).

An initial aspect of popular religion is the intrinsic relationship between belief and grace, meaning that faith seeks miracles. What is asked of God and the saints, or the *orixás* and *exus*, or the spirits? A cure for an illness, the return of a missing family member (unfaithful husband or wife, wayward son or wayward son or daughter), an end to alcoholism, a job, a home, the regeneration of a family member. What is clear in this "system of graces," to use Duglas Monteiro's expression, is their reference to everyday misfortunes, and the desire that life should not be as it is. Those who are familiar with Brazilian medicine (which is highly classist and costly, in terms of consultations, prescriptions and hospital beds) and the humiliation workers experience as they wait in the lines of the institutions for Public Health Care (many of them dying during the long wait), as well as their exploitation by pacts between businesses and hospitals, would agree that cures and miracles are asked for and sought not because of alienation, but because of a perfect knowledge of causes and present impotence, to not do so is certain death. Those who are familiar with unemployment, underemployment, the high turnover in the workplace, the exploitation of wages, would agree that God and his celestial intermediaries and heavenly assistants are turned to not because of alienation, but because of a full knowledge of the cause and a desire for survival.

As Carlos Brandão observes, contrary to the official Catholic dogma or roman theology, in which the miracle is an extraordinary occurrence that ruptures the natural order of things, thanks to the omnipotent will of God, in popular religions the miracle is a simple routine, mutual fidelity between the divinities and the faithful, with or without the assistance of a church and mediators. It is not a rupture, but the return to "the natural order of things" of the concrete life of the faithful, the community, or the world, an order that had been temporarily broken as the result of a challenge imposed by the Gods and saints on their faithful or just servants, or as a consequence of the direct result of evil in the earthly world; the miracle is, therefore, a necessary, accessible, routine, and reordering occurrence. This routine aspect of the miracle means that much of the time taken up by personal or collective prayer is dedicated to its petition or appreciation.

Petitions are not made because a religious itinerary has been chosen, rather a religious itinerary is chosen because of the knowledge that, in the present, there is no alternative. This determines a second aspect of popular religiosity: the simultaneous acceptance of a plurality of seemingly incompatible beliefs. In the search for grace, the individual seeks out Catholic saints, accepts the severity of the Pentecostal ethic, goes to the *umbanda* and *candomblé* terreiro, and meets with a spiritist medium. Conflicts between the faithful followers and leaders (especially in the official Catholic and Pentecostal churches) frequently emerge, when the plurality of beliefs expresses the fragility of one of the religion's social control and the followers' implicit resistance to control, so that individuals organize their own system of faith and belief as Rubem César Fernandes has observed. Another peculiar aspect of this religiosity is transgression. In fact, white Christian religions attempt to keep the miracle within the control of a religious hierarchy, and Catholicism makes an effort to establish a pantheon of legitimate Saints. There are always other "companions" (an expression used by the followers of popular religions), however, spirits, and miraculous entities that do not belong to the official pantheon and escape the official control of the religious hierarchy. The faithful seek out these other companions, transgressing the boundaries of established religious authority.

Catholic and protestant opposition to Afro-Brazilian cults, considered forms of magic, superstitions, and "the work of the devil," is also present. This opposition between "God's religion" and "the work of the devil" seems to be accepted, above all by the Pentecostalists; however, this does not preclude the faithful from turning to the work of the *orixás* and *exus*. For instance, an instance of infidelity can be seen as the result or "the work" of *macumba* or *umbanda*, while God, that is, "God's religion," is turned to, in order to ask for the return of the unfaithful partner, at the same time that the work of the devil is called upon to keep away the third party. What is separated and excluded by religious authority is, therefore, replaced and reunited in popular practices as kind of complement and simultaneity.

Religion takes place as the knowledge of reality, as a practice that reinforces and negates this reality, which combines fatalism (conformity) and the desire for change (inconformity) and whose touchstone is the miracle.

Elaborating a transcendent (destiny, fate, karma, providence, predestination) justification for things that take place here and now, religion converts the future into an ought whose cause is located in a distant past (but repeated in mass) or an uncertain future (but one that is continuously hoped for by theodicy). By extending time (calling it eternity) and by structuring space by recognizable coordinates (via the sacred), popular religion opens up the limits of the world while simultaneously rigidly demarcating it. The miracle is thus spontaneously simple for the popular religious soul (which is distant to theology, which barely tolerates its fringes), because it restores the predetermined order of the world through the force of the imagination and will. Key to popular religions, the miracle is the real cosmic profanation of purified religions, which are internalized and rationalized. In these official purified religions, God is *reason* (preparing to dessacrilize of the world). In popular religions, God is *will*. The miracle reinforces the omnipotence of its own Divinity—which it would have no interest in, if they were unable to restore the path of their decisions, expresses a strictly personal relation with its follower—it makes a distant power close, the visible invisible, and cries and appeals, at long last, audible.

Religious suffering is, at one and the same time, the expression of real suffering and a protest against real suffering.

> Religion is the sigh of the oppressed creature, the heart of a heartless world, and the soul of soulless conditions (...). Thus, the criticism of Heaven turns into the criticism of Earth, the criticism of religion into the criticism of law, and the criticism of theology into the criticism of politics (...). This state and this society produce religion, which is an inverted consciousness of the world, because they are an inverted world.[22]

Eventually, there will come a day when we shall all struggle.

Notes on Popular Culture

For those of us who weathered the historical experience of populism, expressions such as "popular culture" and "culture of the people" provoke a certain distrust and a vague sense of uneasiness. We must bear in mind, however, that these reactions are born from the memory of the political context in which those expressions were abundantly employed. In all of its manifestations, paternalistic or forceful, populism is a politics of manipulating the masses who are attributed with a passivity, immaturity, disorganization and consequently, with a mixture of innocence and violence, justifying the need to educate and control them so that they may appear "correctly" on the stage of history. The populist is obliged to recognize the reality of a crude culture deemed "popular" while also valuing it both positively (as the basis of political and social practices) and negatively (as the bearer of those attributes that were imposed upon the masses). This ambiguity produces the image of an *ideal* popular culture (either in the sense of an idea to be realized or in the sense of a model to be followed) whose implementation will depend upon the existence of an enlightened vanguard committed to the project of enlightening the people. This vanguardist and unconsciously authoritarian form of enlightenment carries with it an instrumental idea of culture and the people,[1] whose most refined expression appears in the 1962 manifesto of the *Center of Popular Culture*.[2]

In another essay, in which I was asked to address the debate concerning "the culture of the people and the authoritarianism of the elite," I initially sought to explore the meaning of the conjunction "and" that joins the two terms of this debate, asking whether it refers to a typological differentiation between "the people" and "the elite" or to an opposition between the dominant and the other, both of which would designate the culture of the people as nonauthoritarian. My familiarity with empirical material gathered by the social sciences tended to negate this hypothesis, however, revealing authoritarianism present in the cultural manifestations both of the dominant and the dominated. I argued that any interest in exploring the opposition, and even contradiction, between the two terms would require at least two approaches. First, a historical and anthropological approach, which would avoid essentialisms by attempting to listen to how subjects themselves interpret their lives in order to determine whether popular practices and ideas are in effect authoritarian.[3] Second, an approach that examined whether authoritarianism possessed only one single meaning for both dominant and dominated. I then proposed an approach that attempted to discern between popular manifestations that conform to dominant culture and those that resist or negate it. My intention was to suggest changing our perspective so that it would be possible to perceive as conservative something that, at first glance, seemed emancipatory, and vice versa. Finally, a third position that would propose politics as the privileged sphere in which to asses the opposition and even the contradiction between "the people" and "the elite," given that even the most diverse events (strikes, revolts, elections) allow us to perceive that the dominant class never fails to identify its enemy. This last observation helps to explain why the dominant classes are interested in conflating notions of the popular and the nation, and why they strive to put forward "popular fronts at moments of conflict." It also asks us why the clear identification of a class enemy does not eliminate an idealized vision of the "good" state. The hypothesis put forward in my previous essay (one that I still maintain) is that this involves not so much a desire to exert the power of the state, but rather a deferred and distant demand for the realization of justice. It is, I believe, in this demand or hope for justice that the nature of the difference between the culture of the people and the dominant ideology manifests itself most concretely.

Popular Culture and Alienation

When popular culture—not the culture of the exploited, but rather dominated culture—is spoken of, there is a tendency to represent it as usurped,[4] annihilated by mass culture and the culture industry,[5] infused with dominant values,[6] intellectually impoverished by restrictions imposed by the elite,[7] manipulated by a nationalistic, demagogic, and exploitive folklore-ization.[8] In short, it is seen as impotent in the face of domination and dragged along by the destructive force of alienation. However, if we look closely at the concept of alienation, we can see that it lacks the necessary explanatory force to reveal the impetus behind the differentiation and identification between popular culture and dominant ideology.

In the first instance, the phenomenon of alienation seems to occur in the sphere of consciousness and, thus, in the mode by which subjects represent social relations as they appear to them, for it is otherwise impossible for them to recognize themselves in the social objects produced by their own actions. One speaks here of a "false consciousness." However, if we pass over the notion of false for that of an illusion that is necessary for the reproduction of a particular social order, the concept of alienation begins to gradually lose its immediately subjective connotation, to emerge as an objective determination of social life under the capitalist means of production, taking possession of both the dominant and the dominated—for even if its content and purpose are different in each case, its *form* is identical in both. For these subjects the movement of social relations generates the impossibility of attaining the universal through the particular, making them create an abstract universality that does not result from mediation upon the particular, but rather through dissimulation and against it. Society (and, therefore, social classes) finds itself inhibited from relating to itself, unless it rejects that which society itself does not cease to replace: the extreme particularization of its internal divisions. This movement is called alienation.

In the economic sphere we need only recall the abstract universality of labor sustaining (and being sustained by) the absolute fragmentation of the labor process, in order to perceive alienation inscribed in the means of production, not only at its subjective surface, but also in its objective process. If the contemporary worker, as an individual worker, recognizes himself in the product at hand, it is paradoxically because he cannot recognize himself as the collective worker he really is; for it is not only his class reality that eludes him, but also the global significance of the productive process as valorization, as well as the partial significance of that process for the resolution and control of capitalism. The abstract universality of the labor process supplements the abstract reality of the system.[9] Furthermore, we must not overlook that ". . . the productive capitalist process, while particularizing itself through the labor process, imposes upon itself a key objective: to participate in the process of valorization. For capital, all products assume the form of merchandise integrated into the movement of self-valorization (. . .) *potentially*, the object of labor, machines and the labor force present themselves as capital, as capital capable of self-valorization. Nothing is simpler, therefore, than taking the part for the whole, accepting the autonomy of each one of these figures, lending it, at each instance of the labor process, the basic feature of the capitalist production process in its totality. Capital loses its *social means* so that its parts may acquire a represented *natural means*. Nature begins, then, to naturally generate income; machines fabricate profit, and labor produces wages. Thus, fetishes are formed."[10] The formal subordination of labor to capital (the "free" contract of buying and selling the labor force) prepares its real subordination. Now, "it is not the worker who employs the means of production, but rather the means of production that employ the worker. It is not real material labor that is produced by material work; it is material work that is conserved and which is added by means of the absorption of real labor, by virtue of the fact it is transformed into a value that is valued into *capital*."[11] No one would doubt that this entire process might be a universal hallucination, yet it is more difficult to accept that it may be maintained by a "deceived" consciousness.

Not being a state or form of consciousness, but rather a production process of an abstract universality, the privation of a concrete universality, alienation reveals the need for every social institution to search for its own universalization, to struggle against lapsing into the particular, which would rob from it the legitimacy to be equally valued by all. This is why, from the beginning of capitalism, one of the biggest problems encountered by the Church was being reduced to the particular (to being simply another institution), which would rob it of its power over men, universally reocognized as citizens and only sometimes as faithful followers.[12] This is why the bourgeois state cannot stop presenting itself as universal, the foundation and limit of an imagined community capable of nullifying, thanks to the formalism of the law, the particularity that defines it, concealing class domination by the simple rejection of the form of the real existence of class, that is, of struggle. Beyond this, it is necessary to recognize that "statism" is not an accident in the histories of capitalist societies, as liberals would like us to imagine, but the production-limit and continuum of an abstract universality in action. Finally, it is not by accident, but rather from necessity, that the initial movement of a class' self-appearance has the form of the particular—to recognize oneself as other—and that it permanently runs the risk of abstractly universalizing itself, for example, as the "real force of the nation."

With reference to ideology as the universalization of the particular, achieved via a *corpus* of norms and representations charged with fabricating social unity by concealing internal divisions, alienation is not only a result (chronologically subsequent), but also the driving force, condition, and end of this process. It is so, not simply because it would be responsible through the inversion of the real (ideology reducing itself to a phenomenon of unconscious consciousness), but because it contains the foolish attempt to imaginarily suppress the fragmentation of real conflicts. It is neither by chance nor by a subjective Machiavellian determination that the dominant class finds purchase in the ideas of administration, planning, and communication: through its intermediary, the universal abstract becomes an "adequate means to an end"—or rationality.

Finally, with regard to dominant culture, taken as condition and result of the radical separation between manual and intellectual labor, we can see that the latter is just as fragmented as the former. However, in the case of manual/productive labor, unity is given in a multiplicity and multiplication of activities, so that they can relate to themselves or to the whole only through fragmentation. In the case of intellectual labor, the privation of the universal initially tends toward a hypervalorization of the particular—known as specialization—so that the moment that follows conversely attempts to overcome the practical and theoretical limit imposed upon every sphere of knowledge by attributing it with a universality. This process—called reductionism—comprises the effort to universalize the particular point of view of a realm of knowledge, giving it the status of the foundation of all of the others and of the real itself.

These observations are intended merely to urge caution when using the concept of alienation in discussing the condition of popular culture, in order to avoid applying a concept that defines the very social totality to a single sphere of society. Caution does not imply, in any way, an abandonment of the concept employed by the vanguard during the past century, imbuing it with the philosophical humanism of the old socialists. On the contrary, it is intended to sustain it, because, once the identity of the exploiters and the exploited is understood, it is possible to pinpoint the difference between them, which is of concern to its contents. For the dominant class, the practice and experience of alienation is a source of self-preservation and legitimization; for the dominated it is the source of historical paralysis. It may be rightly observed that this text has glided from the term "popular" to "class" without making the process of elaboration that has permitted this transition explicit. This process is not just a consequence of the theoretical referent adopted here; it is also the conscious consequence of two key factors. The first intends to make it clear that we are not using popular as a synonym of national. The second is, above all, a precaution against the intellectual obsession of imposing upon the exploited an alienation that is their own, witnessed, for instance, in discussions of the "culture of poverty" imbued with "limited symbolic stock,"[13] stemming from a "simple" life experience. Attributing cultural poverty to the inferior orders serves, in the very least, to evaluate the misery of intellectuals. Such arguments allowed Juan Ginés de Sepúlveda, who "had never seen the indigenous Americans, but knew Aristotle very well,"[14] to legitimize the right of the Spanish to enslave those who "due to their simple nature should be obliged to serve more refined (civilized) peoples,"[15] that "will protect the natives against their own weakness."[16]

" 'The workers don't have any opinions. They vote for whoever you tell them to (a crew worker).' This evaluation of rural workers is representative of large sectors of Brazilian society. It is even sanctioned by legislation that prohibits the illiterate from voting (. . .) 'Elections are a big deal for them, but they don't really matter to us (. . .).' 'The right thing for poor folks to do is to vote for anybody' (a migrant farm worker) (. . .) 'It's all gibberish, bullshit. It's all about kissing the boss' ass. Even Arena kisses his ass. Arena's party says it's all about land redistribution. Those guys that get things done, the MDB (. . .), what do they say? That it's all about the poor folks, but I don't believe any of that' (a migrant farm worker) (. . .) 'Rural folks like us don't figure into that stuff about the election. Go on and vote. I think the election probably matters; for us country folks it doesn't, but for them it probably does, otherwise they wouldn't have an election' (a migrant farm worker) (. . .) 'In Brazil there are no more strikes. You think that if we got together that the police wouldn't beat us? Do you think that the workers would win? The police and the army – they're tough.' (A migrant farm worker) (. . .) If political immobility and appeals to an ideal government can be seen as possible strategies for confronting existing forces, they could also be abandoned in favor, for example, of organized strikes, an alternative option for workers. So, the same person that might say 'once a worker always a worker,' might also believe in the idea of a 'complete strike,' and in resolving the hunger of striking workers by taking possessions from the owners."[17]

A meeting place for construction workers, odd-job men, street vendors, and minor public servants, the *boteco* or neighborhood bar, unlike middle-class bars and other places in which to "see and be seen," is a world of its own.[18] There, the customer-proprietor relationship is not one of camaraderie, it is one of antagonism and tension disguised as reciprocal complacency: the customer *knows* he has the owner in front of him. There, the newcomer is confronted with distrust: regulars *know* that they may be standing next to a policeman. And love, a constant theme of conversation in middle-class bars, is rarely discussed: "brawls" are recounted, but love deserves modesty. There, politics, an obligatory topic in the middle-class bars of the festive Left, is virtually absent: the world of politics is felt to be inaccessible and the politician is despised for his corruption. There, the drunk, in contrast to middle-class bars, is treated as though he were sober: he participates in conversations and he is not excused if he offends someone; there, drunkenness is not a laughing matter because it is not the occasion for a "return of the repressed." The policeman, deemed necessary, is not directly challenged or confronted: his actions are curtailed by those protecting the focus of his threats. For the men of the *boteco*, for whom virility is an undisputed fact, to be macho is to be brave (to challenge society) and to be resistant (to not turn in a peer when caught by some force of "order"). The privileged subject of conversation in the *boteco* is work, associated with technical ability and physical strength. "Any activity that is not manual is not considered work, despite being held in high esteem—or maybe because of this."[19] Simultaneously aware of his identity and value, along with his exclusion from the "civilized" world, the man of the *boteco* knows about things. Machado da Silva's excellent analysis suffers a "slip" in the last paragraph of his text. Interpreting how the men of the *boteco* relate to time, the author concludes that they are incapable of projects and plans, or of reflecting on the future, in such a way that their rigid daily routine is a substitute for their perception of time. There is an interference here of the point of view of the intellectual who does not ask whether or not time possesses the same meaning for these men than it did for Benjamin Franklin. This is related to a similar prejudice toward those who consider the "subaltern" organization of space to be restricted, indiscriminant, and confused, without acknowledging that it is a space whose coordinates are not identical to those of the bourgeois *gestalt*. When the BNH architect[20] is shocked by the spatial chaos of the workers' neighborhood that he so carefully planned, and whose decorative gardens have been dismantled by the construction of vegetable plots, whose façades have been painted bright colors, and whose carefully demarcated sidewalks and enclosed yards have been "confused," it does not occur to him to ask whether or not this destruction of planned space may also in turn be a rejection of it.

"My mom was toasting cornmeal. She spread out white cloths over the grass and started throwing the cornmeal over it so it could toast there. She went into the house and all of a sudden it started to rain, a thunderstorm came. She rushed out to save her cornmeal. The cornmeal didn't get wet, but she caught a cold. My mom went eight days without talking; she didn't say a single word. (...) My mom died, dried to the bone: she used to work the round pan, by the fire. We asked: Will you give me a corn cake, mom? She gave us some of those big ones. Cornmeal is tough to make, girl. Needs lots of work. People see them all made up in those nice little packages, but they don't know how hard it is to make them (...). When my mom ran out she didn't have anybody to save the cornmeal that was in the sun. She closed up her throat and she never said another word."[21] This is how Ms. Risoleta, the daughter of ex-slaves and a housekeeper for more than seventy years, recounts the death of her mother Theodora. As Ecléa Bosi points out, it is through work, through labor, that Ms. Risoleta's memory finds the maternal figure, her life and her death. "Ms. Risoleta meditates on the product of her mother's chores being sold in packages to people who did not value the sacrifice she describes. Spreading out white cloths on the grass, moving the pan in the fire, giving corn cakes to children, saving the cornmeal outside, Theodora went on working and dying. The daughter's narrative blends together scenes of her work and death, of the meal cloths and the bed sheets of the dying."[22]

Poor culture, simple life experiences, a lack of perception of time and space... If these were French *madeleines* instead of corn cakes would the "symbolic stock" of these people still be considered "limited"?

In concluding this section, it is worthwhile highlighting intellectuals' tendency to minimize the role of repression so that the idea of alienation obscures the existence of the exploited. "The notion of 'apathy' or 'depoliticization,' as used by Juan Linz, seems inadequate to me for describing the political attitudes of agrarian workers in Andalusia (and certainly the same could be said for all Spanish workers). It also seems tendentious because it functions to conceal the importance of repression and fear (...). Analyzing fear would require tackling questions of Social Psychology. And I ended up getting discouraged when a bibliographic search through political theory and literature on fear (in Spain and other countries) produced limited results. I think this is surprising, given that the majority of the world's poor are afraid of getting involved in politics (...). The concept of 'mobilization' (or of 'demobilization') cannot capture the political attitudes of the proletariat (...) You cannot say that workers are satisfied *or* dissatisfied with a situation, but you can say that *they are at the same time* satisfied and dissatisfied. On one hand, they see themselves as powerless to change a situation. Instead of taking on that lack of power, confessing their fear and attempting to overcome it, many of them prefer to adopt a fatalistic attitude and show wariness toward militants that attempt to muster them from their inactivity. Yet despite the apparent calm, there is a profound nonconformity that is often difficult to perceive beneath the guise of fatalism. The extent of their action depends upon the repression and persistence of fear. It is, therefore, erroneous to see 'depoliticization' as a given, because it can disappear at any moment."[23]

Popular Culture and Religion

When a young Marx declares: "we are all Jews," affirming that religion is fear and acceptance of a transcendent power; or when an elder Hegel declares: "we are all Greeks," intending to point out the essential determination of religion as visibility and spectacle, they define the field of religion as fear and the irresolvable split between exterior and interior.[24] This is why, from the point of view of reason, religious consciousness appears as the exemplary form of alienation—a theme explicitly developed by Feuerbach.[25]

The fantastic projection of the human into the divine, religion defines an irreparably divided existence: the division between the finite and the infinite, creature and creator, individuality and universality, the here and the beyond, the now and the future, guilt and punishment, merit and compensation. Feuerbach states that the God of religion is not a God-intellect (of interest to the philosopher and theologian, "embarrassed atheists"), but rather a God-will and heart. Unable to satisfy the religious soul, which is essentially anthropocentric, the first is in communion with the universe and is pantheistic. Projected as a perfect moral being, as the absolute self in the form of the ought, God is manifest as practical reality that demands action and creates tension between what we are and what we desire to be. Thus, the consciousness of the pain of sinning can be noticed only by a personified other, made of love and mercy, bridging the gap between His law and our heart. This is the God of religion. Division and separation, projection of the self onto a vast Other, tension and struggle define the essence of religious life and human alienation whose end, the advent of the unity of man with himself, is, simultaneously, the end of religion. Alienation ends when humanism begins, upon our recognition that by water (baptism) we belong to nature, by bread and wine—the fruits of labor—we are humanity. Human life has within itself a sacred meaning whose infinite essence does not need to forget itself, projecting itself into the beyond.

When it is defined as spectacle for not being speculative, as the logic of illusion for not reaching the root of effective history, or as alienation because its humanity is not recognized, religion appears as a generic attitude before the real, making it impossible to establish a qualitative difference between the religion of the dominant and popular religion:

both appear to be mere variants of the same, distinct in degree, not in nature.[26]

From the perspective of the social sciences, however, it appears possible to distinguish qualitatively between the two modalities of religion. *Grosso modo*, for the social sciences, popular religion results from the combination of four variables: the social composition of believers (the poor, oppressed, lower levels), the function of religious sentiment (to conserve a tradition or respond to the loss caused by social changes), the contents of religion (sacred vision of the oscillating world, satisfied with the given option, between rigid ethics and a more fluid magical-devotional attitude), the nature of the religious institution's authority (bureaucratic or charismatic, but always tending toward the formation of sects in opposition to the dominant religion, which is institutionalized in the form of churches). Anthropologists enhance these analyses by underscoring the essentially cultural dimension of popular religion as the preservation of ethical, aesthetic, ethnic, and cosmological values of minority and oppressed groups, so that it functions as a channel for the expression of a group identity and of practices considered to be deviant (and, therefore, repudiated) by all in the society.

In the particular case of Brazil, we can summarize (with some generalization) the following features of popular religion.

1. Popular religion, such as rural Catholicism, which has roots in the institution of the Padroado[27] and Christendom, is characterized by the defining presence of the laity as champions of religious life (brotherhoods, pilgrimages, chapels, devotions, processions, festivals), into conflict with the imposition of Romanization or Tridentine Catholicism, which privileged sacerdotal authority.[28] Romanization confers supremacy to the sacraments and to religious institutions (catechism), beyond censuring previous practices, by abolishing them or by placing them under the supervising tutelage of the official clergy. Under these circumstances, the difference between popular and official religion manifests itself as the opposition between laymen and the clergy, and between festivities and sacraments, in other words, between a spontaneous religious sentiment and a vertical religion, imposed authoritatively. This very opposition will reappear after Vatican II and we can interpret, for instance, the difference between the "Cursilhos de cristandade" or Courses of Christianity and the base communities[29] as a new expression of the previous conflict, in terms of not only social composition, but also theological

terms, the former emphasizing evangelization, the latter privileging a prophetic dimension. This description however, and creates a problem: the emphasis given to the authoritarian character of the Tridentine Church and to those opposed to Vatican II, compared to the spontaneity of the popular, does not explain the way in which the former resolves the issue of class difference, because the idea of the laity serves to identify all believers (in the past) and to minimize clerical authority (in the present). With regard to popular rural Catholicism, for instance, do land barons, colonels, prefects, and merchants belong to the same brotherhoods, worship the same saints, and attend the same festivals, as blacks, tenant farmers, freemen (herders and settlers), minor employees, and servants? Is their distribution in processions random, or does the "geography" of their organization obey hierarchical criteria? These questions become relevant in so far as the identification produced by the notion of laity can suggest that (past) popular Catholicism was an expression of rural community life. Yet this perhaps overlooks the fact that these communities are spanned by two forms of institutionalized violence. The first operates among the poor, deprived, and isolated, amongst whom prevails "the capacity to preserve their own person against any violation appears as the only way of being,"[30] so much so that their relationships are marked by reciprocal challenge and test of bravery. The second, evident amongst the poor and the dominant, expresses itself in a number of institutions whose synthesis and meaning centers on relationships of favor, violence manifesting itself in the concealment of the inequality inherent in the bonds of personal dependence.[31] So, it is not coincidental that the dominant class adhere to Tridentine religion: it reinforces the idea of favor (we can recall here the introduction of communion on the first Friday of every month in order to promise salvation for those who may happen to die in a state of mortal sin); it establishes strict boundaries between the sacred and the profane, producing the same separation accomplished by politics in religion.[32] Similarly, the contemporary Courses of Christianity, a religion of the masses, promote Bible reading, social participation, communal confession, and a spirit of community through an encounter with Christ. The fact that the base communities have a prophetic dimension (not an evangelical one as in the courses) and that they defend social participation not in terms of accommodating the existing order (as in the courses), but of contesting social injustice, however, does not free them of the stigma of a "foreign" conscience; however, neither does it stop them from interpreting social justice as a form of redistribution of wealth through a more "just" capitalism, for when they overcome that boundary they will suffer internal repression (the past idea of the laity does not explain the extent of the "popular" in religion), nor does the idea of the base community in the present allow us to determine the extent of the "social" in Catholic religious life.

2. Popular religion is characterized by a "limited level of consciousness with regard to the values that justify it,"[33] in opposition to an internalized religion in which the believer participates in a conscientious and deliberate manner. There is a modernizing tone in this second modality resulting from the use of scientific advances (particularly in the human sciences and medicine), redefining religious norms and values that are more in harmony with modern society (meaning capitalist) and which stimulate the active participation of believers, conscious of the discrepancy between the egalitarian ideas of religion and society's injustices. On the other hand, popular religion, defined as traditional and, therefore, as conservative, tends to legitimize the status quo through a sacred vision of the world that supports the dominant order. The opposition between internalized and popular religion, in terms of traditional and modern, explains the initial conversion of Catholics (urban middle class) to historical Protestantism, whose modern ethic responds to the individual and democratizing anxieties of men immersed definitively in capitalist society. It also explains the conversion of poor Catholics to mass urban religions (Pentecostalism, Umbanda, Spiritism, *Seicho-no-ie*), because, the way in which Catholicism is internalized and modernized and the fact that Protestantism continues to be modern emphasize the disenchantment of the world and the admission of its rationality. Yet for the poor who do not benefit from scientific accomplishments (medicine in particular), and who cannot tolerate the idea of their misery being rational, the search for religions that respond to their vital concerns becomes a pressing need. Migration and isolation, illness and unemployment, poverty and lack of power drive them from a traditional popular religion toward a different one—a mass religion. This approach can be quite problematic due to its extremely functionalist character. For instance, the "modernity" of Protestantism and of new Catholicism is presented without relating it to the processes of social domination or

to church's maintenance of power. "Modernity," which appears to be intrinsically good, obscures religion's determining function in capitalist society, seen, for example, in the redefinition of gender and familial roles "explained" by the sciences (or, in other words, by the demands of the labor market). Moreover, modernity is an ambiguous term: how can we identify the modernity of the Courses of Christianity or the base ecclesial communities? By stating that members of the former should read the disciples of Parsons and Galbraith, while the members of the latter should read Buber and Marx, Bourdieu and Vasquez? How can we classify Kardec's Spiritism, which defines itself as a "scientific" vision of Christianity? By stating that Kardec should read Comte and that positivism is not modern? In addition, the value attributed to mass communication techniques are also emphasized as a feature of modernity. In this case Billy Graham, a modern, highlights the manipulative character of modern religion, which substitutes television for the pulpit. It would be advisable to proceed carefully with the procession pedestal for the saint is made of clay.

3. Adherence to urban (mass) popular religion is an attempt by the oppressed to triumph over a world seen as hostile and oppressive. Religion provides direction in life, a feeling of community, knowledge about the world, it compensates misery for a system of "graces": a cure, a job, the "return home" for unfaithful husbands, wives, the delinquent son, the prostituted daughter, and the end of alcoholism. It also provides a feeling of spiritual superiority compensating for real inferiority. For some (the urban, lower middle class), it promises social mobility as a recompense for moral rectitude. For others (the poor), whose prize shall be attained one day in the ever after, it reinforces the fatalist vision of existence. Some social scientists set *Umbanda* and *Macumba* apart from other popular sects and from the devotional Catholicism of saint worship, considering the former as religions of transgression and the latter religions of order.[34] The social composition and the difference between order/transgression are inferred from the nature of the solicited graces and commissioned "deeds." But if we examine requests made by the poor (from any of the sects), we can observe an aspect that has been rarely underscored because of the emphasis given to the idea of alienation. Petitions for a cure, a job, the "regeneration" of a wayward family member and for a different life. Those familiar with the situation of Brazil's healthcare (the price of consultations, hospital beds, medication, medical insurance,

medical plans) must admit that this is not attributable to alienation alone; it is also a perfect awareness of the present impotence
that causes one to seek a miraculous cure—to not do so is certain
death. Those familiar with the situation of underemployment,
unemployment, high turnover, and unemployment benefits, must
admit that this cannot only be attributed to alienation; it is also an
absolute awareness of the cause and current impotence that forces
people to seek their daily bread in exchange for lilies that are no
longer of the valley. In his scathing pages on alcoholism and pros-
titution among workers, Marx does not speak of alienated people:
he speaks of degraded people. Petitions are not made because one
"chooses" the religious way, but because under the present circumstances one knows there is no other alternative. It would also
be interesting to ask whether the distinction between the religions of transgression and religions of order is applicable. Perhaps
there is an order in all of them, but a different kind of order as a
consequence of the definition of good and evil and of the time of
reckoning (now in *Umbanda*, tomorrow in Pentecostalism and
Catholicism, in the next incarnation in Spiritism). Conveying
"good" and "evil," religions depend on a bearer to "transport
them" and, therefore, upon an authority invested in that purpose. From the moment that authority is recognized there is a
hierarchy and, consequently, an order. Transgression, if there is
such a thing, is also organized. So, for example, when *bichas* are
favored and valued in the city of Belém's *terreiros*[35]—the spaces
in which *Umbandist* rites are performed—"deviancy" becomes a
source of power.[36] Yet when creating a space that legitimates the
"deviant," the *terreiro* justifies through segregation the values of
the established order. The study of popular and mass religions
should take into consideration three contradictory aspects. The
appeals to a transcendental power as the result of a clear consciousness of a present reality, in which individuals feel impotent. The vision of this reality as final, demanding that man
move exclusively within a delimited space, in such a way that any
change can be conceived of only as a miracle—we should not, for
one minute, forget that the miracle is a possibility of another
reality within the interior of an existing reality. Finally, a collection of transgressions (not using mainstream attire in the case of
Pentecostals, receiving the spirit of light for the *Spiritists*, male
venting of feminine impulses for the *Umbandistas*) organized
around and subjected to authority.

4. Popular religions are organized as sects, in opposition to official religions that are institutionalized as churches. If, at times, the term sect serves to describe the minority character of its followers, the more common use of the term serves to underscore the segregated character of the religious community, whether in ethical terms (Pentecostalism, Spiritism), the magical powers of its leaders (*Umbanda, Macumba,* Spiritism), the miraculous power of its saints (devotional Catholicism), or, its latent or manifest fanaticism. The sect tends to become sectarian through the transfiguration of the social, economic, and political segregation of its members into a spiritual choice. Devotional Catholicism does not exactly appear to correspond to the notion of a sect. Their concept of Christendom, however, is taken as an inferior form of the "true" religion that is professed by the cultivated and dominant classes. Some social scientists and historians tend to value the sectarian character of popular religions for their perceived formidable nonconformist potential—one that tends to "turn the world upside down" to use Hill's expression.[37] Whether assuming a messianic or prophetic form, the social contestation of the religious order is radical, owing to religion's contact with the absolute and the transformation that it demands for itself of making "the sea become the backlands and the backlands become the sea." Perhaps for this reason it may be essential for ecclesiastic leaders to affirm the passivity and pacifism of the people, denying them their rebellious potential. Perhaps too, for the same reason, an effective instrument for suppressing the desire for change may be the transformation of popular religion into mass religion, coopting its leaders for the services of the dominant class. It is here that the expression "opiate of the masses" becomes a truism.

The cosmic order of space and time eliminating chance, separation, and reconciliation of the finite and the infinite, conjuring the fear of death, religion, "universal compendium, popular version of logic" in the words of the young Marx,[38] responds to the terror of desegregation. Elaborating a transcendent justification (destiny, *moirai,* karma, providence, predestination) for what happens in the here and now, religion transforms the everyday into an ought whose cause is found in a distant, more remote, past, or in an inaccessible, yet hoped for, future. Extending time (calling itself eternity) and constructing space in recognizable coordinates (calling them sacralization), religion opens up horizons in the world, while demarcating its rigid limits. Thus, the miracle—the defining gesture of popular religions, one of stunning simplicities for the religious soul—is, *de jure*, inacceptable for theologies and, in fact, is only tolerated by them, for it breaks with the predetermined order of the world through an imaginary effort. Thanks to popular religion, the miracle is the true profanation of purified or internalized religions. In the former, God is will; in the latter, God is reason, the first step in the secularization of the real. The miracle, while reaffirming the omnipotence of the divinity to which it appeals (and which would not have the least interest if it were not capable of altering its ancient decisions), manifests a strictly personal relationship between the supreme power and the suppliant—the only moment in which there is certainty that the suppressed cry has escaped and been heard. "It is the sigh of the oppressed creature, the heart of a heartless world, and the soul of a soulless condition (...). Thus the criticism of Heaven turns into the criticism of Earth, the criticism of religion into the criticism of law, and the criticism of theology into the criticism of politics."[39] Emancipation from religious consolation is the task of history, critique of illusions, for if "religion is the inverted consciousness of the world, it is because this society, this state is an inverted world."[40]

Contrary to intellectual interpretations that see religion as the effect of the ignorance of the absolute's true nature, Spinoza[41] considers religious sentiment to be the originating imaginary form relating to power. Expressing the contradictory play of two passions—fear and hope— religion realizes itself as the coming of an evil when good is hoped for, and as the hope for good when evil is feared. To fear is to hope. To hope is to fear. Fear and hope are effects triggered by the perception of time as fragmented and, therefore, as the source of pure chance. The need to conjure the risks of an uncertain time, fixing them in predictable regularities, and the need to find a visible substitute for challenges to certainty, fixing space into a controllable topology, leads to the appeal to an organizing power that not only creates temporal continuity and spatial familiarity, but that also and above all is separate from the world that is to be organized. In effect, the demand that the supreme being be separated from the world is not only a fantastic projection of man onto an emptiness in the here and after: it is the figuration of the very essence of power conceived as a potential that can act only if it is outside, before, and above the chaos that it should organize. If it were confused with the living, it would not have power over them; it would only be an entity among other entities, impregnated with the uncertainty of the world and unable to govern it. If religion is, as Spinoza affirms, the privileged instrument for political domination, it is not because it presupposes infinite resignation, but because—the religious soul having a secret power placed outside of its own reach, simultaneously felt as implacable (just) and merciful (good)—it prepares the scene so that obedience and resignation may infiltrate into all of existence's manifestations in which power will be represented in the same way. Thus, the sovereign power's omniscience and omnipotence result from its transcendence. Despite this, born of human lack, power is conserved only as an object of belief and adoration if it does not cease to show itself: the enchantment of the world, the ritualization of life, the signs and the miracles, the symbols of an absent presence are not expendable, but rather intrinsic exigencies of religious sentiment. Fear and hope engender transcendence at the same time that faith requires the restitution of divine power in the world. Religion needs to place power beyond the visible and, simultaneously, return it to sight. It is a complex system of signs, through whose mediation religions distinguish themselves without losing their originating identity, which makes liturgy the core of religiosity. Pompous, sober, delirious, or exuberant, liturgy commemorates the separation between the divine and the human and the promise of its momentary reconciliation—it reaffirms the myths of origin (always of transgression and fall, without which human existence would remain inexplicable) and the myths of return (always reconciling, with out which worship would be meaningless). Imaginary response to the adversities of the present and the uncertainties of the future, the failings of the past and the remissions yet to come, it marks the emergence of authority as distant and near, silent and merciful, blind and just, ready to answer the call, from the moment it is made according to its own orders, dissipating graces, from the moment in which the receptacle is docile. It is exactly for this reason that the phenomenon of institutionalization—either as a sect or a church, whether charismatically or bureaucratically, traditional or modern, progressive or reactionary, far from being the loss of religious interiority to an exteriority, either dead and repressive or living and defiant—reveals itself as liturgy, the indispensible corollary of religious life, and not simply because it crystallizes that which religion desires (the establishment of the real), but because it realizes that which religion seeks: the figuration, in the here and now, of separate and invisible power. Thus, as anointment and crowning of the medieval king transfigured his profane body into the political-religious body, so too does the consecration of the *Nagô* priest "transform the human being into a truly living altar in which the presence of the *Orixá* may be invoked."[42]

How can the "affinity" between the religious visions of authority and the profane perception of state power (modern or otherwise) be denied? How can it also be denied that the search for intermediaries to diminish an invisible distance reopens a new span—reproducing in the visible the same separation, such that among the cult officiators, directors of churches and sects, and political elites there is established a type of relationship, opposed to believers and the dominated—that makes it impossible to distinguish between religious contemplation of power and the establishment of political authority?[43] How can it be denied that, for the oppressed, there are in both of these cases the same contradictory effects, that is, the perception of this distance vis-à-vis God and the state as unawareness of the nature of power (or its origin) and as the effective comprehension of the lack of *this* power? Finally, how can it be denied that it is the fear of time and "disorder," that is, of consequence and conflict, in a single word, the *fear of history*, that is found to be on the side of the exploited, because they know the price of defeat, and of the exploiters, because they know what they face losing? The politicization of religion and political religiosity does not possess the same meaning: in the former, it is required that the invisible manifest itself. In the latter, that the visible conceal itself. And this difference is greater than anything that our vain philosophy may imagine.

Whether as the reactionary and rationalized version of Pentecostalism, the militarized cosmos of *Umbanda*, the strictly impersonalized universe of good and evil of Protestantism, the conservatism of the Spiritist "evolution," the bureaucratic verticality of the Tridentine Church, or the modernizing and prophetic line of Vatican II, in its popular variants, religions sanction the dominant version of submission to the hidden plans of a separate power. In all of them, social conflicts are represented as the result of the action of forces external to society, strange polarizations between good and evil that fall upon man, that determine their lives and organize the real. From this perspective, we are tempted to consider the secularization of knowledge and the disenchantment of the world as the first indispensible step in denouncing the powerful of the earth and dealienating the exploited. However, anyone with good sense (*equally distributed among men*, as Descartes once said, and not to be confused with common sense) should agree, without fear of being taken for an obscurantist, that the belief in the very rationality of the real can be a sedative just as harmful as popular religion and, perhaps, even more terrifying. It is not only confidence in the "progress of light," or, so that we be less anachronistic, in "consciousness raising," that can engender a vanguardist and enlightening authoritarianism to justify the existence of elite leaders (whether with, for, by, or against the people matters little). It is, above all, the belief in the very rationality of the real that can legitimate the reigning order, creating opportunities for the staging of "necessary underdevelopment" or for reformism (whether with good or bad intentions, also, matters little), justifying the supposition that the "people as phenomenon"[44] is not capable of following the "correct" path on its own, and requires a *cultural front*, constituted by those that "choose to be for the people," and are *more* people than the people. Taking into account what became, for the West and the East, the "administration of things," the organizational models of industry, health, education, leisure, and the state, nothing keeps us from perceiving the appearance of the diffuse and pervasive belief in a reason inscribed within things themselves. The bourgeois world is lay and profane, a disenchanted world that becomes reenchanted not only by the magic of mass communication (in order to forge a transparent community of broadcasters/receivers of authorless messages), as the speaker is the voice of reason, but also by the magic of a society intelligible from end to end. The gods have exiled themselves from this disenchanted world, but reason conserves all of the features of a concealed theology: a transcendental and separated knowledge, exterior and previous to social subjects, reduced to the condition of manipulable sociopolitical objects (the good souls and the unhappy consciences say, euphemistically, "mobilizeable"), rationality is the new divine providence. Perhaps the heretical hour has arrived: science is the opium of the people.

Winds of Progress:
The Administered University

Taking into account the scope of modern society, the state must revise and strengthen the means of distributing cultural products... Contemporary channels must reproduce the models of large supermarkets, making cultural objects increasingly accessible... For me, cultural politics is an activity that is linked on three levels: the producer, the distributor and the consumer... you flatter the distributor... the consumer is, above all, the formation of new audiences.
    —Eduardo Portela (Minister of Education and Culture during the dictatorship in Brazil)

They have been given a new place in society, but in spite of this intellectuals are unable to carry out a new function. What they can specifically do however, is refuse to remain there. And, to avoid the traps that have been prepared for them, there is nothing better than to begin by examining the new place they have been given.
    —Claude Lefort

Analyzing the 1968 student movements in Europe, many saw the end of the liberal illusion, widely shared by the left, of education as an equal right for all and of meritocratic selection based on individual skills and talents.

Economic strategies (which led to the lengthening of educational courses in order to keep a large part of the workforce out of the market thereby stabilizing salaries and jobs), along with strategies that led to transformations in the social division of labor as well as methods of labor (which led to an increase in technical-administrative jobs),[1] "democratized" the European university, which began to open its doors to a growing number of students who had previously completed their education at high school. This "democratization" triggered a constellation of contradictions that had been implicit in the system but that came to the surface in 1968.

First, it exposed the actual limits of the ideology of educational equality. As soon as the "majority" acquired the possibility of receiving higher education, universities lost their selective function and became detached from their eternal corollary—that of social promotion. If everyone is able to attend university, capitalist society must replace, through administrative and market mechanisms, the selection criteria. This led, second, to the devaluation of degrees, to the depreciation of the labor of university staff matched by a reduction in their salaries and ultimately, to outright unemployment. Third and consequently, the university was exposed as being incapable of producing a "useful culture" (since in reality it provided neither work nor prestige) and of functionality, thus becoming dead weight for the state, which began to limit its resources.

This assessment led to the development of at least three alternative proposals. For some, the solution was to exploit higher education's lack of functionality, to make the most of its independence from the market in order to create a new culture that could destroy the division between intellectual and manual labor. For others, the solution was to develop the absence of productivity in higher education by substituting the idea of a "useful culture" for a "rebellious culture". Many, however, believed that because the university was no longer capable of creating a "useful culture" and was by definition unable to produce a "rebellious culture," it should be destroyed in order to abolish the very idea of "the university" as a "separate culture."[2] None of these proposals or forecasts was implemented—not in France, Germany, Italy, or England. Of course, today's European university is not an exact replica of the system that existed before 1968 (the competent authorities learned their lesson). Despite this, the university did not cease to exist. If it did not cease to exist and if, on the contrary, it was transformed, this was because it was given a new role by capitalism, whose logic is to conserve those who serve it. Exactly what role the European university fulfills after 1968 is still unclear; nevertheless, the fact that it was provided with a new role is patent.

In Brazil, paradoxically, the explosion of the student movement in 1968 questioned liberal and authoritarian ideals, laying the foundations for a critical or "rebellious" university. The institution's subsequent repression by the state, however, led to a process that took place in Europe before 1968: a modernizing reform of the university, which after a twelve-year lag, would produce the same results as Europe 1968, without its prerevolutionary charm, of course.

This summarizes the opinions of many contemporary thinkers who have analyzed the so-called crisis of the Brazilian university. For them, the crisis was simply the end point of a trajectory that had been prefig-ured by Europe. In Europe this narrative had been exuberant; here it was prosaic and monotonous.

While it may be difficult to talk of differences in the contemporary age of global capitalism, where there is only sameness in the endless pro-liferation of diversity, it may perhaps be prudent to start with the partic-ular—the Brazilian university—before attempting a comparison. This is not an attempt to uncover our "national specificity," since this would only lead to useless abstractions. Rather the attempt here is merely to understand how a process whose master narrative is global took place in Brazil. More specifically, this means: how does the transformation of the university take place in the absence of the demands of liberal democracy? What are the effects today of a reform that took place in the shadows of Brazil's military dictatorship, the Institutional Act Number 5 and Decree Number 477?[3]

The fact that today's Brazilian universities have become small ghet-tos of self-referentiality, internally fragmented by political divisions and personal disagreements, increases their similarity to their international counterparts, but it does not determine the nature of its foundations. Nevertheless, it is a sign of the times. I believe that the university today provides a function that many are reluctant to fulfill, one that is indis-pensable for the very existence of the university: to create socially and politically incompetent individuals, to create through culture what businesses create through labor, that is, to divide, fragment, and limit learning, to inhibit thought in order to block all concrete attempts at decision making, control, and participation both at the level of mate-rial production as well as intellectual production. If the Brazilian uni-versity is in a state of crisis, this is simply because teaching reforms have inverted its meaning and its purpose—rather than creating ruling elites, it is now designed to create a docile workforce for an increasingly uncertain market. The university is ill equipped for this new role—hence its crisis.

Guidelines of the University Reform

Devised after 1968 in order to solve the "student crisis," Brazil's uni-versity reform took place under the protection of the Institutional Act Number 5 and Decree Number 477. Its background stemmed from the combined findings of two reports—the *Atcon* report (1966) and *Meira Mattos* report (1968). The first heralded the need to deal with educa-tion as a quantitative phenomenon that must be resolved with maximum efficiency and minimum investment. The most adequate means for achieving this was implementing a university system based on the administrative model of large businesses, "headed by individuals recruited from the business community, acting under a business management system that is separate from the technical-scientific and teaching body."[4] The second report was concerned with the lack of discipline and authority, demanding new structures for higher education that were in line with the new administrative order and discipline. This report refuted the idea of the autonomous university, regarded as the ideal venue for teaching material that could be prejudicial to the country's social order and to democracy (democracy meaning against socialism); and it was interested in forming a young generation that was truly responsible and "democratic," thereby allowing for the reappearance of student bodies at a national and state level. The *Meira Mattos* report proposed reforms with practical and pragmatic objectives that would be "an instrument for speeding up national development, for social progress and for the expansion of opportunities, thereby linking education to the national imperatives of technical, economic and social progress."[5]

Temporarily transformed into a political problem and social priority, the university was to be reformed in order to eradicate the possibility of internal and external dissent, as well as to meet demands for social mobility and social prestige from the middle class that had supported the 1964 coup and was now claiming its reward. Inspired by the *Meira Mattos* report, the Institutional Act No. 5 and Decree 477 fulfilled the first function. The university reform fulfilled the second, extending the middle class' access to higher education. Since this process was to be achieved with "maximum efficiency" and "minimum investment," it will be useful to outline how this was in fact attained.

A key initial revision was departmentalization. The previous project of the University of Brasília, conceived by Darcy Ribeiro,[6] had implemented departmentalization in order to democratize the university, with the intention of eliminating the power of chairs and transferring the decision-making process to teaching staff. Departmentalization in the university reform was different. In consisted in amalgamating a number of related disciplines into one department in order to offer classes in a single space (one classroom), reducing material expenditure (chalk and erasers, tables and chairs), and eliminating the need to increase the number of faculty (a single professor teaches the same course to the largest number of students possible). In addition to limiting costs, departmentalization facilitated administrative and ideological control of professors and students.

Another revision entailed enrollment by courses (courses were split and organized by credits). This entailed a division between compulsory and optional courses, meaning that courses that were compulsory for some students were optional for others. Consequently, students enrolled in different degree programs could study the same courses, taught at the same time by the same professor and in the same class. According to the reports, this reform would increase the "productivity" of faculty, who could now teach the same things to a larger number of people.

The core course was also introduced. According to the reform's report, the core course was implemented in order to make up for the "idle" nature of some courses, that is, courses that had little student enrollment and that were not, therefore, profitable, and to reduce the need to employ more professors in courses with high enrollment. By using professors of so-called "idle" courses for the core course, the lack of profit was dealt with, as was the need to spend money on employing more teaching staff. The core course performed another additional function; it became a veritable *vestibular* or entrance exam, one that was internal and concealed, and thus likely to cause fewer controversies than the explicit entrance exam. In this way, while the entrance exam enables more students to gain access to the university, mitigating possible social dissatisfaction, the core course selects students according to a criterion considered fair by all, that of value.

The standardization of the entrance exam by region, as well as the implementation of a classificatory entrance exam, aimed to fill unpopular courses in degree programs, by forcing students into these courses or forcing them to enroll in programs in private universities that would otherwise have remained less popular. The core course and the entrance exam produced what the educational reform dubbed "the unification of the market of university teaching." The new classificatory system of the entrance exam intended to minimize complaints by students who had been admitted into university (albeit with low grades) by transferring the actual task of controlling "possible tensions in demand" on to individual courses, while ensuring that state spending to meet this new demand was proportionally low.

The fragmentation of the degree program and the dispersal of student and faculty intend to put an end to the idea of academic life as a form of community and communication—there are no classes but rather human conglomerates that dissolve at the end of each semester. The introduction of shorter degrees in the sciences, social sciences, and communication studies caters—in the short term—to the demands of a growing number of students, while keeping consequential costs to a minimum by reducing their time spent in education. In the long term, these shorter degree programs ensure a constant supply for higher education courses and justify the poor remuneration of their teaching faculty.

Finally, the increasing introduction of graduate courses reinstates socioeconomic discrimination that is no longer marked in the degree itself, recuperating university education's verticality. Its ostensible goal is the production of high-level researchers, university professors, and highly qualified workers for bureaucratic businesses and states. Its real goal, however, is very different. It functions to contain the expansion of university teaching, making it possible to control careers and by extension, power and wage structures within the university itself. Outside of the university, it grants symbolic prestige, which fosters discrimination within job market: the graduate earns more and turns the undergraduate into a degraded student—a university peon.

This rather brief description of the university reform highlights at least two key aspects.First, the significance of so-called massification. It is often said that there has been a massification of university teaching because the number of students has increased and the number of courses has decreased. This has led both to the disproportionate ratio between faculty and student numbers and also to the demise of high school education. The fact that a quantitative element now dominates all aspects of the university (from the entirely arbitrary proportion of the number of students to professors, regardless of the course taught, to the system of credits awarded for classroom hours) is proof of this massification. However, this massification contains an elitist notion of knowledge that tends to be obscured by analyses. While the reform aimed to meet social demands for more higher education, opening the university to the "masses," it was not matched by a proportional growth of the university's infrastructures (libraries, laboratories) or faculty. This failure exposes the belief that any old knowledge will do for the masses—there was no need to expand the university in such a way that an increase of quantity would be matched by an increase in quality. Second, education came under the auspices of the Ministry of Planning, rather than under the Ministry for Education. Or rather, the latter became a mere appendage of the former.

The University Profile

Three of the key ideas that guided the reform of teaching in general and of the university in particular were sustained by successive educational reforms, that is, ideas that linked education to national security, to economic development, and to national integration. The first idea, which links education to security, highlights the political dimension of teaching, frequently at play in primary and secondary school in classes dealing with citizenship and *brasilidade*, and in high school in seminars focusing on Brazil's problems. The other two ideas underscore the economic dimension of education. The idea of security performs a clear ideological function, whereas those of economic development and integration determine the form, content, length, quantity, and quality of the entire educational process, from the primary school to the university.

In the past, schools were privileged sites for reproducing class structures, power relations, and dominant ideology. Higher education (according to the liberal concept) functioned differently, because it was a cultural good that belonged only to the ruling classes. Following the university reform, education became a means of training workers for the market. Conceived as capital, it became an investment and, therefore, needed to generate social profit. This explains the emphasis on professional or vocational courses in the sciences, social sciences, and communication studies in higher education colleges and in universities.

In addition to highlighting the economic determinations of education, the ideas of national economic development and integration possess an ideological objective, that is, to socially legitimize the idea of teaching and of education as capital. By emphasizing education as a key component of the nation's economic development, it is said to be equally beneficial for all, in the long term, and its overall growth is seen as an index of democratization. Since development is national, the class dimension of education is obscured. Since integration is national, the reproduction of class relations mediated by the occupational structure defined by education is also obscured.

By separating education and knowledge, the reform means that universities do not need to produce and transmit culture (dominant or not), rather they train individuals and make them productive for employers. The university trains and supplies a work force.

The subordination of the university to the Ministry of Planning, however, means that higher education begins to function as a kind of "fluctuating variable" of the economic model. It is either stimulated by financial investments or disabled by budget cuts, according to criteria that are completely unrelated to education and research, but that are determined exclusively by the performance of capital. Education and culture are in this case linked: culture is regarded as a form of investment and expenditure, a variable of planning. The speech made by the

222 • Between Conformity and Resistance

minister of education, included as an epigraph to this essay, confirms this view of education.

Many have challenged this interpretation, claiming that the university does not create a work force or train workers because this function is carried out more quickly and efficiently by businesses that are capable of creating in little time and at little cost the labor they require. Such views would suggest that, in addition to having lost its previous ideological and political function, the university has not acquired an economic function, making it an anachronistic institution, a dead weight for the state, and an irrational element rather than a rationalizing force. Others have argued that the university could be seen as politically undesirable for the state, to the extent that the ruling class no longer emerges from the educated cadres, but from other social segments. Devoid of all function, the university becomes a permanent focus of frustrations and resentments. Lacking economic significance as well as political expression, it promises a rebellion that has no future. Expanded in order to receive the sons and daughters of the middle class, the university offers them neither material advantages nor social prestige. Unemployment, withdrawal, and evasion—these are the signs of the nonsense of the university.

In my opinion, however, it is not possible to fully agree with these views, because they seem to lose sight of the articulation between the economic and the political, ignoring the immediately functional relationship between them and supposing, in a manner that somewhat resembles the progressives, that only something that advances the political can have an economic function and vice versa. In addition, these views appear to confuse the old liberal university with the reformed university. The new university is incapable of fulfilling the goals of the former, something that is not surprising, but rather necessary.

The liberal university has become anachronistic and undesirable in Brazil. Based on the ideas of country's ruling intellectual elites who were formed and driven by the idea of public place as a space of opinions, of social leveling through education, and of the rationality of social life through the diffusion of culture, the Brazilian liberal university is dying. Its death is so protracted that it appears to be in a state of crisis. Its hasty modernization makes the university seem irrational and useless; incapable of dealing with the demands of the market, it creates a future filled with unemployed individuals.[7] This does not preclude the reformed university's economic determination, since even oscillations in funding, that is, intermittent incentives provided by the Ministry of Planning, are a sign of its variable importance within the framework of the economic model. To simply claim that university finances are not linked to education and research does not eliminate its economic nature. On the contrary, financial dependency appears to be one of the university's only forms of existence. It is impossible to separate the implementation of degrees (short and now long) in the sciences, social sciences, and arts and communications, from the university's economic function.

It is also important to remember that the lack of jobs for graduates does not equate to the university's lack of economic determination, unless we consider the creation of an educated reserve of workers as extra-economic. To negate the university's role in training workers is to ignore the precise meaning of this training: following the diffusion and expansion of secondary education (which was initially charged with this function because it accompanied the expansion of higher education for political rather than economic reasons), the university began to perform a professionalizing and vocational role. This occurred not because of a real need for advanced instruction but simply because the increase in graduates meant that employers began to demand more of job candidates. Thus, by hook or by crook, the university is responsible for an initial and general training that is subsequently completed by businesses.

To claim that the university does not train workers because businesses do suggests that in order to carry out a real economic function the university must create an intellectual work force, which it is incapable of doing. This, however, loses sight of the key issue, which is the particular mode of the articulation between the economic and the political: like businesses, *the university is responsible for producing socially incompetent individuals, easy prey for networks of domination and authority*. The university trains individuals, just as businesses do. The fact that the university degree can be simplified and shortened, and that businesses can "qualify" someone in a few hours or days, proves that as the cultural and technological archive expands, like knowledge itself, *less is taught and less is learned*. The opposite situation would require the university in particular and education in general to offer social individuals the conditions to control their labor and the power for making their own decisions, as well as providing concrete conditions for their participation (either the educational system or the labor process). To ignore the fact that training emerges from economic and political conditions that are geared toward exploitation and domination simply because supply and demand is not always met in the labor market is to lose sight of the new role of the university.

An appendage to the Ministry of Planning, the university is structured along the organizational model of large businesses. Its goal is output, its methods are bureaucratic, and the laws of the market determine its condition. It would be a mistake to reduce the university-industry nexus to the financial complex of research and the production of a workforce, because the university itself is internally organized according to the model of a large capitalist business. As such, as well as participating in the social division of labor (which separates intellectual labor from manual labor), the university creates internal divisions of intellectual labor, that is, it creates divisions between administrative activities and research.

The fragmentation of the university occurs at all levels, from teaching to research, administrative and departmental roles, as well as management. Taylorism is the rule. This means, first, that fragmentation is not random or irrational, it is deliberate because it obeys the principles of modern capitalist industry: to divide and control. Secondy, it means that the fragmentation of education and of research is a corollary of the fragmentation imposed on culture and teaching by the ideas of specialization and of competency. This means, above all, that unity cannot be achieved as a result of intrinsic criteria applied to teaching or research but only by extrinsic determinations, in other words, by output and productivity. Third, the deliberate imposition of a fragmented cultural life, founded on the radical separation between decision and execution, leads to a very specific kind of unity: bureaucratic administration. Bureaucracy is characterized by the functional hierarchy of positions that, in turn, determine a hierarchy of salaries and of authority, creating a system of power in which each person knows directly who is in charge of them and that hinders the possibility of having a vision of the entire group and ascertaining their responsibilities. Administration, a contemporary form of capitalist rationality, involves the complete exteriority between university teaching and research on the one hand and the university's management or control on the other.

In today's world, a universe of market equivalences, in which anything goes for everything and things are worth nothing, to administer simply means imposing onto an object a situation or even a collection of principles, certain norms and concepts whose empty formalism can be applied to anything regardless of its reality. From an administrative stand point, this absence of specificities or differences means that everything is homogenous and can, therefore, be subject to the same principles. According to this way of thinking, there is no difference between IBM, Chevron, Bayer, McDonald's Volkswagen, Petrobras, or the university.

Subjecting the university to bureaucratic administration, the organizational model ultimately leads to a division between the university's management—its deans, chancellors, and principles—and its faculty, students, and staff. The administrative roles of public universities do not differ from those in private universities, although in the latter the ties between management and owners are visible. In public universities, a ceremonious bureaucracy conceals an essential characteristic: those in charge belong to the university in appearance only (they are professors); in reality they are representatives of the state within the university. In addition to the relations between management and education/culture, these administrative and bureaucratic connections mean that state vigilance and protection are determined by the nature of work conducted. Linked to the state apparatus and separated from the university collective, the ruling mechanisms reduce faculty, students, and staff to the passive condition of carrying out superior orders whose meaning and goal must remain secret, because bureaucracy receives its power from secrecy.

Brazil's public university can, therefore, be defined as a completely heteronomous reality. Heteronomy is economic (budgets, endowments, scholarships, research funding, collaborations decided outside of the university); it is educational (curricula, syllabi, systems of credit and attendance, evaluation, terms, degrees, validation of diplomas and certificates, entrance exams, implementation of post graduate courses); it is cultural (criteria for selecting undergraduate and postgradate students, for devising curricula, employing faculty, and services, which are quantitative and determined outside of the university); it is social and political (professors, students, and staff do not decide what services they would like to offer society, nor who they will offer them to, so that the decision to use the instrumental culture produced or acquired is not made by the university). To claim that the university is autonomous is, therefore, both farcical and an impossible ideal.

University and Culture

Defined as unproductive, culture must somehow compensate for its lack of productivity in capitalist society. This compensation can be achieved in a number of ways, but it will always produce the same result: the instrumentalization of cultural production.

Grosso modo, there are three immediate and visible forms of the instrumentalization of culture: first, one that is carried out by education, in order to reproduce class relations and ideological systems and to train workers for the market; second, one that transforms culture into a valuable object in a reification that overwrites cultural production with an image of prestige for those who produce and consume it; and third, one that is achieved by the culture industry, which, as well as popularizing and trivializing cultural works, preserves the myth of culture as valuable in itself, while also inhibiting its actual access to the consuming masses.

There are, however, two other, more subtle and dangerous, methods of instrumentalizing culture. The first emanates from the culture industry and it consists in convincing each individual that they are destined to social exclusion if their experiences are not preceded by the "competent" information that orients people's feelings, desires, and objectives. Culture becomes a practical guide for proper living (providing advice on diets, sexuality, work, tastes, and leisure) and, consequently, a powerful element of social intimidation. The second consists in confusing understanding with thought (or thinking). To understand is to take intellectual possession of a given field of facts or ideas that constitute established forms of knowledge. To think is to confront, through reflexion, the opacity of a new experience whose meaning has yet to be formulated and that has not been provided elsewhere. This must be produced through reflexive labor, the only assurance coming from experience itself. Understanding operates in the realm of the established; thought operates in the realm of creating and inventing.

The Brazilian university is responsible for the instrumentalization of culture. It reduces the sphere of knowledge to learning, ignoring the labor of thinking. Limiting its field to an established knowledge, there is nothing easier than dividing it, fragmenting it, distributing it and quantifying it, or administering it.

Analyzing critiques concerning cultural production made by those working within the university itself, however, takes this discussion to another direction. In the sciences and technology, for instance, it is widely argued that dependency on the economic system blocks all independent research and limits the role of the university to training individuals to become agents of a foreign *know-how*. In the humanities, the common critique is that that the socioeconomic system is contrary to the very idea of culture and has immersed the humanities in a pure technicism, eroding its meaning and relegating it to the condition of an ornament or a relic to be tolerated. With regard to the commensurability between the university and society, many are fascinated by modernization, that is, by administrative rationality and quantitative efficacy, and they oppose those who lament the end of a university where teaching was an art form and research was a lifelong labor.

These observations, which express the disenchantment of university faculty as producers of culture, may be true but they are also partial.

To identify cultural autonomy with national autonomy is, for instance, questionable, not only because this identification opens the floodgates for nationalistic ideologies (generally, statist), but also and above all because it obscures the key issues: on the one hand, the division of classes in Brazilian society, and on the other, capitalism as a global phenomenon that determines particular forms of action that are mediated by the nation-state. Economic heteronomy is undoubtedly real, not because of dependency but because the logic of imperialism as finance capitalism is to abolish any possibility of national autonomy, both for those at the "center" and those on the "periphery" of the system. The important question then is not, how does scientific research help Brazil, but whom does scientific research help in Brazil?

The direct opposition between humanism and technicism may also be seen as illusory. We cannot forget that modern humanism was born as an ideal of technical power over nature (by science) and society (by politics), meaning that so-called early modern Western man is not a negation of the technocrat, but one of his ancestors. Early modern man, as an agent of knowledge and action, is moved by the desire for practical mastery over the totality of the real. So much so, that as an agent of knowledge he needs to elaborate the idea of the objectivity of the real in order to make it susceptible to mastery, control, knowledge, and manipulation. As a subject of knowledge, that is, a conscience that institutes representations, early modern man creates a conjunction of theoretical and practical apparatuses, founded in the modern idea of objectivity as the complete determination of the real, allowing for the Baconian adage: "knowledge is power." If today science and techniques manipulate things and "give up living in them,"[8] this is because they have been transformed into objectivities, that is, into controllable representations, and these representations are activities of the modern subject. To become a subject of representations and of the practical apparatus (as the Cartesian *Cogito* or the Kantian Pure Reason), it was necessary for early modern man to create a space for himself. The subject, as the creator of representations, occupies the place of the pure observer, that is, a place that is separate from things, and thanks to this separation he can control them. Being a sovereign conscience detached from objects, man occupies exactly the same kind of place (separate and external) that power and its figuration, the state, occupy in modern society. The place of power in the modern world is separate from society. Placing itself as separate from things, the subject of knowledge gives himself the very hallmark of modern power. This is the deeper meaning of the Baconian adage, since Bacon stated that the best way to control nature was to start by obeying it, therefore defining the relationship of knowledge and the relationship of technique as one of command and submission, that is, a form of control. Seeing humanism and technicism as polar opposites then is not productive, because they are different outcomes of the same origin. In order to provide the opposition humanism/technicism, with new meaning, a new way of thinking is necessary, one in which subjectivity, objectivity, theory, and practice are open and inconclusive questions rather than preestablished solutions. A way of thinking that, abandoning the point of view of the sovereign conscience, may consider the construction of consciences and social relations, and may always be attentive to the problem of men's power over others, which is called class struggle.

Returning to my initial observation, I would venture to say that we are not producers of culture. Not because we are economically "dependent" or because technocracy devoured humanism, or because we do not possess sufficient funds to transmit knowledge ourselves, but because the university is structured in such a way that its function is *to provide understanding in a way that impedes thinking*. To acquire and reproduce knowledge without thought. To consume rather than produce the work of reflection. To know in order to not think; everything that enters the university has a right to be there and to remain there only if it is reduced to a representation that is intellectually controlled and manipulated. The real must be transformed into a dead object to acquire university citizenship.

This situation produces a number of effects that is useful to examine. Among teaching staff, it leads to a fascinated support for "modernization" and the criteria of output, efficiency, and productivity. For those of us who do not adhere to this modernizing myth, the mindset of colleagues who are excited about classroom hours, credits, rigid deadlines for research, climbing the career ladder (defined bureaucratically), being physically present on campus (to reveal their service to the university), quantitative criteria as an expression of qualitative work, the job market, seems unbelievable. For many, the emphasis on "the modern" seems to be an abdication of the very spirit of culture. But, this is not completely true. Those who adhere to the myth of modernization have simply interiorized the supporting mechanisms of bourgeois ideology: objectively, the acceptance of culture through the bias of instrumental reason, that is, the construction of theoretical models for practical and immediate application; subjectively, the belief in the "redemption by work," in other words, the belief that efficiency, productivity, meeting deadlines and obtaining credits, an emphasis on the publication of papers, vigilance over "relapses," and an increase in the number of publications (even if these always deal with the same topic and are never developed because they are rewrites) are proof of moral honesty and intellectual seriousness. For many professors, modernization, as well as benefiting from funding and contracts, means that the university has finally become useful and, therefore, justifiable. It fulfills the contemporary idea of rationality (administration) and shelters all honest workers. In spite of the petty vision of culture that this entails, as well as the death of the art of teaching and the pleasure of thinking, these professors feel vindicated by their conscience of having fulfilled a duty, however futile. Clearly, we have not focused on episodes of pure and simple bad faith, that is, colleagues who use the university not to hide their own incompetence but to discipline and punish those who dare to think.

The feeling among students is different. Refusing instrumental reason, most students rebel against the modernizing madness. This rebellion tends to adopt two forms: the immediate valorization of pure feeling and sentiment against the false objectivity of knowledge, and the transforming of "Theses 11 on Feuerbach" into a slogan, a touchstone against the university's impotence.[9] Although these attitudes are understandable, they are nevertheless worrying.

The immediate and absolute valorization of sentiment has always been a powerful weapon for political fascists who promote the intensification of affects but impede their reflexive elaboration, producing frustrations that allow affective life to be channeled for politically determined contents. Fascist politics is interested in the explosion of feelings inasmuch as it can impede their natural flow and process, diverting them to objects determined by power. It even manipulates them according to its own rules and designs. Here, infantilization (necessary for the cult of authority) and fear (necessary for the practice of terror) occupy a privileged place. The communitarian sentiment, based on the "immediacy" of affects with no elaboration or reflection, is transformed into a gregarious sentiment, an aggressive passivity, ready to charge against anything and everything that may emerge as other, because whoever is outside of the group can only be an enemy. Sound and fury, dependency and aggression, fear and attachment to authority—this tends to be the balance sheet of a reality constituted only by manipulators and manipulated.

With regard to the dogmatic and equally immediate attachment to "Theses 11 on Feuerbach," this undoubtedly results in authoritarianism.

This presupposes a preestablished knowledge ("theory" as an explanatory model), a preestablished practice (past effects transformed into exemplary actions to be imitated or avoided), and a preestablished discourse (words take on the guise of a proven "formula"). Founded on the already known, already accomplished, and already pronounced, authoritarianism makes thinking in the here and now useless. The dogmatic defense of "Thesis 11" (as well as divesting it of the historical and practical context that gave it meaning) presumes the admission of the uselessness of thought and of reflection in comprehending the real, leading to a belief in the possibility of immediately progressing to its transformation, because a definitive, ready, and complete explanation already exists—a science, as it is often referred to, waiting to be applied. Beneath the transforming activity hides the fear of confronting the real as something to be understood, and that, being historical, is always traversed by knowing and not knowing. Relinquished from the need to think, to unravel the meaning of a new experience and paths for an action to be fulfilled, students tend to reduce theoretical work to the repetition *ad nauseam* of abstract models and to the practice of mechanically applying these models, in the form of tactics and strategies. What is lost as a result is not just the work of thinking, but also the very idea of action as a social praxis, once this activity, beyond the creation of a historical possibility, is consumed by the pure technique of acting within a circumscribed field of the probable and foreseeable.

The Difficult Question: The Democratic University

We are speaking here of academically trained people, people who for professional reasons have some kind of inner connection with the spiritual struggles and skeptical or critical attitudes of students. These people appropriate a milieu entirely alien to themselves and make it their workplace; in this remote place they create a limited activity for themselves, and the entire totality of such labor lies in its alleged utility for an often abstractly conceived society. There is no internal or authentic connection between the spiritual existence of a student and, say, his concern for the welfare of workers' children or even for other students. No connection, that is, apart from a concept of duty unrelated to his own inner labor. It is a concept based on a mechanical contrast: on the one hand, he has a stipend from other people; on the other, he is acting out his social duty. The concept of duty here is calculated, derivative, and distorted; it does not flow from the nature of the work itself. This sense of duty is satisfied not by suffering in the case of truth, not by enduring all the doubts of an earnest seeker, or indeed by any set of beliefs connected with an authentic intellectual life. Instead this sense of duty is worked out in terms of a crude, superficial dualism, such as ideals versus materialism, or theory and practice. (Walter Benjamin, "The Life of Students")

Faced with this escalation of "progress" (understood as the administrative and administered organization of the university), a barrier has been created in order to contain and if possible reverse it. This barrier is the idea of a democratic university.

Professors, students, and staff everywhere have elaborated proposals and practices that aim to democratize the university. Professors have concentrated their efforts in two key areas: the strengthening of teaching associations as a countervailing power and veto of university bureaucracy, and the struggle to diminish hierarchical authority by increasing the representation of teachers, students, and staff in college structures and decision-making associations.

The pressure and demand for greater representation, above all for those at the start of their careers, means that professors are committed to the right to know and control university finances and to the defense of freedom in teaching and research, denouncing the ideological selection and devalorization of teaching and research by means of quantitative assessment. Thus, against the administrative bureaucracy of the university, we have proposed reinforcing university parliaments; against the absence of economic autonomy, we have proposed the transparency and control of finances and funds; and finally, against the lack of cultural autonomy, we have proposed freedom in teaching and research and an emphasis on quality.

Faced with the reigning authoritarianism in universities, these proposals and some of their accomplishments have produced significant cultural and political advances, much to the concern of university administrators who see these as a threat to their power. This is significant, because, when closely examined, our attempts at democratization do not exceed the framework of the demands of liberal democracy!

In fact, our proposals do not go beyond the liberal framework, to the extent that our sights have been focused on a democratization that aims to transform the university structure by increasing representation, but we have not discussed the importance of the greatest obstacle to democracy, which is the radical separation between management and implementation. We want to increase representation in existing structures of power, and we want to participate in them, however, we have never questioned their necessity or legitimacy. On the other hand, we have defended freedom in teaching and research as a defense of the freedom of thought (a monumental task in this country), so that the university can be defended as a *public space* (a space in which there is freedom of thought) rather than a *public thing* (which would assume revising the very nature of classes). If the university is comprehended as a public thing, this would force us to understand that the social division of labor excludes segments of the population not just from public space, but also from the right to produce knowledge and a lettered culture. As a public thing, the university does not make lettered culture more immediately accessible to the uninitiated—this would involve reproducing the ideal of the consumer's instant gratification, inherent in TV culture—but it does highlight the difference between the right to have access to the production of culture, and the ideology that, supported by a number of theories, turns it into a question of talent and aptitude, that is, class privilege.

The idea of democracy is constituted by the articulation of other ideas: by the idea of a political community founded on liberty and equality, by the ideas of social and civil rights, popular power, legitimacy of internal conflicts, elections and the alternation of governments. This means that liberal politics and ideology are, by definition, contrary to democratic principles, because the existence of liberal democracy is not the result of the spontaneous decision of the ruling classes, but the action of class struggle, in which popular forces oblige the ruling classes to this type of system. Liberal democracy is, therefore, not a false democracy, but neither is it the only possible form of democracy. It is merely a historically determined form of democracy.

Liberal democracy defines and articulates the particular mode of ideas that constitute democracy, providing them with a particular context.

Thus, the idea of community, which in the original concept of democracy is defined by the presence of a common standard that makes all of its members equal (this standard is the freedom by which the equality of conditions to participate in power and to redistribute goods will be established) is impossible in a class society, which is divided by conflicts of interests, and also by differences that range from relations of production to participation in culture and power. In liberal democracy, two entities have replaced the idea of a free and equal community: the nation and the state. The first is the subjective expression of the "community" of origins, customs, and territory, producing a social organization that disregards class divisions. The second is the objective face of the "community," figuring, in an imaginary form, general interests over and above particular interests.

Freedom is defined by the idea of independence, whose definition is in reality reduced to the right to private property, the only thing that leads to nondependence in relation to another being (accordingly, dependents are not free). This idea is clearly incompatible with that of equality because everyone's formal right to private property is not a concrete possibility if the social system is founded on the inequality of classes. Equality, therefore, comes to be defined by the private property of the body and by a contractual relation among equals (everyone is the owner of their own body and desires). This contractual relation is seen as a juridical reality and, because of this, equality is defined as equality before the law. Conflicts, not being conflicts of interest but conflicts of class, cannot be worked through socially and are instead routinized by institutional bodies that facilitate their legal expression and, therefore, their control. Elections, which articulate the idea of the alternation of governments, lose their symbolic character (meaning, the periodical revelation of the origins of power, since during the electoral period the place of power is empty, it is revealed as belonging to no one but rather as shared by the sovereign society) by reducing this to a routine of the substitution of governments (so that power is always occupied).

Liberal democracy, therefore, reinforces the idea of citizenship as a right to representation, making democracy an exclusively political phenomenon, concealing the possibility of confronting it as social and historical. The idea of representation obscures that of participation, reducing this to the moment of voting. Freedom is reduced to a voice (opinion) and a vote, and equality is reduced to the right to have a law in one's favor and to possess representatives.

In a country like Brazil, which has a strong authoritarian tradition, liberal democracy always appears to be a great historical and political achievement, whenever it has been periodically implanted. Because of this, it is entirely understandable that, within the university, democratization remains locked within a liberal context. This, however, should not prevent us from comprehending a democratic possibility beyond the limits of liberalism. In doing so, we would need to start by understanding that *democracy is not the form of a political regime, but a social form of existence.* From this point of view, democracy would allow us to understand that power is not restricted to the state, it is found throughout all of civil society in the kind of economic exploitation and social domination carried out by institutions, in the social division of labor, in the separation between proprietors and producers, managers and workers. Democracy, understood as social and political democracy, would also allow us to understand how social divisions operate in the sense of increasingly privatizing social existence, progressively reducing the field of common actions and groups, restricting social space to isolated domestic space (we need only look at contemporary urban landscapes to see the increasing privatization of life), periodically mobilizing individuals in order to depoliticize them.

It would also be necessary to reexamine the idea of representation before immediately linking it to participation. The fulcrum for contemporary power, in the form of bureaucratic administration or organization, is the separation between management and workers in all spheres of social life (economy, leisure, social institutions like schools, hospitals, urban spaces, transport, political parties, and even cultural production). Therefore, rather than a discussion of citizenship as a form of representation, the democratic question should focus concretely on citizenship itself—agents' *right to manage* the economic, social, political, and cultural forms of their own life. Social and political democracy founded on concrete forms of citizenship that begin at the work place marks the passage from sociopolitical objects to sociopolitical subjects.

Seen in this way, democracy highlights the problem of violence, which reduces a human being to the condition of object. Violence is not the violation of the law—we need only mention here violent laws. It is the position, frequently within the law, of the right to reduce a human being to a manipulable object. What is the separation between management and workers if not a form of institutionally reducing a part of society to the condition of object? It is here, I believe, that the university can be questioned.

In previously stating that our struggles and proposals for democracy do not exceed the liberal framework, I did not intend to minimize the importance of these struggles and proposals, especially if we consider the authoritarian context in which they were made. I merely intended to suggest that they do not allow us to analyze the violence that we ourselves are implicated in, often unknowingly. Professors and researchers practice violence on a daily basis and our democratic failure is increasingly alarming because it is reinforced by the university institution and interiorized by each of us. Two situations (taken from many) highlight this: pedagogical relations, transformed into a lifetime possession of knowledge, and research, which focuses on "a history written by winners."

When we look at pedagogical relations within the university, there is little to praise. We are not dealing here with the authoritarianism of university regulations (we know what these are and whom they are for). We are dealing with the use of knowledge to exercise of power, reducing students to the condition of things, and robbing them of their right to be the subjects of their own discourse. Far from accepting that the professor-student relation is asymmetrical, we tend to hide it in two ways: either by "dialogue" or "class participation," promoting the semblance of a lack of difference between us and the students at the very moment that we transform this relationship into a routine; or we acknowledge the difference, not to highlight it as asymmetrical but rather as an inequality that justifies the exercise of our authority. What would the acknowledgment of an asymmetrical relation as difference entail? It would involve understanding that students' dialogue does not stem from us, their professors, but from ways of thinking, so that we are the mediators of this dialogue, not their obstacle. If students are engaged in dialogues with forms of knowledge and culture, and, therefore, with cultural praxis, the pedagogical relationship would reveal the place of knowledge as always empty, and for this reason, everyone could aspire to it equally, since it belongs to no one. Pedagogical labor would, therefore, be labor in the fullest sense of the word: a movement that suppresses the student as a student, so that he can emerge as an equal to the professor, that is, as another professor. Dialogue, therefore, is not the point of departure, but rather a point of arrival, once asymmetry is overcome and equality is installed, thanks to asymmetry itself. It would be necessary to acknowledge here that the place of the professor is symbolic—and, therefore, always empty. As a result it is always ready to be possessed. If we do not think about the very meaning of the act of teaching and of thinking, we will never be able to conceive of a university democracy.

If we examine the field of research, we find little cause for celebration. We are committed to the core to the knowledge of the dominant classes. While this commitment is mediated in the field of science, that is, the content of research is conditioned by money, in the social sciences, this commitment does not even have the alibi of a submission to finance. Brazilian society, in its structure and history, its politics and ideas, is described, narrated, interpreted, and periodized according to visions and divisions that belong to the dominant class. This aspect becomes truly dramatic when the "object of research" is the dominated class itself. In addition to robbing its condition as subject, research treats the dominated's history, desires, revolts, customs, production, and culture, in the *continuum* of a history that is often the history that the dominated, implicitly or explicitly, refuses. In other words, the dominated enter university research through dominant concepts; they are included in a society that excludes them, and in a history that periodically subjugates them, and a culture that systematically reduces them. Involuntary cohorts of the ruling class, the objects of research have neither time nor presence in the space of the university. If we do not think of these commitments that determine the university's very production, our discussions concerning democratization will be converted into a pious vote with no future.

Notes

Theory in the World: A General Introduction

1. Martin Heidegger, *What Is Called Thinking?*, trans. Fred D. Wieck and J. Glenn Gray (New York: Harper and Row, 1968), pp. 166–167.
2. Jacques Derrida, *The Other Heading*, trans. Pascale-Anne Brault and Michael B. Naas (Bloomington: Indiana University Press, 1992).
3. Vincent B. Leitch, ed., *The Norton Anthology of Theory and Criticism* (New York: Norton, 2010).
4. Cited in Henry Louis Gates, Jr., "The Black Letters on the Sign: W. E. B. Du Bois and the Canon," in *The Oxford W. E. B. Du Bois* (New York: Oxford University Press, 2007), vol. 8, p. xvi.
5. Michael Ryan and Julie Rivkin, *Literary Theory: An Anthology* (Malden: Wiley Blackwell, 2004).
6. An example that has stayed with me over the years remains Diane Bell's excellent *Daughters of the Dreaming* (Minneapolis: University of Minnesota Press, 1993), which, in response to requests for inclusion of third-world material, put in Trin-ti Min-Ha and me, longtime faculty persons in prestigious U.S. universities!
7. My most recent experience is to encounter a Maori activist bookseller and an Indian feminist at such a convention, who had never heard of Frederick Douglass, where only in response to my questions did the South African participant admit to political problems with translation between indigenous languages, and the mainland Chinese participant to the barrier between Mandarin and Cantonese. Examples can be multiplied.
8. I have discussed this in "Inscription: Of Truth to Size," in *Outside in the Teaching Machine* (New York: Routledge, 2009), pp. 201–216
9. See Hermann Herlinghaus and Monika Walter, eds., *Posmodernidad en la periferia: enfoques latinoamericanos de la nueva teoría cultural* (Berlin: Langer, 1994).

Introduction

1. For instance, Homi K. Bhabha, *Nation and Narration* (London: Routledge, 1990); Benedict Anderson, *Imagined Communities. Reflections on the Origins*

and Spread of Nationalism (London: Verso, 1983); Eric Hobsbawm, *Nations and Nationalism since 1780. Program, Myth, Reality* (Cambridge: Cambridge University Press, 1991).

2. Marilena Chauí, *Brasil. Mito Fundador e sociedade autoritária* (São Paulo: Perseu Abramo, 2000)

3. Roberto Schwarz, *Misplaced Ideas. Essays on Brazilian Culture,* trans. John Gledson (London: Verso, 1996).

4. Stanley Aronowitz, *The Knowledge Factory. Dismantling the Corporate University and Creating True Higher Learning* (Boston: Beacon Press, 2000); Henry A. Giroux and Kostas Myrsiades (eds.), *Beyond the Corporate University* (Lanham: Rowman and Littlefield, 2001); David Noble, *Digital Diploma Mills. The Automation of Higher Education* (New York: Monthly Review Press, 2001); Sheila Slaughter and Larry L. Leslie, *Academic Capitalism. Politics, Policies and the Entrepreneurial University* (Baltimore: Johns Hopkins University, 1994).

5. As I write this introduction, a number of university departments throughout the UK are being threatened with closure, and faculty members are losing their jobs as management seeks to reduce salary costs by 10 percent in the next two years. Middlesex University, for instance, has recently announced the closure of its internationally renowned Philosophy department. Whilst arguments in favor of such measures link them to the current economic climate, this situation must be seen against the background of the neoliberal transformation of universities over the past three decades that share a relationship with those outlined by Chauí in her essay "The Winds of Progress."

The Engaged Intellectual: A Figure Facing Extinction?

1. Boaventura de Sousa Santos, "A Critique of Lazy Reason. Against the Waste Experience," in *The Modern World-system in the Longue durée* (Colorado, BO: Paradigm, 2004).

2. Pierre Bourdieu, "The Corporatism of the Universal: The Role of Intellectuals in the Modern World," *TELOS* 81 (1989): 99.

3. Jean-Paul Sartre, *Search for a Method* (London: Vintage, 1968), 19

4. Maurice Merleau-Ponty, "The War has Taken Place," in *Sense and Nonsense* (Evanston: Northwestern University Press, 1964), 19. The first version of this essay was published in *Les Temps Modernes* at the end of the 1940s.

5. Maurice Merleau-Ponty, *Phenomenology of Perception* (London: Routledge, 1962), 528.

6. Marshall Berman, *All That Is Solid Melts into Air. The Experience of Modernity* (New York: Simon and Shuster, 1982), 113–114.

7. Ibid., 115.

8. Bourdieu, "The Corporatism of the Universal," 102.

9. Manuel Castells, *The Rise of the Network Society* (Cambridge: Blackwell, 1996), 31.

10. "Wealth no longer resides in physical capital but in the imagination and in human creativity," Jeremy Rifkin, *The Age of Access* (New York: Jeremy P. Tarcher, 2000). It is estimated that more than 50 percent of the GDP of the world's largest economies is founded on knowledge.

11. Castells, *The Rise of the Network Society*, 124.

12. According to Appleberry, cited by José Joaquin Brunner, it took 1,750 years (starting from the birth of Christ) for disciplinary knowledge to spread and to become registered internationally, a rate that soon sped up to 150 and then 50 years. Currently the rate of the spread of disciplinary knowledge is 5 years and by 2020 this will be 73 days. It is estimated that information available throughout the world becomes duplicated every 4 years; however, researches state that we are able to focus on only between 5 percent and 10 percent of that information every four years. See José Joaquin Brunner, "Peligro e promesa: la educación superior en America Latina," in F. López Segura and Alma Maldonado (eds.), *Educación superior latinoamericana y organismos internacionales. Un análise crítico* (Cali: Unesco, Boston College, University of San Buenaventura, 2000). Carlos Tunnemann and Marilena Chauí, "Desafios de la Universidad en la sociedad del conocimiento," paper presented at Global Conference on Education, Unesco, 2004.

13. Some philosophers have even become owners of ethical consultancy firms working for large corporations, while others seek a place in the market as clinical philosophers!

14. See Michael Freitag, *Le Naufrage de l'université* (Paris: Editions de la Découverte, 1996).

15. David Harvey, *The Condition of Postmodernity. An Enquiry into the Origins of Cultural Change* (Oxford: Blackwell, 1989).

16. Paul Virilio, *"Critical Space,"* in *The Virilio Reader*, trans. James Der Derian (Oxford: Whiley-Blackwell,1998), 58–73. A similar analysis appears in Maria Rita Kehl and Eugênio Bucci's *Videologias* (São Paulo: Boitempo Editorial, 2005). They note that the gaze forged by the media has little in common with the perceptive experience of the body, since the media destroys our references of time and space—constitutive of our bodies, and institutes itself as time and space. Space is "here"; it has no distances, horizons, and frontiers; time is "now"; it has no past or future. Or as the authors state, television becomes the space, an undifferentiated space that constructs itself as immensurable, defined by the flux of images. Television is the world. This world is nothing more than the society of the spectacle, constructed only in the unceasing appearance and presentation of images that portray it while obscuring its reality.

17. Ilya Prigogine, *The End of Certainty. Time, Chaos and the New Laws of Nature* (New York: Free Press, 1996), 7, 56, 183.

18. Jean-François Lyotard, *The Postmodern Condition. A Report on Knowledge* (Minneapolis: University of Minnesota Press, 1984).

19. David Ford, "Epilogue: Postmodernism and postscript," in David F. Ford (ed.), *The Modern Theologians: An Introduction to Christian Theology in the Twentieth Century* (Oxford: Blackwell, 1989), 291.

20. Postmodernists appropriate the political struggle traced by Michel Foucault who substituted the modern concept of power with discipline. Postmodernists appropriate the philosophy of difference, elaborated by Gilles Deleuze, and the notion of autonomy elaborated by Felix Guattari.

21. See Lyotard, *The Postmodern Condition.*

On the Present and on Politics

1. TN: This tagline was one of the main axes of the cycle of lectures organized by the philosopher and journalist Adauto Novaes, in the second half of 2006 in Curitiba, Belo Horizonte, São Paulo, and Rio de Janeiro, part of an ongoing cycle of talks in Brazil titled "Filosofia em debate." Papers from the cycle were published in the book *O Esquecimento da política* (Rio de Janeiro: Agir, 2007).

2. TN: The idea of democracy that is developed in this essay is witnessed in the essay concerning the myth of nonviolence in Brazil and Brazil's social authoritarianism.

3. The difference between Brazil and the United States is telling here. In the United States colonization was led by individuals who had participated in the English Revolution and opposed the monarchy, mistrusting all forms of power that were centralized and superior to society. Furthermore, North American independence was not the result of "resounding cry" of a prince; it was the result of a revolution, so that the North American people saw themselves as implementing the power of the state. It is interesting to note that in Brazil, because the state is seen as preceding and superior to society, political change appears in the form of changes in the Constitution (we now have five or six different constitutions). The American constitution, on the other hand, has never been altered. It has simply been amended according to social changes.

4. The comparison with the United States is also interesting here. In the United States, it was always capitalists who as private businessmen invested heavily in all aspects of the infrastructure and they always heavily criticized state initiatives.

Religious Fundamentalism: The Return of Political Theology

An earlier version of this chapter titled "The Return of Political Theology" was published in Sérgio Cardoso (ed.), *Retorno ao republicanismo* (Belo Horizonte: UFMG, 2007). This version has been adapted for the current American edition and its readers.

1. Gilles Kepel, *The Revenge of God. The Resurgance of Islam, Christianity and Judaism in the Modern World*, trans. Alan Braley (University Park: Pennsylvania State University Press, 1994), 13–14.
2. Francisco de Oliveira, "O surgimento do anti-valor. Capital, força de trabalho e fundo público," Os *direitos de antivalor. A economia política da hegemonia imperfeita* (Petropolis: Vozes, 1998).
3. Public spending on production includes agricultural, industrial, and commercial subsidies, as well as subsidies for sciences and technology, form broad state sectors that diminish in the military-industrial context, as does the financial valorization of capital.
4. In other words the guarantee of social rights: free education, universal healthcare, unemployment benefit, transport, food and housing programs, culture and leisure programs, family credits, and so on.
5. Exploring new forms of capitalist economy, David Harvey highlights a difference between the industrial and postindustrial age. During the industrial phase, capital fosters large factories (in which social divisions, class struggle, and organization were visible), along with ideas of the quality and durability of products. The postindustrial age is dominated by the fragmentation and the dispersal of economic production (this affects the working class that loses its form of identity, organization, and struggle), the hegemony of financial capital, high employment turnover, disposable goods (and along with them the end of ideas of durability and quality), the vertiginous obsolescence of qualifications for employment due to the appearance of new technologies and structural unemployment as a result of the high turnover of employment, causing social, economic, and political exclusions. Social and economic unemployment is higher than ever and divisions between rich and poor countries continue and new internal divisions emerge.
6. David Harvey, *The Condition of Postmodernity. An Enquiry into the Origins of Cultural Change* (Oxford: Blackwell, 1989).
7. Paul Virilio, "*Critical Space,*" in *The Virilio Reader,* Ed. James Der Derian (Oxford: Whiley-Blackwell, 1998), 58–73.
8. As we shall see, the contemporary fascination, by both the left and the right, with Carl Schmitt, especially his notion of "decisionism" or his idea of sovereignty as the power to make decisions ex nihilio in states of exception, should not surprise us. A sovereign decision is exceptional—for instance, a miracle, when an exceptional act of God interrupts the ordinary trajectory of things. It is, therefore, unconditional, meaning that it does not depend on and does not subject itself to any condition (economic, social, legal, cultural, historical). It is consequently instant, free from all cultural ties—it is the absolute beginning, and has no ties to the past and no future.
9. This distinction is outlined by Boaventura de Sousa Santos in *A Critique of Lazy Reason.*

10. Boaventura de Sousa Santos, "*A Critique of Lazy Reason. Against the Waste Experience,*" in *The modern world-system in the longue durée* (Boulder: Paradigm, 2004)).

11. I refer only to the religions of the book, not to other great religions such as Hinduism, Buddhism, or Shinto.

12. Carl Schmitt, *Political Theology. Four Chapters on the Concept of Sovereignty* (Chicago: University of Chicago Press, 2006), 36

13. Hans Blumenberg, *The Legitimacy of the Modern Age* (Cambridge, MA: MIT Press, 1995).

14. Baruch Spinoza, "Preface," *Theological-Political Treatise*, trans. E.J. Brill (Indianapolis: Hackett, 198), 1

15. Schmitt, *Political Theology*, , 36

16. Ibid., 5

17. Schmitt, *The Concept of the Political*, 19

18. Ibid., 26

19. Schmitt, *Political Theology*, 36–37

Power and Freedom: Politics in Spinoza

1. Baruch Spinoza, *Ethics* III, Def. 1 of Affect

2. Spinoza, *Ethics*, III, Definition of the Affects, Definition 1, p. 531.

3. Baruch Spinoza, *A Political Treatise*, II: 7 and 11 (Hereafter cited in text as PT, followed by part and chapter numbers)

4. Spinoza, *Ethics*, IV, Ax. 1

5. TN: *Convenientia*—Latin word meaning agreement, consistency, harmony

Brazil: The Foundational Myth

1. Afonso Celso, *Porque me ufano do meu país* (Rio de Janeiro: Expressão e Cultura, 1997), 25.

2. I use the word myth in the anthropological sense, that is, as an imaginary solution for tensions, conflicts and contradictions that cannot be resolved in the realm of the symbolic or reality. I speak of a foundational myth because, as with all foundations, it constructs an internal link with the past, as origin, that is, with a past that does not cease and maintains itself perennially present. I therefore use the word myth also in the psychoanalytic sense, that is, as the impulse to repetition, and, above all, as a block in the passage towards the real. A foundational myth never ceases to find new ways of expressing itself, new languages, new values, and ideas, so that the more it seems to be something else, the more it is a repetition of itself. The foundational myth is the basis of ideologies: it fabricates them in order to simultaneously confront and negate historical transformations, since each ideological form is charged with maintaining the initial myth of origins.

3. Sérgio Buarque de Holanda, *Visão do paraíso: Os motivos edêncos no descobrimento e colonização do Brasil* (São Paulo: Companhia das Letras, 1994).

4. A semophore (from the greek *semeion*, (sign), and *phoros*, (to state, charge, issue) is something or someone, or a place or an event whose value is not measured by its materiality but rather by its symbolic force, by its power to establish a link between the visible and the invisible, the sacred and the profame, the dead and the undead, ordained for contmplation. A semaphore is a unique thing (hence it is endowed with aura) and it is a symbolic significance endowed with meaning by a collectivity.

5. For information on Columbus' letters, see Marilena Chauí, "Colombo, exegeta da América," in Adauto Novaes (ed.), *A descoberta do homem e do mundo* (São Paulo: Companhia das letras).

6. Fernando Novais, *Portugal e a crise do antigo sistema colonial* (1777–1808) (São Paulo: Hucitec, 1985), 102–103.

7. The concept of "possessive individualism" is from C.B. Macpherson, *The Political Theory of Possessive Individualism* (Oxford: Clarendon Press, 1962).

8. The quotation by Pero de Magalhães Gandavo is an extract taken from *Tratado das terras do Brasil* cited in Flávio Aguiar, *Com palmos medida: Terra, trabalho e conflito na literatura brasileira* (São Paulo: Fundação Perseu Abramo/Boitempo, 1999), 35

9. Novais, *Portugal e a crise*,105.

10. Alfredo Bosi, *Dialética da colonização* (São Paulo: Companhia das letras, 1992).

11. Walnice Galvão uses the phrase the Cain complex to refer to Euclides as an intellectual who, initially part of the massacre, repents, feels responsible for the war and ends up referring to the dead as patriots and Brazilians, seeking to understand why Canudos took place. In seeking to understand this political event, Euclides, a man of his era, adopts a form of geographic and geological determinism. Walnice Nogueira Galvão, *No calor da hora: A guerra de Canudos nos jornais. 4a expedição* (São Paulo: Ática, 1974).

12. Euclides da Cunha, *Rebellion in the Backlands*, trans. Samuel Putnam (Chicago: University of Chicago Press, 1944), 13.

13. Ibid., 13

14. Getúlio Vargas' speech is taken from Alcir Lenharo, *Sacralização da política* (Campinas, Papirus: Edunicamp, 1986), 56

15. The quotation from Cassiano Ricardo is an extract from his book *O estado novo e seu sentido bandeirante* cited by Lenharo, *Sacralização da política*, 61–62.

16. Lenharo, *Sacralização da política*, 61–62.

17. Cited in Ibid., 61–62

18. Cited in da Cunha, *Rebellion*, 13

19. Ibid., 13

20. Erich Auerbach, *Mimesis: The Representation of Reality in Western Literature*, trans. Willard R. Trask (Princeton: Princeton University Press, 1953).

21. Father Antônio Vieira, *História do futuro: Do quinto império de Portugal* (Lisboa: Imprensa Nacional/ Casa da moeda, s.d), 209
22. Ibid., 210.
23. Ibid., 54.
24. Ibid., 55
25. Novais, *Portugal e a crise*, 62
26. Raymundo Faoro, *Os donos do poder: A formação do patronato político brasileiro* (Porto Alegre: Globo, 1973), 45
27. Perry Anderson, *Lineages of the Absolutist State* (London: Verso, 1974), 19
28. Anderson, *Lineages of the Absolutist State*, 34.
29. Raymundo Faoro, *Os donos do poder*, 47
30. Laura de Mello e Souza, *Os desclassificados de ouro: A probreza mineira no século XVIII* (Rio de Janeiro: Graal, 1986). The reference to the black population as agents is from Silvia Humbold Lara, *Campos da violência: Escravos e senhores na Capitania do Rio de Janeiro, 1750–1808* (Rio de Janeiro: Paz e Terra, 1988).
31. The expression a Civic-Christ is taken from José Murilho de Carvalho, *Pontos e bordados: Escritos de história política* (Belo Horizonte: UFMG, 1998).
32. TN: *The Inconfidência Mineira* (The Minas Conspiracy) of 1789 was a Brazilian Independence movement. Amongst well-known participants were Joaquim José da Silva Xavier, best known as "Tiradentes," referred to here.

Authoritarian Thought: The Integralist Imaginary

TN: Brazilian Integralism was a far right political movement created in 1932. Founded and led by Plínio Salgado, a literary figure who participated in the 1922 Modern Art Week, the movement adopted the characteristics of European mass movements of the time, specifically of Italian fascism. The movement's slogan was "the union of all races and all people." The party created to support this ideology was the Ação Integralista Brasileira (Brazilian Integralist Action)

1. Sérgio Buarque de Holanda, *Raízes do Brasil* (São Paulo: José Olympio, 1975), 141–142. Regarding Plínio Salgado's reading of Farias Brito, Cruz Costa writes, "This is only a small sample of the euphoric and at the same time the lack of a critical sense that characterized the Integralist mentality." See *Panorama da história da filosofia no Brasil* (São Paulo: Cultrix, 1960), 95.
2. Dante Moreira Leite, *O caráter nacional Brasileiro* (São Paulo: Pioneira, 1976), 231.
3. Ibid., 220.
4. Maria Stella Bresciani, "A Concepção de Estado em Oliveira Vianna," *Revista de História* 94: 639; Evaldo Amaro Vieira, *Oliveira Vianna e o Estado Corporativo* (São Paulo: Grijalbo, 1976), 144.

5. Leite, *O caráter nacional Brasileiro*, 216.

6. Roberto Schwarz, *Misplaced Ideas: Essays on Brazilian Culture*, trans. John Gledson (London: Verso, 1996).

7. Ibid., 159.

8. TN: In Vianna's work, the "legal" country is that which exists only in the abstract, in such documents as the Constitution of 1891. It is a country structured according to the principles of democratic liberalism, a political philosophy and system "imported" from Europe and thus seen inauthentic and contrary to the "real" country.

9. TN: *Bandeirantes* were Portuguese colonial scouts, members of the sixteenth- and eighteenth-century slave-hunting expeditions. In addition to caputuring runaway slaves, they focused on finding gold, silver, and diamond mines. They ventured into unmapped regions in search of profit expanding Portuguese America to the same territory as current day Brazil. *Sertanejos*, the people who inhabit the semiarid backlands of northeastern Brazil known as the *sertão*, are imbued with traditional values, and are seen as maintaining habits from the past.

10. I would like to clarify here that we are not dealing with a psychological (authoritarian conscience) or psychosociological question (authoritarian personality), since it would be absurd, following on from the Frankfurt School, to believe that we may "add" to it. We are dealing with an epistemological, as well as political question.

11. In Brazil, the importation of ideas performs the same role as theology at the height of bourgeois ideology. One of the most interesting aspects of the secular and political uses of Calvinist beliefs by the Dutch bourgeoisie (in the seventeenth century), was demonstrating that the monarchy (i.e., the interests of the House of Orange) was an unjust regime (for the bourgeoisie) because the Bible, a revelation of the divine word, stated (in the Book of Judges) that God was antimonarchical. The difference between Israel and mercantile Holland is irrelevant, what is of interest is finding a pronouncement, in this case absolute, which makes the political discourse irrefutable, as well as the power of those who proclaim it.

12. TN: The tupí word *anauê*, meaning you are my brother, was adopted as a salute by the Integralists.

13. Plínio Salgado, *A quarta humanidade* (São Paulo: José Olympio, 1934), 87.

14. Ibid., 77.

15. Miguel Reale, *O estado moderno* (São Paulo: José Olympio, 1935), 215–216.

16. Plínio Salgado, *O sofrimento universal* (São Paulo: José Olympio, 1936), 47.

17. Plínio Salgado, *Palavras novas aos tempos novos* (São Paulo: Panorama, n.d.), 49.

18. Plínio Salgado, *A aliança do sim e do não* (São Paulo: Editora das Americas, n.d.), 224–225.

19. Salgado, *O sofrimento universal*, 47.

20. Salgado, *A quarta humanidade*, 90–101.

21. Plínio Salgado, *Manifesto de outubro de 1932* (São Paulo: Editora das Américas, n.d.), 96.
22. Salgado, *O que é o integralismo* (São Paulo: Editora das Américas, n.d.), 38.
23. Miguel Reale, *Perspectivas integralistas* (São Paulo: Odeon, n.d.), 28.
24. Salgado, *O Integralismo perante a nação* (São Paulo: Editora das Américas, n.d.), 60.
25. Salgado, *Palavra novas aos tempos novos*, 91.

Ethics and Violence in Brazil: A Difficult Democracy

1. TN: Brazil's Landless Workers' Movement, or in Portuguese *Movimento dos Trabalhadores Rurais Sem Terra* (MST), is the largest social movement in Latin America with an estimated 1.5 million landless members organized in 23 out 27 states. The MST carries out land reform in Brazil, where 1.6 percent of the landowners control roughly half (46.8 percent) of the land on which crops could be grown. The movement emerged in the late 1970s in the midst of Brazil's military dictatorship but was officially founded in 1984.
2. TN: *Garimpeiros* are gold prospectors and miners, who in the late 1970s occupied indigenous lands in Brazil despite orders forbidding these invasions. The invasions led to conflicts, often violent, between the indigenous and the *garimpeiros*.

Popular Culture and Authoritarianism

1. Roberto Schwarz, *Misplaced Ideas. Essays on Brazilian Culture*, trans. John Gledson (London: Verso, 1996).
2. TN: The economic miracle refers to the economic growth experienced in Brazil during some of the toughest years of the military dictatorship. The period also saw an increase in poverty indicators as well as a general worsening of living and working conditions as the difference between the rich and the poor grew.
3. TN: The *Ato Institucional Número 5* (AI-5) or the Institutional Act Number 5 was implemented in 1968 and marks the hardening of the military regime controlling the Brazilian government since the coup of 1964. The Act closed the National Congress and shifted all power to the Executive. It also suspended habeas corpus, enacted censorship, and made illegal any type of political organization opposing the regime.
4. TN: For reasons that will become apparent later in this essay, Chauí's use of *luta de classes* is translated, in this essay only, as "struggle of classes" instead of the more customary "class struggle."
5. Lúcio Kowarick, *A espoliação urbana* (Rio de Janeiro: Paz e Terra 1980), 92–93. "The fact of being a resident of the *favela* disqualifies the individual from being an urban inhabitant, for they are denied the possibility

of defending themselves with regards to housing issues. As an occupant of someone else's land, the *favela* resident is defined by his/her illegal situation. The draconian empire of society's fundamental rights, which are centered on private property, collapse upon the resident of the *favela*, whose prerogatives as a resident are necessarily annihilated by it. Thus, the resident of the *favela* does not appear as an urban citizen in even this essential sense, appearing before society's eyes as a usurper that can be destroyed without any possibility of defending him/herself, for the kingdom of legality hovers over him/her and, with it, the right of expulsion." Ibid., 91.

6. TN: Movimento Brasileiro de Alfabetização (MOBRAL) or the Brazilian Literacy Movement was a military government literacy initiative launched in 1967 and which sought to assure a minimal level of functional literacy through satellite schools.

7. For a description, analysis, and interpretation of SACI/EXERN, see Santos, Laymert Garcia dos, *Desregulagens, educação, planejamento e tecnologia como ferramenta social* (São Paulo: Brasiliense, 1981).

8. TN: The Conselho Nacional de Desenvolvimento Científico e Tecnológico (CNPq) or the National Council for the Development of Science and Technology was formed in 1951 as a government umbrella organization to oversee and administrate various research and development sectors in Brazil.

9. TN: Paulo Freire (1921–1997) is a Brazilian educator and influential theorist of critical pedagogy, whose work has had considerable impact on the development of educational practice and informal and popular education. In 1961, he was appointed director of the Department of Cultural Extension of Recife University in the northeast of Brazil, and in 1962 he had the first opportunity for significant application of his theories, when 300 sugarcane workers were taught to read and write in just 45 days. In 1964, the military coup put an end to his work. Freire was imprisoned and later went into exile, and returned to Brazil in 1980.

10. José Guilherme Cantor Magnani, *Festa no pedaço* (São Paulo: Brasiliense, 1984), 137–139. For a description of the "periphery" see Teresa Caldeira, *A política dos outros* (São Paulo: Brasiliense, 1984); Kowarick, *A Espoliação Urbana*; Sílvio Cacia Bava, *Classes sociais e movimentos populares. A luta por transportes* (Master's Thesis, University of São Paulo, 1984).

11. Magnani, *Festa no pedaço,* 92.

12. TN: *Literatura de cordel*, literally string literature, are popular books sold as pamphlets that recount in poetic form the heroic deeds and marvelous adventures of popular heroes. The books stem historically from Portugal but were also in evidence elsewhere in Europe: the *literature de colportage* in France and *pliegos de suelto* in Spain. In Brazil the form developed primarily in the Northeast.

13. TN: Dialectic of *malandroism* or trickery is a seminal essay by literary critic Antonio Candido that examines the art of trickery in Brazilian literature and society, as a means of exploring how the marginalized use official

discourses for their own uses, often subverting them. The essay appears in *Antonio Candido. On Literature and Society*, trans. Howard Becker (Princeton: Princeton University Press, 1993).

14. Diana Brown, "Uma História de Umabanda no Rio," *Umbanda e Política* (Rio de Janeiro: Marco Zero, 1985); Maria Helena Vilas Boas Concone and Lisias Negrão, "Umbanda: da representação à cooptação. O envolvimento político-partidário da umbanda paulista," *Umbanda e Política*; Patrícia Birman, "Registrado em cartório, com firma reconhecida: a mediação política das federações de umbanda," in *Umbanda e Política*.

15. TN: The war of Canudos took place from 1893 to 1897, between the new Republican administration and some 30,000 settlers in the Brazilian Northeast most of whom were annihilated. The Contestado War was another dispute between settlers and the government in the northeast that took place from 1912 to 1916. Both conflicts were dominated by popular religious leaders.

16. Ralph Della Cava, "Brazilian Messianism and National Institutions," *Hispanic American Historical Review* 3, no. 48 (1968).

17. Duglas Monteiro, *Os errantes do Novo Século* (São Paulo: Duas Cidades, 1974).

18. Marli Auras, *Guerra do Contestado. Organização da Irmandade Cabocla* (Florianópolis: Cortez, 1984).

19. Christopher Hill, *The World Turned Upside Down* (London: Penguin Books, 1975).

20. Caldeira, *A política dos outros.*, The statements were all taken from Caldeira's magnificent book, and despite my own interpretation taking a different approach, I agree with all of her interpretations.

21. Verena Stockle, "Enxada e Voto," *Os partidos e as eleições* (Rio de Janeiro: Paz e Terra/CEBRAP, 1975), 82.

22. Karl Marx, *Critique of Hegel's Philosophy of Right* (Cambridge: Cambridge University Press, 1977), 131–132.

Notes on Popular Culture

1. My original intention was to comment on the CPC's manifesto in the third part of this essay; however, the length of this text made this impractical. My idea was to interweave comments regarding the distinctions between the "people as phenomenon" and the "people as essence" (an interesting method for working with the dialectic of appearance and essence), and between the three forms of art—the art of the people, popular, and revolutionary—suggesting that, perhaps, new anthropological studies in Brazil could make these politically unacceptable distinctions "scientifically" questionable.

2. TN: Initiated in 1961, the Center of Popular Culture of Brazil's National Student's Union attempted to establish a cultural and political link with

the Brazilian people or masses by putting on plays in factories and working-class neighborhoods, producing films and records, and by participating in literacy programs. Along with the National Student's Union, it was banned by the military regime in 1964.

3. Regarding this point, these works were particularly valuable: E.P. Thompson, *The Making of the English Working Class* (London: Penguin, 1976); Duglas Monteiro, *Os errantes do novo século*, USP (doctoral dissertation); Verena M. Alier, "Enxada e voto," *Os partidos políticos e as eleições no Brasil* (Rio de Janeiro: Paz e Terra/Cebrap, 1975); Lúcio Kowarik, "Usos e abusos: reflexões sobre as metamorfoses do trabalho," *Cidade—Usos e abusos* (São Paulo: Brasiliense, 1978).

4. Paulo Freire, *Pedagogy of the Oppressed* (New York: Continuum, 1970).

5. José de Souza Martins, "Viola quebrada," *Debate e Crítica* 4 (1974); Luiz Augusto Milanesi, *O paraíso via Embratel* (Rio de Janeiro: Paz e Terra, 1978); Barriguelli, José Cláudio, "O teatro popular rural: o circo-teatro," *Debate e Crítica* 3 (1974).

6. Verena M. Alier, "As mulheres da truma do caminhão," *Debate e Crítica* 5 (1975); Ecléa Bosi, *Leituras de operárias* (Petrópolis: Ed. Vozes, 1972).

7. Aracky Martins Rodrigues, *Operário, operária* (São Paulo: Símbolo, 1978); Eduardo Hoornaert, "Folclore é invenção de policiais," *Arte popular e dominação* (São Paulo: Alternativa, 1978); Maria Conceição de Incão e Mello, *Os bóias-frias, acumulação e miséria*, (Petrópolis: Ed. Vozes, 1976).

8. See the collection *Arte popular e dominação* (São Paulo: Alternativa, 1978).

9. Harry Braverman, *Labor and Monopoly Capital. The Degradation of Work* (New York: Monthly Review Press, 1974).

10. José Arthur Giannotti, "Formas da sociabilidade capitalista," *Revista Estudos*, Petrópolis, Cebrap/Vozes 24: 78.

11. Karl Marx, *Capital. A Critique of Political Economy*, Vol. 1, Chapter 6, 6:465, tr. 17,

12. Roberto Romano da Silva, *Brasil. Igreja contra estado* (São Paulo: Ed. Kairós, 1979).

13. Oscar Lewis, *Five Families. Mexican Case Studies in the Culture of Poverty* (New York: Basic Books, 1959).

14. Lewis Hanke, *Aristotle and the American Indians.A Study in Race Prejudice in the Modern World* (London: Hollis and Carter, 1959), 82.

15. Ibid., 61.

16. Ibid., 61.

17. Alier, ibid.

18. Luiz Antônio Machado da Silva, "O significado do botequim," *Cidade. Usos e abusos*, ibid.

19. Ibid., 99.

20. TN: The Banco Nacional de Habitação (BNH) was established in 1965 by Brazil's military government as part of its housing policy to carry out

large-scale accommodation initiatives geared toward both middle- and lower-class residents.

21. Ecléa Bosi, *Memória e sociedade. Lembranças de velhos* (São Paulo: Taq. Ed., 1979).

22. Ibid., 709.

23. Juan Martínez Alier, *Notas sobre el franquismo*, Barcelona University Working Papers (1978), 30–32. See also Michael Hall, *Immigration and the Early Working Class* (Jahrbuch für Geschichte, 1975).

24. These references to a young Marx and an elder Hegel were found in Gérard Lebrun, *La patience du concept* (Paris: Gallimard, 1972), 43.

25. "Religion is man's earliest and also *indirect form of self knowledge* (. . .) man first of all sees his nature as if out of himself, before he finds it in himself. Religion is the *child-like condition of* humanity (. . .). Religion, at least the Christian, is the relation of man to himself or, more correctly to his own nature, i.e. his subjective nature, but a relation to it viewed as a nature apart from his own. The divine being is nothing else than a human being, or rather the human nature purified, freed from the limits of the individual man, made objective, i.e. contemplated and revered as another distinct being." (Ludwig Feuerbach, *The Essence of Christianity*, trans. *Marian Evans* (New York: Ungar, 1957), 33–34.

26. For Hegel, for example, the difference between Christianity and Judaism, between Christianity in its true form and its "primitive" or popular form, consists of the difference between a religion whose speculative content is recognized and another that cannot cease demanding revelation and manifestation. Christianity, in reality, is a religion of mediations, of invisibility, of remembering, of the abolition of imagination and representation, of an interiority reconciling the finite and the infinite. On the other hand, the popular version is immediate, sensitive, representative, dogmatic and manifest, contentious. In it, God is an emptiness placed in the beyond, an "object" of devotion and of nostalgic memory.

27. TN: The *Padroado* was an agreement between the Vatican and the Kingdoms of Portugal and Spain that delegated to the kings the power to appoint local clergy, thus cementing a coincidence of localized political and religious authority.

28. Riolando Azzi, "Catolicismo popular e autoridade eclesiástica na evolução histórica do Brasil," *Religião e Sociedade* 1 (1977).

29. TN: The Courses of Christianity originated in Spain in the 1940s as the *Cursillos de Cristianidad* and constituted a movement away from the church hierarchy and toward a lay engagement with Catholicism through projects of charismatic evangelization in which believers would revitalize their faith through three-day workshops or *courses* led by laymen. Liberation theologians introduced the system of base community pastoral work into the Catholic Church in the 1960s, for example, in the *favelas* of Brazil's big cities.

30. Maria Sylvia Carvalho Franco, *Homens livres na ordem escravocrata* (São Paulo: IEB/USP, 1969), 60.
31. Ibid.
32. In Brazil, historical Protestantism was correct in its critique of Brazilian Catholicism for its devotional (the people) and clerical (the dominant class) mentality, but it failed to take into account the objects of clerical devotion.
33. Cândido Procópio de Camargo, *Católicos, protestantes, espíritas* (Petrópolis: Vozes, 1973), 65.
34. Duglas Monteiro, "A cura por correspondência," *Religião e Sociedade* 1 (1977). Monteiro offers the term "religions of order," referencing, for example, how a legitimate spouse asks a saint for the return of their mate while calling upon an Umbandist or Macumbist "deed" to seduce a lover.
35. Peter Fry, "Mediunidade e sexualidade," *Religião e Sociedade* 1 (1977).
36. TN: *Bichas* is a vernacular term for gay men.
37. Christopher Hill, *The World Upside Down* (Temple: Smoth, 1972); Monteiro, *Os errantes do novo século*.
38. Karl Marx, *Critique of Hegel's Philosophy of Right* (Cambridge: Cambridge University Press, 1977).
39. Ibid., 131–132.
40. Ibid., 131.
41. Baruch Spinoza, *Theological-Political Treatise*, Ed. Jonathan Israel, trans. Michael Silverthorne and Jonathan Israel (Cambridge: Cambridge University Press, 2007), preface.
42. Juana Elbein, *O nagô e a morte* (Petrópolis: Vozes, 1976), 44.
43. In her study of the *Nagô* of the Brazilian state of Bahia, Juana Elbein notes the insufficiency of the research on the relations between the organization of the "terreiro" and the originating sociopolitical organization of its practitioners, suggesting that the former reveals a concentration of politicoreligious power. "These similarities (between the 'terreiro' and its origins) were intensified even more after the creation of the 'body of ministers' of *Xangô*, six on the right and six on the left of *Iyaiaxê*" (ibid., 38). The study of the theocratic policies clarifies the inseparability of the two forms relating to power. However, what is more interesting (and more alarming) is the "similarity" of both in a space in which there is supposed to have been a separation between religion and the State.
44. This term comes from the antiproject of the "Manifesto do CPC," *Arte em Revista* 1.

Winds of Progress: The Administered University

1. Harry Braverman, *Labor and Monopoly Capital. The Degradation of Work in the Twentieth Century* (New York: Monthly Review Press, 1974). See in particular the chapter "Productive and Unproductive Labor."

2. André Gorz, "Destroy the University," *Les Temps Modernes* 285 (1970).

3. TN: The *Ato Institutional Número 5* (AI-5) or the Institutional Act Number 5 was implemented in 1968 and marks the hardening of the military regime controlling the Brazilian government since the coup of 1964. The Act closed the National Congress and shifted all power to the Executive. It also suspended habeas corpus, enacted censorship, and made illegal any type of political organization opposing the regime. In the wake of this act, the regime imposed Decree 477, a law that virtually wiped out the independent politics of the university system. Protests and marches were prohibited and campuses strictly watched.

4. Werner Baer, "O crescimento brasileiro e a experiência desenvolvimentista," *Revista Novos Estudos Cebrap* 20 (1988): 17.

5. Marilena Chauí, "A reforma do ensino," *Revista Discurso* 8 (1977).

6. TN: Darcy Ribeiro (1922–1997). Brazilian anthropologist and also the first chancellor and enthusiastic supporter of the foundation of the University of Brasília in 1961.

7. In an interview on Canal 2, TV Cultura in São Paulo, the rector of the University of São Paulo Waldir Oliva stated that the problem of unemployment or the lack of jobs for graduates could be resolved by relocating university places, meaning courses whose supply was greater than the labor market's demand, should be reduced, while those that had a higher demand could be increased.

8. Maurice Merleau-Ponty, "Eye and Mind," trans. Carleton Dallery in *The Primacy of Perception,* ed. James Edie (Evanston: Northwestern University Press, 1964), 159–190.

9. Theses 11 on Feuerbach: "Philosophers have hitherto only interpreted the world in various ways; the point is to change it."

Index